Getting There

A Gulf Islands Adventure

by Michael Matthews

This is a work of fiction. Names, characters, places and incidents are either the products of the author's imagination or are used fictitiously. Any resemblance to actual persons (living or dead), events or locations is entirely coincidental.

Copyright © 2012 Michael Matthews

All rights reserved.

ISBN-13: 978-1477637043

ISBN-10: 1477637044

DEDICATION

I would like to express my love and thanks to my wife Ma Yue who patiently endured through the long hours while I sat at the computer writing. Thank you for all the love and encouragement you give me.

You are my life.

Wa Ai Ni

CONTENTS

1	Irish Bay	1
2	First Meeting	4
3	And So It Begins	8
4	Falling	14
5	Losing Focus	22
6	Party Time	27
7	Down Time	33
8	Investigating	40
9	The Interrogation	47
10	The Things We Don't Know About Our Friends	52
11	Injury To Insult	62
12	The Chase Begins	68
13	Fishing	72
14	Change Of Course	78
15	Getting Ready To Go	87
16	The Long Night	93

17	The Shock Of The Day	99
18	A New Day	107
19	Fei Hu	115
20	Island Life	128
21	An Interruption	132
22	Vengeance	138
23	Good News And Bad News	145
24	A Hammer Blow	150
25	Additional Troops	155
26	Temporary Shelter	158
27	Van Go Searches	164
28	Time To Leave	173
29	Air Search	180
30	A Raft Of Problems	184
31	A Bad Deal	188
32	Van No Go	194
33	New Friends	197
34	Finding The Target	203
35	Rough Weather	211
36	A Long Night	218
37	Searching	223

38	A Serious Mistake	228
39	For Better Or Worse	232
40	Maybe	237
41	Now What?	241
42	The Catch Of The Day	245
43	Plan Whatever	256
44	A Turnaround	265
45	Re-Grouping	268
46	A Bad Day	273
47	Home Sweet Home	279
48	Mao Fifty Four	285
49	Getting Back To Work	287
50	Eddy's Surprise	292
51	The Big Night	295
52	Salvage Work	302
53	Getting Back On The Horse	306
54	The Preparation Pays Off	313
55	A Care Package	315
	Acknowledgements	318
	About the Author	319

Getting There

Chart Of The Gulf Islands Of British Columbia, Canada

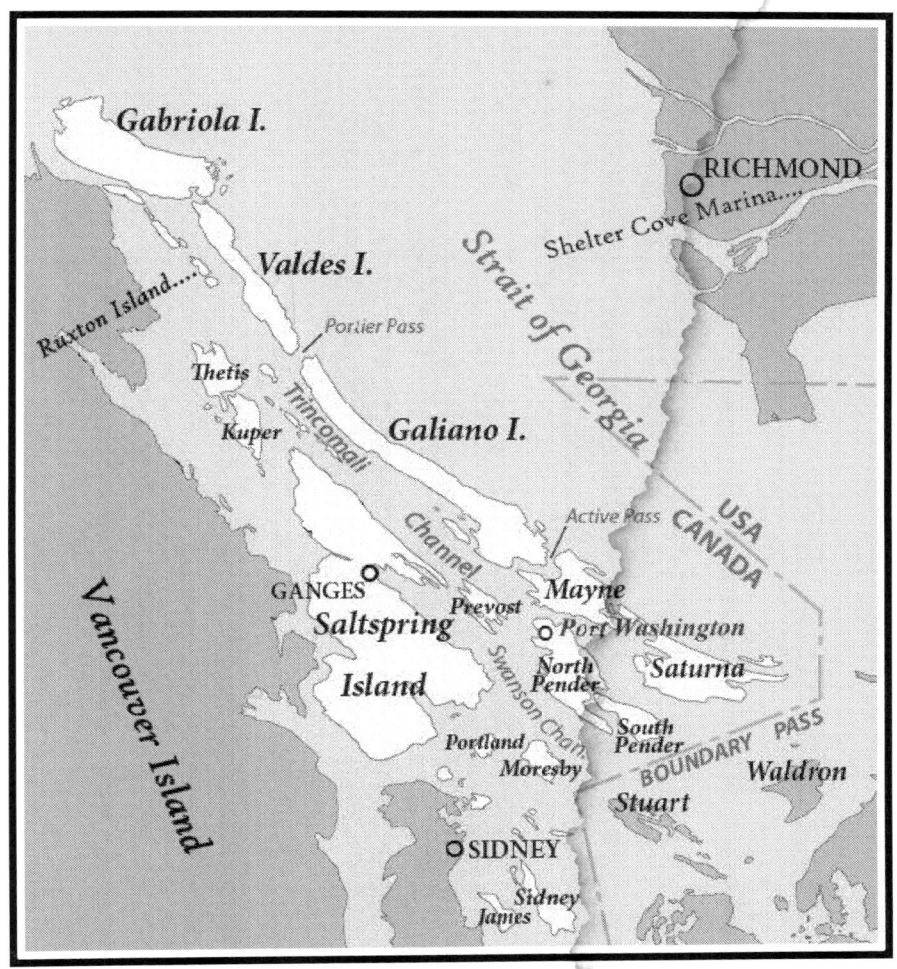

Chart Showing Vancouver Island And The U.S.A

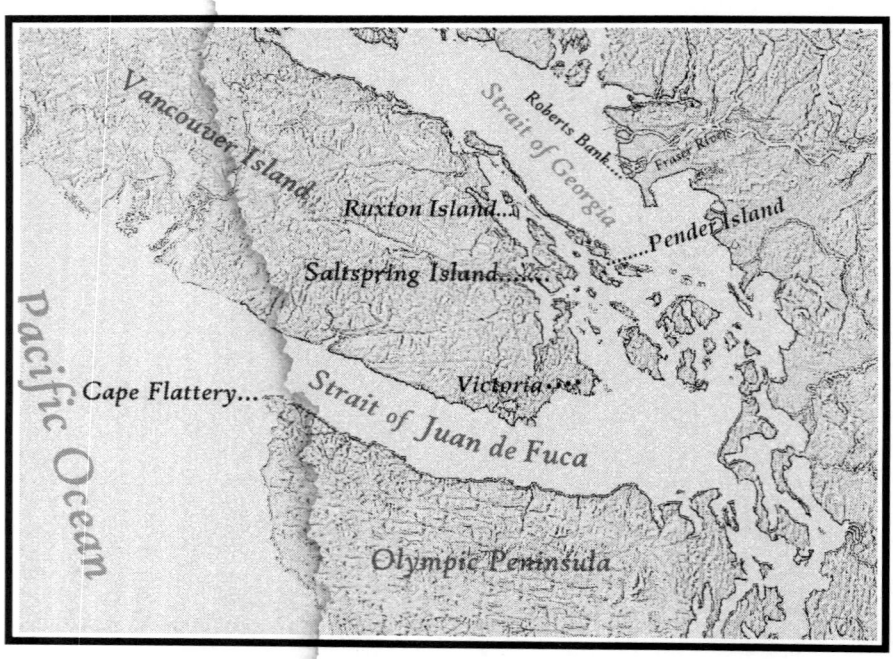

1 IRISH BAY

    A squall, a long misty curtain of gray swept through Navy Channel between North Pender and Mayne Islands and into the wide expanse of Plumper Sound. A procession of white capped waves marched to the west until finally surging onto the beach at the head of Lyall Harbor. To the north in Irish Bay, a sailboat rounded up into the wind and a man in yellow raingear ran up to the bow and loosed a heavy anchor which plunged to the sandy ocean floor.
    A sound symphony was playing; the wet slap of the waves against the hull of the boat, rain hissing down, the wind whistling through the rigging wires. Starlight, the only vessel in the bay, its black hull blending with the monochromatic tones of the surroundings, settled back, doing a lively dance on the end of thirty fathoms of chain and half inch line. The yellow clad sailor made sure the anchor was holding and then walked back to the stern. Stepping into the cockpit, he shut off the slowly thumping diesel engine and took a quick series of bearings to establish his position in the bay.
    Off in the distance, the squall obscured the view of Lyall Harbor on Saturna Island. It was Friday afternoon and the sailor imagined the crowd in the Lighthouse Pub near the ferry terminal. They would be cozy and warm, drinking their Saltspring Ale, wolfing down the delicious burgers and fries. It would be a great place to be if you were in the mood for being with friends, talking and having a good time. But the gray rainy weather in the quiet little cove was much more to his liking than the friendly atmosphere of the pub.

The sailor, Mick Brese, realized he had taken his eye off the ball. All through the years that it had taken to build Starlight, he had steered a steady course. Most of the time when his buddies had come by the shop wanting him to take time off and go drinking or hiking or kayaking he had told them that he had work to do. He had been focused like a laser beam and it had still taken him four long years to finish his thirty seven foot cruising sailboat. Now, when he was just a short time away from going offshore sailing, he had almost sabotaged his dream by falling in love with Claire.

He still found it difficult to admit that it was a mistake. It was more like he had suddenly forgotten what he was trying to achieve. To Mick, offshore sailing was the Holy Grail, the Mount Everest of sailing dreams and a five foot Chinese girl with the sexiest eyes and the fastest half nelson he had ever seen had almost made him lose his way.

He sat down in the cockpit in the shelter of the dodger and looked out at his favorite spot in the Gulf Islands. He had been here in all kinds of weather; from hot sunny summer days to cold rainy spring days just like this one. The rain had started out as a light mist around noon and had developed into a dreary depressing downpour. It was the perfect kind of weather for someone wanting to wallow in misery. He turned and looked down into the cabin. For a fleeting moment, Claire was there, standing at the bottom of the companionway stairs, looking up at him with that ever optimistic smile on her beautiful face. He closed his eyes, remembering her and when he opened them again, she was gone.

It was getting dark, the clouds and rain being driven along by the wind which showed no signs of easing. Mick took a last look around the bay, satisfied that the anchor was holding. He hung his rain jacket from the dodger, headed down below and went about the process of lighting several kerosene lamps which cast a soft warm glow on the teak and mahogany furnishings. He stood for a moment by the diesel heater mounted on the main bulkhead listening to the rain drumming on the cabin top and looked around the cabin while he warmed himself. It was the best place in the world. It was home.

Mick took his deck boots off and put them at the bottom of the companionway stairs making sure they were handy in case he needed them. Slipping his feet into a pair of fleece lined slippers; he took a bottle of wine from a rack mounted over the sink in the small u-shaped galley. It was time for a drink. Maybe that would help. It wouldn't hurt. Sitting down at the navigation station on the starboard side, he filled a coffee mug with the wine and pulled out the logbook to update it.

Flipping through the book, he stopped when he saw a page of fine, precise handwriting. It wasn't his writing that was for sure. It was Claire's. She had even made a few notes in the margins in Chinese, beautifully formed little characters. What it said, he would probably never know. He looked at the date. Two short weeks ago. He shook his head, closed the book and took a sip of his wine. The wine was one that they had picked out together at the town of Ganges on Saltspring Island. It was usually delicious but tonight it seemed a little bitter. He went to the sink and poured it out and set about making a pot of coffee. It was probably the wiser course of action. He decided he would try to get some work done tonight. Put the thoughts of Claire out of his head.

As the coffee brewed, he went forward to a locker on the starboard side of the cabin, just ahead of the main bulkhead. Opening the locker door Mick pulled out a sliding shelf which supported a life size sculpture of a woman's head. This bust was a commission that Mick should have been working on for the last month. Should have been working on. Once it was cast in bronze and delivered to the client, it would be a birthday present from the husband of a well known female pianist. But sculpting had taken a back seat to being with Claire. In fact, everything had taken a back seat to being with Claire. For a guy that was so close to finally achieving his dream of offshore sailing, the timing of the relationship couldn't have been worse. And of the two of them, as it turned out, Claire was the only one smart enough to recognize it.

As he looked at the sculpture, his gaze wandered. There, sitting on the back of the shelf, glowing in the soft shadows of the lamp light, as if calling out to him was a small bronze sculpture. He reached for it and brought it out into the light. It was Claire. He remembered when he had done the original clay model. It was the day that he had first met her at the pub..

2 FIRST MEETING

The Pirate's Den Pub at Shelter Cove Marina was packed with the usual weekday lunch crowd. The regulars were there, a bunch of noisy, grubby looking boat builders from the yard along with an assortment of boaters from down on the docks. A crowd of businessmen in suits had the tables along the east windows. The busboys were rushing back and forth cleaning and setting tables as fast as they were vacated.

Kostis Manos, the owner of the restaurant insisted that all the employees wear pirate costumes. Dressed like actors out of an old Douglas Fairbanks movie, the men wore blousy white shirts without many buttons done up. For the women it was a white t-shirt tied under the bust and fit as tight as possible. Every girl's shirt was at least one size too small. Not the most comfortable wardrobe but from a marketing standpoint it was a success as it brought in a good number of male diners who were content to eat and drink as long as the view was good. Waiters and waitresses alike wore a pirate hat and pants that were torn off at the knees along with knee high stockings and shoes with big brass buckles. The employees thought the outfits were ridiculous but Kostis loved them. As the employer, he won that argument hands down.

Mick and his friend Eddy found a table not far from the gang of boat builders. Everybody knew everybody and there was a lot of good natured banter back and forth with the exception of the surly Pete Peterson who didn't get along well with anybody. He sat at the end of the table; arms crossed over his chest and exchanged a sneer in response to Mick's pleasant greeting. Eddy looked at Mick and shrugged. This was standard operating procedure for Peterson.

While waiting for the waitress to come and take their order, Mick and Eddy chatted. "How are you making out with the electronics Eddy?" Eddy's boat "Seagram" and Mick's boat "Starlight" were out of the water, side by side on the hard. Eddy's boat was there for a simple repaint of the bottom but with the tallest mast in the work yard, she had taken a hit from lightning during a particularly intense spring thunderstorm. Eddy had been next door visiting Mick on Starlight and the two of them had literally jumped out of their seats in the seconds following the lightning strike. The flash and bang of the strike had been deafening and it wasn't until they went down below in Seagram that the extent of the strike had been apparent.

"Well here's what was damaged." Eddy held up his hand and began ticking off the problems. "Radar, radio, depth sounder, refrigerator, masthead antenna, engine alternator and starter, plus all the navigation lights. The wiring for most of that stuff has to be replaced but I have to tell you, I'm not crazy about going up to the top of the mast to pull wires." He shuddered at the thought of it.

"Eddy, I told you I don't mind going up there. I'd be happy to do it for you. Let me finish getting Starlight back in the water and then I'll give you a hand."

At that moment, the waitress showed up to bring beer for the boat builders. It was okay with the boss that they had a beer with their lunch though one beer usually ended up being two or three or four. The boss didn't care so long as the work got done. Mick stared at the waitress. She was Chinese, short and beautiful. Barely as tall as the men who were sitting down, she looked much like a little girl except for the fact that she had a woman's body. Very noticeably a woman's body in her tight fitting t-shirt. Her black hair had been gathered up and stowed beneath her pirate hat but a couple of long strands had escaped and hung down the sides of her face. She had a flawless complexion, high cheekbones and high arched eyebrows over decidedly Asian looking eyes. She was biting her lower lip as she concentrated on offloading mugs of beer from a tray balanced on one hand, one by one around the table. As she reached the end of the table, Pete Peterson felt it was time to let his true nature shine forth. As the Chinese girl was putting beer down in front of Peterson's neighbor, Pete put his hand on her leg and slid it up to her backside. The girl straightened up quickly and in doing so, tipped over one of the mugs on the table. In the ensuing scramble to mop up the spilled beer, Pete took the opportunity to actually slip his hand in between the girl's legs. Her reaction was so fast that neither Eddy nor Mick, who saw the whole episode, could figure out exactly what it was that she had done.

In the blink of an eye, Pete Peterson's hand which had been approaching heaven was now bent, along with the attached arm, behind his back and pulled up toward his head. He was face down on the table and frozen in pain. The fork from the place setting was digging into his cheek. The waitress applied slight additional force and tears began to drip from Pete's tightly closed eyes onto the table cloth. Everyone at the table and the tables nearby were silent and watching in amazement. Pete Peterson was about twice as big as the girl. She leaned over him and said in a quiet voice into his ear, "I can dislocate your shoulder if you move, so don't even think about it. Understand?" Pete nodded as best he could and grimaced in pain. "That was very rude of you, don't you think? The girls told me you're always doing something rude like that." She didn't wait for an answer. "If you ever touch me again, or if you ever touch one of the other girls, I will break your arm and you won't be going back to work again for a long time. Understand?" Pete nodded again.

Not leaving anything to doubt, the girl gave him one more little tweak just to be sure he understood perfectly. Pete cried out in pain as she released his arm. The arm stayed momentarily behind his back until he managed to slowly get it down where it belonged. He eased himself into an upright position and braced his shoulder with his good hand. The amazed patrons all applauded the waitress as she went back to work cleaning the table. Pete stood up, an angry look on his face and headed for the door. His co-workers jeered and laughed at him and toasted the girl. He was going to be even more unpleasant than normal to work with for the rest of the day.

Eddy grinned at Mick. "What do you think about that buddy? Wouldn't she make a fine first mate for your world cruise? You run into pirates, you just turn her loose and they'll be heading for the horizon with their tails tucked between their legs." Mick stared at the waitress suitably impressed with her display of self protection skills. "Where did she come from? I've never seen her around here before."

The girl turned, tucked the empty tray under her arm and pulled out her order pad and a pen which was sticking out from under the edge of her hat. "I'm new here," she said, obviously overhearing the two. "Just started this morning. What can I get you two gentlemen?" She didn't appear to be any the worse for her recent encounter with Pete. She was looking at Mick with a smile on her face.

    Mick Brese had a sudden moment of uncertainty. He had been so careful with his feelings, so determined not to let anything or anyone distract his focus but this girl was so different. Eddy gave him a little kick under the table. Mick looked at him, startled. "A pint of Labatt's and a steak sandwich with fries please."

    Eddy was watching Mick, smiling at his reaction to the waitress. "I'll have the same please."

    Mick tried to get himself together. "I'm Mick Brese. What's your name miss?"

    The waitress looked at Mick for a moment. "In Chinese, it's Xun Xi Pei," she said it quickly. "Sun See Pay" saying it slower this time, simplifying it, making it easier to understand. She leaned closer to Mick and said with a smile on her lips, "But my friends call me Claire."

3 AND SO IT BEGINS

After lunch Mick went back to finish the last of the "to do list" on Starlight. There were a number of things still to be done before putting her back in the water. As he made his way across the work yard he stopped as he usually did to admire his beautiful boat. She was forty three feet from the double ended stern to the tip of the long white bowsprit, thirty seven feet on deck and every inch had been crafted by his own hands. Building her had taken four long years at the same time as he had worked his day job at Freitag's Boats. It had taken every penny of his wages and savings but Starlight was his home, his dream. He had finally found financial freedom when his sculpting hobby had turned into a major money stream after he had accidentally found notoriety with the "P.M. piece" as he called it. In his spare time (of which there hadn't been very much) he had started a practice sculpture, a bust of the Prime Minister and when a reporter friend had done an article about Mick in The Vancouver Sun along with photos, word made it to Ottawa. The Prime Minster himself demanded to see the finished bronze and he had enthusiastically stated in his French Canadian accent, "By God, I want to meet dat artist. If he can make me look dis good, he deserves a medal."

As it turned out, that medal ended up being cold hard cash and lots of it right out of the taxpayer's pockets and the finished work had gone on permanent display at Twenty Four Sussex Drive, the Prime Minister's official residence. After that, the commissions had come like a tidal wave and with them, the money to finish building Starlight and enough to set him up with a good cruising budget. Now, he only had a few odds and ends to clear up and he would finally be able to say goodbye and head offshore. There was only one sour note; one thing missing and the beautiful Chinese waitress had reminded him all about it.

Several months back, Mick had been over at Telegraph Cove in the Gulf Islands and after dark, at anchor he had been sitting in the cockpit under the usual breathtaking display of stars in the clear cold night sky. As he had sat there, a meteor or perhaps a piece of space junk, larger than he had ever seen, had arced across the heavens. It went from one horizon, across the sky to the other horizon in a brilliant blazing arc that left him speechless, almost gasping for air from the sheer magnitude of the display. At that moment he had realized that he wanted, needed someone to share his life with, someone to share the brilliant moments with. Claire had reminded him that he was still on the lookout for a very special "partner" to share all that life had to offer and he had to admit that she appeared to be an excellent candidate.

As Mick started back to work waxing and buffing the hull, he found that he was having a very difficult time keeping his mind off the beautiful Chinese girl. She was amazing. So tiny and yet she had been able to stand her ground against that jerk Peterson. Mick finally gave up working on the hull, shucked his dust mask and wiped the sweat from his face. He climbed the ladder at the stern of Starlight, went down below and from the sculpting locker pulled out a fist sized piece of modeling clay. Sitting down at the dinette table in the main cabin, surrounded by the teak and mahogany that he had so lovingly assembled, Mick started the process of transferring the vision of the Chinese woman from his memory to the clay.

It went easily, his hands moving quickly to rough in the shape of her eyes, ears, nose and mouth. It was easy to remember that mouth, the vermillion forming a perfect little cupid's bow. The hair was a little difficult as she had been wearing a hat which had hidden any indication of her style but after several tries, he decided that long hair worked best. He gave her a part; with the long tresses swept across her forehead from left to right and tucked in behind one delicate little ear.

Mick worked his way down her neck, long and slender, like Audrey Hepburn in Breakfast At Tiffany's. He put in the shoulders and the upper part of her chest. The details came easily to him: they were burned into his memory. After using a number of different shaping tools, Claire was there, in his hands looking at him again with that clear gaze, a slight smile on her lips.

A knock on the hull startled him from his work. Mick put the sculpture down and headed for the companionway.

"Hey Mick, you up there?" It was Eddy, probably coming to ask again if he wanted to go to the usual Friday night party.

"Yeah, I'm just taking a break." Mick called out as Eddy's head appeared at the top of the ladder. Eddy paused, not coming on board.

"I just wanted to see if you were decent. You have a guest."

Mick cocked his head, puzzled. "A guest? Who, you?"

"No, not me you dolt. I wouldn't care if you were decent or not. Besides I have to get ready for the party tonight. I've got to have a shower and make myself pretty for the girls." He waggled his eyebrows and held an imaginary cigar in his best Groucho Marx impersonation. "I'll get out of the way so your guest can come up. I think you're going to be pleasantly surprised."

As Mick started towards the ladder to see who was below, Eddy motioned with a hand to stop him. He slid down the ladder and Mick heard light footsteps coming up and then she was there. First, the jet black hair and then the face that Mick had just finished sculpting. She smiled at him.

"Hello Mick. I hope you don't mind having a visitor. Eddy said that you have a beautiful boat and that I should see it. If you're busy I can come back some other time."

She spoke softly, a gentle sound. She smiled at him waiting for his decision. He grabbed the top of the ladder to steady it.

"No, Claire, I'm not busy. I'm just taking a break. By all means, come on board. Let me help you." She took his hand and stepped onto the deck and into the cockpit. She was wearing jeans and a cable knit turtleneck sweater and a pair of flat soled black Tai Chi slippers.

"I was talking to Eddy in the pub after you left and he suggested that since I'm new around here I should get around and meet some of the locals." Her hand was still in his. "He said that you're planning on going offshore sailing soon. Is that true?"

Mick nodded. This was unusual behavior for Eddy. Normally he would have kept a beautiful woman like this all to himself. "It's true. I've been working towards it for a long time but finally, I'm almost ready to go. I'm going to head for Hawaii first. From there, I don't know. Depends on how well the first leg goes. Do you know Eddy from somewhere?"

"You're sailing to Hawaii? Oh, that would be fantastic. I've seen pictures of it but I've never been there. How long will it take you to get there? You have to tell me all about it. Would you show me around your boat?"

She was an enthusiastic guest. Mick could smell her perfume. It was a subtle fragrance and he was tempted to lean in close to be able to smell it better. It reminded him of a tropical flower. Plumeria maybe? He reluctantly released her hand, though she didn't seem to be minding their touch.

"Maybe I caught you at a bad time? You seem a bit distracted." She smiled as if she realized that she was his distraction.

"No, I'd be happy to show you around." He was reminded of a dream where he wanted to jump out of an airplane to experience the thrill of skydiving but was reluctant for fear of the possibilities. A part of his mind, the still reasoning part suggested that this might be something along the same lines. When you open yourself up to possibilities, you have to be prepared for what comes your way.

The tour started on deck. He showed her how the sails were set up to be operated by one person right from the cockpit. He showed her the autopilot that would allow him to move around while the boat steered herself. She seemed to have a good understanding of mechanical things.

"If you have the autopilot steering the boat, you still have to make adjustments to the sails if the wind changes direction don't you?"

She was smart. All the time that Mick was talking to her, he absorbed the images of her face, her hands and her body. After the tour on deck, Mick led her down below. As Claire stood next to him at the bottom of the companionway stairs, she looked around at the interior of his boat. Her eyes were wide as she took in the details of the carpentry finishing. "You did all this Mick?"

He nodded. "Yeah, everything you see here is my design, my work." He put his hand lovingly on the glossy varnished surface of the navigation table. "It took me way longer than it should have. I didn't really know what I was doing when I started but I learned by doing."

Claire reached out and touched the teak trim of the galley on the port side of the boat. It was smooth and the curves felt good under her fingers. She was amazed. It looked like something out of a magazine, like fine furniture except that the quality went from the floor up to the ceiling. It was a showcase of woodworking skills. She turned and looked at him.

"This is beautiful Mick. I have to tell you, I wasn't expecting it to look like this. It's a work of art." She nodded in agreement with herself.

"Part of the reason it took so long is that my father is a real perfectionist and no matter what it is that I'm doing, I always feel like he's going to drop in and take a look at what I've done. I sometimes wish I could be the kind of person who didn't really care what it looked like as long as it worked. I could have been finished and already gone offshore but for trying to get things to my father's satisfaction."

Claire looked at him. "Well, your father raised you right. If you're going to do something, you should do as good a job as you can possibly do. You wouldn't be happy with a poorly built boat would you? Somehow I doubt that. I have the feeling that you have the same desire as your father, to do a good job."

As they were talking, Mick suddenly realized the sculpture of her was there on the dining table. He hoped that she wouldn't notice it but as she took a few steps into the cabin, her eyes fell on the little bust.

"What's this, Mick? Eddy told me that you were a boat builder but he never mentioned that you were a sculptor. Did you do this?" She picked up the small sculpture, turning it and viewing it from every angle.

Mick was not sure what to say. Would she think it was weird that he had been doing a sculpture of her?

"This is good Mick. You captured my face very well. I'm impressed considering you only saw me for a few minutes in the pub. How did you do that?"

He reached to take the sculpture from her but she pulled it out of his reach.

"It's not very good Claire. I was just taking a break and I sometimes do little sculpting exercises. It's good practice."

"You're being modest Mick. I like it very much. Do you have to fire it to make the clay hard?"

He shook his head. "This kind of clay never hardens. You have to take a mold from the finished work and then cast it in some other medium." He went to the closet, opened it and pulled out the shelf with the nearly finished bust of the pianist.

Getting There

"This one is almost ready. I'll take this to a foundry and they'll make the molds and then cast it in bronze. Then I'll mount it and send it to the buyer out east."

"Oh Mick, it's beautiful. You've really got a lot of ability. I'm very impressed. Would you finish the little one of me and cast it in bronze too? I'd be happy to pay for it. When people look at it I can say that I know the artist."

"You don't have to pay for it Claire. It's not very good but I can work on it some more if you promise to come and sit for me."

She looked at him skeptically. "It seems like I get the better end of that deal Mick. All I have to do is pose for you and I get a bronze sculpture in exchange? That doesn't seem fair. Maybe there's something else I could do for you." She paused in thought. "I could help you work on your boat to get her ready to go back in the water. I could do that." She smiled brightly, excited at the thought.

The ships clock chimed the hour reminding Mick that he still hadn't cleaned up from the days work.

"Claire, I've got to go have a shower over at the maintenance building. It won't take me long and then I could make dinner if you're interested. I mean if you don't have to get going too soon. You could just stay here and relax, listen to some music and have a glass of wine while I shower."

She smiled and nodded. "That sounds very nice Mick. You don't mind me waiting on your boat while you're not here? I could go and wait at the pub if you like."

"No, it's much more peaceful here. I don't mind at all. You can use the head, the bathroom that is, if you need to. I'll show you how to use it. Boat toilets are a little more complicated than regular ones."

After showing her the idiosyncrasies of the marine toilet and explaining that it was hooked up to a holding tank and wasn't going to empty out onto the ground, he gathered up his shower kit and some clean clothes. He got her settled at the dinette table with a glass of wine and turned to go.

"I won't be long Claire. My home is your home. Be back in a flash." Down on the ground, he ran to the showers thinking about what to prepare for dinner for his very lovely guest. At the same time as he was looking forward to having some feminine company, he could hear the voice in the back of his mind telling him to concentrate on the task at hand. But truthfully, it was tiring concentrating so long.

4 FALLING

Mick stood at the bottom of the companionway stairs, his gym bag in hand and looked at Claire. She was standing in the galley, a wooden spoon in her hand. During the time that he had been at the shower, she had somehow figured out how to get the propane stove working and had several pots bubbling and a frying pan sizzling, wonderful odors filling the boat. She had put an apron on, the one that said, "Eat...that's an order!"

A pot of rice began bubbling madly on the stove and Claire lifted the lid and turned the heat down. "Welcome back hard working man." she said, a smile on her face.

Mick turned and put his bag in the quarter berth. "It smells wonderful in here Claire. I was going to do the cooking but it looks like you beat me to it."

She put the lid back on the pot and looked at him. Her cheeks were rosy and she blew a strand of hair away from her face with a little puff from the corner of her mouth. "I love this kitchen Mick. It's so easy to cook in with the stove and the sink so close at hand. I hope you don't mind that I started dinner. I was just going to put a kettle on to boil some water for tea but I started nosing around and found all these wonderful things in your freezer and in the cupboards. You even have rice, so I thought maybe I'd get started before you came back. I wanted to surprise you. You don't mind do you Mick?" She looked at him hoping he wasn't upset. He moved closer to the galley, leaning against the counter.

Getting There

"Claire, I couldn't begin to tell you how nice it is to have you here. You make the place feel so homey, it's a wonderful feeling." He looked at her in his galley and he had to fight the feelings that were happening in him. He had consciously stayed away from women. He had chosen the single life so that he would be able to stay focused on his dream and it had been pretty simple, until now. Most women simply didn't catch his interest. Claire on the other hand had grabbed his attention as successfully as she had grabbed Pete Peterson's this afternoon.

She smiled at him and turned back to the stove to continue cooking. She took a sip from her wine. "Dinner will be ready as soon as the rice is cooked. I must confess that I was a little hesitant to start cooking in someone else's home but I thought that after working hard all day on your boat that you might like having someone do the cooking for you. I hope I wasn't overdoing my welcome." She turned her head and looked at him.

"Like I said, Claire, it's a pleasure. You're welcome here anytime." He said it with feeling.

It was easy to see that this pleased her. "If you don't mind me asking Mick, why do you want to go offshore sailing? I mean, it's a big ocean, don't you think it will get lonely out there, being all by yourself?"

Mick poured himself a glass of wine and started setting the table. He figured this was as good a time as any to break out the good tablecloth he kept for special occasions. He rummaged around in a locker and finally found it. It had yet to be used but tonight seemed pretty special. Of course, if he was going to use the special occasion tablecloth, it also meant getting out the best silverware instead of the plastic handled cutlery. He actually had two complete settings of good silverware and dishes. In this case, one for Claire and one for himself.

"Why do I want to go sailing? Adventure, excitement, personal challenge, those are some of the reasons. The idea really took hold when I was a teenager and I read a book by a man named John Guzzwell. He built a small sailboat and sailed around the world. In fact, he built the boat and sailed from Victoria over on Vancouver Island. There's a plaque dedicated to him in the inner harbor there. I was so inspired by his story that I took up boatbuilding and dreamed about sailing around the world ever since. I don't know if I'll get all the way around the world but I sure want to try. Starlight is a great boat and I'm as ready as I'll ever be."

Claire watched him as he set the table. He was a strong, good looking man, slim and muscular. He looked to be about six feet tall give or take an inch. It seemed strange that he didn't have a girlfriend or wife. Maybe he was gay she thought. One never knew these days. In China, there weren't many openly gay men but here in Canada, there seemed to be a lot. He didn't seem gay if the looks he had given her were any indication.

"To answer your question about getting lonely, yes, I expect that I'll get lonely. But I've just never met the right woman who wants to give up everything and go sailing. I have to admit, it's a sacrifice. You give up the security of day to day life on shore. But I want to go so much that I guess that I'll have to go alone for now. Another reason that I want to go offshore sailing is just to get away from so called civilization. As much as it pains me to say it, Claire, I feel like our society is moving further and further away from civilization every day. Take a look around you. There are a lot of people here in British Columbia who feel that freedom is something that is owed to them, that they should be able to do anything and act any way they feel like. That's not freedom, that's anarchy and chaos and I've had enough of it. I want to go where there's some peace and quiet and I've worked long and hard to be in the position to do just that."

Claire nodded. She understood wanting something and having to sacrifice to get it. There were things in her life that fell into that category. But sometimes the obstacles in your way were too big. She checked the rice and decided it was ready. Mick brought the plates to the cutting board in the galley and she served up the chicken dish she had prepared. A tiny little bit on one plate and a generous helping on the other. She saw the look that Mick gave the two plates. She explained.

"I'm small and I don't take much fuel. You are a strong working man. You need to eat to be healthy."

As they sat down at the table, Mick freshened up their wine and they touched glasses. "Here's to a new friendship, Claire. Bottoms up."

"To a new friendship Mick and may your boat never be bottoms up." Claire smiled and touched the rim of her glass just below his. Mick nodded his head. The food was delicious and Claire ate like a bird which made Mick feel like a pig. She sensed his discomfort.

"Eat, Mick. Eat. It is important for a man to eat to be strong. In China, when we were growing up, we didn't have much to eat and even today it is common when people meet that the first thing they say is "have you eaten?" It's good to have enough to eat and to take advantage of it when you can. You're a hard working man using a lot of energy every day, so don't be shy, eat."

With such encouragement, Mick finished off the delicious dinner while Claire ate sparingly. Finally, Mick pushed his plate away and got up to get more wine. Claire put her hand over the top of her glass signaling that she had had enough. "I'm not much of a drinker Mick. Alcohol goes straight to my head. But don't mind me if you want more."

He started cleaning up the table, taking away the dishes and urged her to sit and relax. "It will just take me a couple of minutes to clean up and I think that's a fair division of labor. You cook and I clean. In the meantime, tell me about yourself Claire. Your English is very good, only a slight accent, so I'm curious to know how long you've lived in Canada."

She looked at her wine glass. He made her feel so comfortable. It was something she had not experienced with a man before. "I, we, my parents and I have lived in Canada for seven years. I learned English in school but I have worked hard since we came here to really speak well."

Mick looked at her wondering if he should ask the next question. "If I'm being too personal, just tell me."

She smiled at him. "Oh, you don't have to worry about that. I'll tell you if you are."

He grinned. "Okay then. Have you ever been married?"

She turned the tables on him. "How about you Mick, have you ever been married?"

He looked at her. Was she avoiding answering? "Yeah, I've been married. Didn't work out very well though. I made a mistake and got involved with a woman who I thought was interested in the same thing I was. Going offshore sailing. But it turned out she was more interested in talking about it than doing it. She wanted to party all the time and tell everyone how she was going offshore sailing someday. She was a lot of talk and very little do and that's the way she'll always be. I didn't figure that out until it was too late. At first she was a lot of fun. But she could party, oh my word, she could party. Finally, I decided I was never going to go sailing if we stayed together, so we parted company. I escaped with my sanity and I guess I'll be going sailing alone. But at least I'll be going. As much as I'd like to find someone to share my life with, going offshore sailing is my first priority right now. I can't let anything or anyone get in the way of that dream. But," and here he looked into her eyes, "sometimes, that's a lot easier said than done."

They looked at each other for a moment and then Claire gave a little smile and nodded as if she understood. Mick had a momentary feeling that she knew a lot more about him than she was letting on. Was that a woman thing or was that a Chinese thing?

Mick continued. "That's my story. How about you?" He looked at her while he finished up washing the dishes.

"Yes, I too have been married. And like you, it didn't work out. My mother and father arranged my marriage."

"You mean they arranged the wedding details?" Mick asked.

"No, they arranged the marriage. In China, it is not unusual even today. My parents were worried about growing old without having a son-in-law who could help to take care of them. You see, my mother felt that I was not amounting to much and that meant that I would not be able to look after them very well in their old age. So they chose a husband for me who came from a reasonably wealthy family. His father was actually a peasant who had worked his way up through bribes to supply fresh produce to the army. He spent money to make money and he made a lot of money. But he was still a peasant and his son was too. But my family decided it was good for their future if I married the son. So, I was married against my wishes and against my better judgment."

Mick finished cleaning up and sat down again with Claire on the settee.

"On our wedding day, we were at the train station when I learned the true nature of my new husband. He had given me the train tickets to hold and I noticed that the tickets were actually dated for the next day and I pointed this out to him. The fact hat I would point out his mistake enraged him and in front of my family and his family and the many people on the platform, he struck me. Very hard and I was stunned. My mouth was bleeding but it wasn't a serious physical injury. It affected me more mentally. It was a shock to know that my husband would do such a thing. As it turned out, it was just the introduction to my new husband's personality. Using violence made him feel more nanxinde," she used the Chinese word and paused, searching for the translation. "I mean more manly, to physically abuse me and it only got worse over time. I decided that one day; I would put a stop to the abuse somehow, no matter how long it took."

Mick looked at her wondering how a man could do something like that to such a beautiful woman. It would be so cowardly in his opinion to do such a thing. "And did you put a stop to it?"

Claire smiled a little smile. "Yes, I did. The first thing I did when we were settled in our new home was to use my husband's money to take classes from a master. My husband did not know, nor did he care what kind of classes I was taking. He just assumed it was something that women would be interested in, so he never asked what they were. And I studied hard. For four years, I studied hard and I waited for my opportunity. And one day, the opportunity came. Oddly enough, it was in the same train station where he had struck me on our wedding day."

Mick nodded. This ought to be good he thought.

"My husband intentionally dropped his wallet on the train platform. In China, people spit on the ground everywhere, all the time. It is disgusting behavior but they do it. There was my husband's wallet, on the ground in the spit. When I didn't immediately pick it up for him, he struck me and pushed me down to pick it up. People started watching. As I was bending down to pick the wallet up, he took the opportunity to put his foot on my backside and push me over onto the dirty ground. As I lay there, looking up at him, I knew that the time had come."

Mick waited, holding his breath. "And?"

"And I turned the tables on him." Claire had a little smile on her lips. "Four years of abuse and four years of martial arts classes. By the time I was finished, he was begging me to stop. There were a lot of people on the train platform and they were shocked. The truth is that I had shamed my husband, caused him to lose face. Big time. His parents found out, my parents found out and everybody took his side. He divorced me and the courts gave him everything. Nobody was interested in my side of the story. My parents, especially my mother went on about the great shame I had brought to our family. She still goes on about the great shame I brought to our family. It is her favorite topic."

"Does this have something to do with you coming to Canada?"

Claire nodded. "Yes, it does. My mother was distraught to the point that she tried to commit suicide. It wasn't a serious attempt, it was more to gain attention than it was to hurt herself but she was hospitalized and it seemed that nothing could console her. She said that the shame was too great to live with. But one of the people who was on the train platform that day had noticed me and went to great lengths to find out where I lived. He solved our problem. He said that he had seen my martial arts moves and wanted to know if I was interested in coming to Canada to be a stunt double in a movie that he was involved with. The money was fantastic and I could bring my family too. When he spoke with my parents, my mother insisted that "we" take the job and in a matter of months, we were living in Vancouver, British Columbia and I was working in the movie business. I did that for the next three years."

Mick was amazed at her story. But having seen her moves in the pub earlier today, he could imagine she was probably good at her job. "So, why are you working at the pub now?"

A little frown crossed her face. "Because I didn't want to spend the rest of my life in the movie business. There are other things that I want to do. I saved up every penny that I earned and I gave most of it to my parents for their retirement. I hoped it would make my mother forget about the shame I had brought the family and help her to forgive me."

"And did it?" Mick thought he could guess at the answer to that question.

"No," Claire replied bitterly. "It didn't. My mother seemed to think it was the least I could do for them. After all, they could still be living in China were it not for me. And she has another potential husband lined up for me again. He's a Chinese business man on the move. He spends half of his time in China and half his time here. Very successful, all he thinks and talks about is making money which is right up my mother's alley. He is helping her learn to play the stock market with the money that I gave her."

"Is she successful?"

"No, but she's like an addict. "Don't worry" she says. "Tomorrow I will do better. I have a hunch." She trusts her hunches. But she is going to run out of money before her hunches pay off." She shook her head with disgust. She began to feel bad that she had opened up so much about her personal life but at the same time, it felt good talking about it. Mick seemed to be so understanding.

"Claire, I understand how parents can get under your skin some times but let me just tell you one thing about my mom. I didn't always see eye to eye with her and even though she passed away a couple of years ago, there are still times when I'll pick up the phone and start to dial her number and then realize I can't talk to her. It's tough because of all the people in the world, nobody understood me quite like my mom." He turned and took a drink of his wine. Maybe he was trying to cover up the emotion that was welling up in his throat or maybe it was just because he was thirsty.

    She decided that they had talked serious stuff long enough. She saw his hand resting on the table and reached out and gave it a gentle touch. They looked at each other and smiled and it was a good moment. Before the quiet became awkward, she said, "Tell me about sailing. I've never been sailing before, it must be very nice."

5 LOSING FOCUS

Mick had a problem. Five feet of problem to be exact. Claire was a remarkable combination of absolute femininity mixed with strength and stamina and was in many ways just like one of the boys. She could show up in the most elegant and sexy Chinese dress looking like a model and then burp or fart just like a guy. She would put her hand over her mouth in a shocked gesture, eyes wide with mock surprise and then burst out laughing. "Too loud?" she would ask, giggling all the while. And despite his resolve to stay focused on the task at hand, it was impossible not to fall madly in love her.

That was the problem. Mick had devoted himself to the single-minded pursuit of his dream of offshore sailing. Then, along came this little wisp of a woman and he was beginning to fall in love. But a storm cloud had come into the forecast. One night while they were relaxing after a hard day of work on Starlight, Mick had asked her about her parents and how they liked living in Canada. It was one of those topics that seemed like a good thing to talk about but in retrospect, he wished he'd never asked.

The mood which had been pleasant and relaxed suddenly tensed up. Claire looked at him for a while before answering. "My father is rather ambivalent about life here. He's a pretty easy going man. I think it's something that came from living through the Cultural Revolution. My mother and father were sent down to the country as so many people were. Uprooted from their lives and made to live in a place and in a manner that they were totally unaccustomed to. My father was in the military and he was sent to another part of China from where my mother and I were sent. My mother was a doctor and was fortunate, if you want to call it that, to be put to work taking care of the others who had been sent to the same place. The people who were sent down were educated people, people who had been successful in their lives but considered the elite, bourgeoisie, and in need of re-education. They were ill suited for working in the fields. They didn't know how to plant rice or do manual labor so they always had many different types of injuries. Needless to say, my mother was very busy and I was left to my own devices most of the time. It was a difficult time for everybody. But my mother and father were separated for a long time and my father was very stoic about it all. He never complained and simply seemed to adjust to the situation. He is like that now. But my mother is a different matter. She complains all the time about life so far from her native land. She always talks about the thousands of years of Chinese culture and the few hundred that Canadians have." Here Claire mimicked her mother saying "the few hundred" with great derision. "My mother is not happy in Canada but to be truthful, she was not happy in China either."

Mick asked Claire if her parents minded her dating a white guy though he had an inkling of the answer before Claire spoke. Claire looked at him and rolled her eyes.

"If my mother knew, she would commit suicide. It would be me shaming the family all over again." She sighed. "It's not that she is a racist. She doesn't see things that way. She just believes that the Chinese culture is so superior to every other culture that it would be wrong to mix races. I've heard her say it. "Chinese with Chinese. I don't care what anybody else does, but Chinese with Chinese." Mick wondered how he was going to resolve this problem.

Claire spent all her spare time with Mick helping him get Starlight back in the water. Then, the two of them turned their energies to Eddy's boat, cleaning and scraping and painting. Claire was completely unafraid of heights and spent a great deal of time in the bosun's chair at the top of the mast helping to repair the damaged wiring. A bonus was that it was so easy to haul her up the mast as she weighed so little.

So far, Mick and Claire had not progressed much beyond the kissing stage. A little touching here and there but Claire had asked that they take it slow and Mick respected her request. Besides, he didn't want to get his ass kicked. Nothing like seeing her nearly rip a guy's arm off to make a gentleman mind his P's and Q's. But they both knew that they were just putting off the inevitable.

When the repairs to Eddy's boat were finished and Seagram was back in the water, it was decided that they should all have a getaway weekend over at Telegraph Cove in the Gulf Islands just across the Strait of Georgia. Claire was excited about going for an overnight sail. All the other girls at work had been amazed that she had managed to interest Mick in something other than sailing. But they all agreed that given Claire's looks it was completely understandable. Eddy was taking his latest girlfriend Penny and her sister Susan. Both girls were models and didn't have much interest in sailing but like most women, they had a lot of interest in Eddy and his big fancy boat. Morris who was Mick and Eddy's neighbor and good friend from down on "B" Dock was coming along in his boat, "Slow Mo."

Mick had taken Claire out on several day sails and she had thoroughly enjoyed herself. She wasn't prone to motion sickness and despite the fact that they had run into some strong winds and heavy seas in the Strait of Georgia, she was eager for more. The sail over to the islands was going to be her first chance to overnight on the boat.

The weather turned out to be perfect with clear skies and mild temperatures. The wind had been pretty light and they had all put their spinnakers up, big balloon sails that helped them make good time across to the islands. Mick and Claire did some fishing along the way and had been lucky enough to catch a salmon which went on the bar-b-cue once they got anchored in Telegraph Harbor.

It was a great day of sailing, eating and relaxing. After dinner, as they sat in Seagram's cockpit, they discussed Sunday's plan. It was a rather one sided conversation, mostly between Claire and Mick. Eddy wasn't paying much attention as he was busy snuggling with his girlfriend Penny. The sister, Susan was sitting on Morris's lap and was nibbling on his ear. Despite the chilly evening, the temperature was heating up.

Mick made a big production out of stretching and yawning. "We're going to turn in early."

Nobody paid any attention and Claire grinned at him and rolled her eyes. It appeared that their presence was not going to be missed in the slightest. They hopped in their dingy and rowed back to Starlight. It was almost dark and the last of the sunset colors were fading quickly from the sky. It was going to be a great night for stargazing.

Getting There

Onboard Starlight, Claire busied herself down below making tea, humming to herself as she worked in the galley. Mick went around on deck, tidying up and getting the boat ready for the night. As he stood in the cockpit, he could see Claire down in the cabin, the kerosene lamps giving a warm glow to her face. She looked up and smiled at him. Finishing in the galley, she came out into the cockpit and stood next to Mick. It was quiet in the bay.

"Mick, I've got some tea ready. Would you like to sit out here for a while? It's so peaceful. I could get used to this."

Mick put his arm around her and held her close, enjoying the warmth of her body. Some kind of sea creature splashed along the shore line. A little burst of laughter came from one of the other boats at anchor. The soft darkness felt ready to swallow them whole. "Sometimes, when I'm anchored out here, I feel like I don't need to sail anywhere else in the world. I mean how could any place be better than this?" Mick gestured around with his free hand at the tranquil scene that surrounded them.

Claire moved tighter to him and put her arms around his waist, her head lying against his chest. "So, why go? Quit working on boats in the marina and come and live in the islands on your boat and sculpt. What makes you feel like you have to go offshore sailing when you just said it yourself that it would be hard to find anything better than this." She already knew the answer.

"Because I want to prove something to myself. I want to experience something that not many people get to experience. Crossing an ocean on your own. Overcoming every challenge. Finding that place where I can find my rhythm and offer myself up for whatever is in store for me. I think you know what I'm talking about."

Claire nodded. She understood about these matters. Proving to yourself that you can overcome all the odds against you. Overcoming your fears. She understood completely.

"Claire, why don't you come with me? We could do it together."

Claire had been expecting this. She knew it was coming and she was tempted to say yes. She wanted to shout it out across this beautiful quiet bay. She wanted this man like none other before. Instead, she moved away from him and stepped towards the cabin doorway and turned to Mick. "Why don't you come with me?"

She held out her hand and led him down into the cabin where she did everything in her power to show him how much she wanted to say yes.

6 PARTY TIME

Eddy looked out the porthole and saw the frost on the dock. He had been drinking since the party started right after everyone got off work and it was now just before midnight. It had been a bummer of a week. The weekend over at Telegraph Harbor had been a blast. On Sunday, Mick and Claire looked like the happiest couple in the world. Obviously, they'd had a great night. Eddy couldn't have been happier for them. Claire deserved a great guy like Mick and vice versa. He was feeling rather pleased with his match making efforts.

Once they had come back to the marina however, everything had gone to hell in a hand basket. Claire had suddenly vanished without any warning leaving only a letter for Mick. Eddy had read the letter that night as he had tried to console the inconsolable man. Claire explained that a family emergency had come up and it was her duty to deal with it. That and the fact that she wanted Mick to go offshore sailing, to fulfill his dream and she didn't want to side track him from that goal. She didn't want him to grow to hate her for stopping him from his dream and she felt that this is what would happen if she didn't leave. She couldn't go with him because she had obligations that she had to deal with and begged him not to try to find her. She had never told him where her family lived and nobody seemed to know. Needless to say, Mick was devastated. But, Claire had succeeded in one thing and that was to give Mick the final push to get going.

Eddy had tried to convince Mick to come to the Saturday night party but Mick was going on one last sail over to the islands so Eddy had gone to the party without him. It was probably a good thing that

Mick hadn't come since there had been a lot of conversation about Claire's sudden disappearance.

Dot and Bill, the boat owners, had invited everyone over for the usual Saturday night get together. Steve and Amanda had the forty five footer in the next berth but were probably going to just stay the night. Jessica from down on "C" dock had come without her partner Dave. They were having relationship troubles and Dave was probably working on their boat. These days, he was less and less likely to show up with Jessica. She was a real hard partier and he was getting tired of it. He wanted to focus more on getting the boat ready for going offshore and it pissed him off that she spent most of her energy and time on partying. But as far as Jessica was concerned, one of the big reasons for life on the water was to party.

Jessica had brought her usual assortment of homemade wines or "high octane grape juice" as she called it. It was delicious stuff but it was nearly toxic in its alcohol content. Most people had the same reaction to it. They would have a sip and utter the same "mmmmm, that's good!" Then they would have a glass, then another and another. Enjoying every mouthful but being totally unaware of the dangers. Then, inevitably it would hit them like a sledge hammer and if they were lucky, they had time to get to the toilet or outside before throwing up. Tonight, during a game of cards, Steve's wife, Amanda, a big strapping girl who could usually hold her own in the drinking department wound up being caught short and had to use the galley wastebasket to throw up in. She apologized profusely while kneeling on the cabin floor with her head poised over the wastebasket. Everyone was pretty toasted and just ignored her. It wasn't unusual when Jessica's wine was involved.

Eddy had years of hard drinking under his belt and was well aware of the potency of Jessica's wine. He had paced himself through the evening and was pleased that he was able to stand reasonably steady. He would not have passed a field sobriety test but since he was just going to walk back to his own boat that was not a problem.

He helped clean up the dishes and stacked them in the galley sink. Amanda was now curled up sleeping on the cabin floor near the wastebasket. Eddy covered her with a blanket.

The card players were in the middle of things so he quietly bid them good night and headed up the companionway stairs. As he slid the hatch back and swung the doors open, he was greeted by a gust of cold air. It was chilly tonight. Stars were out and there was frost on the decks and dock. He stepped out into the cockpit and closed the doors and hatch behind him. For a moment, he stood in the dark letting the cold clear his head. He took a deep sniff of the air. The wind was bringing a tang of the ocean up the river and it smelled good. Despite the cold, he didn't bother putting his jacket on. It was a refreshing change to the heat inside the boat. He felt alive. Living on the water suited Eddy. He had lived on land for most of his life and this closeness to nature always made him feel happy that he had his boat and this new life.

Carefully working his way to the opening in the rail, he stepped down to the dock. It was slippery with the frost but if he was careful and didn't move too fast, he was going to be just fine. His boat, Seagram, was two docks down the river. He walked carefully to the ramp leading up to the road. As he got near the top, he slipped on the frosty ramp and dropped his jacket which he was carrying in one hand. It fell over the side of the ramp and onto the rocks down below. He peered over the railing into the dark shadows. Big rocks, slippery with algae and frost. There was no way he was going after the jacket tonight. He was definitely feeling the wine, no doubt about it. He decided to leave the jacket until tomorrow when he would be able to get it in the daylight.

He opened the gate and as he stepped through it banged shut behind him. It was quiet in the yard except for the clanging of halyards against masts in the breeze. Off in the distance, toward his dock, he could see that the bar was still open and people were coming and going. But here it was quiet.

Just as he started walking along the road, a car suddenly switched on its headlights, shining directly into his eyes. His hand came up to block the bright light and he could see there were people getting out of the vehicle and coming toward him. There was a good hundred feet or so between him and the car but he clearly heard a voice which he recognized immediately.

"Hello Eddy".

It was said in a neutral way. Not threatening but Eddy knew there was a threat coming. No doubt about it, there was one coming. There were two people with the man. The three of them formed a good sized wall blocking the way along the road. They were coming toward him and he stopped in his tracks.

"Did you think we were never going to find you Eddy?"

Eddy took a couple of steps backward and came up against the locked gate. Until he got that gate unlocked, there was no escape in that direction. He called out to them. "You've got the wrong person, I'm not Eddy." It was weak but worth a try.

"Yeah, you're Eddy alright and we need to talk. We've been waiting a long time, freezing our asses off back east while you've been living it up out here. Don't give us a hard time, okay?"

The voice belonged to David Enzio. This was a real problem. Eddy thought he had been very careful in covering his tracks and establishing a new life. He knew Enzio had been living in exile in the east but now he was back. How had they had found him? He was going to have to worry about that later but right now, he had to get away. He pulled the key out of his pocket and turned to the gate. There wasn't much light and he was drunk and cold now without his jacket. Fear had grabbed him deep inside and he was shivering. Shit. The key wouldn't go in the hole. He was a little frantic and thought maybe he had the key upside down but as he rotated it in his cold fingers, it slipped and fell to the ground. He could sense the men coming closer. He looked down and knew that he didn't have time to find the key. He pushed on the gate, rattling it but it was not going to open. He looked back and saw that David and his men had stopped and were watching him. There was nowhere to run and getting down on the dock was the only option. He took a few steps towards the men and saw that they seemed to relax a little though it was difficult to tell for sure as the men were silhouetted against the car headlights. Maybe he could play along, buy some time. Despite the cold, he felt a rush of sweat to his armpits. He started walking towards them until he was about twenty feet from the gate.

"David, I wish I could say it's good to see you but frankly, I was hoping that I'd never see you again." Eddy eyeballed the distance between them. About two boat lengths. Big boats. Then, he turned and sprinted towards the gate aiming slightly to the right. He could hear the men behind him start to run, their shoes making crunchy noises in the gravel. Just a few feet away from the fence he jumped and the toe of his topsider punched perfectly into one of the chain links. Excellent purchase and he grabbed the fence with both hands and scrambled up toward the top. One, two, only one more and he would be able to swing over and down the other side. There was hope on the other side of the fence if he could get down the ramp and head for Dot and Bill's boat again. He could jump in the dingy they had tied up behind their boat and get the hell out onto the river. Then he could head for his boat and get going before they caught on. Maybe Enzio didn't know where Seagram was tied up.

As he was just about to swing up and over the top he began to feel elation, like he was going to make it but his emotions were brought back to earth as one of the men managed to grab his pant leg and pull him backwards. He hung on for a moment but his fingers were only holding onto the thin wire of the fence. Even in his fear and desperation, his fingers were no match for the force applied by the man behind him. He hung on for as long as his fingers could stand the pain until finally releasing and falling backwards. The fear of falling was not as great as the fear of what he was falling towards. Eddy knew it wasn't going to be pleasant.

He remembered the old saying that it wasn't the fall that killed you, it was the landing. This time, the landing was cushioned by the body of the man that pulled him off the fence. Eddy fell backwards with enough momentum that he smashed into the man and the two of them crashed to the gravel, Eddy on top. Eddy's legs were already churning trying to get him into position to start running, somewhere, anywhere. But the man on the bottom grunted and wrapped two beefy strong arms around him and held tight.

Eddy, sensing that he was not going to be able to break free, leaned forward with his neck and shoulders and then brought his head back with as much force as he could muster. He felt the back of his head make contact with something soft and he heard the man below him cry out in pain and Eddy felt the big arms around his chest loosen slightly.

By this time, David Enzio and the other man had reached the two flailing bodies on the ground. Eddy looked up and saw Enzio signal to his sidekick. Eddy knew that there wasn't much point in struggling. The odds were stacked against him. He felt calmness spread through his body as he realized the end was near. He saw the big man above him pull his arm back. In the harsh lighting from the headlights of the car, Eddy saw the man's big fist begin a downward arc. He could see a large ring, a class ring of some kind on one of the man's fingers. Eddy knew it was going to hurt when it contacted his face. Despite everything, he felt a giggle come to his lips as he thought of the coroner taking a casting of the imprint of the ring from Eddy's crushed skull. Good identification material. The ring that cracked his skull could crack the case he thought. But that was the last thought to cross his mind as the ring and the big hand made contact.

7 DOWN TIME

As he sipped from his cup of coffee, the sun was just coming up; touching the tips of the masts of the sailboats along the dock. The frost on the dock was thick like a fuzzy white carpet. It wasn't unusual to see frost this late in the spring down at water level. Here and there, wisps of smoke were coming from chimneys poking up through decks of boats. Out on the river, a couple of seagulls called out, sounding like they were arguing over some scrap of food. A car crunched along the gravel road heading into the work yard. Someone getting an early start on the day.

Mick stood in the open hatch waiting for the sun to get up high enough to warm the decks and melt the frost. He looked across the dock at Seagram and shook his head again. Everything looked normal. Everything looked the same as it did every morning. The river was running to the sea, the way it was supposed to. Boats bobbed and floated as per the rules of hydrodynamics. The sun had come up just like it did every day. Mick rubbed his tired eyes and then felt the stubble of whiskers on his face. Same as always. How could things seem so normal when so much had changed?

Yes, the world was a changed place now that Eddy was gone. If a man is measured by the friends he keeps then Eddy would need a big measuring cup. He was, had been friends with everyone. Good and bad alike. Mick had met some wonderful people during his time with Eddy and he had met some people that he hoped to never cross paths with again. But Eddy drew few distinctions. He was an equal opportunity friend. He was there for everyone at anytime and in any need. If he had something that you needed, he was happy to let you have it.

Seagram was his pride and joy. Mick didn't know how a guy like Eddy could afford a boat like that but he had never asked and Eddy had never volunteered. Maybe he had made his money through his unusual mechanical aptitude. Weak in many areas of personal development, such as being a chronic alcoholic and a womanizer, Eddy was a mechanical genius. He could fix anything, anyplace, anytime. Like a drunken faith healer, he could lay his hands on a balky engine and make that reluctant assemblage of parts fall into line. He didn't need training on a new piece of equipment; he simply knew how it worked. All the bright sparks in the marina who were paid to know how to fix and install things came to Eddy at one time or another for advice or help. Eddy kept their visits to himself so as to not embarrass the pros. It didn't matter to him that they took credit for his work.

Seagram was a mechanical and technological dream. Mick preferred a more traditional vessel under his feet but he had to admire the efficiency and power of Eddy's machine. When they sailed together, Mick usually saw only the stern end of Seagram, if he could see it at all. Eddy was the front man; always the first one to get to their destination. Calling over the VHF, he would report in with the best anchorage locations, the hazards to avoid, what other vessels were in the bay, often making a joke of what time zone he was in. Mick would come sauntering in a while later trying hard to make it seem like he was content to take his time while in reality feeling a little chagrined at being left in Eddy's nautical dust so to speak.

It was good that their last sail together had been so much fun. They had all had a wonderful time at Telegraph Harbor. But the memory of it was tainted for Mick. He had thought that Claire had been so much in love with him. She had given herself body and soul to him but now she was gone. And Eddy was gone now too. And the world that looked so normal was so totally different. How crazy was that?

Mick had gone sailing on Friday afternoon, to try to clear his mind and come to terms with Claire's actions and also to avoid being around people who would ask questions he couldn't answer about where Claire had gone and why. Just before leaving, Eddy had invited him to the Saturday night gathering down at Dot and Bill's boat but Mick had declined. Coming back on Sunday night, he wasn't surprised to see that there weren't any lights showing on Seagram. It wasn't unusual that Eddy might be out drinking or chumming around the marina.

    Not thinking anything might be out of the ordinary; Mick had done the usual post trip chores. After cleaning up, he had gone up to the marina pub for a couple of beers. Walking into what would usually be a noisy evening of dart playing and music from the jukebox, it was a surprise to see a very subdued and tired looking group of his friends. As Mick entered the room, everyone turned to look at him. He stopped at the doorway, puzzled by the strange somber feeling he was picking up. Something was definitely not right. It was his first glimpse of the new world.

    He frowned, wondering what the hell was going on. As he stood there, the door opened behind him and he was immediately grabbed up in a bear hug.

    "Aw man, you're back. I guess you've heard." It was Morris his neighbor from down on B dock. Morris and Mick and Eddy were like the three amigos of B dock. "Man, it's so messed up."

    Mick broke free of the hug and turned. "What the hell is going on Morris? Heard what?" So caught up in his depression over Claire, he suspected the bad news might have something to do with her.

    Morris looked at him and then at the crowd at the tables. He grimaced and grabbed Mick and pulled him towards the bar signaling for a couple of beers.

    "Jeez Mick, I thought you would have heard by now. Come on, let's sit down and have a beer and I'll fill you in."

    They sat and Morris pulled out a pack of tobacco and his papers. As he rolled himself a cigarette he sighed and looked at Mick. "We don't really know for sure what's going on. But one thing we know for sure," Morris took a deep breath and then blew it out. "Eddy is gone."

    Only three words. How bad could that be? How much change could three words make? Mick had a bad feeling growing in his stomach. Kind of like being seasick. That queasy, sweaty feeling. "What do you mean gone? He's not gone. He never mentioned that he was going anywhere and he would have told me for sure. Come on Morris, what are you talking about? Gone where?" He heard a touch of panic in his own voice. Mick looked around at the others in the room. They were all looking grim, tired and defeated. He shook his head for the first time that night. He didn't know the details but he had a bad feeling that he knew what "gone" meant.

What he wanted more than anything was for "gone" to mean all the usual things, all the mundane, normal everyday things. Gone to visit his grandma. Gone to the dentist. Gone to see that bitch ex-girlfriend that had turned all their lives upside down a while back. Gone fishing. Almost any kind of gone except what he feared had really happened.

He knew that Eddy wasn't gone sailing because Seagram was down at the dock right now, right where it should be, right across from his own boat. He wished that he could just get up and head back down to Starlight and turn in and wake up in the morning and never have to hear what gone really meant.

Morris put a match to his cigarette. He took a drag and exhaled out of the corner of his mouth away from Mick. He laid a big hand on Mick's arm. "He's gone Mick. Early Sunday morning, somehow or another, he disappeared. Dot and Bill heard some kind of commotion and they figured out that Eddy must have fallen in the river. They searched as much as they could in the dark but even after searching all day today, we still haven't found anything."

Some news is easier to take than others. Maybe it depends on where you are when you hear the bad news or maybe the time of day or if you've got other things on your mind. Maybe a busy stressed out mind makes it easier to handle the big bad news. It fits in with the pattern of your brain waves better. But Mick had just come back from a weekend of sailing and the possible drowning death of a close friend was too much to comprehend. He stared blankly at Morris for a moment.

"What makes you so sure that he fell in the river?" He finally asked, waving away some of the smoke that drifted his way.

Mo turned his eyes up as he thought back on the details of Saturday night. "Well, apparently he was heading home after partying at Dot and Bill's boat. He'd been drinking pretty heavy," and here he looked at Mick giving a little toss of his hands and a shrug, "like usual. You know Eddy. But apparently he was doing alright, walking fairly steady. He said goodnight to everyone and headed home."

"And?"

Morris took a swig of his beer and signaled to Kostis to bring another round. "And, he went home, supposedly. But Dot said that not long after he left their boat, they heard the gate clang shut and then just a couple of minutes later, they heard a commotion on the road by the gate. When they got up on deck and looked out, they didn't see anything." He left the statement hanging there like it should mean something.

"And?" Mick said again, gesturing a questioning look at Morris. "What's that supposed to mean? So what if they didn't see anything? Eddy said he was going home. The gate clangs shut and when they look up to the road, there's nothing there. So what?"

Morris gave a deep sigh. "The thing is that Eddy didn't get back to his boat. Dot was a little concerned. You know how she worries about everyone, and she went over to Seagram later to see if he got home safely but there weren't any lights on and when she knocked there wasn't any answer and then she found that the hatch was still locked from the outside, so we know he didn't go home. And he wasn't anywhere else, such as here in the pub, or in the laundry room or in the showers. Nowhere to be found. And he hasn't shown up yet."

Mick looked at Morris with a skeptical look on his face. "You don't think there's some other possibility, like he met somebody and went with them? He knows a million different chicks. He could have gone over to some girl's place for the weekend. Hell, he's probably not going to be home until it's time to go to work in the morning. What's everybody so freaked out about?"

Morris looked a little peeved that Mick was not seeing things the way the rest of them were. "Well, we considered the possibility that he might have gone with someone because frankly, Dot did see a car speeding off when she looked up towards the road. It was a black Lexus."

Mick looked at Morris like Morris was an idiot. A few sails short of a full suit.

Morris got an impatient look on his face. "Okay, I forgot to mention that little detail. But the kicker is this. We found his jacket on the rocks at the base of the gate just above the high tide line. We're thinking that he went up the ramp, through the gate, realized he needed to come back down to the boat for some reason and had to climb over the fence to do it. We've all done that before. As a matter of fact, we found his key in the dirt on the outside of the gate. So he must have dropped his key, couldn't find it in the dark, climbed the fence, lost his balance and fell into the river." He looked at Mick like it made perfect sense. "And," he said seeing that Mick was not looking particularly convinced, "and, because the tide was going out and it was maximum ebb at that time of the night, he ended up heading out to the mouth of the river. Don't you get it Mick; he's gone, dead and gone and we can't find his body. All of us," and here he gestured around at the crowd at the other tables, "have been out on the river searching for him, every daylight hour." Morris began tearing up as the reality of it came to him once again. He grabbed his beer and took a large swig.

Mick reached out, putting one hand on Morris's shoulder. He wasn't sure he bought it. There were too many holes in the story. But he could tell that Morris was exhausted and overcome by the whole ordeal.

"Look, Mo, take it easy. It's late. You're tired and there's nothing more you can do tonight. Let's hit the rack and get together first thing in the morning and see if we can't figure out what to do. Have you called the police?"

Morris nodded his head as he rolled himself another cigarette. "Yeah. Fat lot of good that did. We called those bastards right away but they said that unless we had more information, there wasn't much that they could do. They know Eddy, you know." Mick nodded. The R.C.M.P. would know all about Eddy. He'd been in their system a few times for drinking and driving. Of course they would think this was just another of Eddy's drunken escapades.

Mick stood up. "Come on Mo. Let's turn in and get a fresh start in the morning. Let's not assume the worst just yet. I've got fresh eyes and a fresh perspective on the whole thing."

Morris looked at him, a cigarette hanging from the corner of his mouth. He was wasted. Tired and confused and depressed. Maybe Mick was right. There was little they could do tonight.

Morris and Mick left after saying goodnight to the others and letting them know that they would pick it up in the morning. Together the two of them walked down to the quiet end of "B" dock and stood for a moment outside of Seagram. It was too much to handle, so they just stood in silence for a moment and then went to their own boats.

Mick stopped and said to Morris, "You going to be OK?"

"Probably. I think I'll just go to bed and sleep. I remember when I was a deckhand on a tug boat and we did a two week trip, we had a saying. "You're not really here when you're asleep." Right now, I don't really want to be here, so I think I'll try to sleep. Let's get together in the morning and see if we can't figure out what's next. Thanks for bringing some sanity into the situation. It's been pretty chaotic."

Getting There

    Mick looked at him and nodded and as much as he hoped things were going to be alright, the way he was feeling, he doubted it.

8 INVESTIGATING

As the sun eased up and over the trees on Annacis Island, Mick finished his coffee and decided it was time to roust the troops. Time to get things underway for the day. Grabbing his jacket from the quarter berth, he loaded his pockets with a Kershaw Speedsafe knife, his van keys and cell phone. He didn't have much of a plan but decided that it would be best to start where the events of Saturday evening had somehow gone south. He locked Starlight's hatch and then went next door to Slow Mo, Morris's boat. Where Seagram was big, a forty nine foot, high tech marvel and Starlight was a thirty seven foot ocean cruiser, Slow Mo was the little sister of the three. The Dana 24 was a pint sized sailboat, scaled down but in every way as ready for the wide open ocean as the others. Just smaller. Mick stood by the stern and knocked on the hull and almost instantly, the hatch slid back and Morris's head poked up. Bleary eyed, Morris gave a nod of the head and waved Mick onboard. Mick stepped into the cockpit and stuck his head down the companionway. "Hey Mo, how's things this morning?" Morris was pouring a cup of coffee and raised the pot in a questioning manner to Mick. He was obviously not up for conversation just yet.

"Yeah, I'll have a cup. Thanks. I've got a key to Eddy's boat and I'm thinking we should take a look at Seagram and see if there's any indication that Eddy did come home. Then, go over to "E" dock and take a look around." Morris looked at him, paused in pouring the coffee.

"You think you might see something we overlooked?" He looked skeptical but shrugged. "I suppose it couldn't hurt. You never know. I'm hoping for a miracle at this point Mick."

Mick looked at Morris and chuckled. "Morris, the real miracle is that Eddy got this far in his life without killing himself. If we find him and he's okay, it will just be another amazing event."

Morris nodded. "Well, let's hope we find something amazing."

Seagram was tied up just opposite to Mick's boat on a finger that extended out into the river. They finished up their coffee and then walked down the finger to the small set of stairs sitting next to the boarding gate in the railing of Seagram. Mick went first and stepped up onto the side deck, over the coaming and into the cockpit. Morris followed him and together they stood looking over the white fiberglass vessel.

"I never get used to how big this baby is. It's got so much room out on deck compared to Starlight."

The Hunter was a big boat, well designed for offshore sailing and comfort all at the same time. The cockpit area had wide seats with lots of room to lay down and snooze in the sun. A center mounted console had leaves that opened up to form a nice sized table for dining in style. Mick and Eddy had spent many evenings anchored in the island bays sitting at this very table enjoying a card game or talking. Aft, two wheels for steering were mounted, one to port and one to starboard. It was a nice touch to be able to steer from either side. Things on deck looked normal. Mick stepped forward, reached into his pocket and pulled out his ring of keys. He picked through the keys until he found the right one and inserted it into the lock on the hatch.

Mick pushed the hatch back, swung the doors open and peered down the companionway ladder. He stepped over the sill and started down into the cabin. As he reached the bottom, he stopped dead in his tracks. His mouth was actually hanging open with surprise when Morris bumped into his back.

"What the hell?"

Mick moved to the right into the galley so that Morris could get down the stairs. Morris's face immediately matched the look on Mick's. "Wow. Eddy's not much of a housekeeper." The place was a mess. It looked like a hurricane had passed through, churning everything into a wrecked mess. Drawers had been pulled out and dumped on the cabin floor. The contents were strewn in disarray all over. Cushions from the settee on the port side and from the dining nook on the starboard side were strewn about with the stuffing pulled out through long slits in the fabric. Books which had been stored neatly in the lockers along both sides had been thrown to the floor after having many pages ripped out. The flat screen TV which had been mounted on the forward bulkhead over the dining nook had been ripped from its mounts and now hung face down dangling by its power cord.

The galley had similarly been ransacked. At Mick's feet lay a small mountain of opened plastic storage containers with contents such as flour and rice and several types of cereal all mixed together. The cutlery drawers had been pulled out and emptied on top of the food debris on the floor. The doors under the sink had actually been ripped off their hinges and had been walked on showing footprints in white flour. The dishes had been pulled from their cabinet and lay strewn across the floor.

The navigation station was a nightmare. The electronic panel which housed the circuit breakers, power gauges, and a variety of monitoring equipment had been unscrewed and lay hanging by wires. The desktop which was hinged to lift up and usually covered an assortment of pens and papers and tide books and navigating tools was ripped free.

Pretty much everything had been damaged in one way or another. Mick and Morris looked at each other, remaining silent and both shaking their heads. There was an anger building. It was palpable but unspoken. Morris went towards the forward cabin which was Eddy's main sleeping quarters. Mick turned from the damaged galley and went aft into the starboard quarter berth which also included Eddy's office. The door had been kicked open as evidenced by the broken jamb. The desk which was right inside against the starboard hull was completely destroyed. Whoever had done this had been out of control angry, ransacking with a vengeance. The two drawers had been pulled out and dumped on the floor. Both drawers lay broken in pieces further aft near the base of the bunk. File folders, paper, bills, notebooks, photos were everywhere. The mattress had been slashed open and the foam lay in chunks around the small room.

Morris had to push open the door to the forward stateroom. The mattress had been pulled off the bunk and was laying slashed and gutted on the floor. As he entered the room, he was desperately hoping that someone would be hiding there. He was ready to rip someone's head off. Make someone pay for this. Not only was it an outrage to Eddy but so senseless to do so much damage to such a beautiful boat. Morris yanked the door to the head open ready to grab anyone hiding there but he was disappointed. Again, everything had been pulled off the shelves and out of drawers and dumped on the floor. Anything that could be broken was.

They met again in the main salon, looking grim faced and filled with anger. Morris kicked a cup and it ricocheted off of the base of the galley counter and lay spinning in one of the few bare spots on the floor.

"Hey, don't add to the damage." Mick bent over and grabbed the spinning cup and put it on the counter. "Jesus, what could have prompted someone to do this? I mean what the hell is going on?"

Morris picked some books off the port settee and sat down with the books on his lap. He jumped up and picked up a pair of dividers that were hiding in the torn cushion fabric. Sitting down again, he looked at Mick.

"If I find the son of a bitch that did this, I promise, I will tear him to shreds, just like he did to this boat. Jeez, what a mess. What's going on? Who would do this? I mean Eddy doesn't have enemies. Not that I know of. You ever heard anyone say anything bad about Eddy?"

Mick shook his head. He looked around the cabin and let out a sigh. "Wow. I can't believe it. It looks like a bomb went off in here. Whoever did this had to be plenty pissed off to do so much damage. This isn't just vandalism. This is someone looking for something specific but they could have just come in and snooped around without tearing the place up. So, they must have had an axe to grind with Eddy."

"Yeah, and used it too. I guess we should report this to the police." Morris shook his head. "You know, the fact that the hatch was still locked is odd. Do you think that the police might think that Eddy did this himself as some kind of insurance scam? Or," and here he looked at Mick, "think that maybe someone who had a key to Eddy's boat did it to get back at Eddy for some reason." Mick raised his eyebrows and laughed.

"What are you saying Mo? I came on board, let myself in and tore Eddy's boat up because he did something to piss me off. That's a real stretch. And besides, I was away sailing for the weekend."

Morris waved his hand. "Naw, I'm not saying that but don't you think it's pretty weird that the hatch was locked? That means that someone let themselves in, tore the place up and then left and locked up behind themselves. That's pretty strange."

Mick thought about this for a moment and then nodded his head. "Yeah, Mo, it's weird alright. But how about this. They tore the place up, looking for something and then left and locked the hatch so that nobody would see the damage and call the cops. That way, it would buy them some time."

Morris ran his fingers through his hair and sat back against the torn cushions. "Time for what? Are you suggesting that Eddy is mixed up with some bad ass guy or guys and they did this and they kidnapped him? For what? Ransom? Eddy doesn't have any relatives. Who's going to pay ransom for Eddy? Us? Christ we don't have a pot to piss in."

Mick shrugged. "I don't know Mo. I honestly don't know. I'm just guessing but let's go over to "E" dock and take a look around with this in mind." He gestured around. "You just never know what we'll find."

The two of them set off towards "E" dock not really knowing what they were looking for but hoping for the best. In just the short time since that they had coffee on Slow Mo, it had clouded over and begun to rain, just a sprinkle so far but from the looks of the sky, there was plenty more to come. Mick and Mo walked along Dike Road in silence, pondering what they had just found on Seagram. It didn't take long before they arrived at the gate leading down to "E" dock. It was here that something had taken place to cause the disappearance of their friend Eddy. They stood together, hands in their pockets and looked around.

Mo broke the silence. "Well Mick, any suggestions?"

Mick went over to the fence next to the gate and put his fingers through the chain link. He stared down onto the rocks that lined the shore along the river. It was low tide though the water was still fairly high, the ramp leading down to the dock not having much of an angle to it. The water was typically muddy looking, brown and quietly swirling around the pilings of the dock. "Where did you find Eddy's jacket?"

Morris came and stood next to Mick and pointed to a spot not far from the gate and almost directly under one side of the ramp. "Right about where the end of that log is." He turned and leaned up against the fence and pulled his tobacco pouch from his pocket and hunched over, rolling a cigarette in the protection of his jacket.

Getting There

As the two of them stood there taking in the scene around them, Mick thought about the night in question. Eddy had come up the ramp and through the gate. Dot had heard the gate slam shut. Something happened somewhere along the way that had caused Eddy to lose his jacket. Before or after he went through the gate, that was one question. What had happened after he went through the gate? If he had met someone in a black Lexus and drove off in a hurry, why would his jacket be on the rocks by the water? It was cold Saturday night so why wasn't he wearing his jacket? Mick looked at the gravel road in front of the gate. There were lots of muddy puddles along the sides of the road and some trash here and there. A MacDonald's bag, a plastic quart oil container, one of those plastic things that holds six cans of pop or beer. Near the middle of the road was a pack of matches and some change. Mick knelt down to pick up the change. Two quarters, a dime and when he swept a few larger pieces of gravel out of the way, a Looney. And, a damp opened book of matches.

"Hey Mo. Score. I found a buck sixty in change and a book of matches from the Tsawwassen Motel." He was about to toss the book of matches but hesitated for a moment. He stood up and moved back to get a larger view of the roadway. The road had recently been graded judging from the smoothness of the gravel. But in one spot, where the change had been laying, the gravel was disturbed, lots of scuffing and footprints.

Morris watched Mick. "What's on your mind Mick?"

"You ever seen the Tsawwassen Motel? Know where it is?"

Morris shook his head. "Nope. You thinking that maybe someone from the motel came and picked Eddy up? Do you think Eddy dropped that book of matches? Why would he go to a motel out in Tsawwassen?"

Mick shrugged. "Dot says she saw a black Lexus take off around the time that Eddy might have been at this spot. Suppose this fell out of the car or out of someone's pocket that saw Eddy. Suppose we went to the Tsawwassen Motel and found a black Lexus. Maybe Eddy went there with someone." He looked at the front of the match book and saw the address of the Tsawwassen Motel. Ladner Trunk Road, Delta. "It's not far away, just over in Delta."

Morris looked skeptical. "That seems like a hell of a long shot Mick. You're grasping at straws."

Mick nodded. "Yeah, I suppose so but think about it. This matchbook is damp. But it's not soaked to pulp. It rained on Friday and on Friday night but cleared up for the weekend. So, the matches have to have been dropped sometime Saturday or Sunday. I know it's a long shot but other than searching the river along with everyone else, what other bright ideas have we got? Zilch." Morris was looking interested. "We could jump in the van and take a little trip over to Delta, check out the motel, see if we see a black Lexus or maybe run into Eddy and a hot little number. If we don't, we grab some coffee and breakfast on the way back. What do you say?"

    Morris rubbed his belly. "I think I could use something to eat. Let's go.

9 THE INTERROGATION

David Enzio shot his cuffs. Perhaps it was to impress Eddy with his Sazikov guilloche cufflinks or to simply release some of the tension of the moment. He turned and went to the window. Moving the curtain aside slightly, he looked out into the parking lot again. It was raining heavily now, though the morning had started out sunny.

"Bloody rain. What would possess people to live in this part of the world when it rains all the time? One second the sun is out and the next, it's pouring. It's hard to keep from getting depressed with weather like this. Wouldn't you agree Eddy?"

It was difficult for Eddy to comment as his mouth was covered with duct tape and he was groggy from the beating he had received at the hands of Enzio's two beefy assistants. Eddy's nose had been broken and he had blood running down and dripping from his quivering chin. His head hung down but it made breathing even more difficult. He was thinking in his hazy mind that before he succumbed from the beating, he might simply suffocate. It might be the best of the situation. But he had to agree with Enzio, it was hard to keep from getting depressed.

The assistant named Horst grabbed Eddy by the hair and pulled his head back up. He leaned over Eddy's shoulder and said loudly into his ear, "Mr. Enzio's talking to you. Are you paying attention?" He sounded stuffed up like he had a cold. He gave Eddy's head a shake by the hair. It was a little bit of payback for the broken nose he had received when he had pulled Eddy down from the fence at the marina. The back of Eddy's head had made good contact with

Horst's nose and he was pissed off because the blood from his broken nose had dripped on his new leather jacket. He had spent a lot of time with a damp cloth in the motel bathroom trying to remove the blood stains on the front and the mud stains on the back from the hard landing on the road.

Enzio turned and walked back to where Eddy was duct taped securely to the chair. He stood looking down at him and then squatted in front of the chair.

"Eddy, I want to make something very clear to you. I need to know where the money is. You simply must tell me, or I will be forced to let my assistants have at you again. We were very patient waiting for you to come around and we've been over and over this and now our patience is running rather short." He snapped his fingers in front of Eddy's face wondering if he was listening. "Can you hear me Mr. Wainright?"

Eddy began to cry. The tears were streaming down his face. He was embarrassed by the show of emotion but was unable to stop the flow. He had never been in this situation before but he had often wondered how he might react if put in such a position. Now he knew. He had already pissed his pants. That had come quite early in the interrogation when the reality of the situation had closed in on him. That was embarrassing enough but for some reason, the tears were even more so. Perhaps it was the look of disgust on Enzio's face.

Enzio reached up and gripped the duct tape and ripped it from Eddy's mouth. Eddy leaned back in his seat and gulped in a great suck of air. "Oh God. Thank you David, thank you. Please don't tape my mouth again. I can barely breathe through my nose." He bent over again and began to sob.

The two hulks looked at each other and shook their heads. Enzio himself stood up and began to pace back and forth. "Eddy that will be quite enough of the tears thank you. I remember the last fellow I killed." Here Horst and Tommy, the other muscle bound helper rolled their eyes. They had heard it all before. "All the time I questioned him, he maintained a stoic attitude. It was all business. He never cried or pissed his pants, like you, you disgusting worm. Right up till the end, he took it like a man. I was almost reluctant to finish him off but I had to because he wouldn't tell me what I wanted to know. And that's what's going to happen to you if you don't tell me what I want to know."

At that point, Eddy decided to come clean. It was that, or die. "The money's on my boat. What's left of it. I used some of it to buy my boat and I used some of it to live on but the rest of it's there." He sounded earnest. At least he hoped he did.

Enzio stopped his pacing and looked at Eddy over the half frame glasses perched on his nose. "Eddy. It's not nice to lie. Didn't your mother ever tell you that? I know for a fact that the money isn't on your boat because we took a little look there while you were sleeping in the back of my car." Eddy looked confused. "You know, when Tommy punched you on the road, we took the opportunity to search your boat and we know it's not there. Trust me; we were very thorough." Eddy didn't doubt him for a moment.

"I'm telling you the truth," Eddy cried, his head coming up. He looked terrible with various fluids leaking from his nose. "Admittedly, there's not much left. Ask anybody around the marina. They'll tell you what I'm like. I pissed the money away on women and whiskey. You know yourself that I'm a drunk. How the hell do you think I would still have much left? That's the truth and I simply don't know what else to tell you."

Enzio bent at the waist, keeping his distance from Eddy. "Do you think that I'm an idiot? Expecting me to believe you could spend four million dollars in two years on wine, women and song? You are suggesting that I am mentally challenged and I resent the implication. The money isn't on your boat and I know it because we tore the place apart."

Enzio stepped back and motioned to Horst, indicating that he should hit Eddy again. But Horst and Tommy had lost interest in the conversation and were watching the football game on the television. Enzio barked at Horst.

"Horst, for Christ's sake, will you two idiots pay attention." He motioned towards Eddy. "Hit him again" This time Horst came around beside Eddy, pulled his large hand back and punched him in the stomach. The blow caused Eddy to throw up, shooting stuff a couple of feet from his mouth in the direction of Enzio's feet. Tommy snickered. Enzio jumped back cursing. "Bloody hell Horst, what did you have to do that for you stupid bastard."

Horst looked a little put out. "You told me to hit him. I hit him. Don't blame me for what he did after that."

"Get something to wipe my shoes off with you idiot." Horst went into the bathroom and came back with one of the hand towels. He threw it at Enzio. "Clean them yourself."

Enzio glared at him and then looked at Eddy who was breathing heavily and grimacing in pain. He advanced towards Eddy with an angry look.

Eddy started talking. "I'm sorry David. Really I am. I didn't mean to do that." He grimaced as if expecting to be hit again. "I don't know what to tell you. The money is gone. It wasn't all on women and booze. I bought my boat with part of the money too. That was a half million right there what with all the improvements I did to her." He sounded frustrated as though he was unable to get his point across. "The money was partly mine. I earned it and you never paid me. I organized the shipment. I organized the boats. I made sure everybody was in the right place at the right time. It wasn't my fault that the Coast Guard showed up right when we were doing the transfer. I don't know who tipped them off but part of the money was mine." He was sounding very whiney, almost petulant and Tommy and Horst had expressions that indicated that they could almost see Eddy's side of the story. But Enzio certainly wasn't having any of it.

His eyes were bugging out of his head. "Partly your money?" He was shocked at this suggestion. "Partly your money? I was the one that financed the whole operation. It was my money that you stole." He was starting to shout and Horst made little motions with his hands to indicate that Enzio should keep the volume down. This only served to inflame Enzio further.

"I've had enough of this discussion. If you won't cooperate and tell me where my money is, I guess I will have to use a little persuasion. Tommy, go get the toolbox out of the car." Tommy grinned at Horst before going outside and coming back with a small red toolbox. He put it on the nightstand next to the clock radio and the telephone where Eddy could see it. Enzio opened the box and started shuffling through the tools inside. He came out with a pair of vice grips. He looked at them for a moment and then turned to Eddy.

"You know what these are Eddy?" He held the tool up in front of his captive.

"Yeah, vice grips." Eddy said in a shaky voice. He knew only too well what they were and what they could do.

"Vice grips" Enzio repeated. "That's right. Very handy tool, lots of gripping force. Every household should have a pair. But today,

I'm going to show you an entirely different use for this tool." He moved to Eddy's side and reached down and grabbed the little finger on Eddy's left hand which was securely fastened to the arm of the seat. "You right or left handed Eddy? I don't recall."

"Why? What are you going to do? Don't do that. No." He was hysterical, almost screaming. Horst saw what was coming and quickly grabbed the roll of duct tape, ripped off a piece and plastered it over Eddy's gaping maw. Another piece quickly followed. It wouldn't do to disturb the neighbors.

Enzio adjusted the vice grips and placed the jaws right on the knuckle on Eddy's little finger. He started to close the grips slowly. Eddy's eyes grew larger and rounder by the second and he shook his head violently while trying to pull his hand away but he couldn't because his hand was very securely fastened into the chair. That hand wasn't going anywhere.

As Enzio applied pressure and Eddy moaned into the tape, the announcer on the football game on the T.V. was going hyper. Tommy turned the volume up. "It… look… like…he…could…go…all… the wayyyy… Touchdown!" just as Enzio closed the jaws of the grips tightly on Eddy's formerly useful little finger.

10 THE THINGS WE DON'T KNOW ABOUT OUR FRIENDS

Mick's orange Volkswagen van started after a little coaxing and after a quick look at the map, Morris started calling out directions. As they drove towards the highway, Morris began talking. "So, what is it we're looking for anyway?"

"Well, Eddy's either missing or dead. Someone broke into his boat and tore the hell out of it. They must have been looking for something. We don't know a lot of things, so I think we just have to play it by ear and hope that we get some answers and hopefully find Eddy in one piece. How's that sound?" They blazed down the Westminster Highway as only V.W. vans can, fogging up in the increasing rain.

The motel wasn't far from the George Massey Tunnel which was a way of getting from the Lulu Island side where the marina was to the Delta side of the Fraser River. As Mick and Morris entered the tunnel and into the strange yellowish world lit by sodium lights they found that the traffic was at a standstill.

"An accident up ahead, most likely," Morris guessed. At least it was dry and bright inside the tunnel and it gave them time to speculate as to what might lie ahead. "So, let me ask you Mick, suppose Eddy is still alive. We don't have a lot of information but we have a torn up boat. That's a fact. The boat was still locked from the outside. That's a fact. Either Eddy did it himself which is definitely a stretch, or someone else did it. That seems a lot more likely given that it appears like someone was looking for something. From the looks of it, that someone is very violent." He turned and looked toward the back of the van. Getting out of his seat, he moved to the back and rummaged around for a minute, finally coming back to his seat with a tire iron in his hand. "I feel better already." Mick looked at him and thought for a moment before nodding his head.

"Seems like a prudent idea. We don't know what we're getting into. Not that we really know that we're heading in the right direction anyway, but we sailors are always ready for anything, right?" Morris smacked the tire iron into the palm of his left hand in agreement. "The damage to Eddy's boat changes everything Mo. I don't know what Eddy could have done to provoke that.

Traffic started to move and they were mostly quiet now. The long trip through the tunnel ended as the road climbed up and the rain started up again. Wipers clacked back and forth while Morris used a squeegee to keep the front window free from fog. They took Exit 28 towards the B.C. Ferries and then turned left at Ladner Trunk Road. They were now within the circle that Morris had drawn on the map. After only a short distance along Ladner Trunk Road, they saw the sign for the Tsawwassen Motel on the right hand side of the road. Mick kept driving although he slowed down a little as they went by. Since it was the middle of the day, there weren't many cars parked in the motel parking lot and it was easy to spot the Black Lexus. They looked at each other somewhat surprised that they had found what they were looking for. "That's got to be the one Mick. A black Lexus? How many of those could there be?" Morris was excited.

Mick looked at him sideways. "Umm, let me think on that. About a thousand in the lower mainland? That's just a guess." Morris looked disappointed that Mick didn't share his enthusiasm. "I'm just saying. It could be a coincidence Mo, let's not get too excited just yet."

Mick went another block or so and then pulled into a driveway and turned around and drove slowly back towards the motel. He pulled into the electrical substation parking lot on the right and parked so that they could sit in the van and watch the motel and parking lot across the road.

"It looks like you were right Mick. We'd be sitting around with our thumbs up if you hadn't found that match book. We should call you Dick." Mick gave him a blank look. "Dick. Detective. Private Eye, you know? Mick the Dick." Morris laughed at his own joke. "Since you seem to be such a sleuth, I have to ask, have you done this kind of surveillance before?" Morris opened a bag of chips he found in the back of the van. A couple of soft drinks were popped open and they settled in.

Mick looked at Morris, thinking for a moment. "Promise me you won't think I'm weird."

Morris looked at Mick while stuffing chips in his mouth. "Man, it's too late for that; I already think you're weird, so go ahead." He grinned.

"I used to go down to Chinatown in Vancouver and park and watch the Asian chicks walk by. At first, I used to just stand around watching but that was too obvious so I started parking and watching. Sounds pretty weird to say that but hey, I've got a thing for Asian girls."

"Wow. Now I do think you're weird. I was only joking before but now I'm serious. You really did that? Just sat there and watched them? I guess that explains why you took such a shine to Claire. How come you never told me this before?"

Mick looked over at Morris who was shoveling chips in his mouth and getting crumbs all over the front of his jacket.

"Because I didn't want you to think I was weird."

Several hours of mindless chit chat later, they spotted movement. Mick climbed into the back of the van and from a backpack pulled out a pair of Nikon binoculars. He passed them forward to Morris who trained them on the motel. "Nice binoculars. Compact. Lightweight too."

Mick looked at him, "Write a review for the next Optics Magazine. Just tell me what's going on over there."

Morris focused in and saw a well dressed man wearing a fedora get into the driver side and a big linebacker type guy getting into the passenger side of the black Lexus. The driver started up the car and pulled out to 66 Street, turned left and then left again during a break in the traffic on Ladner Trunk Road. It brought them directly in front of Mick and Morris. The two men in the Lexus were talking animatedly and Morris felt safe enough observing them through the binoculars. The driver had tipped the fedora back on his head which allowed Morris to see his face closely. Dark complexioned compared to the passenger who was very light skinned. The driver had a thin Wayne Newton style moustache. He looked big in the shoulders though small in comparison to the gorilla in the passenger seat. The gorilla was wearing a leather style bomber jacket. He was big and strong looking. There were several dark stains on the front of his leather jacket.

"You ever see either one of those guys around the marina?" Morris said, setting the binoculars down on the floor.

"No, can't say I have. That doesn't mean that they're not friends of Eddy. He knows a lot of people."

Morris looked at him. "Friends? Friends of Eddy? After what they did to Eddy's boat, you think their friends?" He shook his head.

"We don't know that they're the ones that tore up Eddy's boat. Let's not jump to conclusions."

Morris looked skeptical. "Tell you what Mr. Head Up Your Ass. I'll go across the street and take a little walk along the front of the rooms. If the window curtain is open I might be able to get a glimpse inside and see what's going on in that room. It's worth a try. You just keep an eye on me with the binos and if anything goes wrong you come and save my ass."

Mick nodded. It sounded safe enough. Not much risk. "Fair enough. I'm waiting and watching. If you see anything interesting just give a wave and I'll come over."

Morris jumped out of the van and made his way across the highway and through the parking lot before getting to the shelter of the protected sidewalk in front of the motel rooms. Nobody else was around. It was raining hard now, so anyone with half a brain was inside and staying there.

Morris shoved his hands in his pockets and strolled along the front of the motel. To Mick, he looked like someone trying to see in the windows but maybe that was because he knew that's what Morris was doing. He hoped it didn't look that way to anybody else.

He couldn't believe it when Morris actually stopped and put his face up to the window of the room in question and put his hands up to shade his eyes for a better look. Then he knelt down obviously trying to get a better look. Freaking idiot. He stood like that for a moment and then turned and started running back through the pouring rain. After crossing the highway and making his way through the puddles of the parking lot, he jumped into the warmth and dryness of the van.

"Man, are you crazy? Sticking your head right up to the window and peering in. What the hell were you thinking?"

Morris grabbed his soda and took a swig. He turned to Mick and was grinning. "It's room 11. Eddy's there. But there's a big guy flaked out on the bed sleeping and Eddy is taped into a chair and looking pretty beat up. The curtain was only open a little bit down near the bottom so I had to get right down low to take a look. Eddy is sitting there with his head hanging down and he's duct taped around his chest, his arms and his legs. There's lots of blood on his face and hands. Pretty nasty." Morris was pumped. He was shaking with excitement. "Shit, I can't believe it man. We found him. I don't know what the hell is going on but we found him!" He leaned across and grabbed Mick in a bear hug.

"Jeez Morris, chill out. We need to think about this for a minute. Are you sure the guy on the bed is asleep?" Mick could feel his heart beating faster and he hadn't even seen inside the room. The reality of the situation was opening the adrenalin valves.

"Yeah, he's laying there with his mouth wide open and his eyes closed. I could hear him snoring even through the window."

Mick sat looking out the window of the van and drumming his fingers on the steering wheel. "How do we know there's only one guy in the room besides Eddy? There might have been someone in the bathroom. Besides, have you got any idea how we could get into the room?"

Morris pulled his wallet out of his pocket and from inside drew out two slender metal wires. "These, my friend will get us into any room. I never told you but I haven't always been this nice guy that you know. I was a little bit of a hooligan in my younger years. Went around tipping over a few rubbish bins, I did. I used to work for a locksmith. Got to know my way around the tools of the trade and still carry a few of them. One of the things I learned was how to pick a lock. I haven't done it for a while but I'm pretty sure I can get us into that room quickly and quietly. I don't know if there's anybody else in the room but I've got a feeling that it's just the guy on the bed. You know what Gretsky says. You can't score unless you shoot the puck. What do you say?"

"You know you could get into a lot of trouble for carrying around lock picking tools."

"You know its dangerous going offshore sailing by yourself?" Morris shot back.

"You know you can get into trouble for breaking into a motel room?" Mick retorted.

"You know you can talk yourself out of doing this a million different ways. Right?"

Mick nodded, took a couple of deep breaths and then started up the van and they quickly made their way across to the motel. Morris reached behind his seat and popped the big sliding door open a crack.

Getting There

Mick shut off the ignition and pushed in the clutch and they did a dead stick landing outside of room 11. The rain had increased now to the point where they couldn't hear much over the noise of the rain pounding on the roof of the van. Mick took the tire iron with him as he got out of the van. He didn't know if he would be able to use it but it looked good and felt reassuring.

As they got out they were careful not to close the van doors completely. Morris went to the door of room 11 and Mick saw the opening at the base of the curtains on the window. He knelt down and put his face to the glass and peered inside. Even through the glass and over the noise of the rain, he could hear the guy on the bed snoring. That was as reassuring as the feel of the tire iron in his hand. Across the room, in the reflection from a large mirror, he could see that there wasn't anyone in the bathroom. He gave Morris a thumb's up and Morris began working on the door lock.

Inside the room, Eddy stirred. He jerked his head up and moaned in pain. Mick motioned to Morris to stop until he was sure that the big guy on the bed didn't wake up. Morris looked at Mick and got another thumb's up. He went back to work. Apparently Eddy could hear some noise from Morris's work and he turned his head and looked towards the door. His eyes were wide with fear. Morris dropped one of his two tools and cursed quietly. He bent down, picked up the tool and went back at it. With just a couple more strokes, he grasped the knob, turned it and gently pushed the door open a tiny bit.

Mick took one more look at the guy on the bed and was relieved to see that he was still sleeping. Mick joined Morris and they looked at each other. Taking a deep breath, they stepped inside and pushed the door almost closed but not quite. Eddy's eyes were bugging out and he was breathing hard making little bubbles at his nostrils. He looked to be having a difficult time breathing with his mouth taped shut. Mick put his finger to his mouth signaling quiet. He pulled the Kershaw knife from his pocket and they both moved quietly until they were beside Eddy. Mick started cutting the duct tape and soon had Eddy's chest, arms and one leg free. He was working on the tape on the other leg when they heard a car pull up outside. All of them froze. All of their heart rates increased dramatically.

Morris stepped to the window and bent down and peered through the small opening. He looked for a moment and then gave Mick the okay sign with his thumb and forefinger. Heart rates declined somewhat. Mick kept cutting. The guy on the bed snorted and rolled over on his side with his face in their direction. Everyone held their breath and heart rates went back up.

Mick and Morris both helped Eddy stand up. It was obvious that he was weak. He smelled bad too. Morris grabbed him by the upper arm and then by the hand and prepared to guide him to the door. Eddy jerked his hand away and made a loud whimpering sound through the tape. They all stopped and stared at the big guy on the bed. Snoring. Mick began to think he could bang the tire iron on the wall and it wouldn't wake the guy. He pushed the other two in the direction of the door. They quietly opened it and looked out. Whoever had pulled up in the car had gone into one of the rooms. Mick went ahead and quietly slid the big side door of the van further open. They grabbed Eddy and rather unceremoniously shoved him into the back and gestured at him to lay still.

Sliding the door almost closed, Mick went around to the driver side and got in. Morris jumped in the passenger side and Mick started up the van. Quickly, they reversed out and then headed out onto 66 Street. At Ladner Trunk, Mick turned right instead of left and they headed east while Morris climbed into the back and slammed the big door shut. Morris helped Eddy get into a seat in the back. He ripped the tape from Eddy's mouth without ceremony and without warning. Better that than knowing it was coming.

From the lack of reaction that he got, Morris realized that Eddy was in worse shape than he looked and he looked real bad. He slapped Eddy lightly on the cheek. "Eddy. Eddy. Are you alright?" Eddy opened his eyes and nodded and smiled weakly. "Man, you are a sight for sore eyes Eddy. What the hell is going on? We figured you were dead and gone. And" Morris added almost as an afterthought, "not to make you feel any worse than you already look, someone tore the living shit out of your boat." Eddy let his head fall back on the seat and nodded slightly.

Mick was trying to stay under the speed limit but he was so full of adrenaline that he was having a difficult time. Morris moved into the front seat next to Mick. They looked at each other for a moment and then grinned and high fived.

Mick tipped his head back and gave a shout. "Man, we are a couple of genuine hooligans now aren't we? You are good Mo. Nice work on the door." Mick was still holding onto the tire iron and shifting with the same hand. He handed it to Morris who placed it on the floor at his feet. In the rear view mirror Mick could see Eddy. They made eye contact in the mirror. "I'm glad to see you again Eddy. I don't know what's going on but I sure am glad to see you."

Eddy nodded and lay his head back and closed his eyes. He coughed and a little froth of blood came to his lips. Mick looked back and forth between the road and the rear view mirror. "Eddy, can you hear me?" Eddy gave a weak nod. "I'm thinking we need to get you to a hospital, pronto. You okay with that?"

Eddy lay still for a moment before lifting his head and looking at Mick in the mirror. He said as loud as he could, "Thanks for saving my ass back there. I think it would be best if we were to take a little boat trip right about now. If Enzio, the guy who did this to me catches up with us, we are in for a world of hurt. Let's go to your boat and get the hell out on the water. It will be a lot harder for him to find us out there. I've got to have a little time to come up with a plan." His eyes were closing; he was running out of energy. Quietly he said to himself, "time to see mama, time to see mama."

Mick turned to Morris. "Fancy going for a bit of a sail? Like as soon as we get back to the marina? I've got a good first aid kit onboard and everything is ready to go. Water, fuel, food, it's all there."

Morris nodded his head. "While you get the engine warmed up, I'll grab some of my gear from Slow Mo and we'll shove off." Morris moved to the back and took some paper towels and moistened it with water from a water bottle and began to wipe the mess off Eddy's face. He was careful to avoid the nose which was obviously broken and very tender. He offered the water bottle to Eddy, cradling his head in one hand and tipping the water bottle with the other. Between the two of them, they managed to get some water into him.

"Thanks for your help Morris. I can't tell you how good I feel right now in an odd way. I honestly feel like I have cheated death, with your assistance of course. It was a very close thing back there. Enzio had only gone to get some food and they were going to be back soon. It would have been very ugly if we hadn't gotten out of there before he got back."

"Yeah, well, let's not think of what might have happened. You'll take all the fun out of our success. Let's enjoy it while we can. Mick and I don't have a clue what's going on here, so we need answers. You just relax and let us get out on the water where we'll be away from Enzio and his crew."

Mick got onto Highway 91 and before long they were going over the magnificent Alex Fraser Bridge heading back over to Lulu Island. In the rain it was difficult to even see the top of the support columns. It wasn't a great day for a sail but once they got going they would be safer.

At the marina, they were all looking for the black Lexus but there was no sign of it. They helped Eddy down from the back seat and Morris held him while Mick locked up the van. It was quiet around the marina which was good in that they didn't run into anyone as they made their way down to Starlight. Mick thought about telling someone that Eddy was alive but thought it might be safest for all concerned to keep things under wraps. He might have to do some apologizing later but for now he thought it was the safest path. Mick and Morris got Eddy onboard Starlight and got him into a change of warm dry clothes. Mick started the engine while Morris got Eddy settled into the starboard settee, snug inside a sleeping bag and propped up where he was comfortable and safely out of the way. He put the lee cloth in place to hold Eddy in the bunk in case they ran into some rough water.

Morris came up on deck as Mick was stepping onto to the dock. "I'm going to get some gear from Slow Mo and then I'll be right back." Mick nodded. While Morris was getting his stuff, Mick made sure everything was ready to go. When he got back they stood in the rain alongside Starlight and had a quick conference. "Mick, let's get out of here before anyone sees us. I don't want to have to explain what we're doing. I feel bad about everyone still thinking Eddy drowned on the river but I don't want to hang around in case Enzio shows up." He looked over Mick's shoulder towards the parking lot near the pub. "I'll feel a lot better once we're moving and out on the river. We'll figure out where we're going once we get underway. Sound OK?" Mick nodded.

They had sailed together enough to feel comfortable with each other and within a few minutes they were onboard and Mick was backing Starlight down river towards the end of B Dock. He drifted far enough until the bow was going to clear and then put it into forward gear. He gave it a shot of throttle and spun the wheel hard over. The bowsprit carved an arc, missing the piling on the end of the dock by a good margin and then they were heading out on the river, Morris going around pulling in fenders and tidying up lines.

Looking back at the marina, Mick could see someone coming down the ramp. It looked like Jessica from the boat next to Seagram but he was too far away to be sure. Whoever it was, he had a feeling that they had gotten out of there just in the nick of time.

Morris stepped down into the cockpit and gave Mick a clap on the back. "I feel a lot better now that we're on the water. It's a little safer out here. I'll go check on our guest and get some coffee brewed up. I'll dig out the first aid kit and start patching him up too. He's got some broken fingers by the look of it. I think he might have some broken ribs too. Not to mention the broken nose and I saw a chipped tooth when he cracked a smile. He's pretty beat up Mick. I hope we never run into that bastard Enzio."

Mick could only second that thought as he steered Starlight down the river and out towards the ocean. Last time he had headed out to the Strait, it had been with a woman on his mind. Now, it was Eddy and a vicious man named Enzio. He was looking forward to getting some answers from Eddy and was trying hard not to think too much about all the things that could have gone wrong back at the motel. He sat down behind the wheel and was soon feeling back in control as he always did on board Starlight.

11 INJURY TO INSULT

David Enzio turned the car into the motel parking lot. He was feeling pretty good. They had decided to take a little break to go and get some food. Tommy and Horst had drawn lots to see who would stay behind to guard their prisoner. Tommy had lost with a shrug. He didn't care. There was a football game on the tube and he said he wanted to relax and watch it. He had asked that they bring back a couple of burgers with beer to wash them down. Enzio had grander plans and they had driven into Surrey to go to an Indian food restaurant. It was Indian food at its finest. Not bastardized western style, but the real thing. When they brought food to the table they didn't bother asking if you wanted mild, medium or hot. They didn't ask because you were going to get the real deal. Bring on the fire extinguishers.

Horst kept bitching all the way to the restaurant about his leather jacket which had gotten soiled and Enzio had done his best to ignore the whining. When they arrived, Horst didn't have a clue as to what he should order so David ordered for both of them. The Chicken Vindaloo had come to the table with steamed rice and some garlic nans. Horst had dug in even before the plate had touched the table. The waiter pulled his hand back like he had just reached into an alligator pit and was visibly relieved to see that he still had all his fingers. Horst waved him away and ate a good portion of his meal without even breathing. Suddenly he stopped and looked at Enzio. David was grinning at him like he had a secret. Horst's eyes were watering and he was unable to speak. He knocked over a vase of flowers in his rush to get the water pitcher. Forget the glass, he drank straight from the big pitcher. After emptying half of it, he took a big breath and stuck his tongue out to fan it with his hand. "Jesus, why didn't you warn me it was spicy? For crying out loud, you trying to kill me?"

Enzio shook his head in disgust. He'd like to kill him. It was the down side of this business that you had to work with such idiots. They had muscles but where had they been when the brains were being passed out? "If you had waited until the plate had actually settled on the table before wolfing the food down, I would have suggested that you eat at a leisurely pace and have some of the rice to temper the heat, you pig."

The waiter brought their Kingfisher beer, in nicely iced glasses. Horst drank his down in one long guzzle. Enzio was embarrassed by this brute. He swore to leave both of them behind next time. He tuned Horst out and savored his food slowly while he thought about the days work. They were getting some information out of Eddy but not fast enough. For a guy who pissed his pants in the first five minutes, he was holding up pretty well. The vice grip treatment had caused Eddy to pass out and they were forced to take a break until he came around again. But they would put the pressure on even more when they got back from dinner. They couldn't afford to drag the questioning out all night.

He was puzzled by the story about the money still being on the boat. They had ripped the boat up very thoroughly and Enzio doubted that there was anyplace on the boat that could hide that much money. Granted it didn't take up a lot of room but they had looked everywhere, hadn't they? Enzio wanted only one thing and he was going to find out where it was even if it did take all night. He felt the need to get back to the questioning and as good as the food was, he pushed it away and signaled to the waiter for the bill.

On the way back to the motel, Horst was whining about the spiciness of the food and how his stomach was upset and also about his leather jacket and his broken nose. It was almost more than Enzio could put up with and he was tempted to stop and kick the bastard out onto the street and make him walk back to the motel. But there was work to be done tonight.

At the motel, as Horst fumbled with the key in the door lock, they could hear the television blaring away and over that the sound of Tommy's snoring. As the door opened, David stepped into the room and in an instant he realized that Eddy was gone. The chair was there but the dangling gray duct tape on the arms and legs of the chair spoke volumes. Enzio's blood pressure went through the roof. He stormed over to the bed and grabbed the snoring Tommy and began slapping him wildly. Tommy's hands came up to protect his face and in the process he deflected one of Enzio's blows into the wooden headboard. Enzio's hand smacked the headboard with tremendous force and he fell back onto the floor yelling and holding one damaged hand. Tommy sat up and blearily looked around at Enzio and Horst. Then his sleepy eyes took in the empty chair. His eyes grew large and he knew right then that he was in deep shit.

Enzio stood up, now cradling his damaged right hand with his good one and began kicking at Tommy's legs. Tommy stood up and quickly moved around to the other side of the bed. Horst ran interference and blocked Enzio's path. "Here Boss, let me take a look at your hand. Let's get some ice on it to keep the swelling down."

Enzio pushed him out of the way with his good hand. "Oh forget the hand you asshole." He glared at Tommy with such intensity that Tommy was actually forced to back up a step. "Where's Eddy?" It was said quietly but the anger dripped from both words. When Tommy didn't answer right away, Enzio began moving around Horst and around the end of the bed. His steps were deliberate and he asked again, this time louder, "Where's Eddy?" Tommy of course had no idea where Eddy was. He didn't want to admit that he didn't know and the admission wasn't jumping off his tongue just yet. He didn't know what to say. There wasn't anyone else to blame it on so his options were limited.

"He was here when you guys left for dinner. Did you bring back those burgers for me?" It came out sounding stupid even to himself. Enzio was coming to a boil.

"Burgers? Burgers? You incompetent bastard, where the hell is Eddy!" He was yelling now. Close to screaming. Tommy had heard the word apoplectic once. It seemed to fit the moment.

"Boss, all I know is that I laid down on the bed to watch the game after you left and I guess I must have fallen asleep. We've been working pretty hard lately you know. Then I woke up when you started hitting me. How's your hand?"

Any attempts at pleasantries were totally lost on Enzio. He launched himself across the few feet separating them and began throwing elbows and knees into Tommy as they toppled to the floor.

Horst jumped into the fray trying to pull them apart. Enzio was no match for the beefy man and ended up on his back gasping for breath and holding onto his injured hand.

For once, Horst had the intelligence to see that this was going to get them nowhere. He helped his injured boss up onto the bed and examined the damaged hand. It was swelling up but since Enzio could still move all of his fingers, nothing appeared to be broken. He went to the little bar refrigerator and came back with a towel full of ice which he used to wrap around the injured hand. "That ought to slow down the swelling. You just keep the ice on it for a while."

Enzio mumbled thanks and then began thinking out loud. "Okay. Somehow someone got into the room while we were gone. I know for a fact that the door was locked when we went out because I personally checked it." He turned to Tommy who had sat up and was leaning back against the wall. He was gingerly touching under his right eye. It felt like there was some swelling from an elbow that Enzio had landed. "Did you go out after we left?"

Tommy shook his head. "No boss. I told you, I laid down and went to sleep almost right away." He realized it was admitting to a major blunder but he thought it might be good to say that he hadn't gone out. He didn't want to piss Enzio off any more than he had already.

Scowling at Tommy, Enzio continued. "Okay, so someone came in and cut Eddy loose and took him away. The door doesn't appear to be forced, so they must have had a key or picked the lock. Horst, you go to the front desk and ask if we had any visitors or if any of the motel staff came into the room while we were gone or if they noticed anyone outside our room. For crying out loud, don't tell them anything." He could imagine Horst explaining to the desk clerk that someone had kidnapped the prisoner that they were torturing. He wouldn't put it past him.

Horst went out and pulled the door shut behind him. They could hear him test the doorknob to see if it stayed locked. It did. Enzio gingerly eased the towel from his hand and stared at the fingers. They were swollen and turning blue. Shit. It was his right hand and he was right handed. This was going to complicate things. He looked at Tommy and his mouth tightened. Tommy looked away and tried to make himself invisible. How long was it going to take for his boss to forget this screw up? Probably forever. Tommy sighed. It seemed like he was always getting in trouble with Enzio, the asshole. Horst was always kissing ass, staying on Enzio's good side but Tommy wasn't into playing that game. One of these days, he thought to himself. The moon, Alice. He could picture himself getting one good shot at Enzio. Pow.

"We almost had Eddy where he was going to tell us what we needed to know, you jerk," he said in Tommy's direction. "Now we're going to have to go find him again. So, who took our Mr. Wainright? Any thoughts on that matter Tommy?"

Tommy shook his head and kept his mouth shut. He leaned over and grabbed a cigarette from the pack on the nightstand and patted himself down looking for a lighter. He spotted a book of matches near the ashtray and lit his smoke while hoping that the floor would open up and Enzio would go straight to hell.

Enzio continued. "I've got a feeling that we should head over to the marina and see if someone from there came and collected our friend. Of course we wouldn't have to do this if you had been a little bit more on the ball. Nice work shithead." Tommy looked everywhere but in Enzio's direction. He was thankful that Horst came back at that moment.

"Nothing from the front desk boss. We didn't have any visitors and they didn't see anything."

Enzio shook his head in disgust. Horst continued with a smile on his face. "However, I did run into our neighbors and asked them if they'd seen anyone while we were out but they didn't see anyone either." He continued grinning until Enzio finally said, "OK, I'll bite. What's so funny?"

"Well," Horst said, about to sit down in Eddy's chair until he remembered the pissing episode. He sat down on the bed looking back and forth between Tommy and Enzio. "The neighbors didn't see anyone, but they did remember an orange Volkswagen van parked outside our room. The reason that they remembered it is that the passenger door wasn't shut all the way and the rear sliding door was partly open too. They thought that was kind of strange considering that it was raining so hard."

Enzio perked up. "An orange Volkswagen van with the doors open in the rain? OK, that's worth paying attention to. Not too many orange VW vans around. Keep your eyes open. Let's get out of here." They gathered up their smokes and keys and wallets and cell phones, grabbed their jackets and headed out the door, waiting while Tommy took a leak. Enzio waited impatiently and then kicked Tommy in the ass as the big man squeezed by him in the doorway. As they got into the Lexus, Enzio realized that he was going to have a hard time driving and keeping his hand iced at the same time. He tossed the keys to Horst. "Horst, you drive." Heading out on the highway, Enzio said to no one in particular. "When I find out who took Eddy from us, he's in for a world of hurt."

12 THE CHASE BEGINS

Mick sat behind the wheel and looked out at the shoreline of the Fraser River going by. It was growing dark now. The rain was easing slightly but it probably wasn't going to stop anytime soon. Starlight made good speed down the river and before long the hatch slid back and Morris stuck his head up. "Ready for some coffee, Skipper?"

"You bet Mo. It's chilly out here. How's Eddy doing?"

"He got his ass kicked pretty good back there. He's got some serious damage to his hands. He's coughing up blood and I think he's got some busted ribs and his nose took some heavy hits. It's not working very good right now, so he's breathing through his mouth. He's going to have a couple of shiners by the looks of it. To make a long story short, he's really screwed up. I patched him up temporary like and gave him some pain medication. He's sleeping now and I think that's the best thing for him. I'm tempted to say that he needs to see a doctor but I think we can take care of him for now. You've got a good first aid kit there."

"Yeah, I've been stocking it up for quite a while. There's a good book on emergency surgical procedures down there too. If we have to, we'll operate on him. It'll be good practice for us." They grinned at each other but it was sobering to know that Enzio and his thugs were capable of real violence.

Morris brought two cups of steaming hot coffee into the cockpit with him and set them into the cup holders on the front of the steering console. He turned and closed the companionway doors and slid the hatch shut. He shrugged into his rain jacket and pulled his toque down tight. Mick took a sip of his coffee and reeled back a bit. Morris caught the face and said, "I thought you wouldn't mind if I added a little rum to the coffee. Might help to keep you warm. Besides, I thought it might be good after all the excitement we just went through." It was pretty much dark now and the running lights cast green and red glows out each side of the boat onto the water.

"You know Mick; we got pretty lucky back there at the motel." Morris sat down on the starboard side of the cockpit and stretched his legs out in front of him. He took a sip of his coffee and made the same face Mick had just made. He grinned at Mick. "That's a good cup of coffee, eh?" He took another sip and then said, "I don't like to think what might have gone down if Enzio had come back while we were in the room or if the goon on the bed had woken up. In retrospect, it's funny to think about how easy it went but it could have really gone south on us in a hurry. And after seeing Eddy's injuries, I sure don't want to ever be on the receiving end of Enzio's hospitality."

"Roger on that, Mo. But for now, the plan is to get somewhere safe and quiet and have a little heart to heart with Eddy and get answers to a lot of questions. I'm really curious as to why Eddy's boat is so ripped up and I sure want to know what Enzio was trying to get out of our friend. Obviously, there's more to Eddy than meets the eye. I hope that when we find out the answers to our questions, we don't feel like turning Eddy back over to Enzio to finish the job." He shook his head wondering what they were going to think once they heard Eddy's side of the story. "I'm thinking that we should head for Telegraph Harbor. It's not too far away and it's nice and quiet there. Maybe we can have a chat with Eddy and then figure out some way to defuse Enzio and get back to our normal every day lives. That's the trouble with these thugs. They don't have to get up and go to work every day like the rest of us peasants. But I've got deadlines to meet and I know you do too."

Morris sat deep in thought, both hands wrapped around his cup of coffee, his face lit by the glow from the radar screen. It was good to have radar around this part of the river mouth. There was lot of commercial traffic, large ships heading for the cement plant and the automobile loading dock as well as fishing boats coming and going.

They followed the buoys as they headed west towards the Strait. The rain eased and then grew heavy again, coming in waves along with the wind. There was a moderate chop on the water but

Starlight's deep full keel kept the motion comfortable. Morris finished his coffee and headed up on deck to take the cover off the mainsail. It was good to be back on the water again. It was a place with a great deal of familiarity and a place where one could always count on the lack of vindictiveness in the elements. The sea might be cruel but that was never her intent.

Morris occasionally slid the hatch back and looked down into the cabin to see how Eddy was doing. He appeared to be sleeping peacefully. Morris went below to get more coffee and made a trip to the head. As he came up on deck again, he worked his way around behind the wheel and nudged Mick out of the way. "I'll take over Mick." Mick stood and stretched to get the blood pumping again. It was a good opportunity to take a look at Eddy and brew up another pot of coffee. It was going to be a long night.

Starlight was now past the last point of land and Morris was looking out at the dark vista of the Strait of Georgia. Before getting into the deeper water of the Strait, he had to be careful to follow the navigational aids to avoid turning in to the shallow water of Roberts Bank to his port side, or Sturgeon Bank to his starboard side. It looked like he would be able to veer south or north from this position and be safe enough but the water is shallow and it's not until getting clear of the last of the nav aids that the water is deep enough to be safe. Both Mick and Morris were well acquainted with the hazards of the entrance to the river having sailed the area for years. The depth sounder began to show the bottom dropping away and Morris eased the helm to starboard to start heading west. As they entered the deeper water the distance between the waves began to stretch out and with the change in motion, Mick came up on deck.

"Are you ready to get some sail on, Mo?"

"Yeah, Mick, we've got a decent wind, so let's do it."

Morris brought the bow up into the wind and Mick quickly hoisted the mainsail, cranking it to the top with the aid of one of the big Barlow winches mounted on the starboard side. Cleating that off, he turned to the line controlling the roller furled jib. This sail, mounted on the forestay, right out on the end of the bowsprit, unrolled just like an old window blind. As he pulled the line in the cockpit, the sail unrolled to the port side of the boat and soon, both sails were flapping in the wind. Morris eased the throttle back and with a nod from Mick, turned the wheel to the left and the sails filled quickly and began powering the boat ahead.

Getting There

As Mick began adjusting the jib, Morris took the engine out of gear. He adjusted the mainsail until it was filled and pulling quietly. Under sail power alone, Starlight settled down, heeling slightly with the light wind and headed for the unseen islands ahead. Morris shut the engine down and the quiet enveloped them. It was dark and peaceful with hardly a sound save for the gurgling of the wake and the occasional splatter of a wave as it broke against the hull and sprayed up on deck.

Mick and Morris looked at each other, their faces lit by the glow from the radar screen. "It always feels good to get the hell away from land and shut the engine off and get under sail, doesn't it?." It was more of a statement from Morris than a question. Between the two of them and anybody who has had the same experience, it's always a relief to get out to sea. The burdens and cares and worries of land seem to blow away with the wind.

Mick just nodded his head in agreement. They sat in silence for a while, soaking up the peacefulness of the night. It had been quite a day and it was good to have nothing to do except sail the boat. Morris broke the silence.

"You know Mick, I get the impression that there's a lot we don't know about Eddy." Mick stared at the cockpit floor and nodded.

"Yeah. I think that's a major understatement. Eddy's never really been all that upfront about his past and I never really felt the need to dig into it."

Morris took a sip of coffee and then put his cup into the holder next to the steering wheel. "Everyone's got some secrets to hide. I do, you probably do. Hell, I bet even Claire had some secrets she keeps to herself." Mick looked sideways at Morris, feeling a little stab of pain at the mention of Claire but nodding in agreement anyway. "Yeah, I know you didn't want to hear that but I'm just making a point. Everyone hides things from their past. But we're going to have to find out Eddy's secrets or we're not going to be able to get Enzio off our backs. When we cut Eddy free from that chair in the motel room, his problems became ours too."

13 FISHING

As they pulled into the marina parking lot, Enzio, Tommy and Horst all spotted the orange Volkswagen van at the same time. Tommy was sitting in the back sulking because he had been bitched out all the way from the motel. Horst had ganged up with Enzio against him which kind of pissed Tommy off. He was under the impression that the hired hands should stick together but the trip to the marina had proved otherwise.

Horst stopped the Lexus next to the V.W. van and Enzio got out and tested the doors to see if any were open. They were all locked and this didn't help Enzio's mood at all. He peered in the windows to see if there were any tell tale signs of Eddy having been in the vehicle. Without a flashlight, it was hard to see but he thought he saw what might have been some pieces of duct tape lying behind the front passenger seat. There just wasn't enough light to say for sure.

Getting back in the Lexus, he had Horst continue through the parking lot and down to the road that ran alongside the river. They turned left out of the parking lot and onto Dyke Road which put "B" dock on the right side of the car and David Enzio looked down at the row of boats. In the glow from the lights along the dock, it was easy to see Wainright's big boat. Enzio felt a rush of pleasure remembering tearing the interior apart. It was small satisfaction though as they hadn't found what they were looking for and the thought of the missing money and the missing Eddy Wainwright sent Enzio into a fit. He began cursing and without thinking, pounded his injured fist against his thigh. This was a mistake as his hand was swollen and hurting badly. He cradled it with his other hand, rocking with pain.

"I think we should get you to the emergency room and have that hand looked at Boss." Horst was always looking for ways to stay on the good side of his moody employer.

"Oh for Christ's sake, what are they going to do for me? Probably X-ray it, put it in a splint, give me some kind of pain medication and tell me to get plenty of rest. We don't have time for that right now. We need to find out where Eddy is and who the hell stole him right out from under your nose" turning and glaring again at Tommy. Let's go into the pub and see if anyone has heard anything. You two keep your mouths shut and let me ask the questions. You got that?" Tommy and Horst, especially Tommy, nodded vigorously.

After parking the car, as they were entering the pub, an attractive woman came up from "B" dock and arrived at the door at the same time. Since she had come from "B" dock, Enzio figured that opportunity was knocking. He held the door open and Horst started to enter but Enzio grabbed him by the back of his leather jacket and pulled him back. He turned to the woman and gave a little bow. "Ladies first."

Jessica gave a little giggle and touched him on the sleeve. "Thank you. It's rare to meet a gentleman these days. Especially around here." She went in and immediately headed for the juke box in the corner of the room. It was already pounding out "Old Time Rock and Roll" by Bob Seger. This crowd was heavy on the classics. Jessica loaded it up with a handful of quarters and started punching in her favorites.

Enzio herded Horst and Tommy over to the bar and told them to sit down and shut up. He ordered a pint of beer each for them and a scotch for himself. As he settled himself onto the bar stool, Jessica came bouncing over to the bar and called out to the bartender for a pint of beer. He was busy and either didn't hear her or was ignoring her. She rolled her eyes and pulled a package of cigarettes from her purse, shook one from the pack and stuck it in her mouth. She wore bright red lipstick, obviously just freshly applied from the looks of it. Enzio pulled a lighter out of his pocket and held it up for Jessica. She slung her purse over her shoulder and put one hand on her hip, the other holding the cigarette. "Well, it's you again." She leaned in and put the tip of her cigarette into the flame. She took a deep drag and then blew the smoke out, the last of the smoke drifting from her nostrils as she looked Enzio over. She crossed her arms, one hand holding the cigarette between two fingers. The filter of the cigarette was the same vivid red as her lips.

"I don't think I've seen you around here before. Are you bringing a boat in or are you looking to buy one 'cuz there's lots of them for sale, what with the economy being the way it is." She sat on the stool next to Enzio still trying to catch the attention of the bartender.

"My associates and I," Enzio said, gesturing at Tommy and Horst who both nodded at her, "are in the market for a boat. We just haven't decided what kind to get yet. Do you have a boat, young lady?" As Enzio talked, Horst hunched over his beer shaking his head. His boss might be smart but he was so uncool with chicks.

Jessica was trying to pick something off of her tongue with her thumb and middle finger, her right eye squinting from the smoke drifting up from her cigarette. "Yeah, I've got a boat down on "B" dock. My partner and I are going offshore one of these days. Are you going to buy me a beer sailor?"

"Well," Enzio smiled. He wasn't used to women being this forward. He wouldn't ordinarily give this type of woman two seconds of his time. She had obviously already been drinking and judging from her bloodshot eyes might well have been smoking some dope too. "I'm not really a sailor, yet. But I'd be delighted to buy a drink for the pretty lady." Horst and Tommy snickered in their beers and nudged each other. Enzio shot them a dirty look and called out to the bartender for a beer. The bartender nodded and started pouring it.

"Are there any boats for sale down on your dock?" Enzio thought he could do a little probing while they waited for her drink.

"Yeah, there's a big sailboat right next to mine that might be up for sale sometime soon. The owner disappeared," and here she leaned closer to Enzio, "everyone thinks he drowned in the river. So if that's the case, his boat would probably be on the market pretty soon. My guess is that it would be around the four hundred thou mark." She was rummaging around in her purse and came out with a tube of lipstick. She reapplied it to the thick coating already on her lips. Her beer came and she promptly put her red mark on the rim of the glass and then gave her lips another touch up job. It looked compulsive and rather disgusting to Enzio.

At that moment, the door to the pub opened and a tall slim man came in. He looked around and spotted Jessica at the bar. He didn't look all that happy to see her but he came over and took the seat next to her. "Hello Jess. Been here long or have you been drinking on the boat all afternoon?" He signaled the bartender to bring him the same as Jessica was having. Jessica barely acknowledged him and continued talking to Enzio.

"As far as I know Eddy didn't have any family, so I would guess that his boat is probably going to be put up for sale."

"That seems a little out of our price range. Anything else you might know of that is in good shape and a little less expensive? Or maybe you know of someone who could show us some boats and give us a little education on what to look out for when buying a used boat."

"There's a guy on my dock that fixes up boats and sometimes hears about real good deals before the brokers do. He'd be the guy to ask. Knows all about boats and how to fix them and what to avoid."

Enzio sipped his scotch and tried to figure out who the tall guy was in relation to the woman. They seemed to know each other and the fact that the guy was now digging around in her purse looking for cigarettes seemed to indicate that they were somehow related.

"By the way, my name is Martin Bradley and my associates are Bill and Edward. We're from Ottawa and we've been visiting the area for a couple of weeks on business.

Jessica snorted at the mention of Ottawa. "Jesus. Ottawa? You guys got a little off course didn't you. If you were back there now, you'd be freezing your balls off. I guess you're glad to be out here where it's warmer."

Enzio didn't quite know how to take this coarse woman. She was salty enough to be a sailor. "Well, it might be warmer here but I think I prefer the cold to all this rain."

Jessica shook her head. "At least you don't have to shovel rain."

Enzio decided not to argue the point. "We've been out on the water a couple of times with a business friend and now we're thinking we should get a boat of our own. We could keep it here and have someone look after it and then we could use it when we came out on business or holidays. By the way, I didn't catch your name."

He held his hand out to the woman. She stuck the cigarette in her mouth and took the offered hand. "Jessica Christian" she said out of the corner of her mouth, "and this is my partner Dave Edmonds. You know, Mick Breese would be the perfect guy to talk to about all this stuff. He's best friends with Eddy and the two of them are always finding out about boats for sale before everyone else does. People come to them wanting to get their boats fixed up before they sell them. Mick lives on B dock close to my boat, our boat," she corrected herself, giving a slight tip of her head in Dave's direction.

At the mention of Mick being Eddy's close friend, Enzio perked right up. He had to hold himself back. Horst and Tommy looked at each other. Horst turned and said to Enzio, "Sounds like we should talk to this Mick guy, doesn't it Martin." Enzio glared at Horst. Horst went back to his beer.

Jessica however, took the bait and went right on talking. "You're going to have to wait if you want to talk to Mick. He went sailing with his neighbor Morris. I saw them motoring out in Mick's boat. They're probably heading over to Telegraph Harbor since that's where he always seems to end up. He knows people over there I think. He's getting close to going offshore sailing, so he's probably out doing some last minute systems checking or something." She rolled her eyeballs as if it was all too much to think about. Her partner Dave looked at her in disgust.

"We'd be close to leaving too if we could both get on the same page. Instead of spending all your time drinking and partying, why don't we focus on getting ready to go offshore like Mick is doing?" He glared at Jessica. She glared right back at him. Enzio felt like he had just stepped into an old domestic argument. In his books, it was rude behavior to be airing your dirty laundry in public. It didn't seem to bother these two in the slightest. Finally, Dave just shook his head, turned and stormed out of the bar.

Jessica looked out the window and watched him heading back down to the dock. She turned and looked at Enzio. "He's such a sanctimonious asshole. He used to party hearty when we first got together but now he thinks it's a big waste of money and time. He thinks we should be saving every last freakin penny so we can go offshore sailing. But what's the point of living if you can't have fun while you're doing it? Can you answer me that?"

Enzio could have given her a couple of chapters of what the point was but realized that his words would be falling on deaf ears.

"So, you said that Mr. Brese went sailing. Do you happen to know what kind of a vehicle he drives and when he'll be back? I'd like to talk to him."

Jessica was busy fixing her lipstick and pouring beer down her throat. It was obvious that relationship problems made her thirsty.

She waved her hand at Enzio. "I don't know about when he'll be back. He's usually not gone for long. As for what kind of vehicle he drives, it's a puke orange van. One of those German things. Can you believe that asshole Dave?" She was obviously upset by the little spat with her partner. "I've got to go. Thanks for the beer and good luck finding a boat. You never know, mine might be up for sale one of these days." Shaking her head, she stood up, shouldered her purse and picking up her cigarettes and her beer, started working her way through the pub stopping at tables and laughing and drinking. Living life and having fun.

Enzio turned to Horst and Tommy. "Let's go. I think we just found out as much as we need to know."

Enzio paid for the drinks and headed for the door. They had to wait for Tommy who had to go to the bathroom again. When he finally came back, Enzio said to him, "Have you got T.B.?" This was met by a blank look.

"T.B? What's that supposed to mean?"

Enzio gave him a push out the door. "Tiny bladder. We're always waiting for you to take a leak." Horst sniggered, Tommy looked pissed off and Enzio grinned. Out in the car, Horst started up the Lexus and turned the heat up full bore.

"Unless I miss my guess boys, Brese and this Morris guy took Eddy and headed out on their little sailboat. Looks like we're going to have to get a boat of our own and go find Mr. Brese." Enzio cradled his hand which was obviously bothering him. "But, first things first Tommy, head for the emergency room. I've got to get this hand taken care of. Then later tonight, when it's nice and quiet, we'll come back and find us a nice boat for a little trip over to the islands."

14 CHANGE OF COURSE

As Mick pushed the hatch back and swung the companionway doors open, he glanced down into the dimly lit cabin. He saw motion in the starboard settee where Eddy was supposedly snug and sleeping. However, as he stepped down into the cabin, he found Eddy just closing Mick's own cell phone and looking sheepish as Mick came down and stood before him.

"Glad to see you're feeling up to talking on the phone. I hope you didn't put me over my monthly talk time or I'm going to send you the bill."

Eddy handed the phone over. Mick snapped it open and hit redial and saw the last dialed number. It didn't mean anything to him. He closed the phone and put it in his pocket. He went to the galley and lit the stove and began to prepare a fresh pot of coffee.

"Frankly Eddy, I don't mind you using the phone but I'm sure I don't need to remind you, you're here by something of a miracle. I don't have a clue what could have made this Enzio guy so pissed off at you but since Morris and I went to a lot of trouble to save your ass, I sure would appreciate it if you would clue us into what the hell is going on."

Eddy raised himself into a semi-sitting position and tried to move the pillow behind him for support. He only ended up hurting his hand and starting a coughing fit that left him gasping for breath. With a wheezing voice, he said, "First things first Mick. I need to get some medical attention and the people that I just called are going to be able to help in that department. They're going to be waiting for us as soon as you can get us there. Once I get fixed up, I'll answer your questions. I'm just not in any condition to do it right now."

Mick stared at him for a moment and then the kettle began whistling. He turned to the stove and began pouring the water to make the coffee. He could feel the motion of the boat as it made its way through the water but Mick was accustomed to balancing and didn't spill a drop. The stove was swinging on its gimbals keeping the burners level but he locked the adjustable metal arms around the kettle to keep it in place just in case they met some unexpected waves. The diesel heater was keeping the cabin warm and cozy. The lights were turned low. It was everything that Mick had worked towards, this life on the water but right now, it felt as though there was a black cloud of uncertainty hovering over his dream.

He finished preparing the coffee. "You want some coffee Eddy? It might do you some good."

"Yeah, that might be just the ticket Mick. If you could help me get into a more comfortable position it would be appreciated."

Mick first took a fresh cup of coffee up to Morris. He took a look around and Morris gave him a thumbs up. "Everything's cool up here Mick."

Mick went below and took a coffee to Eddy after getting him propped up in the settee with a number of cushions and pillows holding him snugly in place. Eddy gratefully sipped the steaming hot liquid.

Mick took a seat at the table on the port settee. He looked across at Eddy. "What the hell is going on Eddy? Come on. We've been friends for a long time. I'm so freaked out by what's going on that I'm worried that we're getting in over our heads. I don't know what the hell you've been up to but Mo and I are not interested in getting the same kind of treatment you got from Enzio."

"Mick, I'm sorry you had to get involved in this. When you have David Enzio looking for you, as he most assuredly is, you are already in as big a jam as you could get into." Eddy began coughing and a grabbed a roll of paper towel which Mick had put close at hand. He tore off a sheet and when he was finished coughing into it, the paper was red with blood. Eddy laid his head down on the pillow and sighed. "Mick, I've got good news and bad news." His voice was weak and raspy. "The good news is that I am alive and eternally grateful to you for rescuing me from Enzio. I don't know how you managed to find me but you came at just the right time. I wouldn't have lasted long after Enzio and that bastard Horst got back from dinner."

Mick stopped with his coffee cup half way to his mouth and looked at Eddy. "Man, you are in bad shape. I don't understand why we can't simply take you to the hospital and get you looked at and then go to the police and tell them all about that bastard Enzio."

Eddy lifted his head and looked at his friend. "The bad news Mick is that I can't go to the police because it would open a can of worms that would land me in jail. I'd rather die free than go to jail. Even if it means Enzio catches up with me and kills me. I don't want to go to jail."

Mick looked at him. The two of them had been friends for several years now. Lots of good times. Mick had never had such a close friend and it pained him to say what he was going to say now. He took a deep breath. "Eddy, you're my best friend. I don't know what it is that you've done that's got Enzio on your case and why you can't go to the police but the least you could do is stop being so selfish. It's not just about you now. Morris is involved now. I'm involved now. If there's some bad shit coming down, it's going to land on all of us, not just you. So, stop thinking just about Eddy Wainwright and start thinking about all of us. Tell me what's going on."

Eddy didn't move. Didn't say anything for a long time. Starlight sailed along quietly with only slight motion, the gimbaled kerosene lamps danced in a small orbit and Mick sipped his coffee. Finally, when Mick thought Eddy had fallen asleep, the words began to spill out. Hesitant at first as if fearful that the truth would irreparably damage their relationship and then stronger as Eddy realized that the truth would sort it all out. He lay there with his head on the pillow; his eyes closed and just started telling his story.

"Enzio used to be my boss. It seems like a lifetime ago but I guess it was only about six years ago, he found me working at Fisherman's wharf in Victoria. I had my own little business, kind of like you do. I was working on an old fishing boat and someone brought in one of those Velocity 410's, you know like the one that Yarner has." Yarner was a guy who raced powerboats on the cheap and was always asking Eddy to help him out and Eddy fit right into Yarner's budget. A bottle of Crown Royal bought a lot of engine repairs as far as Eddy was concerned. "Everybody around town had had a crack at trying to figure out what was wrong with it. They were running the thing at the dock and it was making all kinds of noise and attracting a crowd of onlookers. You know how it is when there's some special kind of boat at the dock. Anyway, nobody could figure out why it was running so rough and not getting the kind of RPM's that it should. Finally someone came over to the boat I was working on and they dragged me over and after listening to it for a while, I..."

Mick interjected. "You laid hands on it, fixed it. Yeah, I've seen it with my own eyes Eddy. There's nobody quite like you when it comes to fixing all things mechanical."

Eddy gave a little shrug. "Anyway, Enzio happened to be there because he was looking for a boat like the Velocity and he needed someone who knew how to work on them. I didn't know why he was looking but when he made his offer, I wasn't about to refuse. I didn't care why; I just knew that the kind of money he was offering would buy me lots of chicks and lots of booze. I didn't even care when I found out he was running drugs. The money was too good to pass up." He lifted his head and looked at Mick, wondering what his friend was thinking but Mick was not giving any clues. Just drinking his coffee and relaxing on the settee.

"At first it was just him and me. We had one Velocity and we made quite a few runs with it down the coast to La Push in Washington State with loads of B.C. Bud."

Mick interrupted him. "B.C. what?"

Eddy looked up. "B.C. Bud. Mary Jane? Weed?" He gave a wave of his hand. "Shit you can't call it weed. It's the most primo marijuana you're going to find. Potent. B.C.'s second largest cash crop. Man, there's a huge number of growers here in B.C. Enzio knew how to get it cheap and he had people down south that would take it and move it east. It's worth a shitload over there. And that Velocity, that boat could go so fast, we didn't even worry about getting caught. We were in and out so fast, nobody ever caught on. We made a lot of money. We could have kept doing that forever but Enzio had bigger plans. He decided it was time to start importing instead of just exporting. He even had business cards printed up. "David Enzio. Import, Export, Agricultural Products." There was a long pause as Eddy reminisced in his memory. "Jeez, we had some great times together."

Mick interrupted the wistful remembrances. "Hey, you wanna invite him over for a beer or two, Eddy? For a guy that just got his ass kicked you seem pretty fond of the ass kicker."

Eddy smiled though it obviously hurt. "Yeah, I know it sounds weird but we used to be real tight. But things went bad on our first cocaine deal. Enzio's a big thinker. He had put together a deal that would put us in the big leagues. It was all coming together nicely. I arranged the boats that would ferry the coke from the freighter back to a place we'd picked out along the west coast of Vancouver Island. It was perfect. Isolated, far enough away from everything that we wouldn't attract any attention at that time of the year. Enzio had put together four million in cash. We had it in two briefcases." He opened his eyes and looked at Mick. "I was surprised. It all fit in two briefcases. I expected it to take up a lot more space." Eddy was running out of gas. He looked exhausted, pale and sweaty. He laid his head back on the pillow in obvious discomfort. Mick was tempted to tell him to just rest but Eddy went on. "Things went bad at the last minute. We made contact with the freighter and had the boats alongside. Enzio and I were in one boat and we had two other boats with us. Enzio had the money ready and they had put out the boarding ladder so we could load the coke. We were just climbing up the stairs and then along came the Coast Guard. I swear to God, I don't know how they found out about us. I sure didn't rat us out. First a helicopter that hovered overhead, shining a searchlight on us and then the cutter came roaring out of nowhere." Eddy began laughing but ended up coughing up a bunch of blood into the paper towel. Mick stood up and moved over beside Eddy, deciding that he had talked enough.

"Okay Eddy. You need to rest instead of talking. I'm going to head up on deck and see how Morris is doing." But Eddy put out his hand, grabbing Mick by the sleeve.

"No Mick. Hear me out. I want you to know everything. You said it yourself. You and Morris are in deep now thanks to me, so let me finish. He motioned to Mick to sit down. "I'll be fine Mick. Sit." Mick sat.

Eddy lay still for moment before carrying on with the story. "It wasn't funny at the time but it seems funny now. It was like Laurel and Hardy, we were tripping all over each other trying to figure out what to do, where to go. Enzio and I jumped into one of the boats and took off in one direction and the other two boats went other directions. Somehow or another, we managed to get to Sombrio Beach and I grabbed the briefcases and took off running up to the parking lot. I thought Enzio was right behind me but I wasn't really paying attention

Getting There

to my rear view mirror. I was focused on what was ahead. The trucks that we'd stashed ahead of time were there with the keys under the floor mats and I jumped in one and took off. I figured Enzio would grab the other truck but I don't really know what he did because I was just focused on saving my own ass. And I got out of there as fast as I could. As I drove along Highway 14, I could see that the helicopter had stayed over the freighter and the cutter was chasing the other boats. I just kept driving for a while, then went up a logging road and dumped the truck. I buried the briefcases deep in the woods and then just started walking. Took me three days before I finally made it to Sooke and I was a wreck. I didn't know what happened to Enzio. I was just glad to have made it out of there in one piece. I got down to Victoria and hid out in a motel for a few weeks. Then I rented a car and went back and got the money in the middle of the night. Of course everything looked different and it freaked me out being in the woods in the dark looking for those briefcases. Once I had the money, I went back to the motel. I didn't have a clue where Enzio had disappeared. I couldn't reach him. For all I knew, his business contacts had killed him for not coming through with the coke. People in that business get very upset when you don't deliver the goods." He lifted his head and looked at Mick. "As you now know. Enzio wants his money back."

Mick sighed. This was his good friend Eddy. Up till now he hadn't known about his history or where and how he had got the money to pay for his beautiful boat. Now he knew and it was more than he wanted to know. And now, Morris and himself were smack dab in the middle of Eddy's old business. "Where's the money now Eddy?" It was a simple question.

Eddy looked at him. Blood was coming from one of his nostrils, a line of red leading down to his upper lip. It dripped down onto his t-shirt. Finally Eddy dabbed at it with the paper towel. "Just like I told Enzio. It's on Seagram. I told him but he wouldn't believe me." Having seen the inside of Seagram, Mick wasn't inclined to believe him either.

It was obvious that Eddy was wearing out from the talking. He began to cough again and Mick went to his first aid kit and pulled out a stethoscope. He knelt down and opened Eddy's shirt. He placed the stethoscope on the left side of the chest and listened and then on the right side. He got a flashlight and had Eddy open his mouth and with a tongue depressor looked down his throat.

"I hear air entering both sides pretty much equally, so I don't think it's a punctured lung. If it was, you'd have other symptoms than coughing up blood. Frankly, I think the blood is coming from your broken nose, draining backwards and now you're coughing it up. But truthfully, I think you need some professional medical attention. I hope whoever we're taking you to knows what they're doing. Are you planning on telling me where we're going? I need to let Morris know which way to head the boat."

Eddy laid his head back on the pillow and took a deep breath. He seemed to be breathing better, now that he was sitting up. He opened his eyes and looked at Mick. "We need to get to Port Washington on North Pender Island. There's a government dock there where you will be able to tie your boat up and my friends will be waiting for us. Trust me Mick, these people will help us."

Mick looked at him for a moment. 'If it's any consolation Eddy, while I can't condone what you did, I can understand why you did it. I mean, you're a boozer and a womanizer so I can see how a lifestyle that would net you large amounts of cash without having to get up and go to work every day would be appealing to you."

Eddy stared at him. "That's harsh."

Mick smiled. "What? The truth hurts?"

"You could be a little gentler." Eddy looked a little put out.

"Well," Mick replied, "compared to Enzio, I'm like Florence Nightingale. Eddy, you're a wonderful guy. That's why you're my best friend. You're generous to a fault with your time and energy. You're a fantastic mechanic and electrical technician. You've got so many good things going for you but you have to admit that you are a little unmotivated by the regular routine way of working for a living, right?" Eddy nodded. "So, I understand why you did what you did. But I still don't condone it. Let me ask you a question. Do you think I like getting up every day and working for a living? You've seen how long my days are. I'm up at the crack of dawn and usually work until midnight. Do you think I enjoy that kind of life? And that's just me. How about all those people on the freeway heading into town every bloody morning? Do you think they're all happy with that kind of life? No. But they still do it."

'That's because they're too stupid to figure out a way to make fast cash." Eddy said it without thinking and then realized he had just insulted his best friend. He started to apologize but Mick cut him off.

"Save it Eddy. Truly, I understand where you're coming from. One of the reasons I want to go offshore sailing is to get out of the rat race. I know, the rat race, it's such a cliché but I'm telling you Eddy, I have to get out of here because I can't take it any more."

Eddy looked surprised. "Wow. I didn't know you felt that way Mick."

Mick looked back at him. "Heading offshore is not just about sailing Eddy. A lot of it is about finding a way of life that is out of the ordinary. An extraordinary lifestyle."

Eddy nodded his head enthusiastically. "Yeah. I know what you're talking about. That's what I was doing with Enzio. A life out of the ordinary." He was excited that they were both on the same page.

Mick laughed. "Eddy, we may both be seeking an extraordinary lifestyle but I want to keep it legal. That's the difference and it's a big difference."

Mick sat back on his heels for a moment looking at his friend. Eddy didn't have much to say about that. After a moment Mick got up and headed up on deck.

As he stepped into the cockpit, he said to Morris, "Change of plans buddy. Let's head for Active Pass instead of Porlier Pass. It will be closer to our destination. We're going to Port Washington on North Pender. Eddy's got some friends there waiting to give him some medical attention."

"Port Washington?" Morris shrugged and swung the wheel over to port and brought the boat around until they were running almost due south. Mick trimmed the sails and noted that the wind had picked up a bit. It was still raining and visibility was dropping but the radar showed a clear path ahead. Mick punched in the new co-ordinates on the GPS unit and it calculated out their time and distance. At this rate of speed, they were going to be spending pretty much all night on the water. But as long as they were out on the water, they were out of harms way. That had to be a good thing.

Mick sipped his coffee and was watching the radar screen when his cell phone rang. He pulled it from his pocket and snapped it open.

"Mick? It's Dave. Dave Edmonds from the marina."

"Dave, what's up?" Mick was surprised to hear one of his neighbors on the phone. It always seemed strange to be out on the water talking on the telephone. He wondered if someone had tried to get into Eddy's boat again.

"Mick, I just wanted to give you a heads up. I was with Jessica in the bar and she was talking to some guy. The guy is thinking about buying a boat and Jessica said that you could answer questions for him. Jessica mentioned that you and Mo were out sailing. Are you looking for Eddy at this time of the night?"

Mick realized that Dave wouldn't know that they had found Eddy and that he was alright. Well, maybe not alright but better than dead. Mick felt his heart rate increase. "Did the guy tell you his name?"

"Yeah, he said his name was Martin Bradley and he had a couple of business partners with him. I can't remember their names but they were big guys. Martin was a pretty sharp dressed guy. That's about all I can tell you."

"Did Jessica tell them where we were going?"

"She said that you often go over to Telegraph Harbor, so she was just assuming that's where you were heading this time."

"OK Dave. Thanks for the heads up. Keep an eye out around there for these three. They are definitely not good guys. As in very dangerous, so don't cross them. Steer clear and call the police if you see them again. Thanks again and call me if you find out anything else."

"Okay Mick. You be careful out there. Talk to you later." He hung up.

Mick closed the cell phone and looked at Morris. "It's a good thing we're not going to Telegraph Harbor, Mo. I'd be willing to bet that Enzio might be planning a little trip there himself. It's good information to have. That Jessica's got a big mouth. Remind me not to tell her any of my deep dark secrets."

15 GETTING READY TO GO

The emergency room was packed with sick people in every state of illness and suffering. Kids were running around unsupervised making a big racket, getting disgusted looks from some of the sick. The people's faces showed the resignation that comes when dealing with a bureaucracy that grinds along at its own slow pace. Three Sikh men wearing turbans, jeans and t-shirts were arguing with the admissions clerk. She kept pushing a clipboard full of forms towards them and they kept pushing it back at her. Partially in Punjabi and partially in English, the argument seemed to be endless.

David Enzio waited impatiently for them to finish but finally lost his temper and using Horst and Tommy as blockers managed to push the surprised Sikhs out of the way. He laid his swollen hand on the counter and demanded to have someone look at it. The Sikhs began to argue with Enzio but Horst was in the way and he straightened to his full height and started advancing towards them. A dark skinned woman quickly stepped forward and tugged on the arm of one of the men. He scowled but allowed himself to be pulled towards a row of seats. The other men followed, none of them looking very happy about relinquishing their place in the line. They sat down and began talking Punjabi and throwing angry looks towards Enzio and his men.

The clerk started to argue with Enzio about butting into the line but upon seeing the look on his face thought better of it and instead presented Enzio with the clipboard full of forms which he promptly pushed right back onto her desk. She sighed.

"I don't have time for all that. I want someone to look at my hand right now." Thinking that she might be a little dense, he pointed at his hand and said slowly and clearly, "Hand hurts. Must see doctor now." The clerk smiled and suggested that someone might look at it tonight and then after looking at her watch corrected herself and said tomorrow morning. Enzio simply glared at her. She shrugged and suggested that he could pass the time by filling out the forms, nudging the clipboard in his direction again. Enzio fumed for a moment and then cursed the B.C. healthcare system and grabbed Tommy and Horst and headed for the exit. The Sikh men jumped up and began their argument anew with the tired clerk. It was just another long night in the emergency room.

Enzio, Tommy and Horst piled into the car and Enzio gave Horst directions back to the marina. "Stop at a burger place and let's get something to eat." A discussion ensued between Tommy and Horst regarding the culinary advantages of Burger King versus McDonalds. They tried to get an opinion from Enzio but his mood was too foul to get anything from him other than a curt "I don't care where the hell we eat, let's just get it over with and get back to the marina."

"You really should have stayed to get your hand looked at Boss." There goes Horst kissing ass again thought Tommy.

"You idiot, we'd be waiting there all night. You saw that robot behind the desk. She'd probably let every bloody person get in to see a doctor before she let me in. Just to spite me. Then maybe they might give me some aspirin and a splint and tell me to make an appointment with my doctor. Do you really think that's worth waiting all night to hear? Stop in at the next convenience store and get me some more ice to put on my hand. Tommy, I ought to kick your ass for causing me to hurt my hand." He reached with his good arm into the back seat and began flailing wildly hoping to land a blow on the cowering Tommy. No such luck.

It was late when they arrived back at the marina. Burger King had won the day and Tommy was getting annoyed looks from Enzio as he sat in the back burping and making rude sucking noises with his soft drink. He was treading on thin ice with Enzio. The whole world was treading on thin ice with Enzio. He felt like everything was going wrong and he was getting no help from anyone. He was close to really losing his temper and he knew from bitter experience that this was something to be avoided at all costs. That was one of those things you

Getting There

woke up the next morning full of regret about. He had to keep his cool even if Horst and Tommy and everyone else seemed to be determined to test him.

There were a few people still in the pub but otherwise it was all quiet around the marina. Enzio had Horst park on Dyke Road down towards E dock. It was nice and dark, so they wouldn't be seen sitting in the car and they could look out at the river and the boats at the dock below. If anything, the rain was heavier now which suited Enzio just fine. The weather was miserable and that would keep nosy onlookers to a minimum. Enzio was interested in a couple of good sized power boats tied up along the outside of the dock. Since they would not be familiar with the boats handling, it would be easier to leave from the outside of the dock and not have to do much maneuvering.

Horst's ass kissing hadn't paid off as Enzio told the big man to get out and climb over the fence and open the gate from the inside. Horst started whining about the rain and his leather jacket getting wet but one look from Enzio and he was gone. For a big man, he was surprisingly agile. He was over the fence and had the gate open even before Enzio could get out of the car. With Tommy in tow, they went through the gate being held open by a grinning Horst.

"Good work Horst. For once."

As they made their way down the ramp to the docks, Enzio looked at the river to see what the tide was doing. The ramp was at a fairly flat angle and there didn't appear to be much current in the river at the moment. One less thing for them to worry about Enzio thought. It was quiet on the dock and they headed towards the outside slips. Enzio stopped at the first big powerboat that they came to. There weren't any lights on and the cockpit was closed in by curtains with plastic windows. A big "For Sale" sign was taped to the inside of one of the windows. It was a Bayliner Thirty Nine. Looking like he owned the place he unzipped the cover at the back and stepped aboard. He had to lean back out and tell Tommy and Horst to get their asses on board.

The cabin doors were locked but they were flimsy looking things. Tommy stepped forward and grabbed the lock in his hand and gave it a vicious pull. With little resistance the thin mahogany door splintered and the lock came away in Tommy's big fist. Enzio clapped him on the back and said "Now that's making yourself useful. Let's see if we can get some power turned on and get this thing fired up." It was cold down below but at least they were out of the rain. Enzio had

Horst go around and close all the curtains and then he found the breaker panel and started switching on some lights. He searched around the cabin until he found what he was looking for. A key on a spongy rubber floating key chain. It was hanging on a hook just inside the forward stateroom. He had Horst open up the engine room hatch so they could open the sea cocks that provided cooling water for the engines. He took a look at the engines, checking the oil and making sure that everything looked serviceable. It smelled a little bit like gasoline down in the bilge, so he turned the engine room blowers on. It was probably a good idea to run them while they got organized.

Horst and Tommy were like a couple of big kids who were in the way while they looked around the cabin. Enzio told them to sit down at the dinette table and shut up while he got ready to go. From time to time he pulled the curtains aside and peeked out at the dock. It was still quiet out there. Bless the crappy weather.

Sitting down at the captain's chair, Enzio scanned over the engine instruments. Plugging in the key, he turned on the power and was able to see that the tanks were three quarters full. Good enough. This was a twin engine machine. Good for maneuvering. He'd seen it all before and was comfortable with the boat. He put it in neutral and cracked the throttle on the port engine. Hitting the starter, it fired up quickly and settled into a quiet rumble. He did the same with the starboard engine and then had Horst and Tommy go out onto the dock and take care of the forward and aft lines. He told them to untie the lines and then toss them on deck and get back aboard before the boat moved away from the dock. He pointed out that he was going to leave them behind if they weren't quick about getting aboard again.

He turned on the windshield wipers and was opening up the curtains on the port and starboard window when he saw someone coming down the dock towards them. Tommy was crouched down on the dock trying to untie the forward line. Horst had his untied and was standing there holding it in his hand trying to look like he wasn't helping to steal the boat. A man wearing a bright yellow rain slicker stopped and began talking to Horst who looked like a kid caught with his hand in the candy jar. Enzio quickly stepped out into the cockpit and stuck his head through the zippered opening. "Good evening," he said. The man had his rain hood up and looked out from under its brim.

"Kind of a crappy night for going out isn't it?"

Enzio looked surprised. "Around here if we waited for good weather, we'd never get out on the water, right?"

Tommy now had the line untied and was giving Enzio a thumbs up. "I'm just showing the boat to these two gentlemen. They're from back east and have to leave first thing in the morning. I'm hoping we can get out for a little spin and then go back to the hotel and finish up the deal before they have to go."

"You guys are going to love this boat," the man said. I've been out on her before. She handles like a dream. Well, I won't keep you." He turned to Horst and looked him up and down. "You might want to invest in some foul weather gear if you're thinking of doing much boating. That leather jacket won't be worth a damn if you wear it around here very much." With that he headed off down the dock.

Horst looked at his beautiful leather jacket which was soaked and started to complain about it to Enzio but was cut short. "Will you shut up about your bloody jacket? Throw those lines on board and get the hell in here. Let's get out of here before someone else comes nosing around."

The tide was just beginning to flood and with the boat no longer tied to the dock, it began to slowly drift backwards. Enzio put the engines in gear and gave them a little throttle and turned the wheel to port. They began to edge away from the dock and were soon moving forward. Flipping some switches on the instrument panel, Enzio turned on the navigation lights and switched off the interior cabin lights. He had Tommy go out on deck and pull up the fenders that were hanging down on the starboard side. Tommy was moving very carefully on the wet deck and when he came back in, he zipped up the curtain in the cockpit.

Enzio turned on the radar and the GPS unit and opened the throttles until they were moving along at a sedate three or four knots. He wanted to let the engines get nicely warmed up before he pushed them. There was a chart book in a rack next to the captain's chair and Enzio pulled it out and found it was already opened to the chart showing their part of the river including the marina. Navigation looked fairly straight forward and he pointed the boat down the river heading for the mouth. Horst was whining again, still going on about his poor leather jacket. Enzio told him that he would buy him a new one when they got back and would he please sit down and shut up. Better still, would he see if there was any food or coffee on board? Enzio was wishing that they had stopped at a Tim Horton's and gotten some doughnuts and coffee. Tommy had to go to the bathroom and Enzio had to tell him from where he was sitting how to operate the toilet. Enzio cursed under his breath. It was just like having kids around.

That they had gotten a boat so easily and the fact that his hand was starting to feel better were the only bright spots in this lousy day. They only had to get over to Telegraph Harbor in one piece and locate Eddy and then they could go about kicking Brese's ass for stealing their prisoner. Once they re-captured Eddy, they would get the answer that they so badly needed. Enzio felt like they were on the right track despite some setbacks. As he looked out at the navigation markers passing by in the dark, he imagined finally getting what he was looking for. It made his heart come gladly.

16 THE LONG NIGHT

It was dark out on the water. Behind them, the lights of the cities of Vancouver and Richmond glowed along the horizon but Starlight was almost across the Strait of Georgia and it was dark. The clouds had dropped low to the water and it was raining hard. With the radar, and the GPS navigator to help them find their way, the rain and the poor visibility didn't really matter except that it made life uncomfortable. Even with the dodger that wrapped around the front of the hatch and covered part way back over the cockpit, it was still uncomfortable. But if you're a sailor in the Pacific Northwest, you put up with it. It comes with the territory as they say.

They were heading southwest until they got closer to Galiano Island at which point they would ease further south towards Active Pass. They had consulted the tide tables and figured that they could probably make the Pass just after slack water and would be able to go through on the ebb. Since it would be after the B.C. Ferries were finished their last sailing, they wouldn't have to worry about meeting up with the big boats in the confines of the Pass.

Mick and Morris sat in the protection of the dodger while the autopilot steered the boat. They both wore floater coats, rain pants, deck boots and toques. As wet and cold as it was, Mick and Morris were enjoying the trip. It felt different than the usual dash over to the islands for a little R and R. This trip had purpose. They both knew that if Enzio got his hands on them, it was going to be unpleasant to say the least. Mick had filled Morris in on what Eddy had told him.

Morris took the news without much surprise. "Four million dollars. Well, that explains how he could afford a boat like Seagram. But it doesn't explain how it is that Enzio didn't find the money and if he didn't find it, where is it? Enzio sure as hell didn't leave any places unexplored down below and I didn't notice two briefcases full of money laying around on deck." Mick nodded, mentally going over Seagram inside and out trying to think where the money might be.

Eddy had really been hurting and Mick had given him a Percocet. The pain, the medication and the excitement of the day had really taken a toll on him and he was now fast asleep and snoring heavily. Morris went below to check on him and came back up on deck with more coffee. The motion of the boat had increased considerably as the wind had picked up and Morris was doing a great balancing act with the cups. He braced himself and passed a cup to Mick.

"You hear that racket down there?" He jerked his head in the direction of the cabin. "I don't think Eddy would wake up even if the ship was sinking."

"It's probably for the best. I'm worried about the blood he's coughing up and the fingers on his left hand look pretty bad. Enzio is one sick bastard. I wouldn't have believed someone could do that to another person. I guess it goes on all the time in some places like war zones or third world countries but it's sobering to see it in person. We lead pretty sheltered lives, compared to a lot of people in the world. Thank God."

Morris nodded his head. He sat his coffee down and made some adjustments to the jib. It was partially reefed now. The wind had picked up and this was as good a sail as they had had for a long time. It was unusual for them to sail at night. "This is kind of like offshore sailing Mick. I mean out there, you sail twenty four hours a day until you get to your destination. I haven't sailed at night for a long time. Usually we're anchored somewhere safe at this time of the night. Good training for when we get going."

"Speaking of getting going Mo, once we get this mess sorted out and get Enzio off our case, I'm going to finish up the last of my sculpting commissions and I'm leaving. I've had enough of preparing. It's time."

"Well Mick, on the one hand, I'm going to be sorry to see you leave but on the other, I'll be happy for you. We all talk about going and talk and talk but so few of us ever manage to cut the ties that hold us here. For every one person that gets going, there are a lot of us that stay behind just dreaming. I'm not ready to go yet but I'm getting close. Maybe we can meet up somewhere out there." He pointed in a westerly direction and then they knocked their coffee mugs together to seal the deal.

Around midnight they changed course as they approached Galiano's steep wooded shores. They pointed the bow towards the southeast with plans to arrive off Gossip Island at the entrance to Active Pass right at slack water. Morris went up on deck and made the rounds, just to be sure everything was in order. Mick looked out the starboard side at the looming darkness of the island. Occasional lights showed from a few houses but it was mostly dark and shrouded in clouds. The wind was dropping and as Morris came back into the cockpit, Mick suggested that they take in the jib and crank up the engine. Since they had no intention of sailing through the pass, it was as good a time as any to get the engine started. While Morris rolled in the jib, Mick got the diesel fired up.

Standing at the wheel, the autopilot turned off, Mick headed them a little closer into shore. The radar screen showed no other traffic in their vicinity and they were right on time as they came abreast of Gossip Island.

The tides and currents in the Pacific Northwest are not something to be taken lightly. With a tidal range of twenty feet or more in many places the current can cause rapids, whirlpools and large rips and eddies. Morris was watching the instruments closely. "Looks like we're doing fine Mick. I'm glad we've got the radar and the depth sounder and four good eyes to get us through." The lay of the land, with Galiano Island on the starboard side and Mayne Island to port, would force them to do a dogleg pattern going through the pass.

Morris slid the hatch back just long enough to see that Eddy was still sleeping which was good. They still had a while to go before they would be tying up at the dock in Port Washington.

"It's going to be pretty early in the morning when we show up at the dock at Port Washington. Eddy said that he had friends who were going to meet us there. Are they just hanging around waiting for us or do we have to contact them somehow?"

"I think we'll just play it by ear Mo. If they're there that will be great, if not, we can call them. I've got their number on my cell phone. Just have to hit re-dial."

It was quiet going through the pass. The few lights on land only helped to emphasize the lonely feel of the night. As they exited the pass, Helen Point was just off their port bow and Mick was biding his time before turning and heading south. The rain had stopped now and it was almost calm. Morris looked up at the big mainsail above them and decided it was time to bring it down. He uncleated the halyard and began to pay it out which dropped the boom into the gallows. As he lowered the main, the lazy jacks kept it contained and in just a few minutes, he had the sail secured along the boom.

As they cleared Helen Point, Mick advanced the throttle and headed towards Prevost Island. Starlight moved through the flat water with ease and they were soon making good speed towards their destination. Mick and Morris were both yawning and Morris held up his coffee cup in a questioning manner. Mick slouching at the wheel gave a vigorous nod. It was going to be a while before they would be tied up at the dock and it was a safe bet that a warm bunk was still a few hours away.

It was a different feeling being inside the islands as opposed to being out in the wide open waters of the Strait. Here, the water was smoother and due to the closeness of land all around them, it felt like they were going much faster. Morris came up on deck and shut the cabin up again. As he handed the coffee to Mick he offered to take over the helm again. Mick moved out of the way and sat down under the dodger as Morris took the wheel.

"I guess we can just head straight for Port Washington now. You can see the light in the middle of the bay just off the starboard bow. You see it there?" He was pointing to a flashing red beacon off in the distance.

"Yeah, I've got it Mick. When I was down below, I checked on Eddy. He's awake now. Not the brightest spark at the moment but he's talking. I asked him if we were going to have a welcoming party at the dock or not. He told me not to worry about it. Everything is under control." Morris shrugged as he delivered Eddy's comment. "He seems pretty calm about it. Maybe it's just the drugs that have him so relaxed but he seems to think everything's taken care of."

"I'm happy for him. Personally, I think we should be ready for anything. I'm going down below. Want anything?"

Morris shook his head. "Naw, I'm fine."

As Mick entered the cabin and shut the hatch, he turned and found Eddy was awake. He was looking like death warmed over. Dark yellowish circles were forming around his eyes, his nose was swollen and red and still bleeding slightly.

"Could I trouble you for another cup of coffee Mick? I'm kind of groggy from the medication. I want to wake up before we get to Port Washington." He sounded all stuffed up like he had a bad cold.

Mick filled the kettle and put it on the stove to heat. He yawned while he counted spoonfuls of coffee into the coffee pot. "We should be getting there pretty soon. Hopefully there's some room at the dock. It's first come, first served, so we might have to anchor out in the bay, or go around to Port Browning. But, if there is a spot at the dock, we should be all stop in about an hour or so. Are your friends going to be there?"

Eddy nodded. "They'll be there, don't worry. I think you'll be pleasantly surprised. Trust me."

Mick shrugged. Trust was in short supply these days. "We'll see. I'm hoping so."

When the kettle signaled its readiness, Mick finished preparing the coffee and poured a cup for Eddy, gave it a shot of milk and took it over to him. "How's the pain?" he asked as he saw the grimace on his friends face as he took the cup.

"Truthfully? I have a feeling it will be a while before my hand gets back to normal, if ever. But the medication you gave me earlier seems to have helped some. I'll live, thanks to you. I want to thank you and Morris again for getting me out of that motel room. I had a feeling I was going to be leaving that room in a body bag. I was scared Mick. I've never felt fear like that before and it's a sobering experience. I hope I never go through anything like that again."

"I hope you never do and I hope I never do too." Mick said. "I've got to get back up on deck Eddy. If you need anything, give a good loud shout." He turned and went up the companionway stairs and into the cockpit. As he turned to close the hatch, he could see that they were getting close to Pender. The island is well populated, so there were considerably more lights than on the other islands. Port Washington was dead ahead and they were making good time. Morris looked cold, so Mick went aft and took over the wheel.

"I'm going to the head Mick. Be back up in a few minutes."

"Yeah, that's fine Mo. Can you get the binoculars for me from the navigation table please? Morris went down below and handed the binoculars back up. Mick throttled the engine back a bit. He had been to the Government dock a couple of times but it had always been full so he had gone elsewhere, either to anchor or tie up at another marina. Through the glasses, he could see that there was plenty of room and it looked like it was an easy approach. He sat sipping his coffee and letting the autopilot do the work. It was always nice to be coming into a dock and it was even better to be leaving a dock. Life on land left a lot to be desired. Out here on the water, it was easier, simpler. There were always lots of decisions to be made but they were simpler kinds of decisions. Where to go, when to leave, tides, winds, sail management, maintenance, eating, sleeping, they were all easy decisions to make. It was good. He couldn't get enough of it and usually didn't. That was going to change soon if he had his way.

Morris came back on deck and saw that they were closing in on their destination. "Which side are we going to be tying up on?"

Mick pointed to the port side and Morris went up on deck and moved the fenders over so they would be ready. He prepared the bow line and then came back and got the stern line ready as well.

"It looks like we're going to be on the outside, just behind the Nordic Tug." It was quiet in the bay and there didn't appear to be anybody waiting for them. "I'm not seeing a welcoming committee Mo, but let's be ready for anything. I don't know who to trust these days."

Mick took a nice long slow arc towards the dock and put the engine in neutral as they were about a hundred feet away. Morris dropped the fenders over the side and stood by with the mooring lines in his hand. At the dock, they had almost come to a stop as Morris stepped off the boat and quickly tied the bow and stern lines. Mick looked up and down the dock but saw no one about. There did not seem to be any sign of the friends that Eddy had promised. Morris came back onboard and the two of them stood in the cockpit yawning and waiting. For ten minutes they waited but still nothing. Mick shut the engine down and followed Morris down the companionway, closing the hatch behind them.

Eddy was sitting up now. Mick looked at him and said, "Well? I hate to tell you this but it looks like your friends aren't on call tonight. Maybe they went to Port Browning, or Bedwell Harbor. There's nobody waiting for us at this dock, that's for sure."

17 THE SHOCK OF THE DAY

At that moment, there was a quiet knocking on the side of the boat. Mick and Morris looked at each other and Eddy said, "That will be them. Go on, let them in." Seeing the hesitancy on the faces of the two men, he added, "I'm sure it's my friends Mick. Go."

That was all it took for Mick to turn and open the hatch. As he opened the companionway doors, he was stunned. He was face to face with one of Eddy's friends who had already come aboard and was standing in the cockpit. Even in the dim light of the dock, it was easy to see that this was not what he was expecting. This was, simply put, a very beautiful young looking Asian woman in a pea coat, her long black hair hanging down both sides of her face. She stepped back a half step and in that quiet voice he was so accustomed to, stated simply, "Hello Mick, is Eddy here?"

Mick's words caught in his throat. He opened his mouth and then shut it again. For some reason, even the simple answer seemed more than he was able to deliver. Instead, he just nodded his head. Claire turned and waved her arm towards the dock. She looked at Mick and with a slight smile, said, "I'm sure you weren't expecting to see me again. I hope you will give me a chance to explain but first we have to take care of Eddy." Mick stepped back down into the boat and shook his head in confusion to Morris's inquiring look. Claire came down first followed by two more people, a man and a woman, Asian and both rather elderly and frail looking. Everyone was wearing rubber boots and rain jackets and the man was carrying a backpack which looked heavy. The woman looked at Mick and huffed. She glared at him and her mouth formed an angry thin line. She blew out through her nose and the only word that Mick could think of was "huffed". Mick was taken aback by her response to him. He didn't have any idea what that was all about.

But as soon as they saw Eddy, it was old home week, except it was all in a foreign language with no subtitles. Chinese. Claire stood out of the way moving into the galley to give the man and woman room to get by. The woman went to Eddy and gently picked up both of his hands in hers. She spoke rapidly to him in Chinese and looked very concerned. She began to tear up at his answer also in Chinese. Mick and Morris looked at each other in absolute surprise. This was definitely not what they were expecting and they both wore looks of amazement.

Mick was reluctant to butt in on the conversation between Eddy and the woman but butt in he did. "Eddy, these are your friends? Claire and let me guess, Claire's parents? And you speak Chinese? Tell me I'm dreaming." The woman and Eddy continued on as if Mick had not spoken a word. Mick glanced over at Claire but she was leaning back against the galley with her hands in her coat pockets and looking down at her feet. The Chinese man ignored him also. They had their own agenda and at the moment it did not include Mick and Morris.

The woman began talking to the old man who started taking items from the backpack and putting them on the navigation table. Claire grabbed the kettle from the stove and began filling it. She lit the stove without difficulty. After all, she knew her way around Mick and Morris sat down next to each other on the port settee keeping out of the way. The two of them looked like a couple of stunned mullets.

The old woman took her rain jacket off and looked around for somewhere to put it. Morris jumped up and took it from her and hung it in the hanging locker in the aft quarter berth. Eddy was now lying back down and the woman was opening his shirt. As Eddy's belly came into view the woman broke into a smile and patted the belly and looked at Mick and Morris and said, "He's a very strong man, good health."

Mick looked back at her and said bluntly, "He's a fat bastard, not good health." The Chinese woman looked at Mick and Morris, "You two are too thin, not strong, you need to eat more."

Eddy spoke in Chinese to her and everyone except Mick and Morris started nodding their heads. The man turned to Mick and

Getting There

Morris and bowed and said what sounded like "See-ya, see-ya." Claire saw the questioning look on Mick and Morris's faces and explained. "Eddy was just telling us that you and Morris saved him from a very bad future. We are grateful. My mother and father and I thank you. See-ya, see-ya, is thank you in Chinese. We are very grateful that you saved our friend."

Mick looked at Claire's mother who certainly didn't look grateful to him. She glared at Mick. He looked at Claire who had a calm, confident look on her face and his heart took a couple of extra beats. He tried to ignore it. Not too successfully he admitted to himself. Claire's mother looked at Mick and then at Claire and a frown came over her face. She spoke sharply to Claire and the daughter went back to work making some sort of hot herbal drink, her cheeks burning.

The woman unwrapped the bandages that Mick had put on Eddy's hand. They were blood soaked and stuck to his fingers in places. Eddy grimaced in pain but didn't say anything. As the woman worked, she kept up a high speed conversation with Eddy. Occasionally she spoke to the old man and he handed her various items which they had brought with them. Surprisingly, they had brought metal splints for Eddy's badly damaged fingers. The woman worked professionally, showing her medical training, applying strange smelling ointment and the splints to two of Eddy's fingers on his left hand. Eddy wouldn't be playing the piano anytime soon if that was his pleasure.

The old man was busy lining up several rows of small glass cups on the table. Mick and Morris looked at the cups and then at each other. Morris shrugged. With help, Eddy removed his shirt. He was a big man alright with chubby breasts and a large round stomach. There were two dark bruises under his left breast, probably from blows from a large fist. The woman touched the bruises, probing gently with her fingers. Eddy grimaced and from the looks of it, he probably had one or more cracked ribs. He was unable to turn over on his own and the old man and the woman helped him to turn onto his stomach on the settee. The sight reminded Mick of a large sea lion lying on the beach.

The old man handed the woman a jar of oil and she liberally massaged the oil into Eddy's back. As she was doing this the old man picked up a piece of cotton batting with a pair of forceps and then dipped it into a jar that contained alcohol. He passed the forceps to the woman and she lit the cotton batting with a lighter and quickly shoved the flaming cotton into the mouth of one of the jars that Claire handed to her. The woman then pressed the cup onto Eddy's back and his skin was sucked into the cup. She slid the cup along one side of his spine, the cup moving easily on the oiled skin. As the cup moved, it left a reddened path of skin in its wake. It looked rather bizarre as she parked the cup at the top of his back, just below his neck on the left side of his spine. She repeated the process until she had all the glass cups lined up one after another on both sides of his spine from his neck on down.

The woman went to the galley and washed her hands and had a quick conversation with Claire and the old man. Claire turned and spoke to Mick and Morris in a soft and quiet voice. "My mother and father will stay with Eddy but it would be best if we do not disturb him while the cupping is going on." In response to their questioning looks, she stated, "Cupping is a traditional Chinese treatment. It is important that the patient be relaxed and have quiet as well. I understand that you have some questions that need to be answered. However, Eddy told us over the phone that you have had a very long and busy day so perhaps you would like to wait until tomorrow to talk?"

Mick took the lead and motioned with his hand that they should go up on deck. "Ladies first." As he followed her up the stairs to the cockpit he could smell that wonderful touch of ginger and tropical flowers. He inhaled deeply and felt like he was being pulled along behind her.

In the cockpit with the companionway doors closed behind them, they sat. Mick and Morris on the port side of the cockpit and Claire on the starboard side. She sat with her hands in her pea coat pockets. She looked at the two of them and then directed her gaze on Mick.

"Mick," she started to speak and then stopped, looking uncomfortable. She looked at Mick and made a slight glance in Morris's direction indicating where her source of discomfort was coming from. Morris caught the look and decided he would go below to watch the cupping process and get the synopsis later on. He could tell when he wasn't wanted.

"If you two will excuse me, I think I'll go below where it's a little warmer and I don't just mean the weather. It's nice to see you again Claire." He grinned and turned and disappeared down below, quietly closing the hatch behind him.

Getting There

Mick almost forgot how angry he was with her for leaving him. Here, so close to her, it was easy to forget. Frankly, aside from the shock of seeing her, he had to admit that he was feeling pretty good. She looked like she might be cold all the way over there on the other side of the cockpit so he stood up and lifted the locker lid and pulled out a blanket. "Claire, it's cold out here. Wrap this around yourself." She took the blanket and draped it over her shoulders and snuggled into it.

"Thank you Mick. I'm so sorry that I left the way I did. I'm sure you are hurt and angry and I don't blame you at all. Oh, I hope I can make you understand why I did what I did." She sounded almost desperate.

Mick shook his head. There were a lot of emotions running through his head and his heart right at that moment. "Claire, I thought we had a good relationship going. In a relationship, people talk. People try to find ways to make things work, that is if they love each other. And I remember clearly that we both used the L word more than once."

Claire went limp and she looked down so that Mick was unable to see her face. She took a deep breath. "Mick, do you think it was easy for me to walk away? There are two reasons why I had to leave. First, I didn't want you to compromise for me and second, my parents won't compromise for me. I want you to go offshore sailing. I don't want you to give that up for me and as much as I want to, I can't go with you because I'm Chinese." Mick looked puzzled by her statement. "I'm Chinese. I have an obligation to my parents. My parents want me to marry a Chinese man. In case you hadn't noticed, my mother knows you and I have a relationship. That's why she is so upset with you. There's nothing worse in her mind than her daughter having a relationship and marrying a Lao Wai." In response to his questioning look, she clarified. "A foreigner." They already have someone in mind for me and he is Chinese and as much as it makes me angry, I feel like I can't disappoint them again." Her eyes were shiny with tears and she felt around in her pockets for a tissue. She found one and dabbed her eyes.

Mick looked at her with a complete lack of understanding. He shook his head. "You're kidding me. Your parents already arranged your first marriage. Look how well that turned out. You would go through that again just to not disappoint them? How could you do that to yourself? Isn't your happiness worth anything?"

Claire realized that there was more distance between them than the width of the cockpit. There was a cultural divide between them that would be almost impossible to span. "Mick, my parents may be able to speak English and they may eat with a knife and a fork and a spoon now instead of chopsticks but they are still Chinese. They are Chinese inside and for them, it is important to carry on the family line as Chinese. They can trace their families back for many generations. They can recite their family histories to you like they were reading from a book and for them, family is everything. I am their only child and if I marry a westerner, the family history takes a turn in a direction that they can't deal with." She was sounding exasperated as though trying to explain snow to a person who had lived in the desert all his life. "I don't agree with their point of view but I understand it. You know, they are the first people in both their families to have ever been outside of China. I know it's difficult for you to imagine because you are from the west. I know you've traveled all over the world and your family has too. But my parents have lived in the same province, the same city most of their lives and so too have their ancestors. And when they think of their daughter marrying a man from a different culture, from a different country it's enough to break their hearts and I can't do that to them. They want to move back to China soon and they want me to go with them. They hope that by coming home with a new Chinese son-in-law, the shame that I brought them will be forgotten. And as much as I love you, I want you to follow your dream and let me make my parents happy." She sat back against the cockpit coaming and began to cry. Deep wracking sobs coming from her small body.

Mick sat on the other side of the cultural divide and felt completely helpless. As much as he was comfortable and happy being who he was, at that moment he was wishing that he was Chinese and he could make Claire happy and make her parents happy too. But he was a big white guy and there was nothing that he could do to change it.

"Claire, I don't believe you for a moment." She looked up startled. "Yeah, that's right. I don't believe you. You say you want me to follow my dream and you want to do what you have to do to make your parents happy but I don't believe you are going to do it." He leaned toward her. "You know that we belong together. You know it and I know it. And I don't know how I'm going to do it but I'm going to make you admit it. To me and to yourself and especially, to your parents."

Getting There

At that moment, the hatch slid open quickly and Claire's mother popped up and looked back and forth between the two of them. Both Mick and Claire were startled. Claire glared at her mother and spoke sharply to her in Chinese and Mick had a feeling that she was giving her mother a bit of flack for startling them. Without a word, her mother took one last look at the two of them and was gone and the hatch slid shut again.

Mick looked at Claire and the fact that she was blushing was evident even in the dim light of the dock. Her gaze was directed down and she was obviously embarrassed.

"My mother is very protective of me, Mick. As I explained, we are a close family." She gave a weak smile and tipped her head in the direction of the cabin. "Sometimes a little too close I think. Family ties are very important to Chinese people and it is a part of our culture that the children take care of their parents. My parents certainly don't need caring for but traditions are traditions. My mother thinks that there is no man who is good enough for me, especially someone that is not from our own culture. It is not prejudice or racism; it is just tradition and she is a mother who loves her daughter very much"

Mick nodded and they sat together in the cockpit in the quiet of the Port Washington night. He decided it was time for a change of topic. He wanted the answers to some other burning questions. Like why did Eddy bring them to Claire and her parents? How was it that he knew her parents so well and how was it that he seemed to be able to speak Chinese so fluently? Mick knew that the answers to these questions were going to shed a lot of light on things. But Claire looked cold and tired and it was already four in the morning.

Mick reached toward her and she let the blanket fall as she reached across to him. He took her hand in his. It was small and warm and familiar. "Claire, we should call it a day. Thank you for the explanation. I know you think it's difficult for me to understand but I do. It's just that I don't agree with what you want to do and I don't think you're heart is in it. And in my culture, we listen to our heart and we try to find a way to make everyone happy at the same time as we get what we want. Now let's see what's going on down below. Your mother doesn't scare me." She let her hand slip from his again. She felt warm just from his touch. Mick slid the hatch back quietly and opened the companionway doors and motioned for Claire to go first. She went down and stopped at the bottom just as Mick came down behind her.

It was warm and cozy in the cabin, the little diesel heater cast a flickering light on the room. Eddy was covered up, still on his belly, snoring gently this time. Claire's mother and father had made up the port settee into a bunk and were covered up and sleeping. Morris had taken the starboard quarter berth, which left only the bunk in the bow stateroom. Claire looked up at him and spread her hands in a questioning manner. Mick went around her and took her by the hand and led her forward. He sat her in the seat beside the bunk and proceeded to remove her rubber boots then motioned for her to stand up. He took off her pea coat and then turned the comforter down on the bunk. He motioned for her to get in and then covered her and made sure she was comfortable. She watched him as he removed his boots and rain pants and floater coat and put them all in the hanging locker. He got an extra blanket from the bottom drawer of the locker and lay down on top of the covers beside Claire and covered himself. She looked pleased that he had been so considerate of the situation. It was like bundling, something they had done in China in the wintertime to keep warm. It was cozy but safe.

He turned out the small lamp at the head of the bunk. "Goodnight Claire, it's good to see you again" Mick whispered. He was very tempted to kiss her but he laid his head down instead.

"Goodnight Mick. Thank you. Thank you very much." She closed her eyes and went to sleep enjoying the closeness.

Mick lay there with his eyes open, listening to her soft breathing. It was a good feeling. He hadn't felt this good in a very long time. He hoped the feeling would last.

18 A NEW DAY

Good feelings come and good feelings go. Mick's good feeling evaporated as soon as he opened his eyes. He was still lying on his back and he could feel Claire beside him on the bunk. But as his eyes focused and he turned his head to the side, he came under the furious glare of Claire's father. The old man's face was beet red as though the blood had all come to his head and was about to explode from his pores.

With more speed than could be imagined, his hand shot out and struck Mick a chopping blow right in his stomach. For an elderly, skinny little man, he managed in one simple move to leave Mick gasping like a fish out of water, just trying to get one breath back into his lungs. While Mick's only concern was how to learn how to breathe again, Claire sat up quickly beside him and the old man began berating her in Chinese. He was like a leaky high pressure valve with flecks of spit coming out of his mouth along with his shouted words.

Claire realized what had happened and began arguing back to her father which only enraged him more. Mick sensed that the old man's attention had shifted and in that moment took the opportunity to send a punch hard into the old man's stomach. The effect was almost comical. The old man doubled over but being rather short in stature and due to the close quarters, his head came down and cracked hard on the edge of the bunk. Apparently it knocked him senseless and he crumpled to the floor like a rag doll. The sudden quiet was all it took to galvanize Claire into action. She scrambled out from the cover and over top of Mick. She hopped down and crouched next to her father on the floor where she cradled him against her. His head was bleeding slightly and a large bump was swelling up on his forehead. His eyes opened, slowly coming into focus and he first looked at Claire and then up at Mick.

Claire was talking in Chinese. Her mother and Morris had both been awakened by the ruckus and had come quickly and were crowding into the narrow entrance to the bow stateroom. The mother was shouting in Chinese mostly at Mick. Morris was shouting in English trying to find out what was going on. It was a chaotic scene and the old man finally shouted something in Chinese, obviously asking for quiet because immediately Claire and her mother were silent. Morris followed suit.

The father put his hand up to his forehead and gingerly felt the lump growing there. He looked at Mick. "That was a good move Mr. Brese. The time to strike is when the opportunity presents itself. I let my guard down for a moment and you took the opportunity." Turning to his daughter, he continued. "When I saw you in the same bed as Mr. Brese, I thought you were sleeping together and I became a little upset." Claire rolled her eyes at this massive understatement. "I thought you were together under the same blanket and I was mistaken." This was apparently about as close to an apology as he was going to get.

Claire stood and helped her father sit in the seat next to the bunk. "Mother could you please get a damp cloth so I can clean Father's forehead." She turned to Mick. "Do you have ice, Mick?"

Morris piped up from the other room, "Yeah we've got ice in the freezer. I'll get some for you." The crowd began to disperse.

Mick lay back on the bunk and rubbed his stomach and the old man sat holding his head in his hand. Claire stood looking at the two of them shaking her head. "When are you going to grow up, Father?" she asked not expecting an answer.

He looked at her. "Confucius say, only the wisest and stupidest of men never change. If I do not "grow up" as you put it, will you think I am the former, or the latter? Your mother and I have tried hard our whole lives to protect you. Is it stupid or wise for an old man to continue to do so? I do admit to you that sometimes I am overprotective but you are my life work."

Claire smiled at him as her mother came in with a damp cloth and a small bowl of ice which Claire used to tend to her father's head. The mother glared at Mick as if the whole incident were his fault.

Mick lay on the bunk trying to ignore the look and said, "What are your father and mother's names?"

Claire looked at him while holding the ice to her father's forehead. "My father is Xun Yuen Shung but everyone calls him Mr. Xun. Xun is correctly pronounced "sue-in" but most people simply say Xun. My mother's name is Lu Huan Lan and everyone calls her Mrs. Lu."

Mick put his hand out to Mr. Xun and said, "Pleased to meet you Mr. Xun." Mr. Xun shook the proffered hand and said wryly, "A pleasure Mr. Brese." It seemed that the crisis had passed.

Mick said, "I got the impression that your mother and father spoke mostly Chinese but I guess I was mistaken."

"Chinese is our native language. My mother and father prefer to speak it most of the time and we have found that it is sometimes very useful not to let on that we speak English. People feel like they can say things around us that they would not ordinarily say. "

Mick said, "And another thing. Last night, Eddy was speaking Chinese like it was his native language too."

Claire turned to look into the main cabin where Eddy was now sitting up. "Eddy is a man of many talents Mick. He does speak Chinese but hardly like a native speaker. I will explain later." Changing the subject, she asked, "How are you feeling Mick? Are you ready for some breakfast?"

Mick sat up and noted that his stomach was a little tender from Mr. Xun's chop but he was more than ready for something to eat. "Morris and I will get some breakfast going Claire."

Morris spoke from the main cabin, "It looks like you and I are going to have to find something else to do Mick. Mrs. Lu has taken over the galley." Claire patted Mr. Xun on the arm and gave Mick a smile that spoke volumes. She turned and went to the galley to help her mother. They appeared to know what they were doing, and Mr. Xun was tending to the bump on his noggin, so Mick and Morris went up on deck.

It was a sunny morning for a change. At this early hour, mist was still hanging heavy in places and wafting through the bay like low flying clouds. The sun was warm and it sparkled across the breeze ruffled water.

As they went around the boat tidying up, Mick dropped a bucket over the side and filled it with seawater to sluice the decks off. While he used a long handled brush to scrub some dirt off the teak deck he filled Morris in on the details that Claire had provided about her reason for leaving him. Morris was not surprised that Claire and Mick had talked about relationship stuff but he was a lot more interested in Eddy and Enzio. "Yeah Mick, that's not surprising. Who would want you as a son-in-law?" He had to duck as Mick took a swat at Morris's head with the brush. "And what's with Claire's mother practically spitting on the floor every time your name gets mentioned? What did you do to her?"

Mick looked at Morris and shrugged his shoulders. "I was born."

Morris shook his head at that answer. "Okay, I can see that. But seriously, what about why we're here and how did Eddy know where Claire lives and you didn't?"

Mick stopped and leaned on the handle of the brush. It was a great question and he had to admit he still didn't have a clue. Last night's talk with Claire had been all about them.

"Eddy used to live here with us." The voice came from the cockpit where Claire was now standing with two steaming cups of coffee in her hands.

Mick looked at Morris with a surprised look on his face. Mick had a feeling that they were about to get a lot of surprises from Claire. "He used to live here? When? Why?"

Claire worked her way up on deck with the coffees and handed one to each of the men. She sat down on the front edge of the cabin trunk. Morris leaned against the port side railing and sipped his coffee and Mick squatted down sipping his. Mick and Morris both looked at Claire, waiting.

"My father teaches Tai Chi at a studio near our house." She pointed up the hill from where they were sitting. "Eddy showed up one day and signed up for lessons with my dad. He was renting a little cabin down near the Driftwood Center and he spent so much time learning Tai Chi that he started coming home to have dinner with us. My mom and Eddy got along so well and she felt so sorry for him living where he was that she offered to let him stay with us. And he did. He lived with us for about a year. He didn't have a job but he always seemed to have enough money for whatever he needed. He made friends with everybody. He told us he was on Pender Island to rest. We didn't ask what he was resting from, it didn't seem to matter. Anyway, he learned Chinese just by being around us. We were always talking Chinese between ourselves and he listened and asked questions. My mom and dad loved having him around."

Mick and Morris understood that. Everybody enjoyed having Eddy around. He was a natural at making people feel comfortable. Mick wondered if Claire and Eddy were more than just friends. He wasn't going to ask, especially in front of Morris. It was a question that could wait until later. Maybe much later. He wondered if he really wanted to know.

They were interrupted by Claire's mother who came up on deck and told them that breakfast was ready. She stood with her hands on her hips and said something to Claire in Chinese and Claire jumped up and scurried down below. Mrs. Lu shook her head. "She should be helping me with breakfast, not sitting around up here gabbing. She needs to have her pigu clapped."

Mick and Morris looked at each other. "Pigu?" Mick said.

Mrs. Lu who was closest to Morris gave him a little swat on the backside. "Pigu." She giggled and turned and went below.

"We better get below before you get more than your pigu clapped Mick." They laughed.

At that moment Claire came up the companionway stairs with Mick's cell phone in her hand. "Mick, there is a call for you."

Mick hurried back to the cockpit and took the cell phone from her. "Hello," Mick said into the tiny phone. It was Dave Edmonds, their eyes and ears at Shelter Cove Marina.

"Mick, it turns out that the three guys I was telling you about turned up again. There was a Bayliner for sale down on "E" dock and last night, it was stolen. One of the boat owners down there happened by as the sharp dressed guy and two big guys were getting the boat ready to go out. From his description, it's the same guys that Jessica was talking to. They said they were just going out for a test drive but this morning it's still gone and it's been reported to the police as stolen. I thought you should know."

It sounded like Dave was in the pub as Mick could hear people laughing and dishes clattering in the background. The breakfast rush. "Damn right we want to know Dave. Thanks a million. What's the name of the boat, do you know? Got a description?"

"Yeah, I stopped in at the marina office before I came in to the pub. The boat is called "Daffodil" and it's, you guessed it, white with bright yellow trim. It's a Bayliner Thirty Nine. It's got nearly full tanks too, so the range is just about anywhere in the Gulf Islands, or the San

Juans. She's got twin engines and she can cruise around 25 knots so it won't take them long to get where they're going. My guess is that they're heading for Telegraph Harbor."

Mick nodded. "Good enough Dave. Thanks for the heads up. We'll keep our eyes open for them. Talk to you later." Mick closed the phone and looked at Claire and Morris. "Well, it sounds like Enzio is heading our way. It seems that he stole a boat and since Jessica told him that we were probably headed for Telegraph Harbor, that's more than likely where he's going to start looking for us first."

Claire looked confused. She was still in the dark about David Enzio. "Who is Enzio and why did he hurt Eddy so badly?"

Mrs. Lu came up the companionway stairs again looking exasperated. She spoke in Chinese again to Claire who began tugging on Mick's arm to pull him down below. Mick swatted her on the backside and she gave a little yelp. "What was that for?" Mick just looked at her. "You've been a naughty girl keeping us up on deck. You needed to have your pigu clapped, that's what." Mick and Morris laughed at her shocked look.

"My pigu? How did you know?" She turned and glared at her mother who was laughing along with Mick and Morris. Claire shook her head. "I see you've already been teaching these two Chinese. Start with the naughty words first. That's how people seem to learn a new language."

They went below and found that everything had been organized. The smell of freshly brewed coffee greeted them as they stood waiting to be told where to sit. Claire was smiling happily looking like she was completely at home on Starlight. She ushered Morris and Mick to the port side of the dinette table which had been made up with the Christmas placemats Mick had stashed away in December. Wine glasses had been filled with orange juice and the Chinese contingent had a tea pot under a cozy in the middle of the table. Bacon and eggs were laid out on everyone's plate along with a pile of toast on a plate. Eddy was now sitting up on the starboard settee closest to the main bulkhead. He didn't look very good. The circles around his eyes had grown darker. He was wrapped in a blanket and sipping a cup of tea and not talking. Mr. Xun and Mrs. Lu sat next to him and Claire sat next to Mick on the port side announcing that if anybody needed anything, she was the go-to girl. Mick picked up his mug of coffee and held it up.

"Here's to the girls for putting a nice breakfast together. Here's to Mr. Xun for not killing me for sleeping with his daughter which would have been a mistake because I was sleeping next to his daughter." Mr. Xun actually looked like he was blushing though he covered it well by offering his own toast.

"Here's to Mr. Brese who will be killed if he is caught sleeping with my daughter and not next to her." This was delivered with a big smile and a vigorous nod from Mrs. Lu.

Claire grinned at Mick and slid her foot sideways to touch up against his. He smiled back and began to eat.

The talk at the table was about Enzio and the fact that he was coming looking for them. They knew what kind of boat he was in for the moment but it was generally agreed that he would be foolish to keep the boat for very long since the police knew about it being stolen.

The talk about Enzio caused Claire to ask again. "Who is David Enzio and why did he hurt Eddy so badly?" Apparently, Claire wasn't the only one looking for the answers to these questions. Mr. Xun and Mrs. Lu both nodded enthusiastically. Mick looked across at Eddy who was looking worse than ever.

Eddy sighed and started to talk but broke into a fit of coughing after only a few words.. He allowed Mrs. Lu to take his tea cup and help him lay down again. He lay on his back wheezing. "Mick, you tell them what I told you last night."

Mr. Xun moved and sat at the navigation table and Mrs. Lu and Claire began clearing away the dishes and everyone listened as Mick related the story that Eddy had told him about his history with Enzio. As the fact that Eddy had been involved in selling drugs, an unbelieving look appeared on every Chinese face in the cabin. It was a total surprise to them and news that they obviously weren't very happy to hear.

As Mick finished telling the story, Mr. Xun was the first to speak. "So, you came to Pender Island shortly after you stole the money." He looked disappointed as if his own son had betrayed his trust. Eddy made a face.

"I didn't steal the money. Enzio owed me. The fact that the deal blew up on us wasn't my fault and I had risked my neck as much as he did. He owed me so I kept the money."

"Why didn't you turn the money over to the police and help them find Enzio? You could have cut a deal with the authorities in exchange for turning in Enzio. Wouldn't that have been the best thing to do? You could have put an end to this whole business." Eddy opened his eyes and looked at the elderly Chinese man.

"Enzio was my friend." At Mr. Xun's astonished look he added, "He used to be my friend but I didn't want to give the money back to him. I figured if he didn't have the money, he would probably get killed by the people he made the deal with and that would be the end of my problems. I didn't want the money but I didn't want him to have it either. I was tired of the whole business so I came to Pender to hide out for a while and that's when I met you." He made a gesture that encompassed Mr. Xun and Mrs. Lu and Claire. "And you were like the family I never had. You treated me so good. You never expected anything from me like everyone seems to. All the time, it's Eddy, can you fix this? Eddy, can you repair this? Hey Eddy, nobody else seems to be able to get this working, let's see you do it. And do they want to pay me? Hardly ever. It's always the same old bullshit. Hey, thanks Eddy. Let me buy you a beer or a bottle or bugger all." He shook his head, anger showing on his battered face. He suddenly seemed to realize what he had said. "But you, you all treated me like a friend. You didn't want anything from me. I had never experienced that before. And when I left to head over to the mainland, it was because I felt so guilty that if you knew the real Eddy, the drug dealer, you'd be so disappointed. And I didn't want to disappoint you. I couldn't. So, I left. And that's when I ended up at Shelter Cove and met Mick and Morris. And bought Seagram. I was starting to think that I had gotten away from Enzio. But I didn't. I don't know how he found me but it probably wasn't that difficult." He lay his head back again and closed his eyes. For the longest time, nobody spoke. It was a lot for Claire and her parents to digest.

Mr. Lu started speaking. "Eddy, as much as I don't agree with what you did, you haven't let me down. All that stuff happened before you met us. It's in the past. And it wasn't difficult to find you. We lost track of you after you left Pender but we did some asking around and that's why Claire went to the marina and got a job at the restaurant. So she could check up on you. We were worried about you Eddy. And it seems like we had good reason to be worried too. But my question right now is what are we going to do about David Enzio? If we sit around waiting, he will find us. It is better to find him first. So," and here he turned to Claire, "I think you should do a little reconnaissance in that machine of yours. You could take Mr. Brese with you."

19 FEI HU

It was a pleasant interlude after the long previous day and night. Eddy was feeling worse which was understandable. Mrs. Lu said that it would take time for improvement. She wasn't worried about anything specific and everything in general. She was planning on spending the day with him, giving him further treatment and keeping an eye on him. Mr. Xun had classes that he had to attend to and he left right after eating to prepare for the day. Before leaving, he asked Claire to talk with him out in the cockpit while the others stayed below.

Morris planned to go with Mr. Xun to see if he could learn some self defense moves. "I get the feeling that if I run into Enzio or his goons, it might be useful to know how to kick some ass the Chinese way." Mrs. Lu was about to make a comment but Morris was ahead of her. "Yeah, I know Tai Chi isn't about kicking ass but Mr. Xun promised to give me some one on one tutoring in that department."

When Claire came back down into the cabin, Mick was cleaning up the breakfast dishes. He knew best how to clean up quickly and efficiently in the small galley and was doing his best to stay out of range of Mrs. Lu while he worked. The sun streamed down the open hatch and the gentle sea breeze was scouring out the lingering odors of breakfast. Mick loved being on the boat on the salt water. It was different than being in the muddy fresh water of the Fraser River at Shelter Cove Marina. It was a treat to have so many people on board Starlight too despite Mrs. Lu's less than friendly attitude. Most of his sailing was done single handed and it was a refreshing change to have so many guests aboard. Especially Claire. There were still a lot of things they needed to resolve but Mick was happy to see her again. As he washed the dishes, he was already thinking about spending the day with her. He had no idea what kind of machine they were going to be doing reconnaissance in but at least he was going to be with her for the day.

Then it was time. Dishes were done. The cabin tidied up and organized, Eddy ready for his continuing treatment. While Mrs. Lu prepared to treat him, Claire tried to help but only got in the way and finally Mrs. Lu suggested rather forcefully that she and Mick get going.

"Just be careful Xun Xi Pei," she said using Claire's Chinese name. "You know how I worry."

"Mother, you know I'm always very careful when I'm out in Fei Hu. " Claire looked like she had had this discussion many times before. "I've set Mick's VHF radio to Channel Sixteen. If we need to talk to you, we'll make contact and then move over to Channel Sixty Eight" She patted her mother's arm and said goodbye to her and Eddy. Grabbing Mick by the arm she fairly pulled him up the stairs and into the cockpit.

"Let me show you my machine Mick. It's not much but I think you'll love her after I show you what she can do. Do you have your floater coat?"

Mick nodded and pulled his deck boots on. They climbed down onto the dock and made their way up the ramp to the shore. Mick followed and as they walked, he asked, "You never told me you had a boat Claire."

"That's right, I didn't. Well, you'll have to be patient for just a little bit longer. Follow me."

Mick followed her along a path which led from the dock up a small hill and skirted the edge of the top of the cliff. Below them, they could see the bay and from where they were, they could look back and see Starlight at the government dock. She looked clean and beautiful in the sparkling water. As Mick followed Claire, he couldn't help but notice that she was very nuxinde. He remembered the word that Claire had taught him. Feminine. It fit her to a T. She was wearing jeans that were tucked into the top of her deck boots. A good portion of her body was legs. Slim looking legs that melded into a very nice looking stern. She had left her pea coat behind on Starlight and was wearing a cream colored fisherman knit turtleneck sweater. Mick was having a difficult time keeping his eyes on the path. When he tripped on a root and nearly went headfirst over the cliff edge, he took it as a warning and reluctantly shifted his view.

"What kind of a boat do you have Claire? What does Fei Hu mean?"

She kept walking but turned slightly and smiled at him. "One thing you must learn about the Chinese, Mick is that they are very patient. It's in the genes. So, if you're going to be with me, you must learn patience also. You'll find out soon enough."

As they came around a bend in the path, they looked down on a large boatshed. It was partially on the shore but opened up to the bay. The path led them down to a door at the back of the shed. Claire took a key from her pocket and opened the lock on the door. She swung the door open and stood to one side of the doorway so that Mick had to squeeze past her to enter the boat house. He only squeezed halfway through and stopped. He turned and was face to face with Claire, standing very close to her. Face to face wasn't exactly accurate as she was so much shorter than him. She looked up at him and he looked down and in that moment, Mick knew what he wanted to do. He slowly lowered his face to hers. He wanted to kiss her but wasn't entirely sure what her reaction would be. He need not have worried as her lips came seeking his. She tasted good, very good. Soft and sweet and they would most likely have stayed there except for the sound of a vehicle coming along the top of the cliff behind them.

Claire pulled away reluctantly and turned to look up at the approaching vehicle. Mick was aware that this island was her home and a place as small as North Pender was a gossip haven. With a mother like Mrs. Lu, it was probably best to avoid being seen in a romantic embrace with her daughter. The vehicle passed and Claire sighed and leaned against Mick. She turned and pulled him into the shed and closed the door behind them.

The ocean side of the boat house was closed in by wooden doors with a row of windows near the top which allowed enough light to see the interior easily. There was only one machine in the shed and it certainly wasn't a boat. Since it had wings, Mick guessed it would be what was known as an ultralight airplane. It had been pulled into the boat house nose first, so they were looking at the front of the airplane with the two side by side seats.

It looked a lot smaller and more fragile than Mick imagined any airplane could. In fact, it looked downright scary. The two seats were supported by nothing more than light tubing and thin wires. The wings were covered by sailcloth in a riot of color with stripes of purple, day glow yellow, hot pink, neon green and black. The airplane was sitting on white fiberglass floats, the most substantial looking part of the whole thing.

"My God, Claire, someone stole part of your airplane. They left just the wings and a couple of seats."

She gave a little giggle. "It does kind of look that way, doesn't it? Do you like it?"

"It's beautiful Claire." This was said somewhat tongue in cheek. "I'm just wondering why you chose such a drab color scheme."

She gave him a little dig in the ribs with an elbow and smiled.

"We couldn't be picky when we bought her and this was what was available in my price range but you have to admit it's unique. If you're not familiar with ultralights, it probably looks like a little toy but it's safe and I really do know how to fly her." She stood with her hands on her hips, looking at him as if she was expecting an argument.

"Claire, if you say you can fly it, I'll take you at your word but I'm not sure I feel very comfortable going up in that. It. Her." He was unsure what term to use.

"I call her "Fei Hu". It means Flying Tiger. In China there was a famous group of flyers during World War Two. They were led by an American and they were called "The Flying Tigers". They are heroes in China and when I was growing up I read everything I could about them. Ever since then, I wanted to fly and when I quit the movie business, I bought her and a friend taught me how to fly."

Mick knew this part of Chinese history. His father had brought a book home when they were kids that told the story of the Flying Tigers led by the famous Claire Chennault. "Is that where you got your name? Claire, after Claire Chennault?"

She was obviously surprised that he knew the name. She reached out and grabbed his hand in hers. "You know about Claire Chennault?"

Mick explained how he knew of the Flying Tigers and their famous leader. As he did, he looked down at their hands. Hers was small and delicate in his. Claire looked down at their hands together. She had grabbed his in excitement and his hand felt so good holding hers. She remembered the feelings when he touched her in her most intimate places. It took all of her strength to keep focused on their discussion. She looked up and their eyes met. "I have never met anyone who knew of Claire Chennault. When I came here, people had such a difficult time with my Chinese name that I wanted to take an English sounding name to make life easier. So, I took the name of my hero. It is a girl's name and a boy's name."

"It's a beautiful name." He was tempted to stay here with her all day but reluctantly he said, "What can I do to help you get Fei Hu ready to go?"

She sighed and nodded. "You can open up the doors and I'll start my preflight inspection. OK?"

Mick gave her his best military salute. As he went around a narrow walkway to open the doors he could hear her humming and talking to herself. He pulled a chain that began rolling the doors open. They folded along both sides allowing the sunshine in. The colorful airplane looked even more garish in the bright light. Through the framework of the tail section, Mick could see that Claire had climbed up on the floats and was checking the engine.

The engine sat exposed with a three bladed propeller pointing backwards. He couldn't quite believe that he was going to go flying in this rickety collection of parts but if Claire could do it, Mick guessed that he could do it too. "What the hell," he thought, "you only live once."

Claire climbed down from the floats and did a walk around of the wings and then around to where Mick was standing beside the tail.

"There's a ramp that the airplane is sitting on that is raised up out of the water. We lower it down and then push her out. We'll both have paddles and when we get her turned around, I'll start the engine and we can get strapped in as we taxi. There aren't any brakes, so we'll be moving as soon as the engine starts."

She could sense some apprehension in Mick so she gave him a hug.

"Don't worry Mick, I've never had an accident and I don't intend to start now. I'm going to take it easy and do my best to make this first flight one that will make you want to come back for more."

With that, she took Mick's hand and led him around to the front of the airplane. She presented him with a black fiberglass helmet which he put on. It was snug but comfortable enough. Carefully he climbed onboard and sat in the right hand seat and she passed him a paddle. Claire took a khaki colored flight suit from a hook near the door and worked her way into it and topped it off with a helmet of her own. She put an orange floater coat on and then cranked a wheel mounted on the wall of the boathouse. The ramp began to lower and the floats of the airplane were soon sitting in the water. Claire climbed on and gave a push with one leg and the airplane slid smoothly out of the boathouse into the bay.

They got the airplane turned and pointing away from shore and Claire showed Mick how to strap himself in with the four point harness. He felt a similar kind of feeling as when he sat in the dentist chair. Tense. Claire strapped herself in and then plugged in wires which led from their helmets to the radio. There was a little boom microphone on each helmet. With this setup, they would be able to talk easily over the noise of the engine. Mick thought it would probably make it easier for her to hear him screaming.

Over the intercom, Claire's voice sounded scratchy but clear enough.

"I'm going to start the engine now Mick. It's pretty noisy but you'll get used to it. While we're taxiing waiting for the engine to warm up, I'll show you a few other things you'll need to know."

On the tiny instrument panel above their heads, Claire turned the key to the start position and held it while the propeller started to spin behind them. The engine caught, died and then roared into life. Mick just about jumped out of his seat from the noise.

Claire grinned, "Like I said, it's noisy but you'll get used to it."

Mick just nodded. He looked down and could see the bottom of the bay through the clear water. It was weird sitting out so exposed. Front row seats to the show.

A small inflatable dingy with an outboard on the back came across the bay towards them. The guy steering the dingy waved and Claire waved back with a big smile on her face. Mick felt a little jealous pang which he realized was completely unreasonable but he had a sudden urge to kick the guy's ass.

Claire was pointing out some other features of the airplane but Mick's attention was on the guy in the inflatable. Claire followed his gaze and cleared her throat over the intercom bringing Mick's attention back to the matter at hand.

"He's a neighbor of ours, married with a couple of very nice kids. He's quite good looking wouldn't you say, Mick?"

He snapped his head around only to find she had a big grin on her face. He had been caught out and grinned sheepishly back at her, "He's not my type Claire. I lean more toward female throttle jockeys myself. There's something kind of sexy about them."

Getting There

Claire continued her pre-flight briefing with a smile on her face as they taxied away from shore. "If we get into a real jam, Mick, we can use the Ballistic Recovery System to bring the airplane down safely. It's just a matter of pulling this handle," and here she reached over her head and touched a red D shaped handle attached to the base of a white box labeled "BRS" "and a rocket propelled parachute goes out to bring us down safely. It takes a good hard pull to activate it but my guess is that during an emergency, I'll be pulling real hard without even thinking about it." She grinned at him. "At the time that we bought it we thought it was a lot of money to pay for something you hope you never have to use." Mick nodded.

"Like the life raft we have on our boats. They sit there in their containers and you hope they never have to be used." Claire nodded back.

"Are you ready Mick?"

He sat up a little straighter which pulled his safety harness snugger. He was as ready as he was ever going to be. The control stick stuck up between the two seats with a throttle control beside each of them on the outside. Claire, being in the left hand seat, was holding the control stick in her right hand and her left hand rested on the throttle. Her feet were planted on the rudder pedals in front of her. The matching pedals in front of Mick's feet moved at the same time as hers did. Mick's hands were grasping the edges of his seat and he was sure that his knuckles were white.

Claire pushed the throttle forward and the engine noise increased dramatically. The little airplane quickly surged forward pushing up a good sized wake from the floats. Almost immediately, they started smacking along like a dingy bouncing over the slight chop on the water. In what seemed like a very short distance, the airplane parted company with the water and they were climbing up into the sky.

Claire looked over at him with a big grin on her face. "What do you think of that Mick?"

Truthfully, he was speechless. The little airplane was climbing quite quickly and for the first time he was looking down on the water that he had sailed on for so long. It was fantastic. He felt like laughing or shouting for joy. He realized he was doing both when Claire did the same, right along with him. The sun was shining on the water. There were boats dotted here and there in the channel between the islands and the view was out of this world.

"Let's do a little pass over the bay and you can see Starlight from up above. I'm so glad you like it Mick."

He nodded his head. He looked at the little instrument panel and saw that they were already at about three hundred feet and doing about forty five miles an hour. Claire banked gently, mindful of her passengers' newness to the sport of flying. She came around in a long gentle turn until they were heading directly for the shore of North Pender. Mick could see the government dock and Starlight beside it. As they approached, a figure came up on deck and began waving at them.

"There's your mother, Claire."

Claire nodded her head. "I see her Mick." They both waved wildly at her as they passed over the dock. Claire began banking again and they turned gently around to the northwest. "Time to head for Telegraph Harbor, Mick. Enjoy the scenery but let's keep an eye out for Enzio's boat."

The little airplane was covering the distance very quickly compared to what Mick was accustomed to when sailing. They leveled off around five hundred feet and Claire throttled the engine back. "It's beautiful up here," Mick said.

Claire nodded. "It's a perfect morning for flying Mick. I'm so glad we have this kind of weather for your first flight. By the way, you can let go of your seat now."

He looked down and saw that he was still hanging on tightly. Mick began to loosen his fingers, one by one from the edges of the seat and shook his hands out in front of him. He looked at his pilot. She was scanning the sky and busy with flying and to Mick, she looked very much like she belonged at the controls.

"I'm telling you Claire, your namesake would be very proud of you." She turned her head and blew a kiss at him.

"You sweet talker."

"Sweet talk is sometimes a byproduct of telling the truth."

They were heading up Trincomali Channel, with Prevost Island off Claire's side of the airplane. One of the B.C. Ferry's was just exiting Active Pass on Mick's side. He was wishing that he had brought his camera along.

"At this rate of speed, it's not going to take long to get to Telegraph Harbor. You don't happen to have a couple of bombs hidden in the floats do you Claire? Something we could drop on Enzio and put him out of commission for a couple of decades."

"No such luck Mick. So, what are we going to do if we spot him?"

"I think it will help us to know where he is and then we can start working on a plan. We'll think of something." He wished he had a gun. That would be a pretty good way of paying Enzio back for Eddy's broken fingers.

Claire asked. "I've been meaning to ask you. Will you be able to recognize Enzio? I mean do you know what he looks like?"

"I've only seen him once and that was from a distance. He's got a couple of big burly guys with him and I'd recognize one of them I'm sure. I hope that we only see the three of them from a distance, size up the situation and the get back to Starlight without any problems." It occurred to him that she knew where she was going without even using a chart. He wondered how well she knew the islands.

"Our weekend trip to Telegraph Harbor wasn't your first time there was it?" Mick had never asked her if she'd been there before and she hadn't volunteered.

"I know these islands like the back of my hand Mick. I've been flying around here for a couple of years in all kinds of weather, so it's important to know where everything is."

It was windy sitting out in the front of the little airplane. It was like sticking your head out the window of a car going down the highway. He was glad he had his sunglasses on to protect his eyes and Claire had a little clear flip down visor that gave her some protection.

It wasn't exactly warm even with his floater coat zipped up but the view was worth any amount of discomfort. Here he was, sitting on a little seat hundreds of feet above the ocean, a beautiful woman beside him and the incredible Gulf Islands all around them. "Thanks for taking me flying Claire. It's better than I could have imagined."

Claire banked around the tip of Saltspring Island and in just a few minutes, they could see the entrance to Telegraph Harbor in between Thetis and Kuper Islands. "I'm going to do a run along the harbor and when we get to the head of the bay, I'll bank right and go out over the cut. We can circle around and come back the same way. I'll stay about two hundred feet up."

Mick was totally into it now that he had gotten more comfortable with the airplane. It was noisy but Claire was right when she said he would get used to it. She throttled back and slowed the airplane down. "I'll keep her just above the stall speed so we have a little more time to look."

They flew slowly up the harbor and went by Thetis Island Marina on the left. There weren't too many boats this early in the season, so it was easy to see that there wasn't a large yellow and white powerboat. "He's not here Claire. Maybe he's at Telegraph Harbor Marina at the head of the bay." Mick was pointing up ahead.

As they approached the marina, it was difficult to say whether Enzio's boat was there. Claire increased speed and banked to the right and headed out the cut. They flew through the narrow passage between the two islands and Claire asked if Mick wanted to take another look.

"Yeah, I think one more pass will do it." It was a simple matter of making a gentle turn and Claire brought the airplane back through the cut. This time he spotted the yellow and white Bayliner, not at the marina but anchored in the bay. Mick made a jabbing motion with his hand which Claire picked up on as she straightened the airplane out.

"I see it Mick. I don't see anyone on deck. They could be down below I suppose but there's no dingy so maybe they've gone ashore."

"There's a place for float planes to tie up at the marina. Do you think we could land and tie up for a few minutes and have a look around?

Claire nodded her head. "You've got it. I'll head down the bay and turn around and land."

Mick tensed up again but Claire got them turned around and throttled back and gently eased them onto the water with only a short distance to taxi to the dock. She made it all seem so simple. With perfect timing, Claire shut the engine off and they coasted the remaining few feet. A skinny teenager in shorts and a t-shirt hustled down the finger and grabbed the wing strut, pulled them in and put a couple of lines to the floats.

Claire and Mick undid their safety harnesses and helmets and the lad fell all over himself to help Claire to the dock with Mick finding his own way. They shucked off the floater coats and the teen recognized Mick.

"Hey, Mr. Brese, I didn't recognize you without your boat. This is a new way for you to arrive here. It's nice to see you again." He was talking to Mick but was paying a lot more attention to Claire.

Claire favored the boy with a smile and put her hand on his arm. "We're not going to be here long. Is it OK to tie up for a little bit?"

The teen seemed to think it was more than OK. "Oh, you bet. We're not expecting any flights in for a while, so you can take your time. I'll make sure nobody bother's your little plane." Another smile from Claire sealed the deal.

"Thank you. I didn't get your name."

"Theodore. But you can just call me Theo." He was blushing from Claire's attention.

Mick grinned at him. "Theo thanks for your help. We're actually looking for someone. They came in on that white and yellow Bayliner anchored out there." He pointed at Enzio's boat. "Two big bruisers and another guy. See anybody like that come in?"

"Sorry Mr. Brese. I just got up. I was doing a little partying last night. Slept in, so I'm in deep shit with the boss, excuse me ma'am, and I headed straight down here to the dock. Haven't seen anybody this morning."

They left their jackets with the airplane and headed up the dock. Thetis Island Marina has a grocery store and a restaurant, so they headed in that direction. Enzio had not met Mick or Claire face to face, so that gave them the advantage of surprise. They kept a close eye out for the three men and it seemed likely that they would be able to scope the place out without being recognized.

"What are we going to do if we spot them Mick?"

Claire asked excellent questions.

"Well, we're sure as hell not going to introduce ourselves. If we can get a good description of what they're wearing, we can radio the R.C.M.P. and they can come and arrest him for stealing the boat."

Claire shrugged. "It might work if there's any police available."

There were quite a few people in the store. A tall skinny guy with a Mohawk hairdo and multiple pieces of metal poking through his lips and eyebrows was arguing with the girl behind the counter about the price of fuel. She seemed like she was close to the breaking point.

Claire went down an aisle, looking at items on the shelves while looking around for Enzio and his associates. Everyone in the front of the store was watching the argument at the counter. As Claire rounded the end of the paper towel and toilet paper aisle and started up the next, she saw movement in the back of the store and turned in time to see Enzio open a door and stick his head into a cooler. From Mick's description, it had to be him. He was looking for a cold drink of some kind and Claire took the opportunity to slip down the next aisle. The two big guys were loading up a cart with potato chips and cookies. The cart was almost full, so they were obviously stocking up the boat.

The argument at the front counter came to a close with the skinny guy telling the girl that things would be different if he were running the country. He threw his money on the counter and stormed out, slamming the door behind him. It was quiet for a moment and just as Enzio pulled a gallon jug of milk from the cooler, Claire clearly heard the girl behind the counter say, "Mick, Mick Brese, is that you? Hey, it's great to see you again."

Enzio's head snapped around and he dropped the jug of milk. It bounced on the floor at his feet and then the lid popped off. Milk quickly spread across the floor. The two big guys were so busy arguing about which was better, Cheezies or taco chips, that they were oblivious to the sudden development.

Claire turned and headed back towards the front of the store. She headed straight for the door and as she opened it, she caught Mick's eye. She gave a little come on motion with her hand and quickly headed outside.

Mick didn't bother finishing his conversation with the girl but quickly followed Claire.

As he got outside, Claire was already sprinting back towards the dock and looking over her shoulder yelling at Mick to hurry up. She was small but she was going like hell.

Mick wasn't sure what was going on but he had a feeling that she must have seen Enzio and he wasn't about to hang around to find out. It was difficult to run in his deck boots but his longer legs helped him to catch up to Claire and they both sprinted together down the dock towards the airplane.

Theo was still by the airplane, sitting on the edge of the dock, picking his nose. As he saw Claire and Mick running towards him he jumped up looking guilty and wiping his hand on his shorts.

Mick arrived ahead of Claire and she yelled at him to jump onboard the airplane. He clambered across her seat and grabbed the two floater coats and helmets just as Claire threw herself into her seat and yelled at Theo to untie them.

Theo stood there looking surprised and it took a second shout from Mick to get him moving. He quickly untied the two lines and gave a little push to move the airplane away from the dock.

Claire started the engine and shoved the throttle forward. The airplane surged ahead and Mick turned in time to see Enzio come into view at the top of the dock. Enzio looked around and spotted the airplane and its two occupants.

"Let's go Claire. Let's go." Mick turned and grabbed hold of the edges of his seat again. Neither one of them was strapped in and Mick had a lapful of floater coats. Claire had to alter course slightly to avoid a sailboat that was slowly heading towards them. As soon as she had a clear path, she pushed the throttle forward and in moments, they were on the step and up into the air. Mick craned his neck and was able to see a frustrated David Enzio come to a halt at the edge of the dock. Theo was still standing there, a look of surprise on his face.

As they reached the mouth of the bay, they passed over the ferry going to Thetis Island and Claire leveled off and headed them out toward the open water. As they settled down, hearts pounding, Mick eased his left hand from his death grip on the seat and put it on Claire's knee. She looked at him and gave him another one of her big smiles. Mick realized that he had never met a woman quite like Claire.

20 ISLAND LIFE

Enzio stood watching the little airplane head out of sight. His blood had reached the boiling point. Young Theo could not be faulted for asking if he could help. After all, that's the kind of customer service the boss expected of him. But it was the wrong thing to say at this particular time.

Enzio stuck his face close up to Theo's, "Get the hell out of my way," and pushed Theo to the side. Theo lost his balance and went into the cold salty water of Telegraph Harbor, arms flailing while Enzio ignored him and stormed up the dock.

David Enzio wondered what the hell was going on. Brese takes off, literally with what appeared to be a small Chinese woman in an ultralight. Where the hell did the Chinese babe come from and where the hell was Brese's boat?

As he made his way across the lawn towards the store, people moved quickly to get out of his way. Those who didn't or were slow got pushed aside. Tommy and Horst were still in the store, completely unaware of what had just taken place. They were standing around like a couple of lost kids, waiting for Enzio to come and get them.

"What are you two shitheads waiting for? Haven't you paid for that stuff yet?" He grabbed the cart from Tommy and pushed it to the front counter, cutting off a lady who was in the way. She glared at him but he gave her a look that changed her mind in a hurry. Enzio started slamming things on the counter but a dirty look from the cashier made him slow down. He needed information, so he took a deep breath and shifted gears.

"I'm so upset with myself. I recognized Mick Brese and thought I could catch up to him but he took off in a little airplane and I missed him."

The cashier was sick and tired of people pissing her off and she stood, arms crossed, leaning back against the front window, tapping her toe impatiently. She was silently daring him to push her one last button.

"You may have missed him but you didn't miss making a big freaking mess back there on Aisle One. You know that you'll be paying for that milk you spilled. Don't even think about arguing with me. I've had all the crap I'm going to take for one day. The jerk with the funny hairdo blaming me for the high price of gas, like I'm the president of Petro bloody Canada. Asshole. And then Brese runs out of here like he's too good to talk to me." She looked at Enzio, her jaw clenched. She started passing Enzio's groceries over the scanner and throwing them into the plastic shopping bag. "Jesus, I came here thinking things were going to be different this year but it's the same thing every season. We should be getting hazard pay for having to put up with some of the customer's we get."

Enzio clucked his tongue in sympathy. He hoped she would just shut up and let him get a word in edgewise.

"I understand Dear. You're having a terrible day and then I come along and spill a jug of milk and act like a jerk. You'll have to forgive me. Any idea why Mick Brese left in such a hurry?"

The cashier eyed Enzio, not quite ready to calm down. She still had some pent up frustrations that needed to be vented.

"Duh. He goes chasing off after that little Asian honey like she's the main course and he hasn't eaten in a week. Men." She looked at Enzio as if he were just like all the rest of the male population. Not to be trusted, interested in only one thing. She shook her head in disgust. What did that little Chinese bitch have that she didn't have? After two seasons of being ignored by Mick Brese, he had the nerve to come in here with that little…

Enzio snapped his fingers in front of the cashier's eyes. He could tell that she had temporarily gone off to some other place.

"Speaking of the young Asian girl, any idea who she is?"

The girl let out a little exasperated sound. "She lives over on Pender Island with her parents." She lowered her voice and leaned in towards Enzio. "Just between you and me?" Enzio nodded and leaned closer.

"Everybody thinks she works for CSIS."

Enzio looked at her, waiting for something more.

She began to assume that she was talking to an idiot. "CSIS. Canadian Security Intelligence Service? Like the CIA only ours, not theirs. She buzzes around the islands here in that little pisspot airplane of hers, snooping on everybody. She's got to be doing something like that."

Enzio stared at her. "You don't think maybe she just likes flying?"

A snort from the girl. "The amount of time she spends up there? Come on get serious. There's something definitely wrong with her. And her dad teaches that weird Chinese Ninja shit and her mom does weird things with little glass jars on people's skin. None of that stuff is normal. Right?"

Enzio was lost. There was something not normal all right and it was standing right in front of him. But at least he was getting some information. "You said they live on Pender Island?"

She nodded and finished bagging the last of his groceries. "Yeah, they've got a studio there. Ask anybody on the island and they'll show you where."

David Enzio couldn't imagine why the management of this place kept this rude woman employed. Maybe it was difficult to get people to come and work on an island. He pulled out his wallet and paid cash for the groceries.

"Thanks very much for the information. We're just cruising around the islands in our new boat. My boys and I will probably head back to the mainland in the next couple of days."

The woman waiting behind Enzio gave her cart a little shove and goosed him with it. He turned and gave her a dirty look. In turn, she scowled at him and asked if he was finished and could he please get the hell out of her way. Enzio wondered what was wrong with these people. They were supposed to be relaxed and happy in the islands. Screw 'em he thought as he loaded the grocery bags into the cart and headed for the exit.

Horst and Tommy were standing around outside chatting up a couple of teenaged girls in bikinis. You could tell it was chilly from the way the girls were hugging themselves and from the goosebumps. Enzio used his shopping cart as a battering ram and herded the two men in the direction of the dock.

"Come on you two. Get your dicks back in your pants and let's get back to the boat. We've got to get a move on." The two teens pouted and waved at Tommy and Horst.

"Where we headed boss?" Tommy always wanting to know what was going on.

"Shut up and get moving." They all headed down the dock and loaded the groceries into the Zodiac dingy that they had found stowed in the deck locker of the Bayliner. Horst and Tommy had taken turns getting it inflated before they had come ashore. Whining all the time about how much work it was. Enzio was going to shoot them both if they didn't shape up soon.

First things first though. Lay out a course for Pender and find out where that son of a bitch Brese was. Enzio started feeling better just thinking about it.

21 AN INTERRUPTION

After landing back at Port Washington, Mick and Claire put the airplane in the boathouse and Claire showed him how to "put my baby to bed" as she put it. Mick had a new found appreciation for the little machine. If it weren't for the airplane, they would have had to make a stand and face Enzio and as far as he could guess, the two of them against Enzio and his two super-sized thugs wouldn't exactly be a fair fight.

As they closed up the boathouse and started heading back to the government dock, Mick grabbed Claire by the arm and pulled her close. "I just wanted to tell you how impressed I am with how you handled yourself back there at Telegraph Harbor. If you hadn't gotten us out of there in such a hurry, we would have had a tough go of it."

She put her head against his chest. "I just did what I had to do."

"Claire, I'm trying to tell you that I think you're awesome. You fly like a pro and you're smart and," he paused.

"And?" She looked up at him with a smile.

"And you're beautiful too. But don't let it go to your head." He kissed her. Soft succulent lips. She tasted good, like she'd been eating something fresh and juicy. She kissed him back with a passion that took his breath away.

Apparently it had a similar effect on Claire as she pushed him away, her face flushed. "Mother will be waiting for us Mick. We've got to go." He nodded and started up the path but she grabbed the tail of his floater coat and pulled him back.

Getting There

"You don't have to agree so easily," she said with a little pout. Mick moved to grab her for another kiss but she skipped away and went running up the path ahead of him.

"Lost your chance, sailor boy." She was fast and kept ahead of Mick, laughing as she ran. Mick felt like a teenager again. Full of passion and love. Jesus, he wanted this woman. Badly. She was everything that a woman should be. Strong willed, beautiful, sexy and brave. He didn't know how, but he was going to win her parents over and take Claire sailing with him. He knew she liked sailing. She was in love with him. There had to be some way to work out these so called cultural differences. As he reached the top of the path, she was waiting for him with her hand out.

"Mick, we have to behave ourselves around my parents but I just want you to know, even when it looks like I'm busy doing other things, I'm going to be thinking about your kisses and the way you hold me." Not waiting for an answer, she turned and led the way along the path.

"I might just risk death and give your mom and dad a little display of my manly affections." She turned and stood with her hands on her hips.

"Don't you dare. I need my co-pilot. You got that mister?"

"Truth is, you're mom and dad might just try to arrange an "accident" for me just to get rid of me." Mick stated bluntly.

Claire looked at him. "I don't think you need to worry about that. At least not too much." She smiled. "Seriously though Mick, just try to ignore them. They're old and set in their ways. Let's just agree to take things as they come. If Enzio is as bad as he seems to be, judging from how he treated Eddy, we've got more important things to deal with right now than our future. " Mick had to agree with the logic in her statement.

When they got to Starlight, it was already three in the afternoon. Mrs. Lu coldly informed Mick that there had been a call from a gentleman regarding some boat repairs that they were waiting for. Mick knew it was the elderly couple back at Shelter Cove Marina. Mrs. Lu had several pots bubbling away on the stove and something smelling good in the oven. Eddy was bundled up in a blanket in the corner of the port settee looking like he was wearing sunglasses but it was just the black eyes. He had a little smile on his face.

"How's the patient doing?" Mick asked.

Eddy held his left hand up with two fingers protected by a hot pink cast. "It's going to take a while to mend but the good doctor assures me I will be able to play the piano again sooner or later. The rest of me is feeling much better. I have a cracked rib which is causing me some pain but Mrs. Lu has been feeding me some rather unpleasant tasting medicine made from who knows what which is helping me breathe easier and frankly has me higher than a kite." With a stoned looking smile he sang the first part of the old James Brown song, "I Feel Good."

Mick and Claire and Mrs. Lu gave him a round of applause and he gave a little bow of his head. Mick edged into the galley and started lifting pot lids. Mrs. Lu grabbed a wooden spoon and threatened to whack his knuckles with it. Claire grinned and Eddy giggled like a loon obviously feeling no pain. Mick thought it was a good sign that she hadn't picked up a sharp knife.

"I'd better call my customer." Mick pulled his cell phone out and Mrs. Lu passed him a sticky note with the phone number. He headed up on deck to talk in private.

While he was gone, Claire filled her mother and Eddy in on the details of their morning adventure. Despite Eddy being pretty much looped, he understood that Enzio was a clear and present danger now.

"Enzio is going to be coming. He may not know where we are yet but he's smart. It's not going to take him long to figure it out. Claire and her airplane are well known in these islands."

Mick came back down into the cabin to find the three of them looking rather glum.

"What's going on here? One minute you're all having a good time and now it looks like the party's over."

Claire began to explain but was interrupted by the arrival of Mr. Xun and Morris which involved re-telling the whole story over again. Morris brushed off the apparent threat of Enzio with a shrug.

"Not to worry. I've been training with Mr. Xun all day and I've got moves now."

Mick looked at him. "Moves? Like Travolta in Saturday Night Fever?"

"More like Bruce Lee in Enter The Dragon. Those kind of moves." He whipped his hands into place in front of his body.

Mr. Xun rolled his eyes. "Sorry to tell you Mr. Morris but your moves are a lot more Travolta than Lee."

Claire finally asked what Mick's phone call was all about.

Getting There

"Apparently, my customer found out that the parts arrived today to finish the repairs on their boat. They're insisting that I get back to work and finish their boat so they can get moved back aboard and get on with their cruise. I guess the gentleman hasn't been doing all that well and they want to get going before it's too late."

Morris nodded. "Yeah, I've met the couple and they are pretty demanding. As in "a pain in the ass". What's your plan Mick?"

"I guess I should head back to the marina and get the work done. It will only take me a few hours to finish the job and then I can get their boat put back in the water and they'll be out of my hair. If I leave this afternoon, I can be back here tomorrow about this time."

Eddy nodded in agreement. "You can stay onboard Seagram tonight. You've got the spare key, right?"

Morris looked at Eddy. "What about Enzio? I thought you said that it wouldn't take him long to figure out where Claire lives. Shouldn't Mick stick around?"

"It's already late in the day. I doubt that Enzio is going to be looking for us in the dark. Does anyone know when the next flight is over to the mainland?" Eddy asked the islanders.

Mrs. Lu spoke up. "I often take clients to Bedwell Harbor to catch the Island Charter flight to Richmond. The next flight is around six, so you could catch that one. If you get the work done tonight, you could take the return flight tomorrow morning."

Mick looked at Morris. "Think you can take care of the boat while I'm gone? Look after these good folks?"

Morris struck a fighting stance. "Ready, willing and able."

They sat down around the table and had an early dinner of steamed dumplings and rice that Mr. Xun had brought back from their house along with a bottle of wine. The food was good and everyone was having a great time. Mr. Xun was pretty quiet to start with but as he worked through the wine, his round face got redder and his grin got bigger. Mrs. Lu kept encouraging everyone to "Eat, eat. Don't be shy, there's plenty of food. Eat!" Mick was glad to note that Claire's parents were a little less hostile towards him than they seemed in the morning. But maybe that was because he was leaving, even if just temporarily.

Claire volunteered to take Mick to catch his flight and they left everyone still eating and laughing. As they waited at Bedwell Harbor for the airplane to arrive, they stood together quietly. Claire hugged him close. "Hurry back Mick. I'm going to miss you."

"Do me a favor and keep an eye open for Enzio. I'm not happy about leaving now that he's seen us. You take care of yourself."

"I promise Mick."

The Island Charter floatplane, a de Havilland Beaver landed and taxied in and discharged a couple of hippie types; all long hair and beads and patchouli oil. As the pilot tied up the airplane he fanned his hand in front of his face. A big smile lit up his face as he spotted Claire. "Claire," he boomed. Years of flying in a high noise environment had damaged his hearing and raised the volume of his voice. "Good to see you again. Your little Quicksilver would have been the best airplane to fly those two around. Open to the wind, you might have been able to breathe without smelling that damned hippie perfume they wear. But that's the Pender crowd. Lord knows I should be used to it after all these years. How are you doing?"

Claire introduced Mick. "Captain Harris has been flying around this part of the country ever since I got here."

"Hell, girl, I've been flying these parts since Mao was a little baby boy."

"Captain Harris taught me to fly my airplane. He is a good friend and the best pilot I know, so I feel safe in trusting you with him."

Captain Harris laughed. "Claire, I bet I'm the only pilot you know. But I'll take good care of your fellow." He looked at Mick. "I've been trying to get Claire to fly away with me for years. Get on board Mick and tell me all about your technique. I'm not too old to learn from a guy who's capable of getting a hug from this hot little chick." With that he gave Claire a smack on the backside and a smiling Claire whirled around and gave him a good swift kick in the pants. Another big booming laugh from the pilot. They obviously felt comfortable around each other. "Time to go. Claire, you take care of yourself. I'll see if I can find the mainland." He pointed to the west. "I just head that way once I get in the air, right?"

Claire looked serious. "Yeah, that's right. Downtown Tokyo is just to the left."

Mick got strapped in, marveling at the secure feeling of the larger airplane. Captain Harris pushed them off from the dock and jumped in and closed the door. The big radial engine coughed to life swirling oil smoke, stealing the quiet. They both put on headphones and Captain Harris headed out of the bay. Mick turned to see Claire waving madly. He waved back and felt a mix of emotions. He had lost this girl and found her again. It felt so good he shuddered from the intensity of it. Captain Harris was looking out ahead as they took off but over the headphones came his booming voice.

"Don't worry about her Mick. She can take care of herself and then some. Way I see it, she's worth three normal women put together. You're a lucky guy, though to be honest I don't know what she sees in you."

Mick looked over at him to see a big grinning face.

22 VENGENCE

As they were loading the groceries into the dinghy for the return trip to the boat, Enzio was feeling good for a change. He passed the last of the grocery bags to Tommy and then handed a five gallon jug of gas to Horst. He stepped down into the dingy and settled himself in the stern seat. All in all, Enzio thought to himself, it had been a pretty good morning. Without even having to do any searching, he had enough information about the Chinese woman and her family to develop the beginnings of a plan of attack. Since Brese was with the Chinese babe, his boat must have been back on Pender Island and Enzio was going to find it.

Back on the boat, while waiting for the engines to warm up, Horst and Tommy got the dingy tied off at the stern and then the two of them went forward to haul up the anchor. On the way over to Pender, armed with all the new information, Enzio was deep in thought as he worked on his plan. Tommy and Horst were bitching about the boat going too fast to fish. Enzio finally exploded in anger, pissed off at having to deal with the interruption to his planning.

"Fish? You want to get us busted for fishing without a license? Then they'll ask to see some kind of proof that we own the boat and then where are we going to be? Besides you shitheads, we're in a hurry. We've got to get our hands on Eddy and that bastard Brese for a number of reasons. About four million of them. If we don't get my money back soon, we're going to piss off our suppliers and we're going to be in deep shit. Again. This time, we might not be so lucky to just be out of business for a couple of years. This time we could end up dead if we disappoint these guys, so get your heads in the game."

The weather had gone downhill all afternoon and it was now full on overcast. By the time they got to Pender it would be dark and probably be raining. That suited Enzio just fine for what he had up his sleeve.

They blasted along at full speed until they got near Stanley Point on the north tip of North Pender Island. Enzio throttled back and they came to a sedate cruising speed. He explained to the boys that they were going to go down the western side of the island checking out the bays along the way. Brese's boat was probably at Bedwell Harbor or Port Browning but might be in any of the bays. He told them to keep a good lookout as he took the boat along the shoreline.

They didn't have to go far. They eased into the bay at Port Washington and spotted Brese's boat at the government dock. Enzio smiled at their good fortune. Not wanting to alert anyone, he headed back out into the channel and took the boat around to Otter Bay where they dropped anchor.

Enzio gathered his boys in the cockpit and they sat down for drinks.

"Here's the deal. We're going to wait until Brese and whoever else is on the boat to hit the fart sack. Then when they're asleep, we're going to pay them a little visit. Either Eddy or Brese knows where my money is and I intend to get it back. I want you two knuckleheads to follow my lead. Total silence and if hear a peep out of either of you, you're dead meat. Do I make myself clear? Brese stole from me when he took Eddy and he is going to pay with his life. But I'm going to make sure that he suffers greatly before he dies."

Horst looked at Tommy. "Ooooh. Tough guy." He smirked and giggled. Tommy had the good sense to ignore him and Enzio pulled his gun from inside his jacket and smacked Horst on the side of the head. Hard and fast. Horst was stunned and grabbed his bleeding ear and began whining.

"What the hell was that for? I was just kidding around." He was pouting and grimacing at the same time.

"I just finished telling you that this was serious business and you start joking around. I'm not going to put up with it, understand?" Enzio was face to face with Horst.

"I got it, I got it. Jesus, leave me alone." Horst got up and went into the cabin and got a towel and some ice to put on the side of his face.

Enzio looked at Tommy and told him to go get some dinner ready. While Tommy bumbled around in the galley, Enzio went to the navigation table and began looking over the charts of the area. They would need a place to hide out for a while. He had heard from one of his suppliers of a place on Ruxton Island that might be up their alley. It was used by a family in the middle of summer for a vacation spot and Enzio's connection had told him where the key was hidden. They wouldn't need it for more than a few days. He laid out the necessary bearings to get there in the dark.

Despite having purchased some good groceries at the store at Telegraph Harbor, none of them could cook worth a damn and dinner was a dismal affair. Horst was sullen and uncommunicative. Tommy tried his best to suck up to the boss but Enzio was ignoring both of them. His thoughts were on other matters.

By the time they were finished eating, the rain had returned with a vengeance. As Enzio was checking on the Zodiac to make sure that it was ready to go, he could hear the rain sizzling down on the water. He looked around at the dark mass of the land. It was a perfect night for taking his revenge on that bastard Brese. It was dark and the rain was making enough noise to cover them. Satisfied that everything was ready, he went back inside and lay down on the bunk in the forward cabin. He told Horst and Tommy to keep the noise down and closed his eyes. He felt better now that they were finally going to get some action.

By the time midnight rolled around, Horst and Tommy were both fast asleep at the table, heads down on their arms, snoring. Enzio woke them and told them to get their shit together and get ready to go. He fired up the engines after running the blowers for a few minutes. He explained to Horst and Tommy what the plan was. Again he emphasized dire consequences for making any noise. They seemed to get the message.

Tommy went forward and brought up the anchor. He came back to the cockpit as Enzio slowly motored the big boat out of the bay. They were moving without running lights and Enzio watched the radar and depth sounder carefully. He used just enough throttle to allow them to creep forward.

As they came around James Point and were able to see into the next bay it very quickly became obvious that Brese's boat was gone from the government dock. Enzio cursed.

"What the hell is going on? Where did that bastard get to now?"

Horst saw it first. "There he is. He's anchored just ahead, close to the shore."

Enzio quickly put it into reverse and brought them to a stop. He could see Starlight at anchor, only the single white anchor light at the top of the mast. No other lights.

"Tommy you get a line out at the stern. At least a hundred feet. Horst, I want you to get in the dingy and row over and cut his anchor line. Tie our line onto his and we're going to tow that bastard out into deeper water."

He hoped that Brese's boat would follow them without veering off course. As Horst was busy rowing towards Starlight, Enzio backed around as quietly as possible. Tommy paid out the tow line keeping it out of the way of the propellers.

Horst was praying that he didn't let the boss down. It was a prayer of self-preservation. He rowed as silently as possible looking over his shoulder to see where the anchor line was. He almost bumped into the bow of Starlight before he could locate the anchor line in the dark. He grabbed it and pulled some of it up over the bow of the dingy where he started cutting it with the filleting knife that they had found in the galley. The knife was sharp and cut through the half inch line without difficulty. He was no boy scout but he managed to tie the tow line and the anchor line together with reasonable confidence that they would hold.

Enzio waited impatiently for Horst to return. He kept putting the boat in and out of gear to hold them in position but finally Horst tied up the dingy and came aboard giving the thumbs up sign that Enzio was waiting for.

Now, the job was to tow them out to deeper water without waking up whoever was onboard. Enzio put the engines into gear and crept forward quietly. The tow line came out of the water and came taught very slowly. They eased ahead and it was soon clear that Starlight was going to tow without difficulty.

In fifteen minutes they had moved well out into the channel between Pender and Prevost Islands. Enzio put the boat into neutral and told Tommy to take the helm. He got into the dingy and had

Horst pass him the five gallon jug of gasoline. He motioned for Horst to get in and they began working their way hand over hand along the tow line. When they arrived at Starlight, Enzio took up the oars and rowed them around to the stern. There was still no lights or sign of life on the boat but that was about to change.

Enzio opened up the jug of gas and began pouring it on the side decks of Starlight. The slope of the decks was sufficient that it ran down towards the middle of the boat. He had Horst row them around to the other side where he did the same thing. They made not a sound and Enzio marveled at the fact that nobody on board had woken yet. So far, so good.

With the utmost care, Enzio lifted the now half empty jug (or was it half full, he mused) over the cockpit coaming and poured more gasoline into the cockpit. He was careful to dribble some over the coaming as well. He then placed the jug with its remaining fuel onto the seat in the cockpit.

He pulled a rolled up newspaper from his jacket pocket and shielding it from the rain he dipped it in the gasoline on the deck. He had Horst back off a few feet from the boat, pulled a lighter out of his pocket and lit the newspaper. It made a soft whoosh and started burning rapidly. Enzio gave a nice underhand throw and the burning paper landed perfectly on the gasoline soaked side deck of Starlight.

There was no time to wonder what was going to happen. The gasoline ignited quickly all the way around the boat and into the cockpit. The flames were bright, robbing them of their night vision. It wasn't all that spectacular until the gasoline jug in the cockpit ignited with a thump. Then the action started to pick up. Lights came on in the boat. Enzio had Horst row quickly back to Daffodil where they boarded and turned to watch the goings on. The hatch burst open and Morris came up on deck or tried to but the flames from the burning jug were so intense that he quickly went below and closed the hatch behind him.

In a moment, the hatch on the foredeck slammed open and Morris came out that way. He stood on deck for a moment looking around trying to get his bearings. He called down into the boat and after a brief pause Mrs. Lu came up followed by Mr. Xun. At that moment, the fire in the stern ignited the propane tank for the bar-b-que mounted on the stern rail. The blast tore open the locker it was stored in and the burning gasoline found its way deeper into the boat.

Starlight was really burning now. Enzio hugged himself with glee. "Screw you Brese" he thought to himself.

Morris had Mrs. Lu and Mr. Xun move onto the bowsprit platform at the bow of the boat. The inflatable dingy was on deck and he quickly untied it and flipped it over the side and pulled it around to the bow. He yelled at them to jump down into it while he went back for Eddy. But he had taken too long and the fire had burned too fast. Thick smoke was now pouring out of the forward hatch and at that moment the second propane tank exploded in the stern. A piece of locker lid came flying low over the deck and clipped the top of Morris's head flipping him backward over the rail and into the water. From his position in the dinghy, Mr. Xun dove into the water and grabbed Morris and held his head up. Morris was babbling incoherently now, bleeding from a deep gash in his forehead. Mrs. Lu pulled the dinghy around to the other side of the boat and between the two of them; they pushed and pulled Morris into the rubber boat. Mr. Xun scrambled in behind him.

They looked back at Starlight. The stern half of the boat was completely engulfed; a mass of flames and smoke. It seemed that there was no way to help their friend Eddy escape sure death.

Enzio pulled Daffodil around to the bow of Starlight, approaching the dingy slowly. As they drifted side by side, Enzio went to the cockpit to help Tommy and Horst get the survivors aboard. Mr. Xun recognized Enzio from the description Mick had given but gave no indication that he did. He spoke in Chinese to Mrs. Lu to that effect. Morris was out cold now. Probably for the better.

Seeing only the three of them, Enzio was furious. "Where's Brese?" This only drew blank stares from the two Chinese people.

"Brese, Mick Brese? Owner?" He pointed towards Starlight but got nothing from them.

"Boss, we've got to get out of here. Someone's going to see the fire and send the Coast Guard. We've got to get going."

Enzio was pissed off that he couldn't gloat about destroying the boat to Mick Brese himself but he congratulated himself on a job well done. As he stepped into the cabin and put the boat into gear they began to move forward and picked up speed setting a course for Ruxton.

Starlight continued burning and began to settle deeper into the water, stern first. Soon, as the engine noise from Enzio's boat diminished, there was only the sound of the flames crackling and popping and the rain drumming on the water. The little dingy that the survivors had been in, drifted close by as Mick's dream boat was slowly consumed by the fire and the water.

23 GOOD NEWS AND BAD NEWS

Claire slept fitfully. Onboard Starlight, they had discussed what course of action to take knowing that Enzio was on to them. Morris planned on anchoring in the bay thinking that this would make them a little less visible away from the lights on the dock. He had talked about moving Starlight around to the marina at Bedwell but the general consensus was that it was unlikely that Enzio would be coming so soon. They all agreed that moving to anchor would be sufficient until Mick got back.

As for Claire, she decided that she would sleep in the boathouse with her airplane. That way, if Enzio came to do damage to her beloved ultralight, she would be there to do something about it. Morris asked what a little woman like her was going to be able to do to protect her property but just got a weird look from all three Chinese people. He shrugged.

Claire had slept in the boathouse many times before. When she first got the airplane, she had spent many hours going over the airframe and engine looking for any signs of wear and weakness. She had learned a lot from Captain Harris who had been kind enough to take the time to help her. He had taught her how to maintain the engine and showed her many tricks of the mechanics trade. As it turned out, she was as good at fixing the airplane as she was at flying it.

She had a foam mattress and a sleeping bag that she laid out on the floor near the door. It was comfortable enough and it was peaceful and quiet in the boathouse.

Sometime during the night, she had woken to a noise. As she lay in the dark, she could hear the rain beating on the tin roof. She could see the wings of the airplane against the row of windows in the boathouse doors but not much else. She listened hard and then began to hear a low rumble over the sound of the rain. It sounded like it was coming from out in the bay. Nothing unusual about that she supposed. Maybe someone was coming into the dock late. But then the sound faded away into the distance. It was probably someone looking for a place to anchor for the night but not finding what they were after.

Something about that thought made her sit up. She hugged the sleeping bag around herself. What if it was Enzio looking for Mick's boat? Perhaps he hadn't seen Starlight at anchor and had moved on. Her mind raced. Perhaps she should get up and take a look, though she had to admit to herself, she would probably only be able to see Starlight's anchor light. It was warm in the sleeping bag and she was reluctant to get up and go outside. The windows in the boathouse doors were too high to be able to see anything but sky.

She dozed off and then opened her eyes. As she sat there, she noticed that her night vision was improving, allowing her to see more and more of the airplane in front of her. Due to some weird quirk of nature, a very faint light was almost dancing on the walls and fabric of her airplane.

She began to get a feeling that something was not quite right. A loud explosion suddenly rattled the windows and shook her body. Her heart raced. "Enzio." She said it out loud and scrambled out of her sleeping bag, grabbing her jeans and pulling them on. Not wasting time to put her socks on, she jammed her feet into her deck boots and yanked the door open. She sprinted around the corner of the boathouse and looked out at the bay where Starlight should have been laying at anchor. Nothing.

It didn't take her long to spot the burning boat out in the channel. It was far enough away that she couldn't tell what kind of boat it was but she knew it had to be Starlight. The stern half of the boat was engulfed in flames, smoke billowing into the night sky. It was raining hard enough that visibility was reduced and it was difficult to see the burning boat clearly. She could tell that there was another boat nearby but it seemed to be keeping a safe distance.

Claire watched helplessly. She had no boat, no way of getting out there to assist. It would take too much time to get Fei Hu out of the boathouse and get the engine started. She could only stand and watch and pray that her parents and Eddy and Morris would be able to escape the flames. Maybe there would be some hope at the government dock. She turned and ran up the path. She was quickly soaked to the skin and shaking from fear and cold. As she made the top of the path, she turned and looked out to sea. She had a better view of the disaster. It was Enzio all right. She recognized the big power boat, holding off at a distance, not offering to help of course. She hoped she would be able to find a boat or a dingy at the dock. Anything that would float that she could use to get out there and help. As she ran, she tripped and fell face first on the rocky path. She went down hard and lay there for a moment, stunned. She pushed herself up and started running again. She could feel something warm and wet trickle down her face and she put her hand up and felt a large cut on her forehead. It was bleeding heavily but she didn't stop running.

As the dock came into view, she could see that there were a few daysailer type boats but nothing else. She came to a stop at the top of the ramp, leaning over, her hands on her knees trying to catch her breath, blood dripping down her face. Another loud explosion came from the direction of Mick's burning boat. A car came skidding to a stop just behind her and she turned to see who it was.

"Claire. Jesus, are you okay?" It was their neighbor who had been out in the dingy earlier in the day when she and Mick went flying. He turned back to his car and reached in through the open door and pulled out a jacket and a beach towel. He handed the jacket to her and proceeded to tear the towel into strips and quickly wrapped her head.

"Do you know whose boat that is out there Claire?"

"It's my friend's boat but I don't know how it got out there. My parents and some friends are on board. Oh, I hope they're alright." Her voice shook and she was on the verge of hysteria. "Where's your dingy Tom? She grabbed his arm. "You were out in your dingy this morning, where is it now?"

"It's right down here at the dock. Let's get going." He grabbed her hand and pulled her down the ramp to the dock. The little dingy was down the end where she hadn't been able to see it. They ran towards it and he told her to jump in while he untied the dock lines.

She got in, sitting on the middle seat and pulled on the jacket that he had given her. Tom untied the lines, jumped in the stern and in moments had the outboard cranked up and he gave it full throttle. Claire wasn't braced and toppled off the seat into the bottom of the dingy. As he steered, he held his hand out and helped her back to the middle seat. They headed straight for the burning boat making good time. They could see that the big powerboat had moved around to the bow of Starlight and was now moving off into the dark. The boat had no running lights on and was soon swallowed up by the rain and the night.

Tom yelled over the noise from the outboard. "What the hell is going on? What's that bastard doing?" He was pointing to where Enzio's boat had gone.

By the time they arrived at Starlight, it was fully engulfed in flames and was settling fast at the stern. Flames and smoke were coming from the hatches and portlights. Claire was sobbing now. It was almost too much to comprehend. Her parents, Morris, Eddy, Mick's boat. What had Enzio done?

Tom motored slowly around the burning wreck. As they pulled around the stern, they could feel the heat radiating from the flames. They had to put their hands in front of their faces for protection. There was no chance of anybody being able to exit the burning boat now. The flames had completely engulfed Starlight. Around the port side of the boat, debris was floating in the water and then, near the bow, they found the dingy. As they pulled up close to it, Claire shouted out to Tom to stop and she suddenly dove over the side into the water.

Tom was stunned and quickly shut the engine off, the dingy still drifting forward until it bumped into the side of Starlight's small inflatable. Claire was on the far side and Tom suddenly realized she was holding on to a person who was completely in the water with just one arm in a hot pink cast draped over the fat rubber side of the dingy.

Claire shouted to Tom. "It's Eddy."

Tom quickly jumped into Starlight's dingy and began to pull Eddy into the boat. It was a ghastly process. Eddy's clothes were in tatters, almost burned off. He was badly burned, his skin blackened in places and raw looking pink in others. Eddy grimaced as Tom grabbed him but it had to be done and between Claire and Tom, they finally managed to get him into the dingy, lying on the bottom. Claire clambered in and gently knelt down beside the burned man. He was trying hard to sit up and Claire gently took him in her arms.

With his last bit of energy, he croaked, "Claire, your parents and Morris are OK. Enzio's got them but they're OK. We'll get them back, don't worry." The message delivered, he lay back and let the cool rain wash over him.

24 A HAMMER BLOW

After being dropped off by Captain Harris at the seaplane base near the south terminal, at Vancouver International Airport, Mick grabbed a cab and headed back to the marina. Within two hours of his arrival at Shelter Cove, he had the new parts installed on the old couples boat and had made arrangements for the boat to go back in the water first thing in the morning. He called the couple and was back in their good graces once again. One of the mechanics from Freitag's was going to do the final sea trials and then they would be good to go.

It was nearly eleven by the time Mick finished up and he went into the pub and had a light dinner and a beer. He talked to a few of the regulars, bringing them up to speed on Eddy's condition. There was a big celebration going on when he left to go down to Seagram. He felt guilty about not having given his friends the information sooner but now that Enzio was over in the islands he felt it was safe to do so.

As he got down to the dock, it was strange to be at the marina and not see Starlight tied up at her usual space. He thought about Morris and Claire's parents onboard Starlight at Pender Island. Mostly he thought about Claire.

Down below in Seagram, it was startling to see the mess and damage again. Rather than sit and get depressed about it, he set to work cleaning it up. At least when he caught the flight back to Pender in the morning, Seagram would be in a little better shape. Eddy would appreciate it when he came back home.

Working hard, he made good headway. The flat screen T.V. was mounted again above the dining area. The navigation station was back together. There had been surprisingly little damage to the wiring and instruments thanks to Eddy's careful installation techniques. The wiring had been bundled and zip tied in enough places to prevent damage when the panels had been pulled out. The panels themselves would need some cosmetic repair but they were at least back in place and everything seemed to be working. He could listen to traffic on the VHF radio and the radar, depth sounder and Sat Nav units were all working.

The mess in the galley took only hard work and garbage bags to remedy. It was a strange feeling to have so much room to move around compared to Starlight which was considerably smaller and more cramped. By the time he finally took a break, Mick had the boat looking much better. The torn upholstery didn't look very good but there was nothing he could do about that. The smashed door and furnishings in the starboard quarter berth would take time and tools to put to rights.

As he sat at the dinette table with a cup of tea, he pondered the mess that Eddy had gotten himself into. Himself and a few other people too he added with regret. The money issue was puzzling. He had been over every inch of the interior of Seagram in the last couple of hours and there wasn't any place that the money could be. His cell phone rang, interrupting his thoughts. He looked at the caller I.D. but didn't recognize the number.

He flipped it open and said "Hello." It was difficult to understand what he was hearing but finally he made out sniffling and hiccupping. "Hello?" he said again. "Who's there?"

Finally a little voice. "Mick?"

"Claire, is that you? What's the matter?"

"Mick, I'm at the hospital with Eddy. He's badly burned."

"Burned? Claire, what happened? Take a deep breath and tell me what happened."

"Oh Mick. Enzio came and somehow he managed to get Starlight out in the channel and," here she choked up and began to cry. Mick got a sick feeling in his stomach.

"Claire. Claire!" he said, trying to get her attention again.

"I'm sorry Mick. Everything has gone wrong. I'm sorry but Enzio burned Starlight and she's gone. He kidnapped my parents and Morris but we rescued Eddy and he's in the Royal Jubilee burn unit over here in Victoria. A helicopter brought us here and he's in critical condition but they say that there's a good chance that he'll live. It will be a difficult recovery. Mick, I'm so sorry."

Mick's mind reeled. He took a deep breath. It was almost too much to absorb. Starlight gone. Morris and Claire's parents in the hands of that bastard Enzio. Jesus. Remembering Eddy's fingers after the vice grip treatment, he didn't want to imagine what they were going to face. "Claire, I'm on Seagram now. I'm going to head over right away. Can you meet me somewhere?"

There was silence on the line and Mick thought the connection had been lost. But Claire finally spoke, this time with a strong voice. She seemed to have gotten a second wind.

"I'll meet you back at Pender, Mick. It's up to us now. The police think that Eddy was the only one on Starlight and they think it was a propane leak that caused the fire. I don't want them involved yet, so I didn't give them any more information. They want to talk to me when I'm more up to it."

Mick thought this over. It was probably for the best. Who knew what Enzio would do if the police started chasing him? Never having had a boat burned and people kidnapped, it was new territory for him. But Claire seemed to have given it some thought.

At that moment, the call waiting feature of his phone beeped. He looked at the display but didn't recognize the number. "Claire, I've got another call. Let me take it and I'll get back to you in a moment." He put her on hold and answered the incoming call. "Hello."

"Hello Mr. Brese. How are you doing this evening? Or, should I say this morning. It's rather early wouldn't you say?"

Mick had a feeling he knew who this was but asked anyway. "Who is this?"

"I'm sorry Mr. Brese. Allow me to introduce myself. I'm David Enzio. You know, the man who you owe four million dollars to."

Mick's heart sped up. "I don't owe you anything, Enzio. I don't even know you." Testing the waters.

"Don't mess with me Brese. I found your number on your friend's cell phone. Yes, I've got your friends and Eddy is dead and your pretty little boat is permanently out of commission. Consider that payback for taking Eddy from me. I don't know why you weren't looking after your boat but now that Eddy is gone, I figure you're next on the food chain. I'm thinking that you know where the money is and

I want it back. We trade, we're done. You jerk me around, or if you get the police involved, your friends suffer. Simple. I like things simple."

"You harm my friends and you will be the one to suffer Enzio. How's that for simple. You've already burned my boat, so the way I figure it, you owe me. In the spirit of keeping things simple, let's just call that half a million."

Enzio snorted on the other end of the phone line. "Screw you Brese. Here's how it goes. You have forty eight hours to come up with my money. If you don't come through for me, you will begin to receive parts of your friends by UPS. I will call you and let you know where to deliver the money. You've already pissed me off once by taking Eddy from me. Don't do it again. And remember, no police." With that, he hung up.

Mick got Claire back on the line and filled her in on the development, leaving out the part about the UPS delivery of body parts. It seemed unnecessary. "Claire, I don't care about the money. If we can find it, we can make the delivery and get your parents and Morris back."

There was a pause from Claire. "Mick, you are a very nice man but you are quite naïve in these matters. I know that someone like Enzio has no intention of making a trade for the money. He will take the money and kill his prisoners. He is an evil man and he won't think twice about hurting or killing people to get his way. You have to remember that. You have to realize that we are involved with a sick criminal, not a normal person. Do you understand?"

Mick chewed this over. It was sobering to say the least. He remembered Eddy's crushed fingers and it was apparent that Enzio seemed to have been ready to kill everybody onboard Starlight by torching it.

"I guess you're right Claire, I am kind of naïve. I have a hard time not trusting people but I have to agree with you that Enzio is a right mean bastard. When it comes to dealing with him, I am going to have to toughen up. So, do you have a plan?"

"The first thing we have to do is find out where Enzio is and where he's holding my parents and Morris."

Mick agreed but didn't think they would have time to search for them with only forty eight hours on the clock. "I don't see how we're going to find out where they are and also find the money in such a short time, Claire. In fact, I think it's almost impossible."

"I would agree with you Mick if it were just up to the two of us."

Mick asked in a puzzled tone. "With Eddy out of action, doesn't that just leave you and me?"

"Mick, don't forget Fei Hu, my airplane. Enzio can run but he can't hide. I will locate my family and you just get over here as soon as you can. I need you Mick."

The last part was said in that little girl voice that made Mick's heart skip a beat.

"Okay Claire. I'll get going and be over to Port Washington as soon as I can. Give my regards to Eddy and tell him we're going to do our best to get that bastard Enzio for him. This has become very personal. I know the police are already investigating the fire on Starlight but Enzio told me not to get them involved. So we are going to have to be careful not to let them know about your parents and Morris being kidnapped. They could probably find him faster than we can but then Enzio might do something…" Mick hesitated to draw a picture for Claire. "Well, he might do something stupider than he's already done. I better get going. Bye for now Claire."

They hung up and Mick stood for a moment absorbing the enormity of what had taken place. Starlight was gone. Everything he had worked so long and hard for was gone. The fact that he was now down to only the clothes on his back was difficult to process. If he thought too much about it, he was going to come unglued. There was nothing to do but to get busy, so he sprang into action. He was glad that he had cleaned things up and the boat was pretty much ready for sea. He had spent enough time teaching Eddy how to sail this beautiful boat that he was able to get ready to go in short order.

It was nearly three in the morning, the rain coming down hard and cold when Mick cast off and backed Seagram into the river and headed for the islands. It was a strange feeling indeed to think that only a short time ago he had left from the same place on his beloved Starlight with Morris and Eddy. Now, Starlight was gone, Eddy was in the hospital fighting for his life and Morris and Claire's parents were up shit creek. He had a sense of urgency that he had never felt before.

25 ADDITIONAL TROOPS

      Claire stood in the doorway to Eddy's room. The nurses were working on him and it was obvious that the pain was overriding the drugs they had given him. Claire wanted to stay with him but she had to get busy. She caught Eddy's eye and blew him a kiss and waved at him. Through the haze of pain and drugs, he seemed to recognize the urgency of her situation. Claire saw his attempt at a nod and she turned and walked down the hall to the bank of elevators. She was doing her best to hold back her tears.

      Outside, she lucked out and found a taxi waiting. She woke the driver and gave him an address in the James Bay area. She was dropped off in front of a shabby looking house on Simcoe Street not far from the inner harbor. The house was a holdout to the good old days of Victoria, gingerbread and trellises sandwiched in between a couple of brand new sterile looking condos. Claire had just started to climb the front steps when the door burst open and out stepped a man resembling an overgrown pit bull wearing a wife beater t-shirt and camouflage patterned shorts. The size of his bare feet made him look like he was wearing flippers. He recognized Claire and held both arms out for a hug.

      Van was a big man. Tall and wide and tattooed on every visible surface. A colorful flame pattern started at the shoulder of each arm and extended down to his fingers. Each digit was on fire. His head was shaved on each side leaving a strip of hair down the middle, swept back and held in place by a Canadian flag bandana. He towered over little Claire by a couple of feet and she hugged him as best she could wrapping her small arms as far around his massive waist as possible. It would have been just as easy for her to hug an elephant.

Van put his arm around her and escorted her into the house. Stacks of newspaper lined the narrow hallway leading to the living room. Piles of books and magazines took up almost every space on the floor not occupied by furniture. Van was a voracious reader and a hoarder as well.

"Claire, it's so good to see you. Sit down." He couldn't help but note the gauze bandage taped to her forehead. The wound from her fall on Pender Island had required several stitches. Van's deep voice was raspy, the sound of a long time smoker. "Can I get you something? I've got some nice Jasmine tea I think you'd really like."

Claire was exhausted. It was early morning now. She sat with her hands folded in her lap, her purse hanging from her shoulder. She looked like she might fall asleep at any moment. "Thank you Van but I really don't have time to stop for tea. I have a favor to ask of you. I need to get back to Port Washington in a hurry."

Van was nodding his head up and down like the puppy dog in the rear window. "No problem Claire. We'll head down to Fisherman's Wharf and get on my boat and I'll take you over there right away. It's a done deal." Van would move heaven and earth for Claire.

"Also Van, someone kidnapped my parents."

Van exploded. He jumped up and started pacing back and forth in the narrow aisles between piles, smacking his fist into the other palm. "Who the hell would do something like that? What's going on Claire?"

Claire and her family had known Van for as many years as they had been in Canada. He had been their taxi driver when they first arrived in Vancouver from China and he had taken a shine to the little Chinese girl and her family. Over the years he had gotten to know them and had helped them in everyway that he could. Since he was in the construction trade, he heard about a lot of property deals before they hit the market and he had helped them find the property on Pender. He was one of the family and he had met Eddy on numerous occasions.

"Van, a guy by the name of Enzio has kidnapped my parents and a friend of ours. He burned a boat belonging to another friend and Eddy is in the Royal Jubilee burn unit. There's a good chance he is going to live but he is in critical condition. We know that Enzio has a

Getting There

Bayliner power boat but we don't know where he went. So, we need to track him down and we have to do it quickly."

Van was gnashing his teeth. "Claire, I'll do everything I can to help and we'll find your parents and your friend. I'm sorry about Eddy but he's tougher than he looks. You know your parents can take care of themselves too. I'll just get my things together and we'll get going."

"Thank you Van. I'm sorry to trouble you." She looked at her watch and saw that it was already four in the morning. Just about the time that her and Mick had gone to bed only twenty four hours ago. Now things were so different.

The trip to the marina was cold and mercifully short. Van had an old Harley Shovelhead. Noisy and fast. To the observer it would appear as though a big tough guy was out with his young daughter. As her arms would not reach very far around Van's waist, Claire hung on tight to Van's belt at the back of his pants. Roaring along the quiet streets of Victoria, Claire imagined that they were waking up people in their warm beds, block by block. By the time they arrived at Fisherman's Wharf she was cold and near exhaustion.

Van's boat, the "Van Go", was not much more than a ski boat, fast but short on comfort. He put her down in the small cuddy cabin and insisted that she get bundled up in the big sleeping bag that he kept there. Once he had the engine running and was pulling away from the dock, Van checked on her just to be sure that she was secure as they motored slowly out of the marina. Claire was in a deep and troubled sleep. As they cleared the breakwater, he poured on the power and had the boat on the step in short order. The water was relatively calm and they made good time towards Pender. Van knew a lot of people in the islands and got out his cell phone and began making calls, waking people up all along the Gulf Islands. Grumbles turned into enthusiastic responses once Van explained the situation. This Enzio guy might be worried about the police finding him but he was going to discover that the red coats would be the least of his concerns.

26 TEMPORARY SHELTER

David Enzio had his hands full with foreigners and invalids. He had Tommy watching over the newcomers with a gun but didn't think that it was necessary to tie them up. Morris had sunk into a coma like state with a wound on his head which had bled profusely at first but had tapered off to a slow ooze. At first he had babbled incoherently alternately shouting and crying, apparently stuck in a cycle of reliving the horror of the fire on Starlight.

Mrs. Lu had cared for Morris trying to keep him comfortable and quiet. Without using English, she and Mr. Xun had managed to get the point across that they needed ice for Morris's head. Mrs. Lu felt that they had Enzio convinced that they spoke and understood only Chinese. She was worried that the swelling in Morris's head would cause brain damage but it appeared that the application of ice had helped considerably. He was resting and quieter now.

Enzio had been smart to plot his course to Ruxton Island ahead of time. The weather was the pits and having the three "guests" aboard was distracting. They made good time and had arrived at their destination without difficulty but it was a very tricky entrance to Naylar Bay and Tommy had gone up on deck to watch for hazards and get the anchor ready to drop. He had argued that he should be the one to guard the prisoners but both Horst and Enzio had put that notion to rest with some rather caustic comments about his lack of ability in that department, referring of course to the events back in the motel in Tsawwassen. He was sulking again up on the foredeck in the rain.

Getting There

As the boat came to a stop, Enzio signaled Tommy to drop the hook and then backed down on the rode to set the anchor. There wasn't a lot of room in the little bay but it provided them with a good place to hide. It was almost impossible to see the boat from any angle except the entrance, so they were as hidden as they could be short of putting the boat in a covered boathouse. If there was any paint up at the cabin, he was going to have Horst and Tommy cover up the bright yellow trim and the name of the boat.

Since it would be light in only a couple of hours, they had to get busy and get everybody ashore under the cover of darkness. There was another boat, a small open speedboat anchored in the bay and only a couple of houses on shore but Enzio didn't want to risk anybody seeing the Chinese couple. Mrs. Lu tried to indicate to Enzio that moving Morris was risky but she couldn't get the point across without resorting to English. As it turned out, Enzio knew exactly what she was trying to say but he didn't care one bit whether Morris was up to being moved or not. Morris was expendable. They were all expendable sooner or later.

Horst and Tommy got the dingy ready and then came back inside. Without much care they manhandled the limp body of Morris over the side and into the bottom of the inflatable. Enzio told Horst where to find the key to the cabin and they were soon making their way to the beach. They had been told not to make any noise that might alert any nosy neighbors. From the boat Enzio watched as the two men rowed the short distance to shore and beached the dingy and apparently argue about how to get Morris up the steep stairs to the cabin. Finally Horst roughly picked Morris up and slung him over his shoulder and began the long climb up the stairs. Tommy brought the dingy back to the boat and Mr. Xun and Mrs. Lu were herded at gunpoint into the inflatable and taken ashore. They all slipped and scrambled over the wet rocks and seaweed and then climbed up the stairs.

The key had been just where they were told it would be. Inside the cabin it was cold and damp and dark. In the living room there was a wood stove with firewood piled up beside it but Enzio didn't want wood smoke raising any alarms with the neighbors. If there had been curtains on the windows they would have closed them but there were just big sheets of glass probably to enjoy the view but it was dark and they could see nothing. They turned on only one light in the hallway between the living room and the kitchen. It was enough to be able to see their way around. Enzio directed the Chinese couple to sit against the wall in the living room and then ran his fingers across his mouth like he was closing a zipper. He wanted them to keep quiet. Morris had been dumped on the floor and was moaning and groaning, rolling his head back and forth. Mrs. Lu started chastising the three men in Chinese, getting more and more agitated before Enzio finally lost patience and stepped forward and slapped her across the face.

Mr. Xun reacted without hesitation, leaping up from his sitting position; he feinted towards Tommy but whirled around in a roundhouse kick that caught Enzio off guard. The kick caught him hard in the temple sending him sprawling to the floor, stunned and unmoving. Tommy seeing a way to redeem himself roared like a bull and charged the diminutive Chinese man. But little Mr. Xun stepped aside and Tommy received a good swift kick in the ass and went straight through the picture window, the glass shattering in large dangerously sharp pieces. Screaming, Tommy fell about thirty feet and ended up face first on the rocks below. He lay unmoving, his neck at a peculiar angle to his shoulders. Several long skinny shards of window glass sticking into key locations on his body helped to confirm that he was dead.

Horst took advantage of the moment to pull his gun and send a well placed bullet right through Mr. Xun's shoulder. Talk about noise and confusion. Mr. Xun staggered backwards and then slumped to the floor, holding his shoulder and moaning and groaning just like Morris. Mrs. Lu took the low road and scrambled across the floor and took Horst down in a shin high bear hug. Falling backwards, he landed right on top of Enzio who was just starting to get up from the floor. Enzio went down again, hard, as Horst landed right on his lower back. More moaning and groaning. Mrs. Lu was all over Horst with every combination of mean vicious elbows and sharp fingernails that any pissed off woman might use. Ferocious would be an apt description. Horst still had his gun in his hand and squeezed off a couple of rounds which went through the ceiling and roof and started a slow drip from the steady rain. The gun blasts had the effect of getting Mrs. Lu's attention and along with a clip on the back of her head from the gun, she ceased her attack. It grew quiet save for the sounds from the injured which pretty much included everyone in the room.

Enzio came around, trying to get up, finally cursing at Horst. "Get the hell off me you shithead."

Getting There

Horst rolled to the side, pushing Mrs. Lu off his legs, giving her a good kick in the ribs in the process. Her eyes fluttered open and remembering where she was, she began crawling across the floor to the injured Mr. Xun. Ignoring her own injuries, she went right into nursing mode and began tending to his bleeding shoulder wound. It was a clean shot, the bullet passing through without breaking any bones but leaving a nasty big exit hole in his back. There was a sizable pool of blood spreading across the floor.

Enzio tried to stand up but quickly fell to his knees, both hands holding his lower back.

"You stupid bastard. Do you think you could have made any more noise? The bloody neighbors are going to be all over us now. Shit. I can't stand up. Come and help me you knucklehead."

Horst staggered to his feet and helped Enzio to get to a chair.

"Where the hell is Tommy?" Enzio asked, unaware of the current disposition of his less than stellar employee. "What the hell happened to the window?" He was looking at the gaping hole in the front picture window.

Horst went to the window and looked down at the twisted body of Tommy on the rocks below. He was careful not to cut himself on the jagged shards of glass still framing the hole in the window. "That old Chinese bastard pushed him out the window and he's laying down there on rocks. His neck looks like it's broken. I think he's dead."

Enzio tried to jump up from his chair but only got as far as a crouched over position. Groaning, he waddled over to the window to see for himself. Sure enough, there was Tommy having the sleep of the dead.

It was while they were standing there side by side looking out the window that Mrs. Lu saw her chance. It was a long shot from her point of view. Two big men and one small woman. But their preoccupation with Tommy's situation gave her an edge that outweighed her disadvantage in size. She took aim at the two backsides staring at her. It would have to be a full arm tackle to get them both in one shot but it was worth a try.

She had to be quick but her usual cat like reflexes honed by years of Tai Chi exercises were a little bit off due to the crack on the head from Horst's gun. She launched herself across the six feet between herself and the two men. They heard her coming but were unable to get out of the way in time and she plowed into them with all the force she could muster. Enzio, being bent over at the waist was driven forward into the window sill, a large chunk of glass breaking free and falling, slicing his left ear nearly completely off. The ear hung there at the side of his head, a piece of gristle and cartilage along with a shower of bright red blood. Horst on the other hand was propelled forward through the window but good fortune was with him. Sort of. He went through the window cleanly, not receiving any damage from the glass fragments still hanging there and at least he didn't land on his head. That was the good news. The bad news was that he landed feet first having done a somersault in mid air. The impact broke his left ankle and his right tibia and fibula and everything else that could be broken below the knee. It hurt like nothing Horst had ever experienced before. It didn't just hurt in the leg, it hurt deep inside his brain, like a hot poker being plunged into that part of the brain that told him to open his mouth and scream like a banshee. He screamed. He screamed long and loud. He even cried out for his mommy. He didn't care if anybody thought he was a sissy for doing it, he wanted his mommy right now.

In the cabin, Mrs. Lu was congratulating herself on doing a half decent job of whittling down the odds. It was a mistake to let her guard down and it was going to cost her. She should have finished the job. Enzio had gone to his knees and Horst had dropped his gun conveniently close to where Enzio's hand was on the floor. It was only a short reach to pick it up which he did and he turned and sat back against the wall pointing the weapon directly at Mrs. Lu's face. He was sorely tempted to pull the trigger and blow the bitch away. But he needed information and by god he was going to get it now. And he wasn't going to be gentle about extracting it. No more Mister Nice Guy.

Using his left hand, he pulled the collar of his jacket up and used it to try to stanch the flow of blood from his nearly severed ear. Enzio motioned with the gun in his right hand, indicating that Mrs. Lu should move back and sit. She did so carefully, mindful of the black hole at the end of the gun pointing directly at her head. Down on the rocks, Horst continued making a racket, combining screams of pain with pleas for help and begging for his mommy to come to him.

"I'll give him his mommy alright." Using the window sill as support, Enzio got to his feet and looked out the window at Horst. Mindful of the Chinese she-devil behind him, he hissed down at Horst,

"Shut the hell up you asshole. You're going to wake the whole bloody island up."

Horst thought that maybe a doctor might be woken from his dreams and would come and make him better. He screamed even louder. Enzio couldn't take any more and fired a shot at Horst, ending the racket and Horst's pain all at the same time. A win-win situation.

Enzio turned and hobbled across the floor to sit down at Mrs. Lu's side. Pressing the gun against her head, he calmly suggested that she start talking.

"Don't give me that bullshit Chinese babble. I know you can understand me and I know that you can speak English. You have exactly one second to start talking sense to me or you will join Chairman Mao in whatever type of afterlife you believe in. Understand?" He pressed the gun harder against her head.

Wide eyed, Mrs. Lu nodded her head and in a clear voice, albeit a little shaky, said, "What is it you would like to know Mr. Enzio?"

Enzio nodded and smiled. Now they were getting somewhere.

27 VAN GO SEARCHES

Van cut the power out in the bay and slowed the boat to a crawl as he approached the dock at Port Washington. It was still dark but there was a suggestion of light over the top of Maine Island. Another day on the way. A Cormorant, black against black did a low pass across the bow, its wingtips barely clearing the water. A seal poked its head up off the starboard side, looking at Van with its big dark eyes before slipping back under the water. Van was thinking that being out here in the islands was a lot better than living in Victoria. It felt great to be back on the water. Being stuck in Victoria doing construction work was hell. It meant that he had to get up at the same time every day and head off to work just like all the other peasants. It really wasn't the work that bored him; it was the regularity of it. The predictability made him crazy. That wasn't how he was supposed to live.

The change of speed woke Claire and she came into the cockpit looking bleary eyed and puffy faced. Her long black hair was messy. She was a wreck and Van's heart went out to her. He always thought of her as a little girl not just because she was so small compared to his giant size, but because she had an air of innocence that seemed rather childlike. Despite her looks, Van knew how tough she was. He had seen her demonstrate her mental and physical strength in many ways. This morning however, she looked very worn down.

After tying the boat up at the dock, Van walked with her up to her parents' house and by the time they got there it was growing light. They stopped outside the door to the house. A dog began barking in the next yard. The rain had stopped and it appeared that the clouds were breaking up. It might be an okay day in the weather department.

"Claire, you need to get some sleep. If I hear anything about Enzio's whereabouts, I'll let you know. I've got some friends in the islands keeping their eyes peeled for the bastard." He took her hands in his, reading the worry in her face. "We'll find him, don't you worry your pretty little head about that." For a big gruff man, he had a sweet side.

"Thank you Van. I really should be out there looking myself but Mick will be here soon. He's coming over in Eddy's boat and then we'll start searching. I've got to get some sleep first so I'll be of some use when Mick gets here. Thanks for bringing me back home. I really appreciate it."

"When this is all over, you can pay me back by inviting me over for a dumpling feast." Van held the all time record for Chinese dumpling consumption. Claire's mother adored the big man for his love of her famous dumplings.

Claire hugged Van and turned and went inside. She lay down on her bed without even taking her boots off and was asleep in moments.

Van made his way back down to the dock and jumped onto his boat and headed out to begin searching. He had full tanks, a fast boat and a burning desire to find the enemy. He tried to put himself in Enzio's shoes. A man on the run in a stolen boat. He had prisoners. Two of them Chinese. They would be easy to notice. Enzio would want to get some distance between himself and where he'd torched Claire's friends boat. There were more people and boats to the south, so Van imagined Enzio would head up to the northern part of the Gulf Islands where it would be quieter.

He circled around the northwest side of Prevost Island and checked Annette Cove and James Bay. Nothing. There were a lot of places to hide in the islands, so he knew he had to be patient. Heading up Trincomali Channel between Saltspring and Galiano, it was getting much easier to see with the growing light. His stomach was growling almost louder than the big engine pushing his boat. He reminded himself, search now, eat later.

As he reached Wallace Island, a long skinny piece of land off the tip of Saltspring, he was just trying to decide if he should search on the west or east side first when his cell phone started vibrating in his pocket. He pulled the phone out. "Hello," he said in his trademark growl.

"Van, its Stevie." Stevie from Ruxton Island just happened to be one of the few women who would be able to wear one of Van's shirts and not look lost in it. Out of the thirty or so homes on Ruxton, only a few had full time residents. Stevie and an ever-changing cast of male houseguests lived near Herring Cove in a cabin with a large airy studio where she painted. Van had met her a number of years back and had found a kindred spirit. Because of her size, she and Van had a natural affinity for each other. But Stevie had a natural affinity for many men which was why they had not pursued a serious relationship.

"Stevie, what's up? You got something for me?"

"Well, we don't usually hear people screaming their heads off in the night, nor do we usually hear a bunch of shooting, so yeah, I think I might have something for you."

"You checked it out?"

"Not yet but I was just going to head up the road and see what the hell is going on. You in the neighborhood, or do I have to do this on my own? I don't have any house guests here at the moment, and I don't have any firepower, so I wasn't looking forward to snooping around by myself. You know what I mean?"

Van nodded his head. "Girl, you just hold your water. I'm just up the street, so I'll be there in a jiffy. I'll pull into Herring Cove and come up to your place. Sit tight, I'm on my way. I'm just off of Wallace but I'm in the Van Go, so it won't take me long to get there."

"Roger that. I'm looking forward to seeing you, you big lug. Maybe you might want to stick around for a month or two and keep a big girl company."

Lust was scrambling his brainwaves. "Let's talk about that later Stevie. There's work to be done first. See you in a few minutes." He closed his phone and kicked the Van Go into high gear. With over four hundred horsepower, it was like he'd lit the afterburners and the boat jumped ahead and in moments was roaring in Stevie's direction.

Seventy miles per hour gets you where you want to go in a hurry and with only ten miles to go, Van pulled into Herring Cove in short order. Stevie spotted him coming into the bay and was down at the little dock waiting as he pulled in. Herring Cove is at the northern tip of Ruxton and as Stevie had explained, during the night she had heard all the commotion coming from the direction of Naylar Bay on the west side of the island, just a short walk from her house.

Getting There

As Stevie tied up the boat, Van jumped ashore. "Good to see you sweetheart," Van pulled Stevie into his arms and gave her a passionate kiss. She responded well and had this been a regular visit, they would have been heading straight back to the cabin for some horizontal exercise. But there was business to take care of first.

Stevie suggested that they walk up the road known as Long Walk Road and then along the beach at Naylar Bay since that's where the ruckus had been coming from.

"Is there anybody else around at the moment?' Most of the cabins on the island were used for weekend or summer visits.

"Not down this end of the island. I think the MacLean's are home right now and the Edwards family are visiting but they're at the other end of the island. There's nobody staying around Naylar Bay."

The two of them walked along the road, passing a couple of cabins on the right and one on the left. Ahead, they could see three cottages at the head of Naylar Bay. As they walked, Van spotted the broken front window at the third cottage which sat high up above the rocky shoreline. He motioned for Stevie to stop.

"See the broken window on the third one?" He was talking in a low, quiet voice.

"Yeah, I see it. That's the Mason's house. They haven't been here yet this year. I came by just a couple of days ago and didn't see any damage."

"Let's be careful. You keep behind me, OK?" He held her hand for a moment and then started out again. She followed close behind.

The end of the road led out onto the beach. The tide was fairly high but they still had enough beach to walk on. The water was quiet, barely lapping at the shoreline. In the middle of the bay was a large powerboat. They couldn't see the name on the stern but the fact that it was a Bayliner Thirty Nine with bright yellow trim meant that it was more than likely Enzio's boat.

Other than the broken window on the Mason's place, everything looked normal. The smell of seaweed permeated the air. They could see out the mouth of the bay to Yellow Point, off in the distance. A float plane cruised by, probably heading for Nanaimo. It was like any other very early morning in the Gulf Islands.

They looked up at the cabin, the front of which stood up on stilts above the beach. A long rickety staircase zigged and zagged its way up to the house. The broken picture window was very odd. Since there wasn't a porch around the front of the cabin, the window must have been broken from the inside out.

They watched the cabin for ten minutes seeing nothing moving. Van decided that they weren't going to get anywhere just sitting there. He looked around the high tide line of the beach until he found what he was looking for. It was a four foot madrone branch. He picked it up and hefted it in his hand. It felt good. At least he wasn't going up there empty handed.

They kept to the highest part of the shoreline. It was rockier and involved more work to negotiate but there was also more cover. As they approached the stairway leading up to the cabin, they came across two bodies, one lying next to the other, both unmoving. Stevie scrambled back to a safer place behind a couple of big rocks.

There were shards of glass around the bodies and looking up towards the cabin, Van could see more loose pieces of glass ready to fall. One of the men had been shot in the throat and had bled profusely on what had once been a very nice looking leather jacket. Aside from the bullet wound, his right leg was obviously shattered and bent underneath the thigh. Van guessed that it had to have been a very painful injury. The other man looked like he had a broken neck, his head at a very odd angle to the body. Van felt for a pulse on both bodies but they were cold and unmoving. He went through the pockets of the man with the broken leg, coming up empty but he found a gun in the jacket pocket of the guy with the broken neck. He checked to see that it was loaded. The gun made him feel even safer than the heavy club did. Nothing like having something that shoots small fast moving pieces of lead to make you feel safe.

He turned and found Stevie right behind him, obviously more concerned with staying close than worrying about a couple of dead guys. He put his finger to his lips indicating that they needed to be quiet. Van turned and started for the stairs leading up to the cabin. They began climbing, slowly and quietly. Stevie was so close; she was like Van's living shadow. With breasts. As they climbed, they watched the cabin. Still no sign of activity but Van had a feeling that behind the walls, this Enzio character was probably waiting with all kinds of surprises in store for them. About half way up the steep stairs, they came across another body. Again, it was obvious that a bullet was the cause of death. Van was beginning to wonder just how high the body count was going to go. Behind him, he heard a sharp intake of breath and then Stevie grabbed him and pulled him backwards down a couple of steps where they huddled together.

"It's Tom Edwards." Stevie was practically hysterical but common sense helped her to keep her voice to a whisper. Van could see the panic mounting in her eyes. He hoped she was not going to fall apart on him. "He keeps his boat in the bay here. Maybe he was checking on the Mason's place. Oh Van, I'm scared."

Van took her hand in his. "There, there, Stevie. You stay here and I'll go up and find out what's going on. As a matter of fact, maybe it would be safer if you went back down to the beach and waited there. I won't be long, okay?"

She looked at him like he was an idiot. "Are you crazy Van? You want me to be by myself? I'm coming with you and when this is all over I'm going to kick your ass for trying to get rid of me and leave me alone when there's obviously a maniac on the loose. Jesus." She didn't look so scared now, just pissed off. Nothing like a little anger to calm the nerves.

Van grinned at her and turned and stepped carefully over Tom Edwards's body. The bullet hole in his forehead reminded Van of the Hindu red dot between the eyes. A third eye, though Tom wasn't seeing anything now. Van turned and looked down into the bay to see if Tom's boat was there but it wasn't. Maybe he had moved it elsewhere.

As they reached the top of the stairs, they could see the side entry door of the cabin. They crept onto the porch and carefully peeked through the window of the door. This was just a hallway that led to the front room on the left and the kitchen on the right. A single light burned in the hallway. The door was slightly ajar and Van slowly pushed it open. It creaked on its hinges and they both jumped when they heard a moan from inside the house.

Van flipped off the safety on the gun in his hand. Since he still had the madrone club in his left hand, he turned and tried to pass the gun to Stevie who pushed it back at him, shaking her head. She pointed at him indicating that he should use it. He crouched down and moved forward, one slow step at a time. Near the end of the hallway, staying under cover behind the wall, Van took a deep breath and quickly looked into the front room. Enzio wasn't there. He looked again, this time seeing the large broken picture window but not much else. The two of them quickly moved into the room, Van with the gun out ahead, pointed and ready to fire. Another moan, this time from the dark corner of the room to their left.

It was Mr. Xun. Propped up originally, he had slid over sideways leaving an abstract trail of copper red on the wall. Pollock by Xun. He was lying on his side in a congealed pool of blood. Van knelt beside him and then noticed the other body lying on the floor beside the Chinese man. He motioned to Stevie to check out the second person while he looked at Mr. Xun. He gently lifted the little man into a sitting position again. He found the cause of the blood, a wound in the shoulder which had been packed with a couple of towels. As Stevie touched the other man, she was startled when he grabbed her hand. His eyes opened slowly and he tried to speak. Nothing came out except a dry sounding rasp. Mr. Xun opened his eyes and looked at Van. Recognition.

"Enzio." A whispered word. "He's gone. Took my wife. Gone."

It appeared to be almost too much for the man. He licked his lips and looked like he was close to death. His skin was pale and sweaty. Van got up and went to the kitchen and came back with a bottle of water. He cracked it open and held it to Mr. Xun's lips. Just a taste was all the man could manage. He passed the bottle to Stevie who gave a little to the other man.

"Stevie, we've got to get some help for these two. Fast."

"Everybody keeps emergency numbers handy Van, probably on the refrigerator."

Van was thinking that there would undoubtedly be a lot of questions to go along with all the mayhem that had happened at the Mason's little cabin. Questions that were going to take time to answer and that would also get the police involved in the whole matter.

"I think it might be best if I take them over to a doctor that I know in Victoria. I built an addition onto his house. Not exactly code, if you catch my drift so he won't mind doing a little favor for me. Let's get these two down to the Van Go and I'll call the doc and have someone meet me at Fisherman's Wharf with transportation. Speaking of transportation, we could do with some of that right now."

Van went outside and found exactly what he was looking for in the form of a red Radio Flyer wagon with oversized wheels. It wasn't great but it was better than trying to carry them back to the dock. He went inside and between Stevie and himself managed to get Mr. Xun out to the wagon without too much additional aggravation to the man's wounds. Mr. Xun was pretty much unconscious through the whole move. The other man, who neither of them knew, was totally out of it. They propped the two men up, back to back, legs hanging over the edges of the wagon. Stevie held them in place as Van began pulling. Taking the high road that ran by the front of the house, it wasn't far to the Van Go and in a matter of twenty minutes; they had the two men safely secured down below and the engine warmed up. Van gave Stevie a hug and a quick kiss.

"Once I get out of here, you should call the police and tell them that there was some kind of ruckus down in Naylar Bay during the night. Don't tell them we were at the cabin or they'll start asking you a bunch of questions. You know nothing. I'll be back as soon as we get Enzio wrapped up. Then the two of us will talk about me moving in here for the summer. I've had it with living in town."

Stevie arched her eyebrows and grinned like the Cheshire Cat.

"Now you're talking. I could use a real man around here for a change. Don't you worry about the mess at the Mason's place. Leave it to me Van."

He knew she could handle it. She cast off his lines and he backed out, turned and headed at top speed back to Victoria. Pulling his cell phone from his pocket, he called his doctor contact and explained the situation in very general terms. It was best not to get into specifics. There was no sense getting the doctor worried in advance. Once he showed up at the dock Van could get him to help out without too many questions being asked. There ware certain advantages to being as big as a mountain.

Van's next call was to Claire. He had to bring her up to speed. The phone rang a long time and then went to the answering machine. He knew she was there.

"Claire, pick up will you. It's Van. Pick up the phone. Hello, hello."

A sleepy sounding voice came on the line after the handset had been dropped and then picked up again.

"Hello Van. I'm here."

"Claire, I'm taking your father and another man to see a doctor in Victoria. They're in pretty bad shape but I think they'll be OK once the doctor works on them. There were two big guys down on the rocks below the cabin where we found your dad. They were dead. Don't know who they were but Stevie had never seen them before, so they must have come with Enzio. Also, it looks like Enzio killed one of the locals, a guy by the name of Tom Edwards. Shot in the head." He heard Claire gasp and he kicked himself for providing that choice little bit of information. "Also, your father said that Enzio still has your mother and he's in a different boat now." Stevie had told him that Tom Edward's boat was a white powerboat, not very big, with a circular seating area in the front and very fast. Usually anchored in the bay, it was gone and Van had put two and two together. The description of the boat didn't narrow it down very much but he passed the information along to Claire.

"There's nothing you can do for your father or the other fellow. Leave them to me and the doctor. I'm going to do my best to get the doctor to hold off on reporting your dad's gunshot wounds to the police for at least 48 hours."

"Do you think he'll do that?" Claire sounded skeptical. "I thought it was the law that doctors had to report that kind of thing right away."

Van was shaking his head. "Yeah, that's what everybody thinks. But that's not the law here in British Columbia and besides, the doc and me, we're like this." He held his intertwined fingers up in front of the phone as if Claire could see. She sounded like she got the point.

"Okay Van. I hope so. We can't risk getting the police involved while Enzio has my mother. Who knows what he'd do if he sees the cops heading his way." She shuddered. "Please take good care of them Van. The other man is Morris. He's a friend of Mick's. The two big men were with Enzio so that narrows the odds for us. I'll pass the information along to Mick and as soon as he gets here, we'll get out and look for my mother. I know she can take care of herself quite well, so she'll be okay. Please call me and let me know how my father and Morris are after they see the doctor. Thanks so much for everything Van. Bye for now."

As the connection ended, Van pushed hard on the throttle trying to get the boat to go a little bit faster. He was going at top speed and only the last couple of feet of the hull near the stern were still making contact with the water. He was flying low and making excellent time. He was as happy as he could be.

28 TIME TO LEAVE

Enzio was having a nice chat with Mrs. Lu. The most difficult part of socializing is getting a conversation started and Enzio felt good that they had crossed that hurdle. They were getting along fine now that they had gotten the ball rolling with the help of the gun in his hand. Nothing like a little help from a forty five to loosen the tongue.

Now that Mrs. Lu had dropped the bullshit Chinese language charade, Enzio was getting all kinds of information. Such as who Mick Brese was and just what she and her husband had to do with Eddy Wainwright. Speaking of Mrs. Lu's hubby, he was pretty much out of it. Mrs. Lu had found a couple of towels in the kitchen and had stuffed them in Mr. Xun's shirt to try to stop the flow of blood from the gunshot wound. Her high level of anxiety for him showed on her face.

Enzio himself was now wearing a turban of sorts in order to hold his severed ear in place and also to stop the blood flow. The left shoulder of his nice jacket was saturated with blood. It had been quite an eventful evening for all concerned.

Enzio's phone had interrupted their conversation just at the point where Mrs. Lu was telling him about Claire and Mick. It seemed that once you got this woman talking, she didn't want to shut up. Maybe it was the nerves. She seemed pleased but torn at the same time that the sailor boy had taken a shine to their still unmarried daughter. Mrs. Lu was worried that this might throw a wrench into the relationship that she had been trying to promote between a young Chinese business man and her daughter. Apparently the girl was resisting the match making efforts of Mrs. Lu. The woman kept telling him that she didn't want her daughter to marry a white guy though she was quick to emphasize that it was not a matter of racism. It was just that the Chinese had thousands of years of culture and on and on she had gone about why she wanted her daughter to marry a Chinese guy and it didn't have anything to do with racism. To Enzio, it sounded like racism. You could dress it up any way you wanted to but it still sounded like racism to him.

The phone call had interrupted this charming little chat. Enzio answered in a peeved tone. "Who is this and what do you want?"

A pause on the other end of the line before a pissed off sounding man answered. "It's your fairy godmother, that's who. I don't know why I'm taking a chance on you Enzio. Maybe I'm just a believer in redemption. "Redeem thy misspent time that's past, and live this day as thy last." Trust me Enzio. If you don't redeem yourself, this day will be your last. I don't have time to chit chat, so let me make a long story short. I've got a boat waiting for you in Narvaez Bay on Saturna Island. It's a forty foot cabin cruiser. There is one ton of premium B.C. Bud onboard carefully packaged to protect it from the elements. You want it, it's yours. I'll throw in the boat for free. Just be forewarned. If you're planning to head down the coast to sell the dope, this is not the boat to do it in. There's no safety gear onboard and it is a coastal cruiser. But I don't give a shit what you do after you pay me my money. Just like we discussed before, you bring the four million in cash and my man will turn the whole kit and caboodle over to you. He's not going to wait long, so if you want it, you better be there today. He will leave tonight and if you don't show up with the money, it will be the last time you do business in this province. I guarantee it."

Enzio licked his lips. Two thousand pounds of premium bud. Once he got it across the border all he had to do was move it across the country and he could be looking at tripling his investment. By the same token, if things didn't go as planned, he could end up in jail for a long time. The U.S. didn't have the same laissez-faire attitude towards drug dealing that Canada did. But what the hell, this would make up for that last debacle and get him back in the business again. About bloody time.

"I'll be there. I'm warning you though, that shit had better be as good as you say it is."

There was a long pause on the line and then a slightly incredulous voice came back at him. "Or what Enzio? You forget yourself asshole. You put some of my boys in the slammer the last time I did business with you. You're lucky I'm not hunting you down and killing your sorry ass let alone taking a chance on you again. Don't you forget it shithead. If it weren't for the fact that your father and my father had done a lot of business together, I would have killed you after that fiasco off Port Renfrew, so don't warn me ever again. Or else."

 The last two words were delivered quietly but came with such unspoken threat that Enzio's hand started to shake and he accidentally hit the "End" button. He didn't want to talk anymore anyway.

 He sat for a moment trying to get himself under control. Mrs. Lu was watching him. He could feel her dark eyes on him and he didn't want to let her see him sweat. Never let them see you sweat the old saying went. This whole deal had been getting more difficult ever since Brese had stolen Eddy from him. It was so hard to make a living these days. He was starting to feel like the victim here, forgetting the fact that Tommy and Horst were dead, and Mr. Xun and Morris were gravely injured. That didn't matter. What did matter was getting the money from Brese and getting that dope shipment and getting the hell down south where he could make some R.O.I. He loved the business acronyms and he loved thinking about a whopping big return on investment.

 Starting to calm down, he decided that it was time that they got the hell out of Dodge. They had made enough noise to wake the dead and it would be light soon. He didn't want to have people nosing around and finding the bodies down on the rocks or the injured people in the cabin. Before they went though, he had to call Brese again and light a fire under that bastard. He had to deliver the money pronto or there wasn't going to be any investment to get a return on.

 After burning Brese's boat, they had found a cell phone on the unconscious guy, whoever he was and though the phone had been soaking wet, Enzio had dried it sufficiently to get it to light up when he pushed the power button. He had gone through the contact list and had found a listing for M. Brese. How convenient. He had stored the number on his own cell phone.

 He had just started to call Brese when he heard footsteps crunching on the beach gravel down below. The advantage of having the big front window smashed out was that he could easily hear any noise outside. He jammed the gun in Mrs. Lu's side and whispered to her, "Don't make any noise. If you do, I will kill your husband. Understand?" Mrs. Lu nodded vigorously.

Enzio crawled to the dark side of the room and took a peek out the window. A lone man looked at Tommy and Horst's bodies and then turned and started up the stairs. Enzio decided that it would be best to meet this threat head on. He stood up as best he could and hobbled to the door. His back was so stiff he could hardly stand. Great, he thought to himself; that meant dealing with the bloody healthcare system again.

He checked his weapon to be sure it was ready and slipped it into his coat pocket, hand on the grip, ready to go. Grimacing, he stood as vertical as his strained back would let him and went out the door and started down the stairs. The man was about half way up the stairs and looked up, startled. He stopped and took a step backwards. There wasn't any reason for Enzio to say anything. The end result was going to be the same. Enzio couldn't let this guy go after having seen the bodies on the beach. The gun came out of his pocket smoothly and he simply pointed it and pulled the trigger. The look on the guys face was almost comical. His hands came up as if he were reaching to feel the wound and his mouth made a surprised "O" and he toppled backwards landing on the steps on his back, face up.

The sound from the gun was very loud. Enzio cursed, wondering why silencers weren't standard equipment on guns. Bloody noise pollution. He turned and went back in the cabin. Mrs. Lu had moved over to her husband and the other guy and was trying to make them drink water. She had Mr. Xun propped up against the wall and was holding a water bottle to his lips. She glared at Enzio as he came back in the room.

"Time to go. I think we've worn out our welcome here. People are going to start waking up and someone else is bound to come snooping around. Believe it or not," he said, noting the dirty looks he was getting from the Chinese woman, "I would rather get going than stick around here shooting people all day." He shrugged, "Call me crazy."

Mrs. Lu started to get Mr. Xun to his feet but Enzio put that notion to rest in a hurry. He decided to throw her a bone, something to shut her up before she started bitching at him. "Leave him. He stays. They both stay. We're getting out of here, just you and me. Someone will be bound to come and help them before too long. They'll get better care here than being dragged down the stairs and out to the boat. Have a little sympathy." He ignored her incredulous look. "Besides, we're going to be busy and we don't have time to take care of them." She started to say something but Enzio advanced towards her and raised his hand in a threatening manner. She shut her mouth.

Enzio didn't give a shit about the two men. They were both looking like they wouldn't last another hour, so he didn't feel it was necessary to finish them off. Between Horst and Tommy and himself, they had made enough noise already. He grabbed Mrs. Lu by the arm and pulled her up and shoved her out the door. As they left, Mr. Xun opened his eyes and turned his head to see his wife leave. As he did so, the motion caused his upper body to fall over, slowly until he was lying on his side on the floor. He doubted that he would ever see her again. If he had had the energy, he would have cried. They had lived through so many difficult times in China and it was sad that it had to end now.

Enzio pushed Mrs. Lu ahead of him down the stairs. She had to be pushed extra hard when they got to the body. Enzio searched the man's pockets and came up with a wallet and a set of keys on a spongy key floater. Boat keys. Looking out in the bay he could see the only other boat there. A small open speed boat. Racy looking thing. He didn't really want to leave the Bayliner but it was probably getting pretty hot by now.

When they reached the beach, the tide was up a bit and the dingy was afloat. It was good that Tommy had tied the tow line to an arbutus branch sticking out over the rocks or they would have lost the inflatable. Just about the last intelligent thing that Tommy had done.

They piled into the dingy and Enzio took the oars and headed them out to the little speed boat. It had a big swim grid on the stern which made it easy to board. There was even a gate built into the transom which they opened to enter the cockpit. Sweet ride. Enzio got Mrs. Lu to sit in the passenger seat next to the helm while he figured out how to get the boat fired up. He lifted the engine cover at the aft end of the cockpit.

"Wow. Check out how nicely laid out this engine compartment is. This is a nice boat. What do you think Mrs. Lu?"

She glared at him, arms crossed across her chest. Enzio recognized this as a woman not pleased with the situation. He was good at reading people. Mrs. Lu decided to give him her two cents worth.

"What is wrong with you?" Actually, it came out as "Hmmmpfh. What is wrong with you?" She was angry. Really angry.

Enzio rolled his eyes. What the hell was her problem? "What? What are you so pissed about? It's a nice boat. We'll be out of here in no time."

"That's not what I'm talking about. I don't care if the boat is nice or not. You just killed a man and you don't even seem concerned about it. What is wrong with you?"

Enzio made a face. "I lost two of my men last night because of you and your husband. I don't see you being too upset about that? What the hell is wrong with you? They're humans too."

Mrs. Lu looked indignant. "That's different. You were trying to kill us, so we had to defend ourselves."

"Wrong. I wasn't trying to kill you. You are my prisoners. The more prisoners I have, the stronger my bargaining position with that asshole Brese. If you had just behaved yourselves, we wouldn't have had to hurt anyone."

Another strong hmmmmpfh. Still with the crossed arms. "And that man on the stairs. Was it necessary to kill him? You're a very good liar. You could have lied to him and sent him away. But you just shot him. He didn't even have a chance."

Enzio was tired of the argument. He should have just smacked her and told her to shut up.

"The man was a witness. He could have told the police what I look like. He was a threat and he needed to be eliminated. It wasn't personal."

Mrs. Lu's eyes just about came right out of her face. "Not personal? Not personal?" She was starting to get loud and obnoxious, so Enzio turned and went back to getting the engine ready to go. He tried to ignore the angry woman.

"I'm talking to you." She had stood up and now had her hands on her hips like his second wife used to do. She was triggering some terrible memories in Enzio. His gaze fell on a roll of duct tape in a bin next to the battery box. Perfect. He picked it up and turned on her.

"Shut the hell up." She made like she was going to argue some more but he tore off a piece of the thick gray tape and using both hands firmly sealed her mouth shut. With the loose end on the roll, he started binding her struggling arms to her body. In moments, she was trussed up snugly. He picked her up and sat her down with a thump in the passenger seat again. He took a turn around her flailing feet and in moments had her under control.

Getting There

"Sit and be still. If you keep struggling, I am going to lose my patience and beat the crap out of you. If you sit quietly, you will avoid getting hurt. Do you understand?" He was close enough to her face that a little of his spit landed on her chin. There was little choice. Seeing the anger in his eyes, she saw the wisdom in his words. She nodded.

The boat fired up on the first attempt and after Enzio cast off from the buoy, they motored out of the bay. Naylar Bay was glad to see them go.

29 AIR SEARCH

Claire decided she couldn't wait for Mick. There was no time to waste. She had no sooner hung up from talking with Van before she went sprinting downstairs and out of the house heading for the boathouse and her little airplane. It was daylight now and as she ran, she was looking at the trees. Big arbutus trees lined the road and the leaf movement was a good way to see what the wind was doing. At the moment, it appeared as though it was a very light breeze. Nothing that would bother her flying plans.

At the boathouse, she went through the preflight checklist carefully. There were some things that couldn't be rushed. Since she was flying solo today, she strapped a few things into the passenger seat. Her father had stored some of his junk in her airplane hanger. She had griped about it from time to time but today she was happy about it. A half dozen bricks and a twenty five pound folding anchor. The five flukes of the anchor folded up and were held in place by a sliding ring near the top of the shank. All of these items would make terrific things to drop on Enzio's boat if she got the chance. She had won first prize at the flour bombing contest that was held each year at the Victoria Air Show, so dropping a brick on a boat would be just a step up from dropping a bag of flour on a painted circle on a runway. She worried that she didn't feel a little bad about doing something dangerous like dropping heavy objects on a human being. But she shrugged; war is war she thought as she carried on with her preparations.

It didn't take her long to get ready and then push the Quicksilver out into the bay. She could tell it was going to be a great day when the airplane hardly required any paddling to get turned around and in position to taxi out. Some days were like that. Before putting her flying helmet on, she put her hands free cell phone headset on. She fired up the engine and started taxiing out while checking for any traffic in the air and on the water. By the time she had finished her warm up and her pre-flight checklist, she was in position and ready to go.

Moments later, she was in the air and gaining altitude, heading towards the last known position of Enzio. Once she had leveled off, she pulled out the cell phone and punched the speed dial button for Mick. He answered on the third ring.

"Mick, its Claire. Where are you now?"

Mick was pleased to hear Claire's voice sounding so strong. "Claire, I'm just heading into Active Pass. Are you at Port Washington? What's all that noise in the background?"

"Mick, I'm up in my airplane. Enzio showed up on Ruxton Island. A friend of mine went up there by boat and found my father and Morris. He's taking them to a doctor in Victoria right now. He says they'll be okay. He's got enough experience to be able to judge these things, so I believe him. But Enzio has stolen another boat. He still has my mother but according to my friend Van, Enzio's two associates are dead. I'd be willing to bet that my father and mother had something to do with that."

Mick was startled by all this news. Claire seemed so calm about it all.

Claire continued. "I'm heading up toward Ruxton to start looking for Enzio." She gave Mick the description of the speedboat that Van had said was Enzio's new ride.

"That's the only description we've got so far but keep your eyes open for him. A fast boat like that could be anywhere by now. Keep your phone handy and I'll let you know if I see anything. Mick, thanks for being there. I'm glad to know that you're not far away now. Be careful. Talk to you later."

"Claire, you take care too" Mick said but she had already hung up.

Claire settled into her seat and focused on the water ahead and below. There was a lot of territory to cover and she felt like time was wasting. Enzio had killed to get this new boat and he still had her mother. Claire shivered, partly from the cold morning air and mostly from thinking about what Enzio might do to Mrs. Lu. He was a dangerous man and he needed to be stopped soon.

It was difficult for Claire to concentrate on the search. Her mind kept imagining the worst about her father's condition and her mother's perilous situation. How was Morris doing? What about the man killed on the island? Enzio had to be stopped at all costs and it was up to her and Mick to stop him. She spotted a small boat zipping along near Atkins Reef, near the shore of Saltspring. It seemed to match the description. She banked steeply to the left and began to descend on a path that would intercept the boat. As their courses intersected, Claire could see a man sitting at the wheel with a woman in the stern. As she flew low over the boat, the man at the helm was looking up at her, eyes wide. The woman in the stern was waving at Claire and it was easy to see it wasn't her mother. The woman was a blond, Scandinavian looking type.

Claire got back to altitude and carried on, periodically diving down to check boats that looked anything like her target. After reaching the point where she had to turn back to refuel, she had still not spotted Enzio. She was frustrated at having to go back to gas up again but there was nothing she could do about that. Reluctantly, she turned around and headed back to Port Washington.

A call came in on her cell phone. It was Van.

"Claire, where are you? I called your house but just got the answering machine."

"I'm up in my airplane searching for Enzio. I have to go back to refuel right now. How are my dad and Morris doing?" The fuel indicator showed less than ten minutes of flying time and she was starting to sweat a little. She wouldn't normally get anywhere near this low on fuel but today was different.

"They're going to be okay. Morris has a fractured skull and he's suffered from a lot of swelling and bleeding. The doc used the term Diffuse Axonal Injury. In layman's terms, he's had a shit kicking of the brain. He's going to recover but it's been a close call. Your dad is alert and talking now. They got him on an I.V. and started pumping blood into him. They bandaged up the gunshot wound in his shoulder and he's going to be fine after a lot of rehab. He's lost a hunk of meat about the size of a pork chop from the back of his shoulder but the doc says not to worry. Your dad is a tough guy."

Claire breathed a sigh of relief. That was one less thing to worry about. She tried to talk but found she was choked up. Point

Liddell on Prevost Island was just below and could see Port Washington now. She was going to make it. The nice thing about flying a float plane was that if you ran out of gas or had some kind of emergency, you could put down on the water pretty much anywhere. But this time, she was going to make it back on fumes and be ready to go back out after a fuel and potty break.

"Van, thanks for the information. That helps me a lot. I have to tell you, I was getting kind of worried about my father and Morris."

"I read you, Claire."

"Thanks Van. Thanks so much for taking care of them. Now we just have to get my mother back and deal with Enzio."

"Don't worry Claire. We'll get your mom back. Ta ta for now."

Claire descended and touched down with fuel to spare. Not a lot, but enough to taxi all the way to the boathouse before the engine sputtered to a stop. Claire hoped that that was not all the luck she would have today.

30 A RAFT OF PROBLEMS

As Mick approached Active Pass, he was surprised by how energized he felt. Despite having had only a few hours of sleep in the last several days, he was feeling pretty good.

In the night, during the trip across Georgia Strait, it had rained quite a bit. Seagram had a good auto pilot system and had steered herself the whole way leaving Mick time to move around the boat. At one point, he had been in the bow stateroom and discovered that the deck hatch was leaking. It appeared that the seal had been damaged so he had gone up on deck to take a look from that vantage point.

On deck, while kneeling next to the hatch, flashlight in hand looking at the rubber gasket which formed the watertight seal on the hatch, his brain had gone back to the puzzle of the money. Four million dollars. Give or take. Eddy had said that the money was onboard Seagram. It was possible he was bullshitting. Lord knows, he certainly hadn't been forthright about his past. Mick sat back on his heels and looked around. He was just forward of the mast, and right in between the two life rafts that he and Eddy had gone shopping for only several months ago.

Eddy had said that the money was on Seagram but he hadn't said where. It certainly wasn't below decks. He had been all through the boat and knew that for sure. Mick swiveled around on his heels and looked at the life raft canister to the right of the mast.

On the day that Mick and Eddy had shopped for the life rafts, several months ago, they had argued whether it would be enough to buy just one life raft, or two. One would be enough for most cruiser's budgets but Eddy had insisted on two. Mick didn't try to talk him out of it because he could see the logic if he wasn't being frugal. Each life raft had cost around thirty five hundred dollars and took up a valuable piece of deck real estate. On Starlight, it would have been out of the question to buy two but on the larger Seagram, two life raft canisters fit just fine. And there were times when there might well have been enough people onboard Seagram to fill two life rafts.

Each canister had a fluorescent red band of reflective tape which wrapped all the way around the middle. The canisters, white fiberglass rectangular boxes were sitting in metal cradles which had been bolted to the deck. The canister itself had a lanyard running from it to the cradle so that if you threw the canister overboard, it would still be tethered to the boat and not drift away. It was designed to self deploy once you threw it over the side.

Mick remembered back to a comment that Claire had made when they went for their first flight together in her little airplane. She had said that they had paid a lot of money to purchase the ballistic recovery chute which was something that she might never use. It was the same thing with these life rafts. More often than not they were just decoration because they would probably never be needed. But they were sealed and everybody just assumed that the canister held what it was supposed to hold. A life raft. He reached out and knocked on the canister in front of him. Thunk, thunk, thunk. He moved over to the canister on the port side of the mast and knocked again. Clunk, clunk, clunk. A definite difference. How much room would four million dollars take? It seemed impossible that that much money would fit in anything less than something the size of a small car.

"What the hell does four million dollars look like?" Mick asked himself out loud. He remembered that Eddy and Enzio had been toting the money in two briefcases. Hard to imagine that amount of money fitting in two small cases. The most money Mick had ever had at one time was ten thousand dollars which he had won in Vegas. He had wanted to hold it in his hands and had insisted the payout be in one hundred dollar bills. It had surprised him at the time at how small the bundle of money was.

He looked at the canisters. Each of them was about twice or three times as thick as a briefcase. There was no way to tell which one held the money, or if he was really on the right track. They were both sealed and the only way to open them would be to jerk the lanyard and trigger the inflation process. Mick reasoned that if the canister held money, no inflation would take place.

Mick was not normally a gambling man. An occasional lottery ticket and the one time lucky trip to Vegas was the extent of his gambling experience. Some would say that going offshore was a gamble but Mick saw that as something different. A challenge, not a gamble. Here, with two life raft canisters and perhaps only one holding money, he had a fifty percent chance of guessing right and thunk sounded more like money than clunk.

Mick took a deep breath, reached out and jerked the lanyard on the canister on the starboard side. He covered his face thinking the raft would explode open like an airbag in a car. Nothing happened. The lanyard dangled from his fingers. At that moment, the cellphone in his pocket started vibrating. Opening the canister was going to have to wait a moment longer. He pulled the phone out of his pocket and flipped it open.

"Mr. Brese. How are you doing? Mrs. Lu asked about you. She hopes you're well."

Mick didn't say anything. Just listened.

"Mrs. Lu would like to talk to you but she's tied up at the moment. Actually, she's taped up. I found a great big roll of duct tape in the boat here and I used that to get her under control. Did you know that she killed one of my men and caused me to just about lose my whole left ear? She's quite the lady. So, to keep her boundless energy under control, I thought it prudent to use a good part of this roll of duct tape on the bitch."

Mick stayed quiet.

"You there Brese? I've got a news flash for you. I'm going to pay a big bill today but that's going to be difficult unless you give me my four million dollars. If you don't, I'm going to get hit with some rather stiff penalties and the thought of that has put me in a rather foul mood. So, the time has come to pay the piper my boy. You're going to meet me and give me the money and then I'll give you this pain in the ass Chinese she-devil in return. If you don't meet me and give me MY bloody money, I will kill her and feed her to the fishes. Piece by piece. And then, you know what? Sweet little Claire is going to be pretty pissed off with you. I know you were making puppy dog eyes with the little chick. Her momma told me so. If you want to get into Claire's hot little pants, you better give me the money or she's going to blame you for her mother's untimely and very painful passing and no nookie for you." Enzio was enjoying this.

Mick was fuming but still didn't say anything.

"Hey Brese. I struck a nerve there didn't I? Cat got your tongue? Tell you what, Micky boy. You better say "Yes, Mr. Enzio, I'll meet you and give you YOUR money back and kiss your ass at the same time," or I'm going to do a vice grip special on Mrs. Lu's pinky finger." He paused. "Talk you son of a bitch."

Mick waited a few breaths and then, "Yes, you son of a bitch, I'll meet you and give you the money. And if you harm Mrs. Lu, I will see to it that you won't be able to use your ass for any natural function, be it shitting or sitting, ever again. You read me?"

Enzio's eyes bugged out. The bastard. Just who did he think he was talking to? Who was in the driver's seat here?

"Let's cut this chit chat short. Meet me at Montague Harbor in one hour and we'll make the exchange."

Mick felt the urge to jerk Enzio's chain, just a little bit.

"I don't have the money Enzio. How can I give you something I don't have?"

Enzio leaned over to Mrs. Lu, her arms and legs securely duct taped into submission. He pulled the rusty pair of vice grips from his pocket and yanked the duct tape from Mrs. Lu's mouth. Without hesitation, he clamped the grips on Mrs. Lu's pinky finger on her left hand. Enzio had a thing for starting on the left hand. It gave people time to think about the future and how difficult it would be to live with a gimped up writing hand.

Mick clearly heard Mrs. Lu's scream. His blood began a fast boil.

"You hear that Brese? That's what you get for trying to jerk me around. You meet me and give me my money or she's going to have the same treatment on more tender parts of her anatomy than her fingers. Mark my words Brese. I've had it up to here with the lot of you. Give me my money or she's dead. Oh, and Mick, like I said before, if you go to the police looking for help to find me, this little lady here is fish food."

As the line went dead, Mick was running back to the cockpit to pour on the power. It was time to go to war.

31 A BAD DEAL

Enzio got to Montague Harbor first. He had dumped Mrs. Lu on the floor in the bow of the boat, keeping her out of sight. He didn't want to have to explain to anybody why his first mate was trussed up like the Christmas turkey. Not to mention the swollen and bloody pinky finger on her left hand. He didn't have anything to ice it with to keep the swelling down, nor did he feel like doing it. These people were so difficult to deal with. All he wanted was his money and he would be gone. Was that too much to ask? Enzio didn't think so.

The first thing Enzio did upon arrival in the bay was to figure out where best to position himself for when Brese showed up. Just like making love, timing was going to be everything. Enzio got a good chuckle at his humor. He was feeling pretty good.

Montague Harbor is just around the corner from Active Pass, so it didn't take Mick long to transit the pass and arrive at the entrance to Montague. He throttled back and entered the mouth of the bay, steering into the channel between Parker Island and Winstanley Point on Galiano. There was virtually no current and as he put the boat in neutral, he continued to move slowly ahead. Dead ahead was a small white speedboat, the man at the wheel waving at Mick.

As Seagram edged closer to the speedboat, Mick took a look at the surrounding area. The bay was quiet, only a couple of boats anchored over in the eastern corner to the right of the ferry dock. The water was nearly calm, it was sunny and it was peaceful. Mick thought that there should be a black storm cloud over top of Enzio's boat.

Enzio was close to the shore in the small cove on Parker Island at the far west side of the harbor.

Mick edged closer until he was within fifty feet of Enzio's speedboat. He didn't want to get too close just yet. He was wary with good reason. Enzio was waving him closer but Mick wasn't biting.

"Hey Mick, get over here and let's make the trade."

Mick had to believe that something was up; it wasn't going to be that easy.

"Tell you what Enzio. Let's move over to the middle of the bay where the water is a little deeper. My boat draws a lot more than yours does."

"Whatever you say. You lead the way, I'll follow." Enzio began moving towards Seagram and Mick turned the big boat to starboard and began to apply a little throttle. The speedboat moved around the stern of Seagram from the port side to the starboard side. Enzio was going quite slowly until he got around to the starboard side. Mick was puzzled when all of a sudden Enzio gunned his boat and began to speed up moving almost straight out away from Seagram's side.

Mick was surprised when Seagram's engine began to labor and bog down. He applied more throttle which turned out to be the worst thing he could do. Once Mick spotted the tow rope trailing behind Enzio he realized what was going on and quickly shut the engine down. The damage was already done however.

Enzio was ecstatic. The weight that he had lightly tied to the end of the buoyant tow rope had done the job. It had pulled the rope down into the depths until Enzio had applied power at which point the weight had broken free and the tow rope had been pulled to the surface. It had cleared the rudder hanging down under the stern of Seagram and floated up, right into the spinning propeller and wrapped itself around the propeller and shaft, like spaghetti on a fork.

Mick knew he'd been had. He had two choices. Either hoist sail and leave or drop the anchor and make the trade with Enzio. He had to get Mrs. Lu, so he ran up on deck and dropped the hook. He looked out over the bow at Enzio who was grinning ear to ear.

Mick called out, "Nicely done you bastard." He had to admire Enzio's clever tactic. It was obvious he was going to have to be a lot more careful in this transaction.

Enzio leaned over the stern and cut the tow rope free. "Aw, shucks, I forgot about my tow rope. Mrs. Lu was doing a little wakeboarding on our way over here and I forgot to bring in the tow line. Sorry about that." He was chuckling.

Mick ignored him and walked back to the cockpit and sat down. Enzio shrugged and brought his speed boat around to the boarding platform built into the stern of Seagram. He had his gun in his hand while he steered. Not taking any chances.

Mick continued to sit; ignoring Enzio's look until Enzio himself got up and tied a couple of lines to hold his boat to Seagram. Mick could see Mrs. Lu bound in tape lying on the floor of the bow seating area. She looked frightened and hopeful at the same time.

"Let's not dick around Brese. Give me the money and I'll give you the bitch. Actually I should pay you to take her off my hands but that's not how it's going to work. Bring the money to me right now."

Mick stayed sitting, one leg casually crossed over the other. Slowly, he stood and went forward and removed the liferaft canister from the right side of the base of the mast. It was heavy. Since there was no handle on the canister, it was awkward to carry but he picked it up in both arms and carried it back to the cockpit. He sat it on the starboard seat.

"What the hell is that? You mean to tell me the money is in that? It was on deck the whole time we searched this bloody boat? You're joking." Enzio was skeptical. "Open it. I don't believe it's in there." He gestured with his gun. "Go on, open it."

Mick found the end of the red reflective tape wrapped around the canister and started peeling it off. This exposed a seam in the canister and after removing the tape, Mick pried the fiberglass halves apart. It was hinged on one side and opened like a big white clamshell full of beautiful green money. Mick was surprised to see that it was all American bills. Packages of one hundred dollar bills, each one wrapped with a purple band of paper. Piles of packages. Oodles of bills. Lots of money.

Mick was almost tempted to dump the money out of the canister right on Enzio's head but the fact that Enzio had his gun pointing at Mrs. Lu in the bow of the boat was a suitable deterrent. Getting Mrs. Lu killed wouldn't do.

"Bring the case over here." Enzio was craning his neck and looking towards the bow of Seagram. "There's another one of those on deck. What's in that one?"

Mick turned and looked forward. The second life raft canister was still sitting in its cradle on the left side of the mast. He turned back to Enzio and carried the case of money onto the stern platform.

"It's a life raft. It's mine, you get this one, I keep that one." He held the case out in his arms offering it to Enzio.

"You think I'm stupid Brese? You bring it onboard and put it down on the floor right here." He pointed at the floor just behind the helm seat. Mick climbed into the boat and put the case down.

"Open it again and give me a quick count. We had it in two briefcases last time I saw it. I don't think it's all there.'

Mick looked at him and knelt down in front of the case. He pulled out a package of bills.

"You're right, it's not all here. Eddy used a half million buying the boat and outfitting it. So, it's only three and a half million. But, since you burned up my boat and injured my friends, I think that's worth a half million dollars, so let's call it even."

Enzio spluttered. "How can you call that even? You said this boat" he pointed with his gun at Seagram, "cost half a million and now you're telling me your boat cost a half a million? Forget it."

"Well, if I was to sue you in a court of law, I'd get a hell of a lot more than that for all the pain and suffering you caused, so unless you want to meet me in court, we will call it even."

Enzio spit over the side of the boat as if to express his disgust with the bargaining process.

Mick carried on. "There are a hundred, hundred dollar bills in each package. That means that there should be three hundred and fifty packages in the case. Each of these rows is eight bundles wide and four deep. That's thirty two bundles per layer and," he counted one pile, "there's ten packages per stack, plus," and he did a quick count, "twenty eight packages." Mick hesitated, trying to do the math under stress.

Mrs. Lu piped up from the bow, "Three hundred and forty eight. That's three million, four hundred and eighty thousand dollars."

They both said thank you at the same time. Enzio looked embarrassed. "Chinese people are good at math."

Mrs. Lu said, "That's a stereotype. My husband is terrible at math. But he makes terrific lasagna. Does that make him Italian?"

Enzio grabbed the roll of duct tape. Mick suggested that they get on with it.

Enzio started whining. "What about the other two bundles. That's twenty thousand dollars. There should be three hundred and fifty bundles there."

Mick looked at him with disgust. "You cheap bastard, you're twenty thou short of three and a half million bucks and you're bitching? Put it in the bank for a couple of weeks and you'll get your twenty grand back in interest." He shook his head.

Enzio pointed the gun at Mick and ordered him to get back on his own boat. Mick closed the case and moved slowly back onto Seagram. This is where it could get tricky.

"Bring me the life raft. That'll make up for the missing twenty grand. Not quite but it's a start. You can pay me the rest later. Hurry up."

Mick wanted to get Enzio gone as soon as possible. He went up on deck and untied the lanyard and lifted the life raft from its cradle. Back in the cockpit, he held the canister out to Enzio but Enzio waved at him with the gun and Mick put the canister in the stern of the speedboat.

"There, are you satisfied? Now let's get Mrs. Lu on board Seagram and you get the hell out of here." Mrs. Lu struggled to sit up but the tape binding her arms in place prevented any movement.

"First," Enzio said, "untie the lines and then I'll give you the woman. I don't trust you as far as I could throw you Brese. Untie the lines first."

Mick looked at the gun pointing at him and tried to figure a way around the problem. He didn't trust Enzio any more than Enzio trusted him. He untied the bow line and took hold of the stern line.

"I'm not untying this one until you bring Mrs. Lu over to the rail where I can reach her."

It was a standoff. Nothing was going to happen until they both reached a mutual point of agreement. Enzio went forward and picked Mrs. Lu up off the floor. She grimaced as her bleeding swollen finger was jostled. With her legs being bound, she could only hop and each hop caused her finger to throb. Enzio wrapped his arms around her and picked her up and carried her to just outside of Mick's reach.

Enzio then did what Enzio was best at. He went back on his word. He put the gun to Mrs. Lu's head and cocked the trigger.

"Untie the boat Mr. Brese. Right now or I shoot."

Mick felt like all the wind had gone out of his sails. It appeared that Claire was right after all. Enzio would get the money and then kill

Mrs. Lu. There didn't appear to be any way out. He had to untie the boat to at least buy some more time. He slipped the knot and still holding the line, stood up.

"Let go of the line Brese and push us off and step back into the cockpit. Do it."

Mick let the line go and gave the speedboat a little shove away. Enzio edged backwards until he bumped up against the helm seat. He pushed Mrs. Lu to the floor, still pointing the gun at her head. Enzio's eyes were darting back and forth between Mrs. Lu and Mick. He sat down at the helm. They were now far enough away that he felt it was safe to turn and get the engine started. As he turned, Mick took the short run available to him and leapt across the gap between the boats. It was almost too far but he managed to hit the boat, mostly in the water, his arms grabbing over the gunwale. He started to scramble over the side just as Enzio got the engine fired up. Mick was at the point where he would be able to roll into the boat when Enzio pointed the gun at Mick's head and pulled the trigger. At the same time, the boat already being in gear and at full throttle, leapt ahead. Fortunately for Mick, he didn't have enough purchase on the slippery fiberglass and fell into the water, Enzio's bullet only plowing a deep crease in his scalp.

The water was cold but Mick's blood boiled as he swam back to Seagram clutching his throbbing head.

32 VAN NO GO

After getting Mr. Xun and Morris into the doctor's care Van hung around long enough to get a rundown of their condition which he passed along to Claire. Since he was already in the neighborhood, he stopped off at the burn unit for a brief visit with Claire's friend Eddy before heading out to continue searching for Enzio. The hallways had the stink of charred flesh or at least it seemed that way to Van. As big and macho as he was, Van was just plain squeamish about hospitals and this visit couldn't be over fast enough. As he searched for Eddy's room, walking along the harshly lit hallways, he got little glimpses through the doorways which made him feel queasy. Nurses were washing burned people on strange steel mesh stretchers, bathing the blackened flesh and doing other assorted medieval looking procedures. Van was ready to give up when he finally came to the room he was looking for.

It took him a moment to summon up his courage to enter the room but Eddy spotted him in the hallway and gave a little nod of his head in recognition. As Van approached Eddy's bed, he realized just how terrible the damage was. Up close, he could see the depth of the burns on the hands and chest and face. The worst part was seeing Eddy trying not to show the extent of the pain. Van was sure that he himself would be crying like a baby. This was going to have to be a short visit or he would lose both his breakfast and his composure.

He decided that humor would be the best tack to take. "Eddy, you always did have a way with the women. Now you've got two babes waiting on you hand and foot." He winked at Eddy and got a pained smile in return. "I can't stay long Eddy. I've got to get back out there looking for Enzio. I just came from Ruxton Island and brought Mr. Xun and Morris in to a doctor friend of mine. He's going to take good care of them. They're going to be just fine." He felt a little awkward talking about these things in front of the two nurses. "Umm, maybe I could have a word in private with my friend, ladies." The nurses decided that they could use the time to go have a smoke break and happily headed out the door.

Eddy took a deep breath and opened his mouth to talk. A wheezy scratchy voice came out. "Thanks very much Van. Just tell me what's happening."

"Oh. Well, like I said, I brought Mr. Xun and Morris in. Unfortunately Mrs. Lu is still with Enzio. Claire is out looking in her airplane and Mick is coming over in your boat apparently. So, I've got to get back out there. We're going to find the bastard, Eddy I promise you that. You going to be okay? Is there anything I can do for you?"

"Just get out there and stop Enzio. Please tell Claire and Mick that I'm sorry that I dragged them into my mess." He began to tear up and he looked like he was going to be unable to speak but after a moment he continued. "I'll be okay. A little body work and a massage and I'll be good as new."

He closed his eyes. He looked like he didn't have any energy left. One of the nurses came back in the room and looked around Van's large body. She quietly suggested that Van leave as "Mr. Wainwright looks like he's had enough visiting for now." Van backed out of the room and then sprinted down the hall; looking for a bathroom or some place he could huck his cookies.

It wasn't until he was back out in the fresh air that he began to get his stomach back under control. He blew fiercely out through his nose to try to clear out the stink from the hospital. He pushed his Harley extra hard trying to turbo charge the air into his system but it wasn't until he was back on the Van Go and heading out into the Strait of Juan De Fuca that he finally felt he could breathe clear again.

As he roared along, he tuned into the weather station on the radio. They were calling for increasing cloud and wind and precipitation. This was something new and would certainly mean that Claire would have to be even more careful than usual in that little flying machine of hers.

As Van rounded Staines Point on the southern tip of the Trial Islands, he took a look behind him and saw a long dark mass of clouds moving in from the west. It seemed possible that Environment Canada might be right for a change. He leaned on the throttle and in short order, only the last couple of feet of hull were still in the water, a big rooster tail following close behind.

Twenty minutes into the trip, as the Van Go came even with Gooch Island; things suddenly came apart. Since there was so little hull in the water, the submerged log had no effect on the hull of the boat but the propeller, spinning at high speed, carved fast and deep into the top of the three foot diameter deadhead.

Deadheads are a part of boating life on the west coast. Essentially water logged tree trunks floating vertically in the ocean just below the surface they are difficult to see at the best of times and impossible to see when you're traveling at seventy miles per hour. The good news for Van was that the hull was not punctured. The bad news was that the propeller sheered off with one of the three blades buried deep in the deadhead. Fortunately, Van was seated and holding on to the wheel or he would have been thrown right through the windshield from the sudden deceleration. As it was, the Van Go carried on for another several boat lengths before settling into the water with a big splash. The engine, freed from the load of the propeller, red lined immediately forcing Van to hit the kill switch.

"Shit, this is another fine kettle of fish." Van stood up with his hands on his hips and looked astern where he could see the very top surface of the deadhead bobbing up and down with the waves. His attention drifted to the dark band of clouds heading his way. It didn't look good. He pulled out his cell phone and started calling for a tow. Then he dialed Claire's number to tell her he wouldn't be in on the search for Enzio.

33 NEW FRIENDS

Mick tossed his goggles and snorkel onto the swim grid and stood on the last rung of the boarding ladder trying to catch his breath. He was not making much progress, even after four trips under the hull of Seagram to cut away Enzio's tow line, snarled around the propeller shaft. At this rate of speed, it was going to take the rest of the day to cut the line free. There wasn't enough wind to sail the boat and have any chance of catching up to Enzio. He desperately needed some scuba gear.

Mick pulled his weary body up to sit on the swim grid with his feet dangling in the water. He kicked the water with his foot. Frustration had set in after his first dive. Enzio was getting away and Mick didn't want to imagine what was going to happen to Mrs. Lu. Now that Enzio had the money he didn't need to keep her alive and the fact that he had shot at Mick was evidence enough that Enzio would do anything to escape and get his load of dope. Mick shuddered, not from the cold but from the sudden realization that Enzio had nearly killed him. That certainly put a lot of things into perspective. Nothing like nearly getting killed to make you realize how precious life is and to wonder about priorities. There was a lot to think about. But he was going to think about that later. First, the rope on the propeller shaft had to be dealt with.

Blood still dripped down the side of his face from the bullet wound in his scalp. He had managed to stop a lot of the blood flow by using a styptic pencil that he had in his first aid kit. It was normally used for small cuts, like you might get from shaving but he had laid the whole pencil against the long gash in his head and kept it there until the bleeding stopped, gritting his teeth against the pain. But diving under the boat had washed the alum away from the wound and it was bleeding freely again. He was glad there weren't any sharks in these cold waters.

Small drops of rain began to pepper down around him. Looking up, Mick could see a long line of dark clouds progressing quickly from west to east. The sun was dodging in and out of the increasing clouds and the wind was picking up.

The sound of an approaching boat motor attracted his attention and his gaze was met with the soulful eyes of a big beautiful redhead. An Irish Setter was perched in the bow of a fine looking lapstrake dingy. In the stern, steering a little British Seagull engine, sat an elderly gentleman with a briar pipe sticking out from one corner of his mouth.

The dingy stopped a couple of feet from the stern of Seagram and the elder mariner simply sat there puffing on his pipe. The dog sat back on his haunches on the front seat with his tongue hanging out and looked at Mick.

"Morning," Mick said conversationally. "You two have a nice looking little boat."

"Yup. Built her myself. I've been watching you from my deck." He gestured with his pipe towards a cabin on the hillside, not far from the ferry landing. "Saw that fellow get his tow rope under your boat. Kind of a sneaky way of slowing you down but clever."

Clever. Yes, that was Enzio. A clever son of a bitch. The dog shifted position, moving to the middle of the dinghy but still keeping an eye on Mick.

"That's a nasty looking bullet wound in your noggin. You might want to get some professional attention for that. You making much headway cutting the line from your prop shaft?" The old boy seemed to know exactly what was going on.

"You can see pretty good from your deck."

A nod. "Yup. I've got a nice telescope on a tripod. Helps me keep tabs on the goings on in the harbor here. See some real interesting things. Thought I was going to be bored stiff when I retired but I could write books about what I see with that telescope. I saw you give that fellow a big pile of money and he took off with the Chinese woman he had taped up. You tried your best but he still managed to get away. You're lucky to be alive."

Getting There

Mick was glad he hadn't been sitting around picking his nose. This guy could see everything.

Pulling his pipe from his mouth, he said, "Know what I think?"

Mick didn't know. "No, can't say that I do but I'm going to have to get busy making another dive. I've got to get that line cut free so I can get going."

The old man leaned forward. "You need something better than that damned snorkel if you're ever going to get that line off." He pointed down to the bottom of his dingy where a duffel bag lay. "What you need is a scuba tank. I could tell that as soon as you started diving. You can't do much with just a snorkel. Wasting your time."

Mick got a rush of hope. Could it be possible that this fellow had what Mick so badly needed?

Pulling open the mouth of the duffle bag, the man reached in and dragged out a single cylinder scuba tank. Still leaning over, he turned his head and looked at Mick.

"This something that might be helpful to you?"

Mick jumped up and did a little dance of joy on the swim grid of Seagram. The dog stood up and barked, tail wagging wildly.

"You must have been reading my mind Mister. What's your name by the way? I'm Mick Brese."

"Pleased to meet you Mick. Abner Simmons is my name and my first mate here is Barkley. Barkley and I figured that you might need some help, so here we are."

Hearing his name, Barkley put his paws on the gunwale of the little dinghy, leaning towards Mick. He allowed Mick to scratch him behind his big floppy ears. Abner pulled the scuba tank out of the bag along with a weight belt and a pair of flippers. He began passing them over to Mick.

"You ever used a scuba tank before? There was a time when I could have done the job for you but I've got health issues now."

Mick nodded. He had taken a course at a pool in Richmond but hadn't ever been in the ocean with a scuba tank. It looked like today was the day. He went through the checklist in his memory to get ready and verified everything with Abner. He put the tank on and cinched the weight belt around his waist. Flippers on his feet, mask on, he was ready to go. He grabbed the big Gerber knife that he had been using to cut the line and sat down on the swim grid one more time.

"Me and Barkley will stay right here and keep an eye on things Mick." Barkley wagged his tail again.

"Thanks Abner. Now that I can breathe down there, I think it should go a heck of a lot faster. See you in a bit." He put the mouthpiece in and pulled his goggles down and slid into the water. As soon as he went under, he knew it was going to be a fast process. He wasn't diving so deep that light was an issue. With the weight belt, he was able to control his depth so much easier. In just a few minutes, he had cut away most of the snarl of line. It took a bit of pulling and careful cutting to clear the last of line from the bearing in the support strut. Then he was done. As usual, success was much easier with the proper tools for the job.

He surfaced to find Abner leaning back in his little dinghy puffing away on his pipe, Barkley lying with his head on Abner's lap. They looked relaxed and happy. Mick climbed up on the swim grid and began removing the gear.

"Well, how'd it go Mick? Get the job done?"

"All done Abner. All thanks to you. And Barkley of course. I don't know how I can repay you."

"Nuts to that Mick. Don't you worry. Barkley and I don't have a lot to do, so we're really quite happy to be useful. What's your plan now?"

"I've got to try to find out where Enzio went. That's the guy you saw. I'm not worried about the money he took but he's more than likely going to do harm to the woman."

"The Chinese woman someone special to you?" Abner looked like he already knew the answer.

Mick hesitated. "Yup. And she might get even more important in the future."

Abner looked satisfied with the answer. "There are too many guys like Enzio in the world. Someone needs to put a stop to them. Barkley and I don't have much to do today. If you need a couple of crewmates, we'd be happy to tag along. Unless you don't have room for us of course."

"You're more than welcome to come along. I have to warn you though, this Enzio guy is dangerous. He's got a gun and he's not afraid to use it."

"I saw that Mick. I'm a retired cop, so I know how to take care of myself and Barkley's got a few weapons of his own. We'd be real pleased to lend a hand."

Mick was happy to hear about the retired cop part. Sensible experienced help would be more than welcome.

Getting There

"What are we waiting for? Let's get a move on."

Barkley sensed that new orders had just come in and barked and wagged his approval. Abner secured the little engine and passed the bag for the diving gear to Mick. The oars were already strapped to the seats and Abner and Barkley transferred to the big sailboat while Mick tied the dinghy in towing position. Mick went down below and put dry clothes on and grabbed his watch cap and some sterile gauze. He put the gauze against the wound on his head and put the watch cap over it. That would help keep the bleeding under control until he had a chance to tend to the wound better.

Starting the diesel engine felt good to Mick. He had been thinking it would be a long time before he would be ready to go but Abner's equipment had saved the day. He showed his new first mate how to put the engine in gear and ran forward to bring in the anchor.

The rain was still tentative but the sky was darkening. The wind was light so Mick didn't bother with the sails. They motored out of Montague, two men and a dog in search of that bastard Enzio. Abner stood at the wheel and seemed to know how to handle the boat. Mick picked up the cell phone and punched up Claire's number. She answered on the third ring. Judging from the background noise, she was flying again.

"Claire, it's Mick. I'm just heading out of Montague Harbor. I hate to admit it but you were right. Enzio took the money and still has your mother. I tried my best to stop him but…" He was at a loss for words to explain how Enzio had outsmarted him. It wasn't easy to admit he'd been duped.

"Hello Mick. I understand. Don't feel bad. Enzio is a horrible man and you are the opposite. It is easy for him to trick you and I am willing to bet that you are not the first person he's tricked." Mick was amazed at how well she seemed to be handling the news. "I imagine that he's keeping my mother as insurance to protect himself. He knows we have to be careful as long as he has her. I just got back in the air after refueling and servicing my airplane. Van's boat is out of commission and it's up to you and me to find Enzio."

"Okay Claire. From the direction that Enzio was going when he left about an hour ago, he was heading east, maybe towards Saturna. I'm thinking that I'll head in that direction and wait for your report. You can spot him easier than I can. The problem is that there's some nasty weather moving our way, so we've got to find him soon."

'Yes, I saw those clouds. I had the same idea and I'm over Saturna Island right now. I'm just about to Narvaez Bay. It's really secluded..."

Suddenly, Mick felt like he had lost the cell connection with Claire. "Claire. Can you hear me? Claire?" Nothing. He looked down at the screen on his cell phone and saw that the call had ended and then the phone began ringing.

"Claire?"

"Mick, I've spotted him. He's in Narvaez, rafted up next to another boat. There's nobody on the speedboat that I can see. I'm going down to take a look."

Mick looked towards Saturna in the hopes of being able to see Claire's little airplane but the tall peak of Mount Warburton Pike was blocking the view.

"Claire, you be careful. I'm heading in that direction now. We'll be there as fast as we can. Keep us informed, okay?"

"Roger on that Mick. I've got to go now. I've got a little surprise for Enzio and I've got to concentrate on what I'm doing. See you soon."

"Claire, I'm sorry I wasn't able to get your mother."

"I know you are Mick. I'm sorry too but we'll get her soon. I'm sure of it. See you when you get here." She hung up.

Mick put the phone down and explained to Abner where they were headed. Abner pointed the big boat in the right direction and Mick pushed the throttle forward to its stop and went down below to tend to his head wound and to take some aspirin. He felt real relief now that they knew where Enzio was. Now they were going to get that bastard.

34 FINDING THE TARGET

Enzio was a happy camper. Everything was going according to plan. He had the money. He still had Mrs. Lu who was a good insurance policy. He was on his way to pick up the dope. All was well with the world.

Seeing the money had been like a drug. After all this time, seeing the money again had put him in a wonderful mood. Talk about a pick-me-up. The sad part of all this was that he was going to have to turn most of the money over to the guy on the dope boat. He'd do his best to screw the guy whatever way he could but he couldn't think of a way just yet.

Getting to Narvaez Bay didn't take long. Mrs. Lu was still lying on the bottom of the boat, not saying anything. What was there to say? She was up shit creek without a paddle. Not many options left except to keep her mouth shut and hope for the best. She had rolled over on her side so that she didn't have to look at her captor. As Enzio rounded the eastern end of the island, he could see all the way up to the head of the bay. One boat, a long low cabin cruiser was anchored there. Enzio throttled back and sedately motored towards the cabin cruiser. It looked like the boat that Fairy Godmother had described to him.

As he approached the boat, a lone man came up on deck with binoculars looking in Enzio's direction. Apparently the man had Enzio's description and waved him over. Enzio didn't like the fact that the guy looked as big as Andre the Giant. That was going to make it more difficult to pull a fast one. Maybe big meant dumb. Always the optimist Enzio was.

As Enzio pulled alongside, the big guy leaned out and politely asked, "Mr. Enzio?"

Enzio nodded. He kept one foot on Mrs. Lu to make sure that she stayed out of sight. It would be hard to explain his creative use of duct tape if this were an innocent boater though this guy knew his name so he wasn't just out here for the fresh air.

"Yeah, that's me. You got a name?"

"Lars. Lars Thorson. I'd like to suggest that you tie up alongside and bring the money onboard so that I can take a look at it while you examine the merchandise I have for you down below. When we're both satisfied, we can trade boats and conclude our transaction. Sound OK to you?"

Enzio started to get the impression that this guy was not a dummy. He spoke well and seemed to have a brain between his ears. Too bad. He shrugged. "Yeah, that's fine with me. Let's just do it."

Narvaez Bay is a quiet place although it is exposed to winds from the southeast. Because of the heavy forest and the fact that there are no houses around the bay, this was a dandy spot for doing business. Enzio wanted to get this transaction done with so he could get on his way before the weather crapped out completely. On the way from Montague Harbor, he had noticed the weather front approaching rapidly and already the rain and wind were increasing.

Enzio tied up to the cruiser. He used the duct tape across Mrs. Lu's chest as a handle and stood her up. If Lars was curious about the woman, he did a good job of not showing it. She was passed across to the cruiser like so much cargo and her whimpers of pain from her damaged pinky were ignored by both men. She was pushed down the two steps into the cabin and told to sit and shut up. As she was so securely bound, she had no other choice but to follow orders.

Enzio went back to the speedboat and passed Lars the two life raft canisters. It was difficult to tell which one was which except that the tape had been removed from one of the two. Enzio had his back to Lars and pulled his gun out of his jacket pocket thinking that he would get the drop on the big man. He turned and pointed the gun at Lars only to find himself staring right down the barrel of an even larger gun. A standoff. Mutually assured destruction.

"What," Enzio said looking hurt, "You don't trust me?"

"Just as much as you don't trust me I guess," Lars said with a smirk.

At that moment, a loud noise and a sudden flash of color roared low across the top of the two boats. Both men, caught by surprise, dropped to their knees and ducked their heads. They looked like a couple of guys searching for a lost contact lens on the cockpit floor.

"What the hell was that?" Lars was the first to stick his head up for a look around. Enzio followed suit and the two stood and craned their necks around the sides of the cruisers cabin to see where the noisy object had gone. Both of them had their guns at the ready.

Claire in her little ultralight was climbing steeply, looking back over her shoulder at the two boats together in the middle of the bay. She banked sharply in a rough approximation of an Immelman turn and began diving back towards the boats. She grabbed one of the bricks from the passenger seat and held it at the ready.

While she had been talking to Mick on the cell phone, she had searched for Enzio along the length of Saturna where she was able to see both sides of the island. As luck would have it, as she came in from the west, over the land and down into Narvaez Bay she spotted the two boats rafted together. She could see Enzio and another man in the cockpit of the larger boat but could not see her mother which caused her much concern. Was she down below in the cruiser? Claire prayed for this to be the case. The only other option was too grim to consider. She didn't know who the other man was but he had to be involved in whatever deal Enzio needed the money for. Claire had a strong feeling that whoever he was, he was on the wrong side of the law.

As she dove down towards the boats for the second run, she tried to remember her winning techniques from the flour bombing contest at the Victoria Air Show. She guessed that the brick weighed more than the bag of flour. What would that do to the trajectory? She was sure that she wouldn't get too many good opportunities to catch the boat when it wasn't moving so there wasn't much time for practice. Maybe she could cause enough damage to stop Enzio from leaving or at least slow him down until Mick got there.

She remembered the fighter pilots adage, not to shoot until you saw the whites of their eyes. In this case, she figured that was good advice. She pushed forward on the stick as she came within range and just as she crossed an imaginary point about one boat length in front of the cruiser, she let the brick go. She pulled back on the stick at the same time as she turned her head to follow the brick. It struck the middle of the cabin roof and bounced off into the bay, not making much of a dent. Seeing Enzio and the other man run into each other trying to get out of the way of her bomb was the only good to come of her first attempt. Plus she had gained some tactical knowledge. As she began her turn for her next run, she reached over and grabbed another brick. One last try before going for the big guns.

This run was from the other direction, from the stern towards the bow, so it would make aiming for the cockpit a little easier. As she lined up for her run, she could see the two men, both of them down on their knees and pointing at her. Little flashes of light told her they were shooting at her. That was not good news but there was no turning back now.

This time when she let the brick go, she decided to stay low, not pulling up after dropping her load. She took a quick look behind her but couldn't see where the brick landed. A hole suddenly appeared in the fabric of the wing just to the left of the center section. It was entirely too close for comfort. Claire realized that each bombing run was increasing the odds of taking a bullet in a critical location.

She continued to stay low until she was sure that she was out of range and then climbed steeply, circling around to the left. The wing fabric was holding and it appeared that the bullet hole was not going to be a problem. As she came even with the cruiser, she could see Enzio pointing his gun at her, not shooting, just tracking her waiting for another chance. She squinted, trying to make out what had happened to the other man when she finally spotted him lying on his back on the floor of the cockpit with a large dark stain spreading around his head. She realized that she had scored a direct hit and she was suddenly dizzy with the thought of having hurt the man. But this was war. Enzio had to be stopped. He had kidnapped her father and mother and Morris. He had caused horrible harm to Eddy. He had burned Mick's boat. He had to be stopped.

She reached over to the passenger seat and lifted the folding anchor into her lap. It was heavier than the brick. Folded up it was about a foot and a half long and only about three inches in diameter. It was going to drop like a missile.

Claire was gun shy now. She wanted a little more height for protection. As she turned onto final approach, she could see Enzio had started the engine and had cast off from the speedboat. He was

Getting There

standing at the wheel in the front of the cockpit looking back and forth between her and the boats course. Now she was dealing with a moving target. This was uncharted territory for her. If she slowed down it might give her a little more time to get a feel for the right moment to release her weapon. Of course that would make her an easier target for Enzio too.

The rain had increased considerably and without any windshield the raindrops were like little bullets striking any exposed skin. It hurt like hell. She didn't want to think what a real bullet might feel like. The wind had picked up too and she noticed that she was crabbing through the air trying to stay in line with her target. It would be a big help to have another person sitting beside her to drop the anchor but she was glad that she wasn't exposing anyone else to the risk.

As she got into position behind Enzio, she could see that he had turned and was firing at her now. There wasn't time to waste. She pushed the throttle forward and held the anchor at the ready. She was about a hundred feet up and she had to factor the altitude, the wind, the boat's speed and her own speed and fly the airplane at the same time. Complicated stuff but this was the time to make her namesake proud. Using her experience and a lot of guess work, she let the anchor go and overtook the cruiser. She looked down between the seats and saw Enzio, arm pointed straight up at her, a flash coming from the barrel of his gun. At almost the same moment, she saw her folding anchor strike the deck just a short distance from Enzio's feet and disappear like a bunker busting bomb right through the deck. At the same moment, the bullet from Enzio's gun penetrated through the oil pan on the Rotax engine of her airplane. The bullet continued on a little bit further, striking a connecting rod on one of the pistons.

Claire turned her head in time to see a spray of oil spew out of the engine and the propeller, normally a whirling invisible disc, come to a grinding halt. The loss of power and the fact that she was flying directly into the wind caused her to lose speed quickly. She pushed the nose down and was aiming for a landing spot just to one side of Enzio's course when another of Enzio's bullets struck her in the right thigh. The pain and shock caused her to jerk the stick to the left and with so little altitude; she and her little airplane went into the trees along the north side of the bay. Branches whipped her face and clawed at the wings and dragged her down.

Enzio was delighted. Ecstatic. He'd never shot an airplane down before. How often did you get a chance like that? But the bitch had done him a big favor. She had killed Lars and now Enzio not only had the dope, but he had the money too, thank you very much. He looked to see what had happened with the girl and the airplane but she was deep in the trees and he wasn't about to stick around and check on her. It didn't look like she was going to get out of that one. She was probably on her way to meet her ancestors. Tough shit.

It was time for a damage assessment. Lars had to go, pronto. The old cruiser didn't have an autopilot but it seemed to be well balanced and steered herself when he let the wheel go. At least long enough to get rid of the body. He bent down and grabbed Lars by the feet. He didn't want to work from the head end of the body. Judging from the amount of blood and other material on the cockpit floor, Lars wasn't' going to be looking so good. He cursed the man for being so big. Bastard could have gone on a diet and made this a little easier. He dragged the body over to the rail and with a great deal of huffing and puffing and swearing managed to finally get enough leverage to tip the body into the ocean. Big splash. Good riddance.

The waters off the tip of Saturna Island are called Boundary Pass for good reason. The boundary between the United States and Canada runs through the area and Enzio did not want to enter American waters just yet. He had to clean up the boat first and get himself organized. His plan was to head out through the Strait of Juan de Fuca and run down the coast of Washington State to his old drop off point in La Push. He was pleased with himself for getting the life raft from Brese's boat. Being out in the ocean in this old cruiser would be a lot safer with a life raft aboard.

Periodically checking on his course, he found a bucket and began sluicing water on the cockpit floor. He noticed that the water was not only running out through the scuppers of the cockpit but was disappearing down through a jagged hole in the wooden floor that he hadn't noticed before. This was cause for concern. He peered down the hole but couldn't see anything. It was too dark. He suddenly realized that this hole might have been caused by something dropped by the girl from the airplane. He had been so busy shooting at her that he hadn't noticed her making another drop. Since he had found only one brick, the one that had struck Lars, he now realized that she must have dropped something else. But what?

Getting There

Leaving the boat to steer itself, he went down below into the cabin. Mrs. Lu was sitting on the settee looking very distressed.

"What?" Enzio was busy worrying about the hole in the boat and was not concerned with the woman's feelings. That he had just shot her daughter out of the sky worried him not one bit. So what? She'd been dropping bricks on them for Christ's sake. It was self defense as far as Enzio thought.

Dropping to his knees on the cabin floor, Enzio stuck his finger into a ring pull on a floorboard and lifted it up. "Holy shit, we've got a problem here" he exclaimed out loud. There was six inches of water sloshing back and forth with the motion of the boat. He dropped the floorboard and turned to the electrical panel and searched for a switch for the bilge pump. There had to be a bilge pump. Enzio was freaking out. The last thing he needed was to sink and lose his valuable load of marijuana.

The electrical panel was a simple affair and it only took a moment to find the switch. It was already in the on position meaning that there had to be a float switch somewhere that automatically turned the bilge pump on when water rose above a certain level. He was pretty sure that there was enough water to trigger the automatic switch, so either the switch was jammed or the water was coming in faster than the bilge pump could get rid of it. He hoped for the former rather than the latter. But where was the float switch?

He looked out the forward windows and was shocked to see the sky completely covered in dark looking clouds and the rain coming down hard. The sea had built up quickly along with the wind. "Great. A storm, the boat's sinking and I just barely got going. What next?" Enzio was sorry as soon as he said it. He knocked on wood.

It was logical that there had to be access to the engine and the area below the cockpit floor and it only took a moment to find it. The quarter berth on the port side had a door that opened and let him look at the area in question. As soon as he turned on the light for the engine room, he saw the cause of the problem and the solution. Whatever the girl had dropped on her last pass had gone through the relatively thin wood of the cockpit floor and had enough force to go right through the hull as well. The water was spouting in through a hole in the hull. Enzio grabbed a blanket from the quarter berth and jammed it into the hole. It took a little work to get the blanket stuffed into the hole and staying put but he succeeded. He hoped it would stay until he got the boat down south. He crossed his fingers.

Back in the main cabin, he looked under the floorboards again and saw that the water was now receding. That was better. One less thing to worry about.

Mrs. Lu took the opportunity to ask Enzio to remove the duct tape from her arms and legs. She had to go to the bathroom and she didn't want him to have to help her.

"I've got a gun and you know I'll use it if you piss me off. Understand?"

She nodded. "I can make us some food and make myself useful and I won't do anything stupid. I don't want to get hurt anymore."

Enzio looked at her for a moment and then began taking the tape off. It was difficult to unwrap, so he pulled out his pocket knife and simply cut the tape leaving it stuck on her clothes but freeing her arms and legs. He went back on deck and headed the boat towards Stuart Island where he would then turn towards his ultimate destination. The weather had changed so fast that he was feeling great comfort in knowing that they had a life raft onboard if they should get into trouble. Jesus, what a day it had been so far. And it wasn't over yet.

35 ROUGH WEATHER

The noise from Claire's airplane crashing through the trees died down leaving only the ticking sounds of the engine cooling and the sound of the gasoline trickling out of the broken fuel line. Birds had been startled out of the crash zone and could be heard squawking in the distance. A gray squirrel chattered from its perch on a cedar branch not far away.

The force of the crash had snapped the tubes holding the cockpit in place and the front half of the airplane had actually been folded under so that the seats were upside down. The two white floats had detached, still with enough momentum to carry them another plane length past the crash site. There was not a lot left of the wings and brightly colored fabric was dangling in strips from branches along the crash path. Claire was unconscious, arms hanging straight down, her body still strapped into the seat. The lap portion of the four point harness was pressed tight against her legs, providentially slowing the flow of blood from the gunshot wound in her thigh.

She groaned in pain but did not come around. Fortunately for her, the fuel was not dripping on her or the hot engine. It appeared not to be a threat. The rain was coming down hard but the forest cover was dense enough that it was still relatively dry at the crash site. Claire's cell phone rang. The muted sound came from the pocket of her floater coat. After a short time, the ringing stopped.

Mick closed his cell phone. It was odd that Claire hadn't answered his call. She usually wore her headset while she was flying so that she could talk over the noise of the airplane.

"I don't get it Abner. Claire called earlier while she was flying so I know she's got the phone with her." Abner noted the worried look on Mick's face.

"You know how unreliable cell phone coverage is Mick. We know she spotted Enzio in Narvaez Bay, so she might be down near the water and maybe not getting reception where she is. Call her again in a few minutes."

Abner and Barkley had made themselves right at home on Seagram. Abner was steering the boat, comfortably holding the wheel in one hand and his pipe in the other. He fit right in. Barkley had done an inspection tour of the deck as well as down below and was now sitting on the starboard cockpit seat, tongue hanging out, his long red hair blowing in the wind, happy as could be. From time to time, he would close his mouth and lift his nose into the wind and sniff vigorously, picking up something the humans couldn't smell.

Mick punched the redial button and listened again while Claire's phone rang and rang. Still no answer and Mick could feel a growing knot of anxiety in his chest. She was a good pilot, so he had to trust that she was not in trouble. The weather was a real concern though. The wind had picked up and in Mick's mind had to be above the limit for flying in the little lightweight airplane. Something wasn't adding up.

Mick pointed out the Java Islets to Abner giving him a course to steer that would take them into Boundary Pass where they would turn to port and into Narvaez Bay. As they turned around Monarch Head, they were traveling broadside to the waves and the motion of the boat increased dramatically. They began rolling from side to side and Mick was surprised by how much the seas had picked up in the short time since they had left Montague. Just a little further and they were able to see into Narvaez Bay. Just as Claire had said, a small speedboat was there although it looked as though the boat had washed up on the beach. There was no sign of the cruiser that Claire had mentioned and worse than that, there was no sign of Claire's airplane.

"Maybe in the time it took us to get here, the cruiser took off and Claire is chasing him." Abner was pointing with his pipe towards the south.

Mick nodded, scanning the shoreline with binoculars. "It's a possibility but let's go check out the head of the bay first and see what's going on with the speedboat."

Getting There

Abner turned Seagram and motored deeper into the bay. The motion smoothed out a little as they presented the stern of the boat to the waves. Narvaez Bay is almost a mile and a half long, and it was considerably more sheltered towards the head of the bay. Much quieter. Barkley suddenly snapped his mouth shut and began sniffing the air, his ears pricked forward. He was looking a lot like a bird dog who had smelled game. Abner noticed and gestured to Mick to pay attention.

Barkley stood up and looked back and forth between the woods to the right of the boat and his master. He was clearly excited.

"What, Barkley, what do you smell. Do you smell something?" The dog was whining and ran up on deck to stand by the starboard rail. Eddy had installed netting all along each side between the top wire of the lifelines and the edge of the deck. It was a good method for keeping sails from slipping over the side of the boat and into the water. Barkley stuck his nose through the netting and sniffed towards the shoreline. He ran back to his master. Clearly something was demanding his attention.

What Barkley did next surprised both Mick and Abner. The dog turned away from his master's hand and ran up on the deck and leapt over the lifeline and plunged into the water and began swimming rapidly for shore. It wasn't a long swim. The head of the bay shallowed quickly and Mick had kept to the north side where the water was the deepest.

Mick put the engine in neutral and ran up on deck and let the anchor go. With the forward motion of the boat, the anchor grabbed and slowed them and Seagram turned and stopped, pointing out to the mouth of the bay. They were close enough now to see that the little speedboat was abandoned and pushed up on the gravel beach.

Abner was already in the dinghy getting the little outboard ready. Mick ran back, shut the engine down, untied the dinghy, jumped in and cast them off. The little Seagull engine started on the first pull and Abner gave it full throttle and they headed for where Barkley could be seen scrambling out of the water.

Barkley didn't even stop to shake the water from his long red hair. He disappeared into the woods at full tilt and they could hear him barking and snapping branches as he made his way up the hill through the trees. Not far behind, Mick and Abner ground to a halt on the shingle beach and jumped out. Mick took off while Abner found a branch to tie the dinghy tow line to.

Mick was puzzled. There was nothing to see except trees. The shoreline was steep and it was difficult to catch up to Barkley who was up ahead barking wildly. At the top of a small rise, Mick looked up and spotted some color in the branches. Not the greens and muted oranges of the fir trees and arbutus trees but neon pink and black. His heart sank imagining what he was going to find ahead. He could smell gasoline now and the smell grew stronger as he topped the last rise. There in front of him was Barkley sitting on his haunches, looking up at the wreckage of Claire's once proud little airplane.

Barkley stood on his hind legs and was able to just reach Claire's hand with his long pink tongue. He sat back down and barked again and wagged his tail, waiting for a response. Nothing. The smell of gasoline was intense but the tank had run dry by now. Unless someone threw a match on the forest floor the danger was minimal. Mick could see that Claire was held in her seat by her harness and realized that it would be difficult to support her weight and undo her harness at the same time. He would have to wait until Abner arrived. Meanwhile, he felt for a pulse in her neck. It was there but not strong. Mick could see that the harness was helping to staunch the flow of blood from a nasty looking wound in her thigh.

Mick looked down the hill and could see Abner toiling up the last steep stretch. Turning back to Claire, he was surprised when her eyes opened. She looked up, which in this case was down. She looked at Barkley and then turned her gaze on Mick.

"I didn't know you had a dog. Is it a boy or a girl?" It was good to hear her talking. Barkley barked and Claire gave a little jerk back in surprise.

"Oh. Hello to you too doggie. Mick, why didn't you introduce us?" She was frowning as if a little peeved that this formality had not been dealt with.

"This is Barkley. Barkley," he said, gesturing with his hand to make the introductions, "this is Claire. How are you feeling Claire?"

She looked at him with a puzzled look on her face. "I'm fine Mick. How are you doing?" Clearly, she didn't have all her faculties together but at least she was conscious now. Abner came puffing up over the crest of the hill and stopped, hands on his knees to catch his breath.

Not wanting to be accused of forgetting formalities again, Mick made the introductions.

"Claire, this is Abner a friend of mine. Abner, this is Claire." Abner looked up and extended his hand, which Claire shook. It was a very surreal situation.

"Abner, it's going to take the two of us to get Claire down. Her harness is holding her in but she'll take a nasty fall if we aren't careful. We don't know what kind of injuries she has, so we're going to have to try to go slow."

The two of them got into position, Mick under Claire, bracing her as best he could while Abner got ready to release her harness. Mick's face was close to Claire's and she made little kissing motions with her lips. Mick ignored her and on his nod, Abner pulled the locking lever on the center of the harness and eased the four sections apart. Mick took her weight and slowly eased her down, laying her outside of the circle of gasoline soaked ground. Barkley was quick to move where he could get a couple of licks in on Claire's face. She giggled.

The wound on her leg began to ooze as the blood began to circulate again. Mick pulled off his belt and put it around her thigh above the wound. It didn't take much tension to slow the flow of blood. He knelt down beside Claire and asked her if she had any pain or if she was able to move her extremities. Apparently, the bullet wound and a slight concussion were her only problems.

Lying on her back, looking up, Claire could see the airplane above her.

"Oh my gosh Mick, my airplane is a mess." She began crying, the tears mixing with the rain on her face. One would have thought that she would be more concerned with the bullet hole in her leg or the fact that she had just narrowly escaped death but her broken airplane seemed to be the most important thing.

"Claire, we're going to have to get you to a doctor. I think there must be a road close by. If we can find someone with a car, we can take you down to Lyall Harbor and maybe get a chopper to take you to the hospital."

Claire grabbed him by the arm and pulled him close. She had a surprisingly strong grip. "No. No Mick. There's no time for that. We've got to stop Enzio. He's got my mother and he's getting away. We've got to follow him in your boat. He's got a slow cruiser and your boat can catch up to him but we've got to get going. I'll be fine. Let's go."

She tried to get into a sitting position but Mick pushed her back down. "Claire, listen to me. You've got a bad wound on your leg. You've got a concussion. Those are two things we know for sure but there could be other things wrong with you. We've got to get you to a doctor. Let's notify the police and the coast guard and they can go after Enzio. You need a doctor."

She was adamant. Shaking her head from side to side. "No Mick, we have to finish this ourselves. You told me that Enzio said not to get the police involved. We have to catch up to Enzio on our own. Please, I'm begging you Mick. For me, for my mother, I'm begging you." She was crying again and clutching his arm. It was heartbreaking but common sense dictated that they should get medical help and let the authorities take over.

Claire's phone began ringing in her pocket again. Barkley woofed and put his nose close to the sound. Claire released her grip on Mick and reached into her pocket and pulled out the phone. As she opened it, she heard a beep indicating low battery power and then her mother's voice in a low whisper.

"Claire, its mummy. I'm fine but I don't have much time to talk. Enzio is outside steering the boat and idiot that he is, he left his phone inside. We're heading towards Victoria. Right now we're in between Moresby and Stuart Islands. There's a hole in the bottom of the boat but Enzio did something to slow down the leak. We're not going very fast because the weather's getting worse and Enzio is worried that the boat…" At that moment the battery died on Claire's phone.

"Mother. Mother." Claire was shouting into the dead phone. She snapped it shut.

"Enzio is heading south. I'd be willing to bet he's going to head down the coast to try to peddle his dope in the States."

Abner had been busy finding a couple of long stout poles from the fallen wood around the forest floor. Kneeling nearby, he had removed his coat and zipped it up and slid the poles inside it. Mick got the idea and shucked off his coat as well. Soon, they had a serviceable stretcher.

"Claire, we're going to get you on the stretcher and then we're going to get you down to the beach. It's not going to be easy because the hill is steep. Are you up for it?"

In reply, she scooted over and got herself in position on the stretcher.

"Well, I'm ready, what are we waiting for. Let's go." She sounded strong but they both wondered if she was going to be strong enough for the bumpy ride down the hill.

She was, although the trip tested all three of them and they were exhausted by the time they got to the beach. Barkley had led the way, enjoying himself immensely chasing squirrels and birds as Mick and Abner labored down the hill. It was Abner who summed it up as they stood on the beach, mopping sweat from their flushed faces.

"Well, that was fun. I'm glad you don't weigh more than you do though. I'd probably need the stretcher now myself if you did."

Claire's face was pale and she looked exhausted. It was easy to see that the trip had been very painful for her. They had had to adjust the tourniquet several times to keep her leg wound under control. They got her into the dinghy, the four of them bringing the gunwale almost to water level as they made their way out to Seagram. Getting her onboard and situated down below was easy in comparison to the journey down the hill. Mick showed Abner where the first aid supplies were and went on deck to get the anchor up and get under way. They knew where Enzio was but would they be able to catch up with him and what was going to happen when they did?

As Mick headed out of the bay, he could see the large seas ahead in Boundary Passage. It was going to be a rough ride but it would be even rougher for Enzio and Mrs. Lu in the cruiser. Seagram was built for heavy weather but Mick wondered if Enzio had any idea what he was up against in the lightly built coastal cruiser.

36 A LONG NIGHT

David Enzio was worried. He was worried that the boat might sink and that he might lose his ton of marijuana. He was also worried that there were going to be seriously bad repercussions over the death of Lars even though it wasn't his fault. But who was going to believe that a little Chinese girl flying a dinky toy airplane had dropped a brick on Lars head and smashed his brains to pulp before they could finish their transaction. He could imagine trying to explain that to Fairy Godmother. One thing he wasn't worried about was losing his cash. He was going to protect that with every fiber of his being. He was not going to get cheated out of his money again.

After leaving Narvaez Bay and disposing of Lars's body and cleaning up the brains from the cockpit floor, Enzio had decided that it was probably safe enough to transit U.S. waters before making the journey through Juan De Fuca Strait to the open ocean. He had cut in behind San Juan Island and the seas had moderated somewhat. It was five in the afternoon but the rain and clouds made it seem much later. Darkness was going to come early tonight which was just fine as far as Enzio was concerned. It would be safer to travel in the dark.

It sucked not having an autopilot and Enzio was glad that he had freed Mrs. Lu from the duct tape. With all the wind and rain, he was reluctant to leave the wheel, even for a moment but all he had to do was open the door to the main cabin and she would bring him whatever he needed. He even had her steer the boat while he went to the can where he found his phone laying on the floor at the base of the toilet. It must have fallen out of his pants pocket when he had taken a dump earlier. He was glad that Mrs. Lu hadn't found it.

It was during one of these times away from the wheel that he had checked on his repair on the hole in the hull. He had had to make some adjustments to the blanket he used as a plug as quite a bit of it had gotten pulled out through the hole. He had pulled it back in and secured it better. It wasn't a great fix but what the hell was he supposed to do? He was a businessman, not a boat repairman.

The weather seemed to have moderated quite a bit and after leaving American waters they had made good time. It would have been nice to head in to the Inner Harbor at Victoria and tie up for the night. He could imagine having a pleasant dinner at the Empress, maybe heading uptown to check out a club or two. But it was too risky. He had to use the weather and time to his advantage. Sooner or later, the police were going to get involved no matter what he had told Brese.

Around the time that they were going by Victoria, Enzio's phone rang. Like an idiot, he answered it without thinking.

"It's your Fairy Godmother again. Where's my money asshole?"

So much for pleasantries. Not even so much as a hello, how are you doing? Enzio was at a loss for words. This is what he had hoped he wouldn't have to explain. Why had he answered the phone? Who invented cell phones anyway? He remembered when there wasn't such a thing as a cell phone. Those were the days.

"I'm talking to you Enzio. Where's my money? What happened to Lars? I can't reach him and I'm starting to get a little pissed off."

Enzio decided a balls first approach might be best. "What are you asking me for? I gave him the money and he gives me this crappy boat in return. This thing doesn't even have an autopilot. What's up with that? I thought we were friends."

"David, I doubt if you have any friends at all and what do I care if you don't like the boat. I want my money and I've got a sneaky feeling that you pulled another fast one on me. If you did, I will personally come and shove that boat right up your ass. Think about it."

Despite the cold, Enzio was beginning to sweat. "Look, I left Narvaez Bay around three and Lars was leaving in the other boat. It's a white speedboat with red trim. Nice little thing. Much better than this piece of shit you gave me."

"Yeah, but you've got a ton of bud and the boat, so stop your bitching. I'm going to go out there and look for him and if I don't find him, consider getting some KY jelly baby because I will come looking for you next."

He didn't even say goodbye. He just hung up. Enzio hated impolite people. Jesus, when Fairy Godmother got to Narvaez, he was going to find the boat and no Lars. Enzio's butt began to clench up. He leaned on the throttle a little harder and was rewarded with another couple of RPM's. What he needed was an afterburner. Or a one way ticket to Bolivia.

He also knew that Brese was going to be hot on his tail since he still had the Chinese woman with him. He regretted bringing her along but he had not been able to resist the temptation to cheat Brese in Montague Harbor. It had been worth it at the time. He thought about getting rid of her now but what good would that do? Brese would still be chasing him. Better to keep the woman as a bargaining chip just in case. He needed to press on and get down south in the U.S. where he could get the dope on a vehicle and get it moved across the country. Once that was all taken care of, maybe he could work on placating Fairy Godmother.

The trip out to Cape Flattery was long and stressful. With a little work, Enzio had managed to coax seven knots out of the old tub. Big deal. He wished he still had the Bayliner. Then they would have really been flying. It might have been his imagination what with the darkness and fatigue but it seemed that the weather had worsened again. As they had approached the open ocean, Enzio had grown considerably more nervous. The boat was definitely not designed for open ocean travel. It was old and creaky and the leak didn't make him any more confident. He had the life raft but still, who wanted to abandon ship and get into a rubber raft in the dark? In the midst of a storm too? Not David Enzio, that was for sure.

Enzio was surprised at the amount of traffic in the strait. What were all these people doing up in the middle of the night when they could be home, warm in bed? Assholes. He wondered if any of the boats were looking for him. He hoped not. It would be tough trying to outrun them in this old tub.

Around three in the morning, he was finally able to see the light on Cape Flattery ahead on the left. Jesus, he was tired. It seemed like hours ago when Mrs. Lu had opened the door and pushed a plate of food into his hand and had taken over steering the boat. He had to give her credit. She was tough. Boy, she had been a wildcat in the cabin on the island. Ass kicking China girl. And she didn't whine about her finger. She had found some first aid gear in the cabin and had done a pretty good job of bandaging herself up. He almost felt guilty about doing the vice grip thing on her. Almost.

From time to time through the night, she had brought coffee to him and he was thinking how difficult this trip would have been on his own. Maybe he should keep her for a while. Why not? She wasn't bad looking and she could cook and she was a good fighter and she was a woman. He'd have to think on it.

Cape Flattery got closer and the weather continued to deteriorate. Blasts of wind and rain buffeted the boat. That was bad enough but it was the size of the waves that really had him worried. He had slowed their speed, trying to avoid breaking the bloody boat in half. One wave had punched into their bow almost stopping them dead in the water and then the wave had rolled right up and over the deck, smashing against the cabin windows. Mrs. Lu had been pretty calm up to that point but the big wave had stunned them both and now she looked extremely worried. Not to mention the fact that she was seasick and throwing up frequently.

David Enzio was a fair weather sailor. He preferred the confines of the islands where the seas didn't have the chance to build up into the small mountains that they were facing out here at the mouth of Juan De Fuca. His big concern was what to do once they got out into the open ocean. He wanted to turn south and stick close to shore but given the weather, they would probably have to head out to sea and get some distance from land. The wind was blowing straight at them and that would mean that if they tried to head south, they would be broadside to the waves. If it didn't sink the boat, the motion would be wild and they would certainly be too sick to think straight. It would probably be best to just keep going straight ahead through the rest of the night and hope that the weather would moderate. Once the sea calmed down, they would then be able to head down the coast. If the boat lasted that long.

At some point, before they had spotted Cape Flattery, he had thought about turning around and heading back to Victoria. Then they could just tie the boat up and get some sleep. But when he had attempted to turn the boat they were nearly rolled over. Mrs. Lu had screamed her head off as she had been tossed around in the cabin along with dishes and everything else that was loose. Enzio was so scared that he had been unable to make any sound but he had been screaming inside his head. After nearly losing the battle with the big waves, he got the boat straightened out and heading bow first into the watery mountains once again. His nerves were not quite the same after that. If Brese weren't chasing him, he would have turned back hours ago when it was still possible. Now they were at the point of no return. There was no turning back until the weather moderated. Realizing how precarious their situation was, he made sure that the two canisters that held the money and the life raft were close at hand. Enzio wanted the life raft to be ready in case they needed it. He decided that the next time he had to move some merchandise, he was going to move it by air or by car or carry it on his back if need be. No more boats.

He could see that Mrs. Lu was on her last nerve. He didn't want her falling apart, so he ordered her to get some more coffee made and to clean the boat up. The galley was a mess but she was grateful to have something to do other than watch the white tops of gigantic waves come barreling towards them. She had to admire the way that Enzio was handling himself and the boat. He seemed fearless. She felt like he was going to get them out of this situation. If they could just make it through the night, daylight would surely bring better weather.

Making coffee wasn't an easy thing to do. It was like riding a seesaw. Mrs. Lu was holding on for dear life. One hand for making coffee and one hand for herself. The bow of the boat would rise up on a wave and then crash down into a deep dark trough. Before it could recover, the next wave would hit them and ride up over the decks, smashing against the windows. It was amazing how strong the glass was. Then the boat would shake off the water and rise up on another wave and the whole process would repeat again. Mrs. Lu and David Enzio hoped that the weather would get better and the waves would go away. Dreaming about flat calm water was one thing that they had in common.

37 SEARCHING

Leaving Narvaez Bay, Mick was surprised at the state of the sea. Whitecaps and squalls were now the order of the day. Mick had called down into the cabin to make sure that Claire was secure. Abner had rigged the lee cloth on the port settee and packed a number of pillows around Claire so that she wouldn't get bounced around. Mick was of the mind that they should get her to a doctor rather than risk waiting but Claire would have none of it. She was too worried about her mother and by God she was determined that they were going to catch up to Enzio. She had gotten Abner to plug her phone in to charge in case her mother tried to call back. It was close at her hand.

Mick hoisted the main sail with a reef in it and rolled out the jib part way. The motion eased considerably as they got under sail and Mick shut the engine down. The boat heeled over to starboard and they began picking up speed. This was great sailing weather but it would be hell on Enzio's cruiser. Mick was worried about Mrs. Lu which was funny considering how badly the two of them had gotten along. Right about now Mick would have been happy to have her glare at him.

The boat was sailing itself and Mick asked Abner to take over on deck while he talked to Claire. Down below in the relative quiet of the cabin, he knelt down beside the settee and took Claire's hand in his.

"Claire, how are you doing?"

She looked tired and it was obvious that she was in pain. Abner had been reluctant to give her more than some ibuprofen. He had removed her boots and pants and had done a first rate job of binding up the gunshot wound in her thigh. There was some bleeding but it was under control.

"I'm going to be fine Mick. Thanks for coming to the rescue. It was difficult hanging upside down like that. All the blood went to my head and I kept passing out. I don't think it was a concussion so much as just being upside down. Boy, I really messed up didn't I? And I think I killed a man today. I know they're bad people but..." She began to tear up and Mick put his arms around her and hugged her gently. She felt so small and fragile in his arms. He didn't want her dwelling on bad stuff right now. There was time for that later when she would be stronger.

"Claire, let me look at your eyes for a minute." He got a small pocket flashlight from the first aid kit and checked her pupils. They were equal, round and responsive to the light which was a good sign.

"And I thought you wanted to look deep into my eyes in a loving gaze, Mick." She smiled at him.

"Trust me Claire. I would like nothing more than to gaze into your eyes and a lot more but right now I'm more concerned with your health. Considering how much damage there was to your airplane, I'm amazed you're in one piece. I think you're a pretty lucky girl."

She nodded. "To tell you the truth Mick, that scared me. A lot. I'm going to have to do some serious thinking about whether I want to do any more flying. Maybe I'll take up sailing instead." She smiled at him.

"I'd be happy to be your instructor, Claire. Why don't you try to get some rest now and Abner and I will keep an eye on you. If you need anything, one of us will be close by. Okay?"

As he bent over her to arrange her blankets, she noticed a trickle of blood coming from under the right side of his watch cap. She reached out and touched it and then looked at her finger. "Mick, this is blood. What's wrong? Did you hurt your head? Take your cap off and let me see."

Mick didn't want to alarm her about the bullet wound in his head for fear that she would worry even more about her mother being with Enzio. "It's nothing Claire. It's just a scratch. Don't worry about it." She was having none of that though and pulled him closer.

"Take your cap off and let me see please." She spoke sternly and was beginning to become agitated. Mick sat down on the edge of the bed and gently removed his watch cap which dislodged the bloody gauze covering the bullet wound. It was difficult to see through his dark tousled hair and Claire reached up and carefully touched the wound. "What happened, Mick? This isn't a little scratch and it's swollen up quite a bit."

She wasn't going to let it go and he didn't want to lie to her. "When I was trying to make the money exchange with Enzio, as he was getting away, he, um…"

She gave him an impatient look. "Did he hit you with something Mick?" The realization of what had happened dawned on her and her expression changed to surprise and then to one of fear. "Is that a bullet wound? Did he try to shoot you Mick? Enzio shot you, didn't he?" Her hand flew to her mouth to go along with her look of surprise. "Oh my God Mick, you could have been killed. Are you okay? You need to see a doctor. Oh, damn that bastard Enzio." She clenched her teeth and her mouth was a thin line. If Enzio had been close at hand she would have torn him apart.

Mick took her hands in his. "I'm just fine Claire. Don't worry. It's not that bad. I'll get it looked at when you get your wound looked at. We might get a two for one price from the doctor." She shook her head and laid back on her pillow.

"We've got to stop him Mick. We've got to get my mother back and stop him. Please take care of yourself Mick. Bring me some fresh gauze and let me put some ointment on your wound. Please, let me do something for you." She was getting slightly hysterical and Mick wanted her to calm down and just rest. He got up and got the first aid kit and Claire proceeded to clean and dress his wound. Being able to take care of him seemed to calm her down.

He thanked her when she was finished and then helped her to get comfortable and sat with her for a few minutes to make sure that she was resting easy. He kissed her and then got up and made some coffee, watching her while he worked in the galley. She was beautiful and it felt so good having her here with him despite the circumstances. With a coffee cup in each hand he went back up on deck to take over from Abner.

As he opened the companionway doors, Barkley slipped past him and went and sat down beside the port settee, staring at Claire. She had her eyes closed but sensed his presence and looked at him and then patted the bed beside her. He carefully climbed up and snuggled up next to her with his head on her stomach. She patted him and lay back with a smile on her face. Mick closed the doors and passed a coffee to Abner.

"Thanks Mick. So, what's the plan Skipper?"

"We heard from Mrs. Lu saying that they were heading towards Victoria so my guess is that he's going to try to go out to Cape Flattery and then down the coast to offload his dope in the U.S. We got the phone call around four and she said they were off Stuart and Moresby Islands." Mick was looking at a chart of the area and had a pair of dividers to measure distance.

"From the description of the boat that Enzio has now, it can probably only do about six or seven knots maximum. That works out about right for where they were when she made the phone call." He looked at his watch. "It's quarter after six now, so they've gone about fourteen or so miles. That's a pretty good lead on us but Seagram is fast. We can catch up but we're not exactly sure where they are or where they're going. It's going to be dark pretty soon and the weather conditions aren't getting any better. I'm hoping we can find them before they get to Cape Flattery. It's going to be even harder to find them once they make the open water."

Abner nodded and sipped his coffee. It was blowing hard now and the rain was coming in concentrated bursts, rattling against the canvas dodger. Seagram was making good time even with reduced sail. The wind was allowing them a close reach all the way down Boundary Pass where they would change tack and head south.

"She sails real nice Mick. I've never been on a boat this size before. Most of my sailing has been on Thunderbird's and Santana's. Small stuff but this is a whole different way to sail. Could grow on a fellow."

Mick grinned at him. Foot-itis was a common boating disease. "The great thing is that we can take the foul weather and it's only going to slow Enzio down. We've just got to keep our eyes open and hope we don't go by him without seeing him. We can see almost every boat on the radar screen but we're going to waste a lot of time if we start chasing after every one of them to make sure it's not Enzio's boat. So, we're going to have to go on the assumption that they are trying to go as fast as they can to get out to Cape Flattery and not go into port somewhere. Or drop anchor in some bay somewhere to wait out the weather."

Now that Abner had some coffee, he shooed Mick down into the cabin. He could tell that there was something between the two of them. Who could blame the guy; she was a very attractive woman. Would that he were younger. "There's not much point in both of us being up here. You should go below and get a bit of rest. It's going to be a long night Mick. I'll call you in a bit."

    Mick went down below into the quiet of the cabin. Compared to the noise from the wind and rain on deck it was very peaceful below. Claire looked like she was resting comfortably. He moved over to Claire and leaned down and kissed her gently on her mouth. Her hand came up to the back of his head and she held him to her lips. It was a long kiss finally interrupted by Barkley's impatient nudging with his cold wet nose.

38 A SERIOUS MISTAKE

As dawn crept up from behind, it slowly lit the chaos that was the Pacific Ocean. "I thought that Pacific meant quiet and peaceful." Mrs. Lu shouted at David Enzio over the howl of the wind. She was bringing him another cup of coffee, though most of it had spilled in the short distance from the galley. Enzio took it gratefully.

"I remember from my social studies class that this ocean gets it's name from the Latin words "Mare Pacificum". Peaceful sea. It doesn't look very bloody peaceful today. I was hoping it was going to calm down but I think it's getting worse. Keep pumping girl."

Around four in the morning, during one of his inspection trips to check on the condition of the boat, Enzio had lifted one of the floorboards and got the shock of his life. Water was right up to the underside of the floor and it didn't appear that the electric bilge pump was able to keep up with the incoming water. He checked the float switch and the actual pump itself and everything was working properly. It was simply a matter of too much in and not enough out.

The good news, and they were desperate for some good news, was that there was a manual bilge pump mounted on the aft bulkhead just beside the door to the cockpit. Enzio had put Mrs. Lu to work as soon as he found the handle for the pump which some bright spark had stowed in a locker in the forward cabin. When he explained that the water had to be kept below the batteries which were mounted low in the engine compartment, only a few scant inches above the sloshing water, she had started pumping like a woman possessed. She might be small but she had stamina, or maybe it was just desperation spurring her on. She had pumped for an hour straight and was rewarded with a whopping one inch reduction of the water level.

Enzio had told her to steer and she was happy to take a break from pumping while he looked around to find where the leak was. It wasn't the hole in the hull that her daughter had made that was the problem. It was the age and condition of the boat and the fact that they were traveling as much under water as they were traveling above water. Two thousand pounds of premium B.C. Bud was a lot of extra weight which had already set the boat lower in the water plus the fact that every seam in the boat was leaking. Deck, hull, windows, if there was a place for water to come in, it was coming in. Slowly but surely, they were sinking.

They had options. Keep pumping and hope they could keep ahead of the incoming water. Or, sit back and relax and hope that the weather and the seas moderated, soon. Or, abandon ship and get into the inflatable life raft and hope for the best.

With dawn, option two appeared to be out of the question. Nothing was moderating. Not the weather, not the waves and not the amount of water coming into the boat. If anything, the wind was picking up and with it, the waves were getting bigger. Both Enzio and Mrs. Lu had lost their amazement at the size of the waves. They were numb to the horror of it all. If they had seen these waves yesterday, both of them would have fainted from terror. Today; so what? Just more waves; some big, some bigger.

For now, they just had to keep on pumping, taking turns until their arms couldn't move anymore. They were making a game out of it. Who could pump the longest without stopping? Mrs. Lu was the champion. She was like a machine. Under ordinary circumstances, Enzio would have been embarrassed to be beaten by a woman half his weight and a lot smaller than him. But the sexist part of him had given way to the survival side and he was proud as hell of her for whipping his ass at this challenge. As long as they stayed afloat, who cared whether it was a man or a woman who was doing most of the work? Of course, if they got out of this alive, he would be sure to re-write history to his own benefit. Right now however, history was up for grabs.

They hadn't seen another boat for hours which wasn't surprising. Who in their right mind would be out here in this kind of weather? Not David Enzio. If he had a choice right now he would be in bed with some little hottie to keep him warm.

Radar would have been helpful to be able to see if there was anybody nearby that could come to their rescue if need be. Enzio shook his head at the thought. A few hours ago he was hoping that everyone would stay away and now he was hoping there would somebody close by. Go figure. But if there was a way to keep this old tub afloat, Enzio was going to do his best to do it. He did not want to lose the dope or the money. Or his life he added as an afterthought.

With daylight, Enzio had been hoping that there would be some indication of a break in the weather to the west. But all around them, the gray clouds were kissing the gray water. It was depressing. This was a hell of a way to make a living. Being on the run from Fairy Godmother and Brese and probably the cops, it was tiring. He was feeling sorry for himself. Probably just from lack of sleep. Normally he didn't dwell on these kinds of things.

He was jerked from his reverie by a sudden change in the sound from the engine. What had been a steady dependable rumble all of a sudden missed several beats. The engine was the heart of the boat and immediately his own heart began beating erratically as if in sympathy. He scanned the dashboard. Nothing alarming there. Again, another couple of missed beats. Mrs. Lu heard them too. It was more like they felt the change rather than heard it. They had been so in tune with the steady drone from the big diesel that any change was instantly felt and noticed. Enzio broke into a cold sweat. If the engine failed, they would totally be at the mercy of the waves. They wouldn't last long in that situation.

He was about to call to Mrs. Lu but she appeared at his side before he could even complete the thought. She must have been reading his mind.

"Take over the wheel. I've got to take a look at the engine, see what's going on."

Mrs. Lu had been ready for a break from the incessant pumping. She had been ready to fall asleep on the job but with the sudden engine problem, she had received a massive jolt of adrenalin. She was on high alert now. Ready for anything.

Enzio quickly opened the access door to the engine room and took a look around. Nothing looked out of place. It was warm and the water in the bilge had been pumped down to a decent level below the batteries. God bless Mrs. Lu, Enzio said to himself. All the hoses leading to and from the engine were OK. Nothing seemed out of the ordinary until his gaze fell on the fuel filter. The fuel filter was normally filled with clear, amber colored diesel fuel. Now however, the bottom third of the filter was filled with something that didn't mix with the fuel. It was water. Not clear looking water. This was dirty sediment filled water sitting in the bottom of the filter and the story that it told was of impending disaster.

The fuel filter had been clear earlier on. Enzio had made a point to look at it during the early stages of the storm. Now, the fact that it was partly filled with dirty looking water indicated trouble. This had to mean that water had either been sitting in the bottom of the fuel tank, ready to be stirred up and picked up by the fuel pump, or that water had somehow started to get into the tank during the storm. Regardless, water in the fuel was a ball buster. A deal breaker. As much as the politicians and environmentalists wanted an engine that would run on water, this one certainly wouldn't. And if the engine quit, they would most likely end up broadside to the waves and it would only take a couple of those big suckers to hit them from the side and they would roll over and head for Davy Jones locker.

Enzio looked at the filter. If he had built this boat, he would have put two filters in the system. One could be bypassed and cleaned while the other one fed the engine. But that's not how this boat was designed. No redundancy. And it could easily cost them their lives. Enzio didn't think there was much time before the engine sucked up a snootful of water from the filter. The question was, should they get the life raft in the water before it happened, or should they wait?

Wait for what? Enzio pondered that weighty topic while he crouched on his heels staring at the water sloshing around in the fuel filter bowl. It was warm in the engine room. He was exhausted and as he sat there his eyelids slowly descended like the blinds on two dark windows. Wait for what? He sat down with a thump and slumped over against the engine room door. His eyes closed and sleep wrapped around him like a warm cozy blanket. Sleep. Warm happy sleep. He drifted off, smiling and thinking warm cozy thoughts of nothing. Nothing at all.

39 FOR BETTER OR WORSE

Mrs. Lu was angry. Enzio had disappeared to check on the engine but had yet to return. She could not leave the wheel for fear of the boat turning broadside to the mountainous waves and rolling over. Just taking her hands from the wheel for a moment gave her the distinct impression that the boat would veer off course.

She found she could steer with one hand and she took her left hand off the wheel to pull her hair back behind her ear. Mrs. Lu looked at the hand. The pinky finger was still bandaged. Sort of. It had bled quite a bit and as she looked at it, she realized that it still hurt. But the finger was the least of her worries and she hadn't been paying attention to it. By chance, the lighting conditions were just right and she saw the small scars on her fingers. Something she had looked at every day for a good part of her life without consequence but this time it set her off. Just a little sniffling at first, then a few tears and then the dam burst and years of memories and repressed emotions came gushing forth. A hard life in China symbolized by the small scars on the fingers of her hands. The same scars borne on the hands of her beloved daughter Xun Xi Pei whom she was beginning to think she might never see again.

As a little girl, it had been Mrs. Lu's job coming home from school each day, passing through the train yard in Changchun, to stop at the big mound of coal ashes emptied from the engines of the steam trains. Not all the coal was ash. Hidden like glowing nuggets amongst the ash were sizeable pieces of coal not completely consumed that could warm them at home and heat their food and water. It was her responsibility and that of many other children to find these pieces of black gold and bring them home. It was also the responsibility of the train yard soldiers to chase them away. Every day was a challenge to see who would find the most good coal pieces before the soldiers came running and shouting at them. There wasn't any kind of container to carry the coal pieces in, just a damp rag to wrap them in. Sifting though the hot coal ash was difficult. Picking up the still burning lumps of coal was harder. Without gloves, it was inevitable that her small fingers would burn. And scar.

Life in China had always been difficult but the Cultural Revolution had been the worst of times. Not just for her but for the whole country. Before the revolution her husband, Mr. Xun had seen the handwriting on the wall. He had joined the army and the communist party and had been an outstanding soldier. His good party attitude had made life a little easier for them though they had still been sent down to the country for re-education. Mrs. Lu had been a headstrong young woman and had resented their treatment but her husband had helped her through the difficulties. Later she had thanked him a million times. Still, life had been bleak. She had hoped that by the time that Xun Xi Pei was born, their situation would be better so that she would not have to stoop to the level of picking coal from the train yard. It had not worked out. Life was the same for the daughter as it had been for the mother.

But now, it looked like it might all be coming to an end. Enzio, the pig, had forced her to leave her husband when he needed her the most. And as for her daughter, what would become of her? Without her parents, who would help her to remember her heritage? Who would help her to keep the memories of their ancesters alive? Who would see to it that she married a good Chinese man and had children to carry their history forward? Without her mother to guide her she might just marry the big white man and the xiao bao bao, the little baby would not be pure Chinese. Fresh tears came. How could her daughter make the right decisions without her mother to help her? A bitter anger welled up inside her breast that it had come to this. Out here on the raging ocean with an evil man. If she was going to die, she would make him pay. Pay for taking her away from her daughter and her husband.

She opened the door to the main cabin. "Enzio," she shouted. Nothing. Again, louder this time, "Enzio." Still nothing. She stamped her foot on the cockpit floor. Bang, bang, bang on the wooden deck.

Nothing. She growled in her throat. "You've got a lot of nerve, leaving me here all alone. Enzio, you get out here right now!" She screamed it at the top of her lungs into the cabin. That tone of voice had always made people come at a run to her. He was either dead or was trapped somehow and unable to respond.

She slammed the cabin door shut just in time to look up and see the largest of all the waves rear up in front of the boat, pause and then crash down on the deck. It was deafening. A huge sound engulfed the boat. The crashing of the wave was terrifying but it was the sound of wood cracking and splintering, that sent cold stabs of fear into her heart. Whatever was happening to the boat, it wasn't good.

The cacphony woke David Enzio. That plus the cold salt water that swirled into the cabin and found his sleeping body at the entrance to the engine room. He had never before woken so quickly and so completely. He slammed the door shut to the engine room trying in vain to keep the rising water from the heart of the boat. His last view of the engine before the door closed was the spray of water coming from the fan belt as it began to submerge in the rising water. The flood had already risen to the bottom of the engine and it wouldn't be long before it reached the batteries. Then, it would be lights out and power off.

Enzio splashed his way to the cabin door, taking a quick look forward to see water cascading in through some kind of damage to the foredeck. Hundred pound bags of marijuana, carefully wrapped in green plastic were starting to float around the cabin. Nothing short of a gigantic pump was going to save the boat now. It was time to go. It might already be too late.

When he opened the cabin door, Mrs. Lu was ready and waiting. She chose to turn her fear into rage and she let go of the wheel and attacked with everything she had. Enzio was not prepared for the onslaught. He went down under her furious attack covering his head and his damaged ear with his arms. He saw a foot and grabbed it and rolled away from her. Mrs. Lu crashed down but took an opportunity to drive a knee into the back of his head. He passed out from the blow but was instantly brought around by the invigorating icy cold sea water that his face went into. Unconcious to concious in a microsecond.

The two of them grappled and rolled around in the swirling waters slowly filling the floor of the cockpit. He got to his knees and shouted at her. "We've got to get out of here. Now."

Getting There

That got her attention. In a heartbeat, she was her co-operative self again. "What do you want me to do?" They helped each other up and looked around. The boat was sinking. No two ways about it. The bow was already under water and amazingly enough, the engine was still running, pushing them deeper. Enzio throttled back and pulled the gearshift to neutral. He had a fleeting image of the captain of a sinking ship signalling "All Stop" and telling the engine room crew to get the hell out.

David Enzio was wondering if they would have enough time to get the life raft launched and be able to load any of the marijuana into it but another wave smashing onto the roof of the boat was enough to put that thought out of his mind. He began to think that they might not even have time to save themselves let alone any of the marijuana. "I'm going to throw the life raft cannister over the side."

Mrs. Lu looked at him like he had lost his mind. "What do you mean throw it over the side? We need it." She grabbed at him like he was about to kill them both.

"No, I don't mean throw it away. I have to throw it in the water and it will start to inflate. There's a rope that we have to hang onto so it doesn't get away from us. If we let go of the rope, we're finished. Do you understand?" They were screaming at each other. Partly because of the noise from the wind and the waves but also because they were both terrified. The thought of getting into a little rubber boat scared the hell out of both of them. The water was freezing, they were soaked and shivering and there was nothing to be calm about. They shared the same grim thought. This could be the end. Neither one was ready for that.

Mrs. Lu grabbed the line from one of the two cannisters laying on the cockpit floor but she had grabbed the line from the one that held the money. Enzio snatched it from her hand.

"Not that one. This one. Hold this line and don't let it go." He thrust the rope from the life raft into her hand. "Better still, let's tie it to the rail." He quickly tied the line to the railing on the port side of the sinking boat. It was questionable as to whether they would have enough time to launch the raft before the boat sank right out from under their feet. Enzio took hold of the life raft cannister and picked it up in his arms. He threw it over the side of the boat where it sank into the water and then surfaced again. It reached the end of it's tether and the cannister burst apart and they were rewarded with the beautiful sight of the raft inflating before their fear struck eyes. Mrs. Lu pulled it close as it finished unfolding. It wasn't what either of them were expecting. As opposed to an open rubber dingy which they were both familiar with, this was two bright yellow rubber tubes forming a square with a bright red cover that would help to keep them dry. It even had an inflatable boarding ladder in front of the entrance.

Mrs. Lu wasn't waiting for an invitation. She jumped in the water and in one quick movement grabbed the boarding ladder and was up and inside, turning and looking out at Enzio. She yelled at him. "Come on, don't just stand there. Jump." From her vantage point, she could see the powerboat was going down qickly. Enzio grabbed the other cannister and balanced it on the rail with one hand and pulled Mrs. Lu and the liferaft closer with the other. As soon as she was near he handed the cannister full of money to her, making sure that she got it inside where it was safe. Safe was a relative term. Safer than on a broken down sinking boat. He untied the liferaft line and holding on to it tightly, jumped into the ocean. His breath left his body all at once. He didn't feel like he was going to be able to get the next supply of air into his lungs but somehow managed. His teeth began chattering. He realized that a human wouldn't last five minutes in water this cold.

He didn't have far to go to get to the boarding ladder of the raft but it took every ounce of strength to do it. The wind was pushing the raft and it was moving away from him almost as fast as he was able to swim towards it. Being in the water made him realize just how big the waves were. With what felt like his last bit of energy, he gave a mighty kick and grabbed onto the raft. Mrs. Lu got hold of his jacket and a good bit of skin underneath it and pulled him up and into the raft.

Enzio lay gasping and wheezing on the floor. He rolled over onto his back and pulled his feet inside and then scrambled over to kneel next to Mrs. Lu at the doorway of the raft. Together they looked out at the sinking powerboat. The little rubber liferaft was drifting away from it quite quckly. They watched as the boat sank deeper and deeper and then turned broadside to the waves. It was just as they had imagined. Once the boat was sideways to the waves, it took several punishing blows and then rolled over on it's side and then onto it's back. Even at a distance, they could hear crashing and breaking of wood and Enzio imagined the two thousand pounds of premium B.C.Bud falling through the roof of the boat.

The last thing they saw was the shiny bronze propeller rise up out of the water and then slip beneath the breaking waves.

Getting There

40 MAYBE

Mick watched Claire and Barkley sleep. Barkley was chasing something in his sleep, his legs twitching as he ran down his prey. Claire tossed and turned, disturbed by thoughts of crushed skulls and branches smacking across her face as she plunged into the tree tops over and over. The motion of the boat was adding another level of realism to both dream worlds.

Abner and Mick had been taking turns in the cabin watching over Claire. They hadn't really needed to do so. The combination of exhaustion, the pain from the gunshot wound and the medication that Mick had finally given her had sent her into a deep but troubled sleep.

Abner had insisted that Mick get some sleep too. He seemed to know how to handle the boat. There wasn't much to do except keep her pointed in the right direction and watch the sails. Gratefully, Mick had lain down in the quarter berth and had fallen asleep instantly. Abner had let him sleep for two hours before waking him as they approached the mouth of Juan De Fuca Strait.

Mick woke feeling groggy and achy all over. Two hours of sleep was only a tease to his system. He checked on Claire and found that she was still sleeping. Barkley was awake and wagged his long tail but wouldn't leave Claire's side. Mick quietly made a pot of coffee and washed his face. He was rudely surprised when he looked in the mirror and saw the stubble of his unshaven face and the fatigue in his red rimmed bloodshot eyes.

He took his coffee and sat for a few minutes at the navigation table, watching the radar screen. He could see a few boats back in the

Strait but Seagram was out in the open ocean now. This was where they had decided to search for any sign of Enzio and Mrs. Lu. Mick had bet the farm that Enzio had been forced to steam due west into the oncoming waves. To do otherwise would be sheer folly in the coastal cruiser. There wasn't any way they could survive a broadside attack from these boat killing waves.

Seagram on the other hand was making good progress despite the weather. She was under reefed main and storm jib and while the motion wasn't exactly comfortable, it was tolerable. Mick did the rounds, stowing anything that was making noise or threatening to break loose. He checked the bilges to make sure they weren't taking on any water. Everything was dry. He couldn't help wondering how Starlight would have handled these big seas out on the open ocean. He choked up a little remembering his beautiful boat but that was then and this was now.

Taking a fresh cup of coffee to Abner, he slid the hatch back and stepped out into the cockpit. Abner sat on the starboard side, his hat pulled low over his eyes, his pipe sticking out of the corner of his mouth turned upside down protecting it from the shots of spray that occasionally reached the cockpit. He looked completely at home on the sea. He stood and stretched, taking the proffered cup from Mick. They stood close together, rolling with the motion of the boat.

"I haven't seen another boat since we left the mouth of Juan De Fuca. It appears we've got the whole ocean to ourselves Mick."

Mick looked around at the vast scene before him. Bullets of spray from the bow waves rattled off the dodger windows. Steep curling waves, a surfers' smorgasbord, rolled in steady succession towards the east, any one of them looking big enough to swallow Enzio's boat. For all they knew, one of them might have already done just that but they had to keep searching.

Seagram had a second radar screen mounted out in the cockpit and Mick and Abner both kept their eyes on it while staying out of the rain and spray under the protection of the dodger. Abner packed his pipe with fresh tobacco and used a mini torch lighter to get it fired up. He puffed vigorously until it was burning properly. Aromatic clouds of Captain Black swirled momentarily before being whisked aft.

Mick noticed a white dot show up on the radar screen. It was at the twenty four nautical mile edge of the unit. It was off to the south of them, heading west but going so slow as to be almost at a stop. It was the first boat they had seen since leaving the Strait. Mick nudged Abner and pointed at the screen. As they watched the small blip, it suddenly became two blips, like an amoeba subdividing.

Seagram was on a port tack, trying to stay as close into the wind as possible while allowing them to take the waves at a slight angle. This gave them a better chance to sail over the waves as opposed to bashing through them which they would have done if they took them head on. The problem was that their current course was angling them away from the other boat, increasing the distance between the two of them. It was possible that it was Enzio that they were watching on the radar scope. A long shot but possible.

One of the two blips suddenly vanished from view leaving the other target drifting slowly eastward as if being blown and moving with the wind and the waves. If it was Enzio, had they lost engine power?

"I think that's a life raft we're seeing now. That might well have been Enzio's boat that disappeared and now we're looking at the life raft." Abner was pointing with the stem of his pipe at the remaining white blip on the screen.

Mick thought it sounded plausible. Who else would be out here today and why would one target become two and then back to one? Abner's explanation covered the bases.

"Let's head in that direction. Take the wheel Abner and I'll handle the sails. When I give you the signal, you crank the wheel over to port as fast as you can." Mick was glad that they were in these kinds of seas in this kind of boat and not the one Enzio was in.

"Now Abner." He waited as the boat turned to port and then let go the sheet from the storm jib. The main boom shot over to the port side of the boat and Mick quickly ratcheted the port storm jib sheet in on the big winch. The move had taken only seconds and they were now gathering speed again on the starboard tack. It looked like a good intercept with the target and judging from the speed, they would make contact in a couple of hours.

Abner reset the autopilot and then came back under the protection of the dodger. He was wet and his cheeks were red. "Tis a fine day for sailing Mick." He rubbed his hands together and wiped his face dry with the towel hanging by the companionway door.

Mick looked around the horizon. Abner was right. Given the fact that they had a comfortable boat and everything was working properly, it really was a fine day for sailing. This is what it was all about. A self contained world, all the ocean theirs to explore. He felt alive, exhilarated and as happy as he had been in a long time. Now, if they could just find Mrs. Lu and save her from Enzio, the day would be perfect.

41 NOW WHAT?

    Mrs. Lu was trapped in a sixty four square foot floating hell with a raving maniac. If being on the powerboat had been frightening, this was beyond description. The little rubber raft lacked the substantial feel that the boat had. They were being pushed around by the huge waves, riding up and down like some kind of bizarre carnival ride without the feeling of safety that even a rickety carnival ride had. As they looked out the small doorway on the hell that was the Pacific Ocean, Enzio raged on about losing his precious marijuana.

    Mrs. Lu could care less about the dope. She cared about getting back on dry land and never, ever getting on the water again. Never. Not even on one of the big B.C. Ferry boats. It would complicate living on an island but she had made her mind up. When the boat sank and they had had to take to this little inconsequential piece of rubber real estate, her mind was made up; no more water, no more boats. But that decision hinged on getting out of their current situation. And as she honestly admitted to herself, that seemed more unlikely by the moment.

    Enzio was experiencing a range of emotions. He was happy that they had managed to get off the boat before it sank. But he couldn't get over the thought of his precious load of marijuana being lost. They had drifted quite quickly away from the scene of the sinking, so he hadn't been able to see if any of the dope had broken free and floated to the surface. He was pissed off about that. If they had some way of controlling the life raft, they might have been able to stick around long enough to grab a bundle or two or three of floating dope.

Thousands of dollars of floating dope. He felt sick just thinking about it.

Mrs. Lu had looked at him with disgust and pointed out to him that he still had the money. He was tempted to smack her. It wasn't her ton of dope going to the bottom of the ocean. It wasn't her that was now going to have to explain to Fairy Godmother what had happened. He caught himself. What was he thinking? He couldn't risk meeting Fairy Godmother again. The guy was probably waiting for him to do just that. And then shoot him dead. Or worse.

The ride in the raft was wild. There were times when they had clung to each other for fear that they were going to die. Down in the trough, in the valley between two big mountains of water, it was relatively calm but the view was enough to make you piss your pants. Enzio wanted to cover his eyes but it was like trying not to look at a wreck on the freeway. He looked and regretted it for the fear it generated in his watery bowels.

The raft would begin riding up the next wave, going higher and higher. They could see the curling top coming towards them. Up, up, up they would rise and as they neared the top, the raft would begin to buffet in the raging wind which was suddenly tearing at them. It felt like they were going to be blown right out of the water. At the top of the wave, the view was dizzying. They couldn't see that far but in every direction, it looked the same. Low scudding clouds moving swiftly to the east and everywhere, water being blown to shreds by the wind. The rain drilled sideways at the top of the wave and became part of the maelstrom of froth as they surfed down the roller coaster into the trough again. The process repeated over and over.

Mrs. Lu and David Enzio hung on for dear life. There wasn't much to say and talk was difficult due to the racket from the waves and wind outside. They had zipped the door closed which at least shut out some of the noise and the terrible view but Mrs. Lu quickly became seasick, not having an outside reference point to focus on. The motion was too much for her and she lay down on the floor and wretched her guts out until she had nothing more to give. Still she continued trying, her equilibrium so out of whack that her stomach went into an almost continuous spasm. Eventually she lay still. Enzio thought that she might have died but from time to time she moaned or twisted indicating to him that she was still among the living. Barely.

Enzio on the other hand was busy trying to figure out what the hell his next move was going to be. The fact that there was nothing he could do was a big pain in the ass. He now had to get to land and get out of sight. Again. He had just come from a long exile in Eastern Canada. Granted, he was lucky to have lived long enough to go into exile but the east had it's limitations for a west coast boy. He was not going to do that again. He could go anywhere he wanted. He would have to buy some papers that would allow him to travel but that was mox nix. He had money now.

    The problem was, the money wasn't going to last forever and he was after all, a business man. He wanted to get into the dope peddling business but every time he tried, something seemed to go wrong. It seemed like he was jinxed. He looked at Mrs. Lu. She had a lot to do with his lack of success. He should kill her but he couldn't. Truth be told, he admired her more than any woman he had ever met and most men too. She was probably going to die from puking herself to death, so he didn't feel it was necessary to shoot her. The thought that they both might die crossed his mind but he was quick to think about something else.

    He looked at the canister of money. He had been sure to tie it to a d-ring on the inside of the raft. He didn't want it falling out if they got tipped over by one of the big waves. Since they hadn't seen any other boats all morning long, Enzio assumed that everybody had clued into the fact that it wasn't a sunny spring day out on the water. Just like he should have done. The good news was that he had the foresight to get the raft from Brese. Probably the smartest thing he had done in his life. The bad news was that he hadn't gone into Victoria and simply waited out this god awful storm. What an idiot. He shook his head at his stupidity. If Tommy or Horst had done something this stupid, he would have shot them.

He reached into his coat pocket, sodden and damp and pulled out his gun. There was no bloody way he was going to drown. No way. He had heard that drowning was like going to sleep but he didn't believe that for a second. Since when did you go to sleep gagging and coughing and suffocating for lack of air, lungs filling up with water? If it came down to it, he was going to shoot himself. If he felt the raft tipping over, he was going to hold on with one hand and get the gun ready in the other. And if he thought that the raft was going to sink, he would blow his own brains out before he would go through drowning. A shudder went through him. Probably just from the cold and wet. "I hope I don't catch a cold from this." Enzio wondered if he had said that out loud or just thought it. Talking to yourself was a bad sign he guessed. It wasn't any wonder he might start talking to himself. He hadn't had any decent sleep for a long time. He tried to remember when he had last slept. The little nap in the engine room wasn't long enough to count. God damn it. What he would give for a nice warm bed. He wouldn't even share it with a chick. He just wanted to sleep. Sleep. Perchance to dream. He giggled and leaned back against the soft rubber side of the raft drifting off to sleep in the midst of chaos.

42 THE CATCH OF THE DAY

Claire woke as Seagram changed course. Barkley seemed to sense that she was awake and put his cold wet nose into her ear and licked her cheek. She grinned and threw her arms around him, hugging him close. He pulled free from the embrace and sat back and barked. It would seem that he was announcing to the world that his work was done.

She was feeling refreshed after her sleep and she was glad to be alive. She reached down and felt the wound in her thigh. It wasn't feeling too bad. She vaguely remembered Abner undressing her and treating her wound. The dressing was kind of tight but not unbearable. She knew she was lucky that the bullet hadn't hit the bone or especially the femoral artery. She wouldn't be laying here now if that had happened. Life was sometimes a matter of inches, often a matter of luck.

The hatch slid open and Mick stuck his head down and looked over at the port settee. Barkley's announcement had not gone unnoticed. "What's all the noise down there?" Mick said. Abner's face showed up alongside of Mick's. "We're trying to get some rest out here; can you keep it down please?" Abner's voice caught Barkley's attention and the dog leapt to the floor and raced up the companionway stairs and pushed his way into the cockpit. Mick went down below and put the kettle on and prepared some tea for Claire. While the water was heating he went and sat on the edge of her bunk after letting the lee cloth down.

"How are you feeling Claire?"

She answered by grabbing him by the front of his jacket and pulling his face to hers and kissing him roughly on the mouth. "Fine Mick. Thanks to you and Abner and Barkley I'm feeling much better. Any sign of Enzio yet?"

Mick didn't want to get her hopes up just yet. "We're heading towards a target that might be Enzio. We don't have any way of knowing until we get closer. This is the first traffic we've seen since we left the Strait but it's promising. We'll keep you informed. You have to rest though. Let me take a look at your leg."

Claire turned the blanket down from her leg, not shy about Mick seeing her in just her panties. Mick's gaze was not focused entirely on her wounded leg and she knew it. He looked at her skimpy black lace panties thinking she would make a good model for one of those sexy Victoria's Secret catalogues. "How's it look Mick?" she said with a little grin.

He didn't notice that she was on to him. "It looks terrific Claire. I mean it looks fine." He looked up to see if she noticed. She was grinning at him. "Your wound, I mean the bandage. Um, Barkley, I mean Abner did a great job of bandaging it up." He closed his mouth. He smiled back at her and then the two of them began laughing. "You want to know the truth Claire? You look hot. Even though you've got a bandage on your thigh and your shirt's all wrinkled and your hair is all messed up from sleeping, you look great. I took a look at myself in the mirror this morning and got the shock of my life. I looked like an old man and you wake up looking like a model. What's up with that?"

Claire blushed and took his hand in hers. "That's kind of you to say Mick. I don't feel so hot though. I feel like I've been through the wringer and it's only thanks to you and Abner and Barkley that I'm here at all. I want you to know I'll always be grateful. I will never forget it."

Mick covered his embarrassment by examining her wound a little closer. There had obviously been some bleeding while she slept. The bandage needed to be changed, so Mick went and talked to Abner and made sure that he was on course and the boat was trimmed properly. Abner was fine with maintaining the deck watch.

Mick returned and cleaned and re-bandaged Claire's wound. As he was applying the last couple of strips of tape he made sure to hold her thigh, savoring the softness and warmth of her skin.

"If you don't stop that this instant, Mick, I'm going to have to give you a big kiss," she said, smiling at him.

"I'm going to have to stop Claire. If I don't, we're going to be in trouble with Barkley. He thinks he's your number one boyfriend around here. I don't want to get on his bad side."

Claire did a little pout but didn't argue as Mick finished his work. She asked if he could help her get up so that she could go to the bathroom. He picked her up and carried her to the head in the master stateroom.

"Do you think you can manage by yourself, or would you like me to help you?"

"I'll be fine Mick, thanks very much. I'll call you when I'm finished, OK?"

He closed the door behind him and went and straightened up her sheets and blankets and pillows. He sat down and watched the radar until she called that she was finished. As he carried her back to her bunk, she put her arms around his neck and lay her head against his shoulder. Mick had never thought of himself as handsome or desirable or particularly manly. Right now she made him feel like he had ample quantities of all three traits. She made him feel very good.

As he was tucking her back into bed, Abner slid the hatch back and suggested that Mick get his butt up on deck pronto. Claire gave him a kiss and then pushed him away.

"Get going Mick. You be careful out there. OK?"

He smiled at her and then turned and went up on deck. It was a different world from the warmth and quiet down below. Even though it was only early afternoon, it was dark enough to pass for much later. Still the wind blew and the waves had not diminished. It was a storm the likes of which Mick had not seen before along the west coast.

Abner was pointing to a spot just off the port bow. There wasn't much to see except a succession of large breaking waves, one right after another.

"If you watch long enough, you'll see some kind of a light flashing against the clouds. It's not easy to see. Maybe my eyes are playing tricks on me. I started seeing it about ten minutes ago."

Mick stared. He stood on the port cockpit seat to be able to look over the top of the dodger. The wind and the salt spray made him cup his hands around the sides of his face to shield his eyes. He looked for a few minutes feeling Abner behind him waiting for verification.

He imagined Enzio and Mrs. Lu looking out at these same waves and not having the luxury of a seaworthy boat under their feet. It wouldn't be a good feeling.

"I don't see anything Abner. Let's..." There. There it was. Like the beat of a heart. Flash…flash…flash. Faint white pulses against the slate gray of the torn sky.

"I see it. I see what you're talking about. It's a strobe. It's got to be from the life raft. They must have had to take to the life raft. I know that there was a white strobe light as part of the emergency package on the raft. We're on a good intercept right now Abner. Let's just keep heading on this course." He turned to the grinning face of Abner.

"I was thinking I might be imagining things. You know how you can start to see things if you stare long enough."

Mick understood about self doubt. Even now as he looked back, he couldn't be sure he had seen the flashes. Didn't matter. As he looked at the radar screen he could see that they were now only about five miles from the target.

He tried to imagine what they would do when they got close to the life raft. It was, after all, David Enzio that they were dealing with. He might be down to his last card but he would still be dangerous. He had a gun and he had Mrs. Lu.

Mick sat down and closed his eyes, trying to prepare in advance for how to approach the life raft, if it was indeed the life raft. It would probably be best to continue to run into the waves and try to get the raft alongside. It would be drifting towards the east and Seagram would be on a south westerly course. Would Enzio be ready and willing to come aboard Seagram, or would he be difficult right to the bitter end? Only Enzio knew for sure.

Abner tapped him on the shoulder and pointed to the radar screen. Another white blip had appeared at the bottom of the screen about twenty miles behind them, leaving Juan De Fuca Strait. Judging from the size of the return, it had to be a large vessel, maybe a big fishing boat or a small freighter. Mick picked up the binoculars that Abner had been using and looked in the direction of where he had seen the flashing light.

He looked long and hard and saw the pulsing strobe against the clouds and then briefly, a small flash of red, there and then gone. He held still, focusing his energies on the same area. There it was again. Red and yellow this time and a sharp icy white flash of light. It was the raft. Enzio.

Mick couldn't believe how small the raft looked against the waves. Without any point of reference, the waves had looked impressive enough but now that he could see the little life raft riding up the face of a wave he realized just how big the waves were. And how small the raft was. And how difficult it was going to be to rescue the occupants of the raft.

They were quickly closing the gap between Seagram and the raft. Mick didn't have any experience in rescuing people from a small raft in huge waves. "Got any suggestions as to how we should approach the raft, Abner? Above them or below them?"

Abner stared then shook his head. "If we come alongside the raft on our port side, we'll be above them. It will give them some protection in the lee of the hull. As light as the raft is they'll be drifting away from us though. If we come at them on our starboard they'll drift down against us."

Mick nodded. It would be tricky and they might not get a second chance if they screwed up the first time. These were not the kind of conditions where you could tool around and try different techniques. "Let's get them on our starboard side so they'll drift down on us. We can get into position and then try to line up so they come right to us. I'm going to get the engine fired up so we've can maneuver better."

With the engine warming up, Mick took the wheel and turned as far to port as he dared without broaching. Abner went below to brief Claire on the plan. Barkley went with him. When Abner came back up on deck he smiled at Mick.

"Barkley is staying with her. I told him to make sure she didn't leave her bunk. She wanted to come up on deck and help but as I pointed out to her, she'd be more of a hindrance with her gamey leg. She's not too happy about being kept out of the excitement."

Mick could understand. It was her mother out there. Being this close and not being able to help would be frustrating for her. But it was best that she stay in bed and protect her leg. He hoped Barkley would keep her occupied.

"I also brought these." He held out two safety harnesses. Bright orange webbings with d-rings and coils of line clipped to them.

"I should have thought of that myself Abner. Thanks. Safety first. You get a gold star beside your name today for thinking of that."

They both put the harnesses on, Mick helping Abner to adjust his. With the lines clipped to eyebolts in the front of the cockpit, they would have room to roam but would still be attached to the boat if they fell into the water. It would be difficult to get back aboard but it was a lot better than the alternative. Mick put a life jacket on over top of the safety harness.

They could see the raft clearly now. It was riding up and down the waves, looking like it was going to lift off as it went over the crest of each big breaker. Thank God Enzio had taken the raft from him. Mick shook his head. He had been so pissed off at the time thinking that Enzio had gotten the best of him. Now it turned out that he was going to end up trying to save the life of the guy who had caused so much mayhem in their lives. But they could turn him over to the police and he would spend a long time in jail. There was no guarantee of that though. These days, the judicial system wasn't quite as harsh on criminals as it used to be. Enzio might find a loophole and get off with only a couple of years behind bars.

It was clear that they were on a good course to intercept the raft. They could see the doorway was closed on the red cover. Mick reached inside the companionway doors and brought out the air horn. This little compressed air horn made enough noise to be heard over the roar of the wind and the waves. Mick gave it a couple of blasts which made Abner duck his head and cover his ears. It was loud.

With the engine in gear, Mick was now powering ahead at a slight angle to the oncoming waves. He wanted to get into position so that they could turn slightly to port and have the raft run into the side of Seagram. It would allow them the maximum amount of time to get hold of the tow rope on the raft and try to get Enzio and Mrs. Lu onboard. They were close; it wouldn't be long now. Mick gave another couple of long blasts on the horn. Nothing. No indication that they had been heard. The doorway on the raft was still closed. Abner stood close by Mick as they made their final approach.

"Take over the wheel Abner. As we get close enough, I'll tell you when to turn to port. Not too much mind you or we'll broach. I'll get up by the rail and use the pike pole to try to reach down and grab the tow line or some part of the raft."

"Roger on that Mick. Good luck." He took the wheel and Mick made his way to the starboard side deck and un-strapped the pike pole from its place along the rail. It had a hook on the end of it, an extra fifteen feet of reach for Mick. As they closed the distance to the raft, Mick could see that they were not going to have much time to make the catch. The wind was pushing the raft towards them quickly

Getting There

and they had to keep enough speed on Seagram in order to maintain headway against the seas. Despite the cold and rain, Mick could feel the sweat under his arms, a rush of stickiness. With the windblown spray and the rain, he was soaked to the skin despite wearing his foul weather gear. The only part of him that was dry was the inside of his mouth. He stuck his tongue into the rain for lubrication.

Now. He signaled to Abner to turn slightly to port. The raft was in a trough, just below the bow of Seagram which was riding on the crest of a wave. As the wave rolled under them and Seagram headed down, the raft started up the face of the next wave in line. It was going to be close, very close. What Mick was hoping for was that they could both get into the same rhythm which would give him the most time to grab the raft. Seagram came down into the trough and rose up again just as the raft reached the top of the wave and then they were together. The raft bumped and bounced off the steep side of Seagram, then was pushed hard against the boat. Mick reached down with the pike pole and hooked one of the ropes hanging in crescent shapes between anchor points all around the outside of the raft. It was an easy snag but what he was looking for was the tow line. Without that, he wouldn't be able to keep the raft close long enough.

As Seagram reared up to the top of the next wave, the wind picked up the lighter raft and pushed it hard against the hull of the boat. It slid along the hull and the pike pole lost its grip on the line. As the raft moved past Mick, he saw the towline near the entrance door of the raft, dangling in the water. Reaching deep, he managed to bring the line up, precariously snagged on the hook of the pike pole. It was now or never. Mick brought the pole inboard and as he did the line fell free but draped over Seagram's lifelines long enough for Mick to grab it before it fell back into the water. He quickly tied the line up short to a cleat and the raft did another half turn before jerking to a stop at the end of its tether.

Now that they had the raft under control, Mick yelled down to the red cover. "Hello, hello." No answer from the occupants of the raft. Maybe they hadn't been able to get onboard before the boat sank. It was a chilling thought. Mick knew that nobody would last very long in the freezing cold water. Abner straightened Seagram out and applied a bit more power.

Mick tried to reach the raft without falling into the water. If he could just get the door opened, he would know if Enzio or Mrs. Lu were on board. As he was trying find a way to hold on to Seagram and still get to the raft, he was startled by the sudden blast of the air horn. Another one followed close behind. It was loud even against the howl of the wind. The raft door suddenly started to open. Unzipping slowly, a little bit at first, then enough to allow a head to poke through. It was David Enzio.

Mick was surprised that under the circumstances, the wind and waves, the danger that they were all in, that his first reaction to seeing Enzio would be to want to punch him in the face. If he had been close enough, he might have done it. But he was out of reach and Enzio quickly brought out one arm and pointed a gun directly at him. Mick was so surprised that he burst out laughing. "We're here to save your sorry ass and you point a gun at us? You bastard. I ought to just cut you loose and let you fend for yourself."

"Screw you Brese." Enzio had to yell over the wind. He wasn't looking too good but he was his usual irritating self. "You want to see the Chinese bitch alive; you'd better be nice to me."

"Enzio, we don't have all day to chit chat." As Mick spoke, he looked down at the attach point where the towline was held to the raft. It was under huge strain. Mick knew it wouldn't hold for long. "Pass Mrs. Lu over and let's get the two of you aboard. Hurry up."

Enzio let the door close and turned to Mrs. Lu. She was face down on the floor, looking for all the world like she was dead. He grabbed her by the back of her jacket and pulled her to him. She moaned. She was a mess. Vomit had dried around her mouth; her hair a snarled tangle of black. She opened her eyes and looked at Enzio without seeing. He pulled her close. "You're going home. Help is here. Just between you and me…" He left the rest unsaid. What was the point? She was out of it and he was never one to let people know what he was thinking. It took away from his control. Enzio liked being in control. He knew as soon as he gave the woman over to Brese, he wouldn't have any bargaining room and if he got on the sailboat, he was as good as in jail. No more control.

He dragged Mrs. Lu to the door and opened it again. Brese was leaning over the rail of the sailboat. Enzio shoved the woman out. She was light enough that he was able to hold her almost at arms length and Brese took her jacket collar in one hand. At that moment, the towline attach point on the raft ripped free. Now, the only connection between the raft and Seagram was Mick's grasp on Mrs. Lu's collar and Enzio's hands around her ankles. The raft, now free, bumped down the remaining length of Seagram's side. Mick struggled to move along the side deck, still holding on to Mrs. Lu's collar and trying not to fall overboard. Enzio yelled at Brese.

"I can't hold her, don't let go." By now, Enzio only had her by her feet. Then one foot. Mick realized that if he let go, Mrs. Lu would fall in the water and he could tell that Enzio wasn't going to be able to hold her. Mrs. Lu appeared to be unconscious, or at least so weak that she was unable to assist in any way.

She was being pulled horizontal over the water, stretched tight between the two men. Enzio finally lost his grip on Mrs. Lu who dropped feet first into the turbulent ocean. She was light but her weight was increased by the pull of the water on her legs. Mick held on tight, one arm on her jacket and one arm behind him holding on to the railing of the boat. Mrs. Lu's arms came up over her head and her jacket began slipping off over her head. He was losing her and if she fell into the water, they would never be able to find her. She would be gone.

Enzio watched the scene without being able to do anything to help. The raft slipped behind Seagram and dipped into the trough behind the big sailboat. Enzio sat back and looked out the door at the waves. He was alone. Just him and the money.

Mick realized that there was only one choice. The first step is a real doozie. Where had he heard that before? Some comedy. Turns out, it was true. The first step from Seagram was long and frightening. When he hit the water, he knew he didn't have much time to grab hold of Mrs. Lu. If he lost his grip on her, he might not be able to find her again in the swirling tumbling mass of freezing cold water. He threw his arms around Mrs. Lu, holding her in a grip so tight he heard her gasp for breath. Or maybe it was just the icy cold water which took the breath away from both of them. It didn't take him long to reach the end of his safety line and he jerked up with a snap. He was then pulled face first into the water, Mrs. Lu's body pulling him down, threatening to drown them both.

Abner watched in horror as Mick plunged out of sight from the side of the boat. He had forgotten that they had clipped Mick's lifeline to the eyebolt in the cockpit. He forgot until the line jerked taut and swung around to the stern of the boat, coming dangerously close to decapitating him in the process. He ducked in time and then stood and looked aft to see Mick face down in the water dragging along behind. He couldn't see the woman. He reached down and throttled the engine back and hoped it would be enough to slow the boat and allow Mick to at least turn over.

Mick tipped his head back struggling to get a breath, struggling to pull Mrs. Lu up high enough for her to get air. He realized that it would be simpler if he rolled over onto his back. This brought Mrs. Lu up to the surface and Mick gave her a big squeeze which kick started her breathing process. She spewed out seawater and then sucked in a deep gulp of air. They were in a bad position. Mick could feel the cold water sucking the strength from his muscles. If he didn't get back aboard the boat soon, he wouldn't have the strength to do it. As he looked around, trying to get his bearings, he realized that his boots had been pulled off his feet. He looked past his toes sticking up out of the water and saw the life raft. Enzio was framed in the doorway watching him.

Abner had seen the predicament that Mick was in. He looked around and saw the big winch on the starboard side of the cockpit. The problem was that Mick's lifeline was pulled so tight that there was no way to get it wrapped around the barrel of the winch in order to pull Mick and Mrs. Lu in to the boat. There was only one option and it scared the hell out of Abner. He reached into his pocket and pulled out his pipe cleaning tool. It had a very sharp blade on it. Not big, just sharp. He was going to have to cut the lifeline and in a hell of a hurry get it wrapped around the winch without loosing his grip and the precious cargo on the end of the line. A high stakes gamble. With other people's lives.

He didn't hesitate. Seagram was on autopilot, they were throttled back as slow as they could go and there wasn't time to bugger around. He needed help. "Mick," he screamed as loud as possible. "Mick, kick as hard as you can right now. I need your help. Kick you bastard." He felt the line slacken slightly. "Harder," he shouted. He grabbed the line with one hand, got the best grip that he could get given how taut the line was and then began sawing it, close to the eyebolt. It wasn't a thick line and it cut through and parted with a snap. He dropped the knife and as quickly as he could wrapped the line around the winch and began cranking.

Kicking with all his might, holding Mrs. Lu with one arm, Mick reached behind his head and grabbed the lifeline. He felt a jerk, jerk, jerk and they were being pulled in closer to the stern of the boat. The water kept washing over the two of them, making them cough and gasp for air.

"You're there Mick, give me your hand. Reach man, reach." Mick stretched his arm out as far as it would go and felt Abner's hand grasp his own. He was surprised at how warm the hand was. Abner pulled him close and then Mick felt the hard surface of the swim grid on his back. Finally they were there. Relief flooded through his body like the warmth from a shot of whiskey. Abner reached across Mick's face and pulled Mrs. Lu from his grip and then helped him to get aboard. The two of them crawling, dragging the limp body of Mrs. Lu forward to the safety of the cockpit.

Mick stood and looked around. He was shivering, his teeth chattering. He wanted nothing more than to go below and get into some warm dry clothes and have a hot cup of coffee. But there was Enzio to deal with before anybody could rest.

"Abner, can you get Mrs. Lu down below and take care of her? I'll try to get us turned around and see if we can get Enzio. It's going to be a bit hairy when we turn around. It will seem like we're going to roll over but I'll try to do it as quick as we can. I'll give you warning."

Abner nodded, tight lipped. He wasn't looking forward to them turning around. The thought of getting broadside to the waves even for a short time was frightening. He picked Mrs. Lu up in his arms and Mick held the doors open long enough for him to get her inside. He heard Claire's exclamation. "Mummy!"

Mick closed the doors and prepared to head for Enzio.

43 PLAN WHATEVER

Truth was David Enzio didn't want the Chinese woman around. She would only complicate his escape. By the same token, he had grown to admire her toughness and courage. So, it wasn't a difficult choice to turn her over to Brese. If she had fallen in the ocean and been lost, that would have been her tough luck but it appeared that Brese had managed to hold on to her despite having to go in the drink to do it. Big hero.

It wasn't easy to watch Brese's boat disappear in the distance. When the towline had broken, his heart had sunk but in looking back, it was for the best. He had been planning on shooting Brese and whoever else he had to in order to make his escape. But now, he was going to have to fall back on Plan B.

"Plan B." He rolled his eyes and uttered a bitter laugh. "You have to have a Plan A before you can have a Plan B. This whole thing has been nothing but a mess, right from the word go." He was talking to himself, out loud. It was comforting to hear his own voice, something normal and familiar over the roaring, hissing, seething sound outside the door of the raft. He shook his head. "I don't mind telling you David, old boy, you've really screwed up this time."

It didn't bother him being honest out here in a raft in the middle of a hellish ocean storm. Nobody was going to hear him, so what did it matter? He stretched out his legs and pulled his jacket tighter around him. "Let's just pretend that you had a decent Plan A. Face it, your idea to go down the coast and try to get the dope ashore and move it to the east coast was a pretty haphazard plan." He gave a thoughtful tip of the head and shrug of the shoulders. "I guess it qualified as a plan. Even if it wasn't carefully thought out, it still had the elements of a plan. OK. So, there's your Plan A. But it's in the tank now. Fine, no dope, no Plan A."

It was surprising how easy it was to say that when there was nobody else to hear. He was just getting warmed up too. "So, that means that you can move on to Plan B. No Plan B? No problem. We've got the finest minds in the planning department, right here, right now." He thought that the first thing he should do is to take an inventory of his current situation. That was pretty simple. One life raft slightly damaged but still floating. He looked around, murky reddish light from the canopy coloring the inside of the raft. The inflatable floor was pretty messy over on the other side, away from where he was sitting. A sticky, stinking mess where Mrs. Lu had been sick. Not nice.

Beside him, one fiberglass canister containing approximately three and a half million dollars in cash. American dollars. Nowhere to spend it at the moment and nothing to buy. He could think of a few things that he would like to spend some money on right about now. First thing; one set of dry clothes. Right out of the clothes dryer. Nice and warm and cozy feeling. He loved that when he was a kid and his mom would dress him in his little pj's right out of the dryer. They were the kind of pj's that had the little feet and he remembered feeling warm from top to bottom. His mother; smelling all boozy, that bright red lipstick she always wore, her makeup thick and pasty looking. Him; afraid that she would hit him again for some unknown reason, for something he had or hadn't done. But when she put him in those nice warm cozy pj's fresh from the dryer and tucked him into his nice warm cozy sheets, again fresh from the dryer, he was willing to forgive her anything, anything at all. Maybe tomorrow she'd be different. He'd peck her on the offered cheek as she bent down over him in bed and then as soon as she left, would pull the covers over his head and dream that he was back inside that warm place that he came from in the first place. All he wanted was that nice warm place. It was safe there. Nobody could hurt him there. Nobody could hit him.

Second thing he would spend some of the money on, right now, would be lots of hot coffee. He always made a big deal about how much he hated those coffee places like Starbucks with their frou frou drinks and their spiky haired "barista's." But he'd do some serious tipping right now just to get a nice, whatever they called the largest sized cup of just about every kind of coffee on their menu. That might just perk him up enough to get through the rest of whatever the hell Plan B was.

But there weren't any dry clothes out here and there wasn't any coffee of any kind either. So, forget that. No, he was going to have to wait to spend his money. But he had lots of it to spend. He just needed some dry land under his feet and he'd spend like a drunken sailor. You could take that to the bank.

What else did he have? Not much. Oh, his gun. Nice gun. Solid and powerful and heavy and ready to blow someone's ass off if they got in his way. "Well, folks, that's about it. The end of the inventory. A lot in some situations, not much at the moment." But at that moment, a place to spend money came rolling right up to his front door and blew the loudest horn that David Enzio had ever heard.

"Ooooooooooooooooooooohgah." He just about shit his pants. If he'd had any food in his system, he might just have done that very thing. He thought his heart might rip right out of his chest from the fright. He pulled the door to one side and looked out and up at the looming wall of a small freighter. Steel plating, rusty and peeling, great big rivets going up and down as the raft surfed the waves along side the ship. Enzio shook his fist at the ship.

"You assholes! You trying to scare me to death?" It was futile, nobody could hear him over the noise from the storm but that wasn't about to stop Enzio. He spotted a face on the wing sticking out beside the bridge. He had to crane his neck and look almost straight up. He shook his fist again. "Asshole," he shouted at the face.

They had a P.A. system and he heard a voice in thickly accented English. "Ahoy there. There is a ladder just aft of your position. You must come aboard for your safety. Thank you."

Thank you? Ladder? Enzio looked to the left and sure enough, a long rope ladder hung down, dangling in the water. His raft was drifting slowly alongside the ship and would reach the ladder in moments. This was both good and bad. Good because he could get out of this bloody rubber raft. Bad because he was never going to be able to climb that ladder and hold the canister of money at the same time. He wondered if they could hear him shouting from the bridge of the big ship.

"We're sorry to have frightened you, please come aboard by the ladder aft of you."

Getting There

That answered that question. He leaned out and cupped his hands around his mouth and shouted up at the face again. "I have a," he paused. He didn't want to say a canister of money. "I have some important belongings. One container. Please send a rope down."

"Roger that" was the reply and in moments a cargo net at the end of a long line slid down the side of the ship's hull. The motion of the raft in the huge waves was emphasized by the proximity of the ship. Enzio estimated that he was going about twenty five feet up and down with the passing waves. It was going to make it very difficult to get the canister into the net and get himself onto the ladder. But this was apparently what Plan B was. What else was he going to do? Wave them on and say he'd wait for the next boat to come along? Not likely. It was getting dark now and Enzio didn't relish spending the night on the raft.

Enzio brought the canister close to his knees and made sure it was securely fastened shut. The last thing he wanted was for the canister to open and money to scatter all over the bloody ocean. He leaned out the doorway and pushed his hand against the steel hull of the ship as the raft bounced alongside. Then the ladder was there. He grabbed hold and just about had his arm ripped out of its socket as the raft went down in a trough. He let go and realized this was going to be a very difficult and dangerous proposition. But it had to be done.

He grabbed the bottom of the ladder this time, which slowly angled back along the side of the ship as the raft drifted towards the stern. Once he came to the end of the ladders length, he came to a stop, only moving up and down with the big waves. He grabbed the net on the end of the line and shouted up at the deck. "Give me lots of slack."

Enzio realized that time was of the essence here. No dilly dallying. It was difficult holding on to the ladder with one hand but he stuffed the canister in the net as fast as he could and then yelled, "Pull, pull!" The canister was yanked from him and disappeared from his view. He said a little prayer for its safety.

The next thing to do was get his ass out of the raft and onto the rope ladder. He knew it was going to be painful and dangerous. He waited until the raft was at the top of a wave and grabbed a rung as high as he could and held on tight with all his might. The raft dropped away below him and he was left dangling and scrambling halfway up the side of the ships hull. With the wind and the motion of the boat, the ladder whipped in and out from the ship, slamming his body and raking his knuckles on the rusty steel.

He wasn't going to be able to hang by his arms very long; his old hand injury which he had got back at the motel in Tsawwassen was sending Morse code signals of pain to his brain. His legs were flailing around, like a man peddling an invisible bicycle, until he finally managed to find a rung with his right foot, then both feet. Just in time he was able to push up with his legs and take some of the strain from his hands. He was more comfortable but he was still swinging around on a rope ladder precariously hanging over the cold black ocean. He had two choices; up to safety or down to a watery hell. He started climbing up. Pull with one hand, lift a foot and find another rung. Push up with that leg. Move the other hand up and pull. Lift the other foot and try to find another rung. Slowly and carefully and painfully he climbed as he smashed repeatedly into the hull of the ship, one time twisting and banging his damaged ear against the steel.

Despite the cold and the rain and the spray, he could feel something warm oozing down the side of his face and neck. Blood from his torn ear. Insult to injury. He worked his way up until finally, at the end of his reserves of strength and running out of steam, he came to the edge of the deck. He hoped that he would get some help to make that last few feet. His eyes came level with the deck.

Shoes. A pair of well polished, black, thick soled oxfords to his left and a beat up looking pair of combat boots to his right. Two men, medium height but beefy looking reached down and grabbed him under the arms and pulled him up and through the gap in the railing and onto the deck where he lay, gasping for air like a beached fish.

The two men ignored him while they hauled up the dangling rope ladder, stepping on his legs and generally treating him like he was in the way. He rolled over onto his back and used his elbows to pull himself across the deck where he lay propped up against a locker along the side of the deckhouse. The two men were talking to each other, in Spanish he guessed, as they rolled up the rope ladder and then dragged it across his legs and began to stow it in the very deck locker which he happened to be leaning against. They seemed not to notice or care that Enzio was even there despite his protestations as the heavy pile of rope was dragged over his body.

A door opened to his left and a dark, heavily bearded man in a dirty turtleneck sweater leaned out apparently looking for their new passenger. Spotting Enzio laying on the deck, he gestured with one hand to come.

"What, no time to even catch my breath?" Enzio muttered. As he stood, weakly, he looked out at the sea from which he had just been rescued. It was a long way down to the water. From here, the ocean didn't look as wild and chaotic as it did from down on its surface. These guys probably had no idea just what kind of hell he had been through. He would be sure to bring them up to speed. He staggered on shaky legs towards the bearded man who turned and led the way into the deckhouse.

As the door closed behind him, Enzio was, for the first time in many long hours immersed in warmth and quiet. The sound of the wind and the crashing waves went away with the closing of the door. The warmth surrounded his wet cold body and he felt like sinking to his knees from the absolute bliss of it.

To his right, was the bridge of the vessel. The only lights were from the instruments, glowing green and red. Someone chattering on the VHF radio. One sailor standing at the wheel, another, to the right looking intently at a radar screen. They ignored him. Both of them had a bundle of American money sticking out of the back pockets of their dirty looking jeans. Alarm bells went off in Enzio's head. Like the opening bell on the stock exchange. Clang, clang, clang.

A hand grabbed Enzio by the front of his jacket and pulled him forward. Ahead and to his left was a door which the man opened after knocking and indicated that Enzio should enter. Enzio hesitated. The man gave him an impatient push.

The room was harshly lit by a buzzing fluorescent light fixture on the ceiling. A brass porthole looked out the port side of the room onto the dark clouds and rain that Enzio had just left. The man put his hand on Enzio's shoulder and forced him to sit in a wooden chair near a small desk built into the wall under the porthole. As he sat, Enzio looked around and was surprised to see his canister of money sitting on a small desk against the opposite wall. Sitting in a chair beside the desk, was a tall, slim, dark skinned man in a uniform. He wore a white shirt, gold on black shoulder boards, a couple of spots of ketchup or some reddish substance on the front next to a narrow black tie. He sat in a chair, the same as Enzio's, leaning forward, elbows on skinny knees, his balding head gleaming in the bright overhead light. He looked at Enzio for a few moments before finally offering his hand. Enzio hesitated, then took the proffered handshake.

"Captain Martinez. Melvin, please call me." He leaned back in his chair and pulled a package of cigarettes from his breast pocket. It was a new pack and he began banging it against his other hand. After a few good whacks, he opened the pack and offered a cigarette to Enzio. He took one and the Captain reached across with a shiny Zippo and lit the cigarette for Enzio and then one for himself. He ignored the other man.

He smiled at Enzio. "Excuse me, your name?" A little tip of the head, eyebrows arched.

"David. Look, I want to thank you for rescuing me. Now, if you would be so kind as to turn around and take me back to Victoria, I would be most grateful."

"Victoria? Turn around?" Captain Melvin Martinez laughed. "I'm sorry. So sorry. But we are on our way to San Diego, not Victoria. We have a schedule to keep and we can't take you back to Victoria. Already, slowing down to rescue you from the harsh and dangerous storm when you are in distress," he shrugged, hands outstretched, palms up, "we are already running behind our schedule."

Enzio sensed a bargaining session was now underway. He shrugged. "And I thank you for rescuing me. I would be happy to pay you to take me back to Victoria. It's not far, it won't take you long. I have business to attend to there."

The Captain looked taken aback. "Pay me? For doing what a good mariner is supposed to do? Obliged to do? Someday it could be me in a life raft," and here he crossed himself, "you would do the same for me, yes?" He had a slightly hurt look on his face.

"Yes, I certainly would do the same for you Captain. What I meant to say was that I would be happy to reimburse you and your crew for the lost time if you were to take me back to Victoria."

The Captain smiled at that. It was good news indeed. "Oh, excuse me. I apologize for the misunderstanding. You see, English is not my first language and sometimes I don't understand the subtleties of the conversation. Please forgive me. Yes," he shrugged, the corners of his mouth turned down, eyebrows up in counterpoint, "compensation would be good."

Enzio thought they were halfway there. Now it was just a matter of the amount of compensation.

The captain continued. "However, I am sorry, but we cannot take you back to Victoria. We must proceed to San Diego. You can compensate us for the time you spend on the ship but we must proceed. We can radio the officials that you are a shipwrecked sailor without papers and we can arrange for you to meet with a representative from the Canadian Embassy in the U.S."

Enzio's shoulders drooped. There appeared to be some negotiating technique that he was missing here.

"We are not set up to carry passengers, so you will have to bunk with the crew. Perhaps it is not the kind of accommodations you are accustomed to but it is all we have to offer."

Enzio was not going to bunk with a bunch of dirty sweaty sailors. No bloody way.

"Unless," the Captain offered.

Enzio sat up straight and leaned forward.

"Unless, Mr. Gonzalez here, the First Mate could be persuaded to offer the use of his private cabin. He looked at Mr. Gonzalez who had a look that clearly stated he was not about to relinquish his room without a serious argument.

"I would be willing to offer Mr. Gonzalez five hundred dollars for his cabin for the duration of the trip. I think that's a reasonable rate." Enzio looked back and forth between the two men.

Gonzalez and the Captain looked at each other for a moment, blank faced and then both burst into gales of laughter. It was several moments before they were composed enough for the Captain to speak again. "Five hundred dollars?" Here he gestured to the open case of money on the table. "Five hundred dollars? My dear sir, with so much money, it seems to me that you could be a little more generous than that. After all, the man would be giving up his own cabin which he has worked long and hard to achieve as a perk of his station in life. Please, don't insult the good man." The good man himself stood taller and looked quite aggrieved.

These bastards. Enzio knew he had to play along. "I'll tell you what Captain. On my way in, I couldn't help notice that the two men on the bridge each had a packet of money from my case. If you get the money back from those two, I will give one of the packets to the First Mate here. That should be more than adequate payment for a man of his station in life."

Captain Martinez looked at Enzio with cold steely eyes. His mouth had tightened to a small line under his thin moustache. "If you are suggesting that my men have taken money from you, I hope you are prepared to back that statement up with proof. Do you think that if we go to the bridge that the men, my honest hard working men, will have your money? I am insulted that you should make that kind of allegation. What have my men ever done to you except to rescue you from a very bad situation on the stormy ocean?" He leaned forward, his face close to Enzio's, "Well, are you prepared to back up your accusation?"

Enzio leaned back, away from the Captain. He was getting nowhere. The bastard had all the cards here. Enzio had none. Other than the money, he had few options. "Captain, you have to realize. I just came aboard from the cold and the wind. Look at my ear. Bleeding all over my shirt. I'm sure it's the combination of lack of food, sleep, loss of blood. I don't know what I'm saying. I apologize."

The Captain looked at the First Mate and smiled. The First Mate smiled back. The Captain leaned back and spread his hands in a benevolent gesture. "David, your apology is accepted. I'm sure that you are fatigued. We must let you get some food and some rest. But I don't believe that we settled the matter of accommodations just yet." The man was not going to let it go.

Enzio sighed. He took a drag on the forgotten cigarette. This was a no win situation. "How about one of these packets of money for the First Mate's cabin for the duration of the voyage? Would that be acceptable to him and to you?"

The Captain spoke rapidly to the First Mate in Spanish. Enzio was sorry that he had learned French as a second language. That might be useful in Quebec but he wasn't in Quebec now, was he?

"Mr. Gonzalez will have his belongings out of his, excuse me, your cabin in just a moment." The First Mate left the room. "In the meantime, we can discuss the compensation for the loss of time for the ship and the crew."

Enzio groaned. He thought that might have been forgotten or at least put off till later. He decided to put it up to the Captain first. "What do you think would be a reasonable reimbursement for helping a fellow mariner lost at sea?" That was a clever way of putting it Enzio thought.

"I think that the crew would be more than happy with half of the contents of this container. A reasonable amount under the circumstances, don't you think David?"

At that moment, David Enzio was sorry that he was not back on the life raft.

44 A TURNAROUND

Claire tried to get out of the bunk to help Abner with her mother. Abner was forced to raise his voice in order to get Claire to stay put.

"Claire," he snapped, supporting Mrs. Lu with one hand and removing the woman's dirty clothes with his other. "Stay in bed. You are not going to be able to help me here and it's not going to do any good if you re-injure your leg,"

Claire sat on the bunk, her hands clasped together under her chin, looking on breathlessly as Abner worked. She was clearly anxious and it was not without good reason. Abner had sat Mrs. Lu on the lower step of the companionway stairs while he undressed her. The Chinese woman was shivering, unable to speak and apparently not recognizing her daughter. Her clothes reeked of vomit and she had both urinated and defecated in her pants. It was an unpleasant scene. As a policeman, Abner had seen much worse than this, so he hadn't thought too much about it but Claire was horrified to see her mother in such a state.

"She's going to be okay Claire. She's dehydrated, and bordering on hypothermic. I'm going to get her undressed and get her in the shower and cleaned up. Then we're going to put her into bed with you and Barkley and slowly start putting fluids into her."

Claire was shocked that this man, practically a stranger was undressing her mother and was he suggesting that he was going to get into the shower with her?

As if reading her mind, Abner continued talking to Claire as he worked. "I would have you do this if it weren't for your leg but rest assured, I've seen a naked woman before and believe it or not, I am able to control myself." He had a garbage bag into which he was depositing the soiled clothes. A pair of very dirty panties were the last item to go in the bag. "Now Claire, I would suggest that you avert your young and innocent eyes unless you want to see what an old naked man looks like."

Claire's eyes widened. "You're not going to..." She left her statement unfinished as Abner pulled his shirt over his head and began undoing his belt.

"Claire, I'm going to give your mother a shower and I'm not going to get my only set of clothes all wet. Relax, okay? It's going to be alright." He grinned at her.

Claire turned away and began petting Barkley who was lying with his head in Claire's lap, completely unconcerned with the goings on with the new guest. It was no big deal to him.

Abner, naked now, picked the woman up and went into the head on the port side. He sat Mrs. Lu on the toilet. She shivered extra hard as her skin made contact with the cold toilet lid. Abner turned the water on in the shower and made sure it was only luke warm to start with. Turning, he picked Mrs. Lu up under the arms and gently eased her into the stream of water. The woman moaned and collapsed forward against Abner's chest. He held her and stroked her hair and slowly began turning up the heat. Every muscle in the woman's body was clenched tight. The shivering began to ease off and Abner felt her begin to loosen up a little. Mrs. Lu raised her hands up and gripped Abner's arms weakly. Abner smiled. It was the beginning of a big improvement that was about to take place.

Up on deck, Mick was freezing, his wet clothes sucking the warmth and strength from his tired body. He looked around the horizon at the stormy waters surrounding them. He was happy that they had found Mrs. Lu. It must have been a hellish experience for her and Enzio. He shook his head. To leave a sinking boat and get into a small rubber raft in seas like the ones he was looking at now must have been a frightening experience.

After Abner had taken Mrs. Lu down below, Mick had looked astern, wondering if he would still be able to see the raft but even with the binoculars he was unable to find it in the turbulent seascape. Turning to the radar screen, the raft was still there though, a small dot slowly moving to the east while Seagram continued on to the west. The other target, the larger vessel, was moving directly towards Enzio, perhaps having made visual contact with the raft or maybe just sensing that the radar contact was someone in trouble.

Mick picked up the microphone for the VHF radio. "Securite', Securite', Securite', this is the sailing vessel Seagram, I say again, the sailing vessel Seagram approximately thirty miles west of the entrance to Juan De Fuca Strait." He paused for a moment. "There is a life raft with one person onboard, due east of my position, approximately twenty five miles west of the entrance to Juan De Fuca Strait. Any vessels in the area, please respond, over." He sat back and shivered and waited. It didn't take long before a voice came back over the radio.

"This is the Motor Vessel Rio Bella, Motor Vessel Rio Bella. We have the life raft in sight and are slowing to render assistance. Out."

Out. That meant the end of the conversation. He pressed the send button on the microphone again, paused and then released it. He shrugged. Enzio was going to get picked up. It was a big ship, perhaps a large number of crewmembers. They could probably handle one guy. As he sat watching events play out on the radar screen, his teeth chattering, he saw the large target, which they had assumed was a large fish boat or small freighter, merge with the dot that was Enzio in the life raft.

Mick sat and pondered. What would happen with Enzio? Would the ship take him back to port or would they carry on, or would they call for the coast guard? Did he even care what happened to the bastard? Obviously Enzio had lost his load of dope. It was possible that he still had the money but what could Mick do about that? Did it matter? As he sat and shivered, he saw the two merged dots separate again. At least Mick didn't have to worry about trying to turn Seagram around to rescue Enzio. It was time to take care of themselves now. Time to get into some warm dry clothes.

45 RE-GROUPING

After Enzio had been rescued by the crew of the freighter and after getting Mrs. Lu settled onboard Seagram, Mick had scared the crap out of everyone getting the boat turned around and headed towards the relative safety of Juan De Fuca Strait.

They had decided that it would be wise to get medical attention for Claire and Mrs. Lu and Mick and they had called Van and arranged for him to meet them at the inner harbor in Victoria. While Seagram surfed the big waves towards safety, Mick had time to reflect on the last several days.

It was a shocking turn of events. He was now homeless. All he had were the clothes on his body. He didn't have a passport though he did have the identification that he carried in his wallet which included his driver's license. Thank God for that. At least he wouldn't have to deal with the Motor Vehicle Branch.

Starlight was gone. He shook his head over that one. The many years of sacrifice building his beautiful boat, the money and sweat and hardship, were all for naught. He had insurance on the boat but Starlight was now in about a hundred fathoms of water and if he was going to collect on that insurance it was going to involve proving that fraud wasn't part of the picture. Good luck with that. He suspected that it would be a big hassle and probably end up in court.

He could still work though his current sculpting project was down there with Starlight and the buyer was going to be expecting results pretty soon. He was going to have to start from scratch. He was even going to have to replace all his sculpting tools. And the little bust of Claire was gone too.

And Eddy. His best friend, Eddy was in the burn ward thanks to David Enzio. According to the reports he had received from Claire, Eddy was in bad shape. They expected him to recover but there was always the risk of infection and other complications.

Mick sighed. On the positive side, the glass half full side, they had rescued Mrs. Lu and she was going to be fine with a little rest and some repairs to her finger. It was hard to say how much mental recovery she was going to need but she was a pretty tough woman. Claire was going to need some care to make sure her leg was okay. Mr. Xun was apparently going to recover from his gunshot wound. Morris would be back to his old self without any permanent damage. That was all good news. And, Claire still loved him though there was that whole cultural barrier to deal with as far as her parents were concerned. And what family would want a homeless guy courting their daughter.

It had been an eventful week. As he looked out on the ocean, the turbulence of the seas mirrored the workings of his mind. It was difficult to believe that it was a little less than a week ago that he had gone sailing on Starlight for a peaceful weekend sail and now, everything was changed. "I guess I'm going to have to get an apartment and get busy sculpting to pay the bills." He was talking to himself and the stormy waters around him.

Seagram was doing a great job of sailing herself with Mick simply keeping an eye on things. He looked up as a seagull went rocketing by and then wheeled and fell into formation just off the port side, riding the invisible currents of the sky, looking down on him in the cockpit. Mick picked up the uneaten part of the sandwich Abner had given him earlier and threw it skyward. The seagull unerringly snatched it from midair and swallowed it without so much as even tasting it. It wasn't about taste. It was about filling a need and that's what Mick was going to have to start doing as soon as he got everybody back on shore safely.

In the early hours of the morning they docked at the Inner Harbor in Victoria. It was quiet, the tourists asleep after a night of drinking Molson's and Labatt's in the many bars. The skirl of bagpipes had gone silent, the lone piper at rest in his wee bed, fingers twitching, arm pumping in his dream of playing for a few loonies from the crowd by the Parliament Buildings. The panhandlers were not on duty yet, building up their strength in preparation for another day of hassling the tourists on the quaint streets of Victoria.

Van was there to transport the wounded to Victoria General Hospital in a borrowed SUV. Abner said that he would stay with the boat and took Barkley for a little walk around the inner harbor. Barkley was delighted to finally get some shore leave.

At the hospital, a subdued and weary Mrs. Lu was admitted for observation against her wishes but was more than pleasantly surprised when Van wheeled Mr. Xun into her room. An awkward reunion followed until Mick ushered everyone out of the room to give the couple some privacy.

"It is not easy," Claire explained, "for a Chinese couple, especially of my parent's age, to show affection in front of others. It is difficult even in private but I think under these circumstances it may be a little easier. My father very nearly lost his life and my mother could have lost her life several times over. I am sure that they are sharing how special this reunion is."

Claire and Mick were admitted and examined by Dr. Knights, the same doctor who had taken care of her father's gunshot wound. When he found out Claire was Mr. Xun's daughter he raised his bushy eyebrows.

"I don't know what you folks are up to but it's damned inconsiderate of you to drag me in here in the middle of the night. I hope you're not going to push for a group discount because I'm already working on the cheap. That will teach me for trying to get something built without the proper permits." He grinned at Mick and Claire. "On that same topic, the police have been quite interested in what you people have been up to. They've been around talking to Mr. Xun but the strange thing is that he only seems to be able to speak Chinese when they're around. And their interpreter has been having a devil of a time getting any information out of him. They will be most happy to meet with you Mr. Brese."

Mick nodded tiredly. "I was expecting to have to talk to them sooner or later. The person who caused all the injuries gave us specific instructions that we were not to notify the police but we don't need to worry about him now. As soon as everyone is taken care of, I'll sit down with them and fill them in on what's been going on. I imagine they've talked to Eddy by now."

The doctor's brow furrowed slightly. "Well, Mr. Wainwright has not been in much of a mood to talk to anyone lately. He's been very sick. By the way, I understand that there are some personal belongings of his to pick up from the burn unit. It's a shame about him. I'm really sorry."

It didn't take the doctor long to realize that he had just dropped a bomb judging from the stunned looks on both Mick and Claire's faces. He mentally kicked himself.

"I'm sorry. I thought you knew." He realized that being straightforward was the only way to get through this one. "Eddy passed away about midnight. The burns were really too much for him to overcome." He reached out and put his hand on Mick's shoulder. "I know you two were close friends because he left a letter for you. He seemed to know he wasn't going to make it and he made some arrangements earlier in the day and dictated a letter for you. I'll arrange for everything to be brought down here. But first we need to take care of the two of you." He was glad to be able to get to work on Claire.

As he removed the field dressing that Abner had put on Claire's wound, Dr. Knights appeared to be pleased with the situation. "This isn't looking too bad. With gunshot wounds, there's always some infection as most people don't sterilize bullets before they shoot you." He grinned at his little joke hoping that it might lighten the mood. "Claire, we're going to take you up to surgery to examine and clean the wound and be sure that there isn't any fabric contamination and to assess the muscle condition." He looked at Mick. "You mentioned that you had given her antibiotics to control infection but we really need to get in there and clean the wound thoroughly. I'll go get the ball rolling and someone will be here shortly to get you Claire. As for your noggin Mr. Brese, I'm going to send you down to E.R. to have a couple of stitches put in. When you think about how close that bullet came to your brains, you ought to count yourself a very fortunate fellow. But then so should all of you. Either you came up against a very unlucky shooter or you're just very lucky people."

Van could tell that Mick and Claire needed a little privacy, so he wandered off in search of the cafeteria. Mick was stunned by the doctor's news. He didn't know how to react, so he simply carried on. He would deal with it later.

"Claire, I'll go get my head attended to and then I'll wait here until you get back from surgery." She looked tense and Mick took her hand in his as he stood beside the examining table.

"Mick, you really don't need to wait. I'm so sorry about Eddy." She began to cry. She was exhausted and this latest piece of news threatened to send her over the edge but she saw that Mick was shocked at the turn of events. "Go back to Seagram and get some sleep after you get your head taken care of. You've been up for such a long time. You must be dead on your feet." From the way she held his hand, he could tell she was hoping that he wouldn't go.

"I can sit in the waiting room and have a little nap. Once you get back from surgery and settled into your room, then I'll go back to Seagram. There's no hurry for us to go anywhere now. We've got your mom and dad together, safe and sound, more or less and everything's under control. You concentrate on getting better and don't worry about me."

A knock on the door was followed by the entrance of a gurney pushed by a pony tailed male nurse. He announced, "I'm Steve and I'll be your driver tonight. Let's have you slide on over onto my magic carpet and we'll have you up to surgery in no time. Dr. Knights awaits you. He's cool, so rest assured, you're in good hands." He helped Claire get transferred over to the gurney and started rolling the unit back into the hallway. Claire grabbed hold of Mick's jacket and in a little girl voice, tinged with apprehension said,

"Mick, thanks for saying you'll wait. I'm looking forward to you being there when I get back. And Mick, thanks for rescuing my mother. I didn't get a chance to tell you earlier but I want you to know how grateful I am. I wanted to tell you, just in case."

She was babbling, exhausted and worried. Mick took her hand again and squeezed it tight.

"Claire, I'll be here waiting. Everything is going to be just fine. I'll see you when you come back down." He grabbed hold of the gurney and brought it to a stop. While Steve protested, saying they needed to get going, Mick kissed Claire. A long kiss. Claire was smiling and relaxed as their hands parted and she was wheeled away.

46 A BAD DREAM

     David Enzio was dizzy from exhaustion. As he stood under the hot water in the small shower in the first mate's cabin, he had to brace himself against the wall with one hand to stay standing upright. To say that he was pissed off about the Captain taking half of his money was a massive understatement. As soon as he had some sleep and some food, he was going to start plotting his revenge against every last person on the ship. He was going to get his money back. Right down to the bundles in the back pockets of those two bastards on the bridge.

     But first things first. He finished his shower and tumbled into the bunk, still wet, too tired to dry himself. He wrapped himself in the sheets and was instantly asleep. It was a troubled sleep though. Images of giant waves, windblown spray peppering his face caused him to wince and cry out in his sleep. He was soothed by the small soft hands of a Chinese woman, naked and pressing against him, warming his cold body. Her lips and tongue caressed his skin like a warm wet balm. He kept replaying the sinking of the boat and over and over saw the canister of money breaking open and all the bills being blown across the surface of the tormented water.

     Several times, he had jerked awake, hearing the tail end of a scream and realized that it was his own voice. He sweated, tossed and turned through the night and half of the morning. Sheer exhaustion had finally won out and he had slept for several hours, unmoving, as still as a corpse. Not until two in the afternoon did he finally wake, groggy and disoriented and starving. He had another shower to try to revive himself. He felt like he would be able to sleep for days if not for the hunger in his stomach.

Enzio was getting dressed; disgusted to have to put his dirty clothes back on but at least they were dry. A knock at the door startled him and he growled out, "Go away. I'll be out when I'm good and ready."

"Captain says you come now." A heavily accented voice raised loud enough to be heard through the door.

"Bugger off. Tell the Captain I'll see him later." Enzio was surprised at how tired he was and how much effort it took to sound tough.

"Captain says you come or he come get you himself."

Enzio sighed. What the hell was so important that the Captain wanted to see him? "Yeah, yeah, yeah. I'm coming. You tell the Captain I'll be there in a minute, savvy?"

Apparently it was enough to make the pest go away. Enzio put his watch on and with shaky hands, lit a cigarette from a pack that the first mate had left behind. The bastard had cleared out everything else but had overlooked the smokes. The nicotine went straight to Enzio's head causing him to have to sit for a moment to get his bearings. Another knock on the door.

"Captain says you come or else."

Enzio staggered to his feet and jerked the door open. He leaned down into the face of a short and surprised crewman. "You tell the Captain I am getting ready and I will be there in a minute. Now get lost." He pushed the small man hard and was satisfied when the crew member stumbled and fell on his ass. He missed the hateful look as he slammed the door shut.

Enzio turned and picked up the canister of money. It was considerably lighter after the Captain had taken half of the cash last night. Enzio wasn't going to just leave the remaining money lying around in his cabin while he wasn't there. These vultures would pick him clean before he had finished breakfast.

As he left the room, he looked at the tangle of bedding on the bunk. As messy as it was he was looking forward to getting back to sleep as soon as he ate and dealt with the Captain, whatever he wanted.

The small crewman was waiting for Enzio, standing just outside the Captain's cabin. As Enzio approached, the man opened the door and leaned in, apparently talking to the Captain. He stepped out and held the door open for Enzio.

Getting There

The Captain was sitting in the same chair as before. Beside him on the table was the pile of money. As Enzio came into the room, the Captain held up one of the hundred dollar bills and lit it with a match and proceeded to light his cigarette with the flaming green bill. Enzio's eye's bugged out of his head. The Captain must have gone money crazy. There was no other explanation. Who would do such a thing except someone who thought they had too much money?

Taking a deep drag from his cigarette and leaning back in his chair, the Captain dropped the burning bank note to the carpet and stepped on it, grinding his foot back and forth slowly. He watched Enzio as he exhaled a cloud of smoke.

"Hello Mr. Enzio. I trust you had a good sleep? Is everything to your liking in your cabin?" There was an exaggerated emphasis on "your cabin." "We want you to be comfortable while you are with us. After all" and here he gestured to the pile of money on the table, "you paid handsomely for your passage, did you not?"

Enzio sat down and placed the canister of money close by his feet. He pulled out a cigarette of his own and waved off the Captain's offer to light it with another one hundred dollar bill.

"Apparently Captain, you think you have money to burn. You only had to pluck me from the raft to get it whereas I went through hell to get that money in the first place. So, do me a favor and show some respect for what I "paid" you for my passage."

The Captain smiled and spread his hands in a benevolent gesture. "I'm sorry Mr. Enzio. I certainly did not mean to show you any disrespect." He took another drag on his cigarette and slowly exhaled. He tipped his head back and the smoke curled from his nostrils as he looked at the ceiling, thinking. "I'm curious Mr. Enzio. Do you think that just because we are foreigners, don't speak the language as good as you, because we are common sailors of a," here he shrugged and put his hands in the air, "how shall I say it, working vessel that you can trick us? What is the expression? Pull the wool down over our eyes?"

Enzio squinted at the Captain wondering what was going on. The bastard should be treating him like royalty. It's not every day you literally stumble on someone in the middle of the ocean who makes you a rich man. Over a million and a half dollars was more than this schmuck would make in a decade of driving this shit heap around the ocean.

Enzio stood up, picking up the canister of money. "I'm going to get something to eat and then get some more shut eye. I don't know what the hell you're talking about. I don't care if you're a foreigner or speak Martian for that matter. You've got your money and I've got mine and when you drop me off in California, we'll both be happy men." He turned to leave only to find the doorway blocked by one of the deckhands, arms crossed over his big chest. "What the hell is going on here, Cap." The answer to his question was a hard fist from the Captain, delivered right to the side of his head. Enzio went down like a rag doll, his ears ringing, everything blurry from the tears of pain that sprang from his surprised eyes.

The Captain leaned down over Enzio's prostrate body. He put his mouth close to Enzio's ear and spoke quietly. "You made a mistake trying to fool us, Mr. Enzio. We're off the coast of Oregon now and your money and our good will has run out. It's time to disembark." He stood up and gestured to the deckhand who grabbed Enzio under the arms and pulled him to his feet.

"What the hell are you talking about? Captain, I gave you all that money and you said you were going to take me to California where I could go to the Canadian Embassy and arrange to get back home. I expect you to hold up your end of the bargain." Enzio was in a panic now. Sweating and struggling to stand up on shaky legs. What was going on? Since when was over a million and a half bucks only enough to get a guy to the Oregon coast?

The Captain picked up one of the bundles of money from the table. He turned and smacked Enzio across the face with it. A forceful blow, it rattled the teeth in his head. Enzio's hand flew up to hold his burning cheek. The look on his face was one of total incomprehension.

"This," the Captain said, shaking the bundle of hundred dollar bills in front of Enzio's face, "is worthless. The only thing it's good for is lighting cigarettes or wiping your ass with. As a matter of fact, it's too coarse for wiping your ass." He was shouting now. He broke the band on the bundle and threw the money at Enzio who fell to his knees trying to gather up the precious bills. The guy was crazy. Wipe your ass with it? Light a cigarette?

The Captain turned again and scooped up a large quantity of bundles in his arms and dumped it on Enzio's head, knocking him to the floor. More bundles followed until Enzio was partly buried in money.

Getting There

"You are an idiot if you think this is real money and you are an idiot if you think that you can use it to make us do your bidding. Either way, it's the end of your journey with us. We risk our ship to pick you up and this is how you repay us?" He stepped down on one of Enzio's hands which were scrabbling like crabs over the bundles of bills. Enzio's eyes bulged as the Captain increased the weight on the foot.

"I don't know what you're talking about. It's real money. It's my money. I earned this money. Brese gave me the money. It's…" A light went on in Enzio's scrambled brain. His gaping mouth snapped shut as realization flooded over him making him want to vomit. He'd been tricked. That son of a bitch Brese. At no point in the process, no point in the whole dangerous journey had he stopped to take a close look at the money. He'd been on the run the whole time, busy as a bee, up to his armpits in it the whole time and simply had trusted that it was his money.

Enzio yanked his hand from under the Captain's foot, ignoring the burning pain in his fingers. He picked up one of the loose bills and brought it close to his face. A hundred dollar bill. There was old Ben Franklin staring out at him, his mouth a grim line, the balding head, the dickey sticking up from his shirt. One Hundred in numbers on each of the four corners, the seals where they were supposed to be. He flipped it over. There was Independence Hall, In God We Trust, the color was green, the paper was… it felt a little odd, a little stiff, a little too smooth perhaps. He looked up at the Captain, searching, pleading for an answer.

"You fool. Can't you feel the difference? It's a photocopy for crying out loud. A bloody photocopy or something printed from a computer printer. It's good but that all it is. It's a counterfeit bill you idiot."

The Captain was kind enough not to do further insult to the senseless Enzio before he had two crewmembers throw him over the side. They threw the canister and all of the counterfeit money after him. The whole crew, not including the man at the wheel, stood at the rail and shouted and jeered at Enzio splashing and gasping in the cold ocean. He looked up at the big ship seeing the angry men yelling down at him. He knew he was going to drown and he didn't have his gun with him. It was up there on the ship, in his cabin where the bed was, where the sheets and warm blankets were. He wanted to pull the covers over his head and pretend he was back inside the warm place but it wasn't warm. It was wet and it wasn't safe and it was so terribly cold. Even the rage inside couldn't warm him.

47 HOME SWEET HOME

     Pender Island was buzzing with concern and speculation after the wreckage of Claire's airplane was found over on Saturna. That was until a thoughtful Mr. Xun called a neighbor and explained what was going on. Mr. Xun had received the information about the crash from Van and from his bed in the hospital realized that friends would be worried about Claire. It wasn't until talking to the neighbor that it was brought to his attention that people were worried about the whole family, not just Claire.

     So, it was with a lot of excitement that the community welcomed the family back home, one week after Claire's surgery in Victoria. Van had loaded the walking wounded and Claire in her wheelchair into the SUV and drove them home. Mrs. Lu protested strongly about having to take the ferry but the desire to be back in her own safe home again won out. Thankfully the water was as smooth as it could be and the trip had gone well. It wasn't until arriving on their street after the ferry trip back to Pender Island that any of them realized that they had been missed quite so much. Trees and bushes along both sides of the street had red ribbons tied to branches and a big crowd of neighbors and friends stood waiting for them in front of the house.

     "What's all this about?" Mrs. Lu asked from the back seat where she sat in between Claire and Morris. Mr. Xun in the front seat looked astonished at this outpouring of attention. Claire had one hand covering her wide open mouth, eyes wide in surprise. None of them realized that they had so many friends; none of them realized that there would be so much concern. They were after all, just another family, or so they thought.

Mrs. Lu's calligraphy club, a group of elderly ladies who met with her several times per week to practice Chinese characters under her patient tutelage had made a sign saying "Welcome Home" in big Chinese characters. She would never have the heart to tell them that the sign read "Your Home Is Being Welcomed." After all, it was the thought that counted.

A group of Mr. Xun's Tai Chi students were in the middle of a routine on the front lawn. Upon the arrival of the SUV bearing their instructor, they all stopped and lined up and put fist to hand in front of their bodies and bowed.

Sitting on the front steps was Claire's instructor, Captain Harris. He was smoking a cigarette, a big boyish grin on his face. He had brought the broken propeller from Claire's airplane and had nailed it up above the porch. A sign below it read, "Any landing you can walk away from…is still a crappy landing if your prop looks like this!" Claire read it from the back seat of the vehicle, smiling with tears coming from her eyes.

As the SUV came to a stop, there was a rush to open the doors and help them all out. Claire was picked up and placed gently in the wheelchair, which was carried up the front stairs and into the house. The smell of cooking permeated the air, red lanterns and Chinese New Year decorations, the only ones available upon short notice, hung on the walls and from the ceiling.

The whole family was made comfortable in the front room with great care and attention to the shoulder of Mr. Xun and Claire's leg. Mrs. Lu tried without success to shoo the ladies away as they sat her in the big recliner in the waning sun from the front window. A new quilt from the Quilter's Guild was wrapped around her with a great deal of fussing and adjusting. Morris with his head still wrapped in gauze, sat on a comfy armchair to the left of Mrs. Lu, not saying much but smiling happily at being included in the celebration.

Captain Harris had brought a big cooler full of Tsingtao beer and he had also done some shopping on the mainland and had come up with a number of bottles of Maotai Jiu, China's famous liquor. Bottles were opened and glasses were filled and when Captain Harris saw that everyone had something to drink he called for attention. He had to finally give a big shout to be heard over the hubbub.

Getting There

"Ladies and Gentlemen, I'm not much of a speech maker." He had to give another big shout to be heard over the catcalls and hoots from those who knew better. Grinning, he carried on. "OK, I read you five by five. However, I will keep this short and sweet." He raised his bottle of beer, "Here is to our good friends and neighbors, Mr. Xun, Mrs. Lu and sweet Claire and our new friend Morris, all of whom we are proud to know and very grateful to have back with us, all in one piece, more or less. To their good health." He made a toasting motion with his bottle towards the three family members and everyone echoed, "To their good health."

The calligraphy ladies broke for the kitchen and a great deal of giggling and clanging of pots and pans announced a wide variety of culinary activity. Along with the calligraphy classes, several of the women had also taken cooking lessons from Mrs. Lu. More accurately they had been learning "The Secrets Of Chinese Dumplings" and they had pulled out all the stops in their preparations today. After all, they were cooking for the master. Soon from the kitchen came plates of Jiaozi, their little pleated edges holding in savory meat and vegetable filling. Pot stickers, pan-fried first, then steamed, little golden brown pockets of delight. Har Gow followed close behind, plump little snacks of shrimp and bamboo shoots. One of the ladies, Mrs. Toth was particularly gifted at making Siu Mai which was well received by the crowd in the living room. Mrs. Toth waited apprehensively in the doorway to the kitchen as Mrs. Lu picked up one of the basket shaped dumplings, paused and tasted. Her look of satisfaction was all Mrs. Toth needed before heading back, all smiles, into the steaming kitchen to the congratulations of her peers.

Captain Harris had brought a bar of medals which he ceremoniously pinned on Claire's sweater. He proclaimed that she was now one of the fraternity, having lived to tell the tale. He told everyone that she would soon become just as boring to have at a party as he was. Van, between mouthfuls of dumplings and beer said that he doubted that anybody could ever become as boring as the Good Captain. Captain Harris made like he was going to attack the gigantic Van. Despite the pilot's own large stature, Van simply plunked a big ham sized hand on the Captain's head and kept him at arm's length.

It soon became evident that the family was running out of energy. Despite a week of rest in the hospital, they had still not regained their former strength. Claire, seeing her father struggle to keep his eyes open, cleared her throat and spoke.

"Thank you everyone for your wonderful friendship. It is so nice of you all to come out today to welcome us back. My mother and father and I are grateful to you and we hope that we can repay your kindness." This was followed by a chorus of "no, that's not necessary" and "don't mention it" and simply "you're welcome."

Van, seeing what Claire was leading up to, started to move around the room rounding up plates and glasses along with subtle suggestions to finish up. His lead was followed by the Tai Chi students who, one by one, thanked their teacher and his wife and daughter for their hospitality and headed for the door. The hubbub died down until only a few voices could be heard from the kitchen along with the clatter of plates and dishes being washed up.

Van helped Mr. Xun from his chair and assisted the small man up the stairs to his room. Mrs. Lu sat for a few moments silhouetted in the fading light from the picture window behind her. It was good to be home again. She was remembering that there were times on the boat with Enzio that she thought she might never see home again. It certainly gave her a greater appreciation of the simple pleasure of sitting in her warm and cozy living room, a place she had long ago taken for granted. As she looked around the room at the family photos on the mantle above the fireplace, at the decorations and furniture that she had brought from China, even the very house that they sat in, she realized that none of these things were as precious as their own lives. And as she looked across the room at her daughter, she understood that her daughters' happiness mattered more than ever.

Van came back down and took the quilt from Mrs. Lu and helped her up. She tried to shoo him away but he would have none of it. Like an overgrown mother hen, he carefully helped her up the stairs and ushered her into the room where Mr. Xun was laying on the bed. He waved off their thanks and headed back downstairs to see if Morris needed help finding his room. Morris was saying goodnight to Claire and declined Van's offer of help before heading upstairs where he turned in, grateful to be in a real bed instead of a hospital bed.

One of the remaining ladies had made up a bed for Claire in the office room in the back of the house. It had its own bathroom and would serve Claire well enough until she was able to get around better on her injured leg. Captain Harris picked Claire up from the couch and carried her to her new room and gently placed her on the bed. As Claire got comfortable, Captain Harris sat down on the side of the bed.

"Claire, how are you feeling?"

She lay back against the pillows and sighed. She looked down at the medals pinned on her sweater. She unpinned them and extended them out to the Captain.

"Robert, I have to be honest with you, I don't deserve these medals. Truth is I messed up big time. I should have just throttled back and kept going straight ahead and I could have landed the airplane quite easily. Instead, I ended up in the trees and wrecked my beautiful little airplane and nearly killed myself." This was something she had been thinking about ever since getting back on dry land and it hurt. It hurt a lot to think it and it hurt a lot to say it. But it was the truth and she began to cry. It started with little sniffles which she tried to cover up by looking in her sweater pockets for a Kleenex to no avail. In a moment, she was bawling like a little girl. Captain Harris moved closer and took her in his arms, holding her head to his chest, gently rocking her and patting her back.

"Claire, it's not your fault. You can't second guess what happened out there. You're forgetting a couple of things. Your airplane got hit in the engine; a bullet went right into the oil pan and stopped the engine cold. That's enough to have caused all kinds of problems for any pilot." He paused while she hiccoughed and started sobbing some more.

"Second, you got shot in the leg. That could have ended your life right there. The combination of the engine quitting and you getting shot would have finished any pilot. Me included. I've crashed a few more times than I'm willing to admit and I've never been shot. So, you're one up on me."

Claire pushed away from Captain Harris's chest. Her eyes were red rimmed and puffy. Her nose was running and he reached for some tissues from the nearby desk. She blew her nose. "I don't think I'm going to be able to fly again Robert." Her face crumpled and she fell against him again sobbing into his shirt.

"Claire, I'll be willing to bet that you'll fly again. But you don't have to think about that now. You just have to worry about getting better, that's your main concern. Later, we'll talk about flying. When you're good and ready. But my bet is that it will be sooner rather than later. I know you a lot better than you might think."

He held her until her crying came to an end. When he finally eased her back against the pillow, he saw that she had fallen into an exhausted sleep. He took the tissues from her hand and gently stood up so as not to wake her. As he turned, he discovered that Van was standing in the doorway watching him. The big man looked concerned but Captain Harris gave him a thumb's up and carefully covered the sleeping girl with a blanket. The two men quietly headed back into the living room where they sat down and opened another beer.

"She hasn't been getting much sleep lately," Van said by way of an explanation of Claire's tears. "Mick and I have been taking turns staying in the room with her at the hospital and she's been having some terrible dreams. Nightmares I guess you would call them. A lot of the time she just laid there with her eyes open, afraid to sleep. She says that the crash is like she let everyone down. The cost of the airplane and letting Enzio get away."

The Captain looked at Van. "One crash and she thinks she's a failure. She's fallen off the horse but if I know Claire, she'll get back on one of these days. It's just going to take some time."

The last two ladies finished up in the kitchen and quietly said their goodbyes to the men. Captain Harris got up and gave each of them a big hug and escorted them out into the evening. It was pleasant out on the porch and Van joined him where they stood in silence. The smell of wood smoke added a touch of flavor to the soft darkness.

"Mick will be here in a little while. He's sailing over from Victoria. I'm going to go down to the dock to meet him." Van pushed off from the post that he was leaning against. "You know, Claire's really taken a shine to him."

Captain Harris nodded. He was a little jealous but he was happy for her. She had been so focused on flying that she had blocked out every advance by every guy that had come along, including his own and especially the Chinese businessman. But Mick had found a way into her heart and that was a good thing. It was about time that a sweet, beautiful woman like Claire had a good loving man in her life. Even if it wasn't Captain Robert Harris.

Getting There

48 MAO FIFTY FOUR

Dear Mick.

Well old buddy, I've got bad news and good news. The bad news is that I'm dead. If you're reading this letter, for sure I'm tango uniform or tits up as they say. I'm going to miss you Mick. You were my best friend and I thank you for making my last years the best of my life. If not for you, I would probably have just drunk myself to death instead of having found Seagram and learned a new way of life. It's true, I still have a fondness for the spirits but you gave me a purpose that I would never have found on my own.

The good news? The good news is that Seagram is now yours. I had a lawyer transfer the title and you now own her lock, stock and barrel. I'm really sorry about getting you involved in all of this. I'm sorry that you lost Starlight. I really am. I know you prefer Starlight and often mocked the complexity and luxury of Seagram but you know she's a fine vessel and I hope you don't just sell her outright and piss away the money on wine women and song. But she's all yours to do with what you will.

As you know, I've worked and lived with Claire and her family and they are the best. Mr. Xun and Mrs. Lu may look and act like a couple of elderly foreigners but don't let looks fool you, they are amazing people. And Claire is something else again. She's a super nice person, she's sexy and beautiful and she doesn't even know it. From my point of view, the only problem with Claire is that she's intelligent too. You know how I am. I like my woman to only know one and two syllable words and Claire knows big words in more than one language for crying out loud. But we get along like brother and sister.

You, on the other hand get along with Claire like boats and water. The only problem is that you've got plans and I know you're so focused on your goal that you might let her slip through your fingers. It's your life buddy but just a little word from the dead; don't. She's perfect for you my man. She's Chinese and Chinese women are as loyal to their man as the day is long. And since I happen to know the kind of luck you've had with women in your past, take it from me; if she let's you in the door don't let her get away no matter how badly you want to go offshore sailing. And don't let Mrs. Lu scare you either. Just don't turn your back on her.

I left a little something for you with Mrs. Lu. In the envelope you have in your hand, you will find a Mao button. Yeah, that's what it's called. A Mao button. You can see it's a lapel or jacket pin featuring none other than your garden variety mass murderer, Chairman Mao Zedong. Mrs. Lu gave me this button. Give it back to her and whatever happens beyond that, it's all yours.

One last thing before I go. I'm feeling kind of worried about this death business. I'm reminded of that old joke. You know the one about the atheist who's lying in his coffin wearing his best clothes. He's all dressed up with nowhere to go. Well, that's kind of my take on dying. I never believed in a power greater than myself. So, I always imagined death to be a trip to nowhere, a black void forever. It's kind of scary. I wish I could talk to you Mick because you always had a knack for making me feel better. Thanks for everything old pal.

Eddy

49 GETTING BACK TO WORK

After the family had been released from the hospital, Mick had arrived at Pender Island and had been warmly welcomed by Claire's family. Especially Mrs. Lu. He and Mrs. Lu shared a special bond, one that only they understood. She had insisted that he stay with them at their home until he got organized on his new boat. One morning when Mr. Xun was already gone to teach a class and Claire was still asleep in the back room, Mrs. Lu made breakfast for Mick and herself.

She had come to know his preferences over the past week and had learned how to make coffee to his liking. She even had a friend bring some of his favorite coffee beans from the mainland. As the sun crept into the cozy kitchen, while a couple of cats wound around her ankles looking for affection and food, Mrs. Lu talked of the harrowing events on the high seas.

"I never thought I would live to see this house or my family again, Mick. In all my life in China, I never believed in God, I never prayed. On that boat, I prayed a lot. The whole trip on the boat was like going to hell and David Enzio was the evil devil. After the boat sank and we were in the life raft, I really don't remember very much at all. When you rescued me, I was delirious. I found myself suspended over the water and I imagined it was God himself holding my hands and the Devil holding my feet. It was like being caught in a tug-of-war between good and evil."

Mick sipped his coffee, trying to cover his embarrassment at being even deliriously mistaken for God himself. "Well," Mick said, setting his cup down, "I've done a fair bit of praying and talking to

God too when I've been out on the water. I think it has something to do with how big the ocean and sky seems and how small it makes us feel. And it really was a hellish storm, Mrs. Lu."

Mrs. Lu brought a plate of pancakes to the table and set them in front of Mick. "Eat, eat. I'll make you some more when you finish these. Eat."

Mick had learned that this was a common encouragement around the dining table. Mr. Xun said it, Mrs. Lu said it and Claire said it too. It seemed to be a Chinese thing. Regardless, he didn't need too much encouragement and loaded three golden brown pancakes onto his plate. Mrs. Lu herself poured the syrup and topped up his coffee. If he wasn't careful, she was going to take over cutting the pancakes and putting them in his mouth.

"I never really got a chance to thank you for everything you did Mick. For rescuing me and taking care of Claire." She put her hand on his forearm, stopping him for a moment. "Thank you Mick." She gave his arm a squeeze and smiled at him. Tears welled up in her dark eyes and spilled over and down her cheeks. She pulled a tissue from inside the sleeve of her sweater and put her head down slightly and dabbed at the tears.

This was not the first time that this scene had taken place. It was the first time that she had mentioned praying and God but she had already thanked him numerous times and frequently got a little weepy when doing so. As he had done before, he patted her free hand and then went back to eating.

Mr. Xun had done similar things. Late one afternoon, he had come by the studio where Mick was trying to finish the commission for the pianist's husband. The bust was coming along quickly as this was the second time Mick had done the piece. Mr. Xun had introduced Mick to a sculptor who had a studio not far from the Government dock and Mick had been working long hours on the clay bust getting it ready to cast a bronze from the finished work.

Mr. Xun had stood nearby, not saying anything while Mick worked. It was a companionable silence between the two men. Classical piano music played in the background and it seemed like Mr. Xun was merely there to observe. But eventually and looking rather awkward, he had asked Mick to stop for a moment.

"Please Mr. Brese, I wonder if I could say something to you." He was not the most communicative man on Pender Island so this was difficult for him. Mick put his tools down and picked up his coffee cup and took a sip as he looked at the small Chinese man. This was a man better suited to giving instructions on Yang Palm and Wu Bow Stance or other Tai Chi forms than in opening up to a Lao Wai, or foreigner.

"Mrs. Lu and Claire are…" here Mr. Xun paused, looking uncomfortable. "They are my life. I am not here in Canada for any reason except to give a better life to the two people who mean the most to me in the entire world. I am in your debt Mr. Brese, because you have given to me what was taken away. An evil man tried to take away my reason for living and you stopped him. Thank you so much Mr. Brese." It came out sounding like "Sank you so much." Mr. Xun put his fist to his palm in front of his chest and bowed deeply to Mick who jumped up from his stool and raised the man to a standing position again. There were tears streaming down the cheeks of Mr. Xun.

"Mr. Xun, you don't need to thank me. I'm sure that anybody would have done what I did. I'm happy that I was able to be there with Abner to help Claire when she crashed and I'm glad we were able to locate the boat with Enzio and Mrs. Lu. We just got lucky, that's all."

Mr. Xun grabbed Mick's hand with his own and held on. "Mr. Brese, you are so mistaken. You did more than get lucky. I know what you did involved a lot of skill and determination and bravery. Regardless of what you say, I am forever in your debt. I brought a little something to celebrate with." Here he pulled out one of the bottles of Maotai Jiu from inside his coat and placed it on the counter. "Do you have two glasses please?"

A part of Mick was touched by this man's thankfulness and show of appreciation. Another part of him went "Oh, oh." It was a big bottle and Maotai Jiu was potent brew.

Once the drinking started, all thoughts of sculpting were out of the question. Mick finally ran out of diplomatic ways to try to get out of "just one more toast" and simply followed Mr. Xun's lead. For a small man, Mr. Xun sure could drink. A lot more than Mick who started feeling woozy by round three and was completely knackered by round six or seven. And that was just the first hour. When they staggered down the road to Mr. Xun's home it was well into the early hours of the morning. The little Chinese man had finished off the bottle himself, telling Mick that it was a good sign that his future son-in-law wasn't much of a drinker.

It wasn't until the next morning as the hellish aftereffects of the night's libations wreaked havoc with his system that Mick vaguely recalled the "future son-in-law" statement. He wasn't one hundred percent sure that he had heard it or whether he had imagined it and he couldn't think of a way to broach that subject with Mr. Xun, so he just let it go. If it had been stated, he was pleased to be so accepted. If it had been in his imagination, he thought that the thanks that he had gotten from Mr. Xun would probably stand him in good stead when the question came up. When they had finally arrived home that night, or more accurately early in the morning, Mr. Xun still had the energy and stability to make up a bed for Mick on the couch in the living room. Then at the crack of dawn, Mick had woken to the sound of whistling coming from the kitchen along with the clang and clatter of pots and dishes.

Mick pulled the pillow and covers over his head in an attempt to block out the cheerful sounds and drifted back into a tortured sleep. He was rudely awakened by insistent shaking from Mr. Xun. Mick grabbed the hand on his shoulder and in a raspy voice said, "Ni Hao, Mr. Xun. Please be careful. I feel like my head could explode at any moment now."

Mr. Xun peered closely into Mick's face. "Yes, Maotai Jiu is very strong drink. You did okay for Lao Wai. I will keep in mind for the future that you are not a strong drinker. It is good. It will make my daughter happy. Come now, to the table. I have made a nice congee. It is good for your stomach. Good for your health. Make you feel better." He grinned at Mick and held out his hand to help the ailing man to his feet.

Two bowls of congee were in place at the dining table along with a pot of tea. Mick started to prepare coffee but Mr. Xun herded him to the table and forced him to sit.

"Eat, Mr. Brese. Eat. Drink the tea also. Tea will be better for your stomach and your head. This is tea from chrysanthemum flowers and mint leaves. I will make up a thermos of it for you to drink during the day. Soon you will feel better. Now eat the congee. No bacon and eggs this morning." Mick winced at the thought of greasy bacon. The congee was not something that Mick was used to eating but after a few spoonfuls, he had to admit that the rice porridge was going down just fine.

After a quick breakfast, Mr. Xun placed a large green metal thermos of tea on the table next to Mick. "Remember Mr. Brese, drink the tea and lots of water. You will have smiling mood quite soon." He turned and headed out the front door. A smiling mood? It seemed an impossible concept at this stage of his hangover. How was it possible that Mr. Xun was in any condition to teach a Tai Chi class after drinking so much last night? He still wore a sling to protect his left shoulder but that didn't seem to slow his teaching down. He was the one armed Tai Chi master at least for a while longer.

  Later in the day, while working high up on the mast of Seagram, he had to admit that most of the hangover from the night's drinking was gone. Whether it was the tea or the congee that made him feel better was anybody's guess.

50 EDDY'S SURPRISE

That evening as everyone relaxed in the living room after dinner, Mick finally gotten around to presenting the Mao Zedong button that Eddy had left with him to Mrs. Lu. She looked at him. "Where did you get this?"

Mick answered, "From Eddy. He said that I should give it to you. Do you recognize it?"

Mrs. Lu nodded. "Of course. I gave this to Eddy." She began to tear up at the mention of his name. "Poor, poor Eddy. I wish we could have rescued him from the fire."

Mick sat on the couch, unsure of what he was stirring up with the presentation of the Mao button. It seemed like a simple thing but it appeared to be opening old memories.

Mrs. Lu got to her feet. "Let me show you where this comes from. Would you help me, Xun Xi Pei?"

Claire and Mrs. Lu stood up and moved over to a large Rosewood armoire standing against the wall. It was a handsome piece of furniture, perhaps a little taller than Mick. He watched as Mrs. Lu opened the doors on the front of the cabinet. There were several shelves with an assortment of placemats and dinner napkins and candles. Below that were two drawers, side by side. Mrs. Lu opened one of the drawers and reached inside with her fingers. She wasn't taking anything from the drawer but was instead reaching near the back of the drawer where the tips of her fingers found a small brass pin. She pushed hard on the pin with one finger until the pin sank flush with the surrounding wood. At the same time, the two drawers together popped up about a half inch at the front. Mrs. Lu used both hands and lifted the whole drawer assembly from the cabinet. It took a bit of twisting to get it clear until with a bit of help from Claire, the drawers were placed on the floor nearby.

The drawers concealed a hidden storage area which took up the width and depth of the armoire and was about ten to twelve inches deep. From the front, just looking at the cabinet, it appeared as though there was just empty space below the drawers. A person would actually have to look or feel under the armoire to discover that there was a compartment below the drawers.

Inside the compartment were a couple of items. The first thing was a wooden box, wide and thin, practically taking up the whole top space of the compartment. Mrs. Lu took it out and placed it on the dining table. She rotated the two catches on the front of the box and opened it. Inside were a wide variety of badges carrying the image of Mao Zedong. It was an impressive collection. Mrs. Lu turned to Mick and began to explain what they were looking at. "This is my collection of Mao badges. Everyone in China used to wear them. Some of these come from the time before China was liberated by Mao. They are rarer than the others. Most were made during the Cultural Revolution when they were manufactured by factories, work units and army units. It became all the rage to have a little red book in one hand and a Chairman Mao badge pinned to your chest."

Mick stared at the badges. "Let me guess. There's one missing from this collection."

"There used to be fifty four but when I showed my collection to Eddy, I gave him one. Now I have fifty three."

Mick nodded and looked closely at the badges. "Have you always kept your collection in the hidden compartment? Was the collection in the compartment when you showed it to Eddy?"

"Always. I don't take the collection out and I don't like to have it around because it carries too many memories of what I think are the worst times of my life in China. But they are collector's items and I thought that they might be worth something someday. Eddy was with me when I opened the compartment to show him the collection."

Mick pointed into the compartment. "And has that case always been in there?"

Mrs. Lu shook her head. "No, I've never seen it before. But there are only four people that know about the secret compartment.

Well, five now, including you Mick. So if it wasn't put there by any of the four of us, it had to be put there by Eddy."

Mr. Xun spoke up. "Well, let's see what's in it. What are we waiting for?"

The case fit the compartment so well that it was difficult to get it out. There was a small amount of room on the front but not enough to tip the case and grab the handle. Mrs. Lu slid her fingers down one side and Claire did the same on the other while Mr. Xun lifted on the front. Between the three of them, they managed to slide the case slowly up until Mr. Xun was able to slip his hand underneath and then twist the case and pull it free from the armoire.

This was not your ordinary every day suitcase. It was black, made from some kind of plastic with ridges molded into the top and bottom for strength. Mick understood that it was made from carbon fiber which was expensive and strong. It had the look of something that Eddy would own.

Mr. Xun grunted as he took the weight of the suitcase and he quickly set it down on the floor. He tipped it upright and picked it up by the handle and moved it to the middle of the floor so that everyone could go sit down and still see.

Claire sat beside Mick, perched on the edge of the couch and watched as Mr. Xun and Mrs. Lu knelt down beside the case. Mr. Xun tried to open the case but there were combination locks holding it shut. He looked at Mrs. Lu who shrugged.

"Don't ask me. I don't have any idea what the combination might be."

"Try 7253," Mick volunteered. "It was Eddy's key number at the marina."

Mr. Xun dialed the combination and the locks snapped open. There were smiles all around. There were even bigger smiles when Mr. Xun laid the case down and lifted the lid. Everyone leaned forward to get closer and see what was in the case. They were stunned by the sight of all that money. And what a lot of money it was. Nice rows of neatly packaged bundles of one hundred dollar American bills.

51 THE BIG NIGHT

Mick had everything ready and was just waiting for his guest. Dinner was in the oven, Apricot Szechwan Roast Duck along with steamed white rice and asparagus. The salad was ready and the wine was chilling. The refrigerator also held a delicious candied apple pie cheesecake for dessert. Mick had cooked this menu twice in preparation for this special occasion. Practice made perfect and he didn't want anything to ruin the evening.

Candles glowed in little nooks and cranny's which gave the cabin a cozy feeling. Soft music played over the sound system. Everything was ready. The weather had gone back to the typical west coast spring shenanigans. Wind and sheets of rain outside made it seem all the more cozy inside. All that was missing was Claire. Mick wiped his hands on his apron and checked his watch for the umpteenth time. She should be here any moment. He took a big gulp of his wine.

"Calm down man. You've been through all kinds of stressful situations before. You can get through this." He leaned against the galley counter, closed his eyes and took in a long deep breath, paused and then let it out slowly.

It had been a busy month since finding the cash. He had wondered if he should turn the money over to the police but after a lot of soul searching and conversation with Claire and her family, it was decided that if they did that, it would just disappear into some bureaucratic hole. And Mick had a better use for it than that.

There had been a lot of things to take care of prior to departing for offshore. The sculpting commission was finally finished and shipped back east. It had been received with such glowing praise that several new commissions had been proposed. Mick had so far been able to postpone a decision on whether to accept more sculpting work but the business was there if he wanted it.

A lot of time had been spent being questioned by the RCMP about the loss of Starlight. There had also been questions about the bodies found on Ruxton Island though Mick could accurately say that he didn't know who they were. The police and the insurance company were not entirely satisfied with his answers, nor were they happy with the silence that Mr. Xun and Morris were keeping about what had happened to them.

The pressure from the police had become rather intense but had eventually petered out for lack of any charges to bring to the table. The insurance company was pleasantly surprised when Mick simply accepted their statement that they wouldn't pay out on the policy on Starlight.

There had been some speculation about what had happened to David Enzio but since the real money had been discovered in the secret compartment of the armoire, it must have been counterfeit money that had been in the life raft canister. They all had a lot of different ideas about what Enzio might have done with three and a half million dollars worth of counterfeit money but they hoped they would never learn the real truth. Just as long as he never bothered them again.

Mick had spent a lot of soul searching about whether Seagram was really the kind of boat that he wanted to go offshore sailing in. It was a beautiful boat for sure but it was so different from Starlight. While Seagram was certainly a spacious boat and had a lot of high tech equipment, Mick preferred a boat that was smaller inside. In heavy seas, it was important to be able to have tighter quarters down below and Seagram was a palace. Then, a strange coincidence had occurred. Mick had Seagram out of the water over in Canoe Cove for a final inspection. Right next to where Seagram stood on the hard, an elderly man had a Passport Four Seventy. It was beautiful and in magnificent condition. The owner wanted a bigger boat and drooled all over Seagram. Mick in turn drooled all over the more smaller Passport. It was much more what he dreamed of going offshore in. Over a dinner in the pub, a trade was arranged and the two captain's shook hands then and there. Paperwork was dealt with the next day and suddenly Mick had his dream boat. He changed the name of his new boat to

Starlight Two. Without breaking a sweat, Mick's offshore dream was about to come to fruition.

Mick was brought back to the moment by the sound of footsteps coming on board and a gentle knocking at the companionway doors. He put his wine glass down and went up the steps and opened the doors. Claire took off her shoes in the cockpit and then came down below.

She was wearing a Burberry Poncho, creamy beige that went well with the long traditional Dragon Brocade Cheongsam that Claire had spent hours working on. It was her own handiwork; something that she had started a long time ago and never had the occasion to wear. Tonight however seemed like the right time and she had spent the afternoon finishing it. The silk glowed in the candlelight as Mick took her poncho. The mandarin collar accented her slim neck and the form fitting shape made Mick remember that despite her small stature, she was all woman.

The dress reached almost to the floor and had it not been for the slit on the side that went all the way up to the top of her thigh, it would have been a very difficult dress to walk in. But the slit did more than make it easier to walk. It showcased a leg that Michelangelo would have sculpted on his best day. Mick was not aware of the fact that he was staring but Claire took note and she smiled a pleased smile. The afternoon had not been wasted.

Claire's long hair had been pulled up into a bun with streamers of raven black draped down both sides of her face. She looked stunning and Mick was rendered speechless. This was the same woman that he had seen in a flight suit laughing joyfully as she got them out of a jam at Telegraph Harbor. This was the same woman that he had seen hanging from her safety harness in her busted up airplane in the woods off Narvaez Bay on Saturna Island. This was the same woman who could get down and dirty changing the oil in her airplane who now stood before him looking as elegant and cool and sophisticated as a model. Her versatility was amazing.

Truth be told, Mick felt totally inadequate beside this beautiful woman. It was not that Mick was ugly. Some might even think he was a ruggedly handsome man but beside Claire, he felt plain. But, he reminded himself, hadn't she told him she loved him? Wasn't this the woman that had nearly passed out from the passion of their kisses? Who was he to argue with her taste in men?

Claire opened her bag and presented Mick with what was obviously a gift wrapped bottle of some kind of alcohol. She also pulled a pair of gold, embroidered slippers from her bag and slipped them on her feet.

Mick hung her poncho in the hallway to the aft cabin and then turned to his duties as host. "Claire, may I get you a drink? I have some nice wine from a vineyard on Saltspring."

Claire nodded. "That sounds good. It's so wonderful you found your dream boat Mick. It really is beautiful. Not as beautiful as your woodwork," she said as she ran one hand over the mahogany trim "but I know it's much more to your liking than Seagram was." He nodded in agreement. She looked at him in the soft light. "You look nice tonight Mick."

She put her hand on his arm. He took her in his arms and kissed her. They kissed for a long time until she finally broke away from him and laid her head against his chest. She smelled good and felt good. His heart was beating fast. This was going to be a night to remember. He had waited a long time for this and it seemed as though the stars were aligned just right.

The dinner was perfect. His culinary expertise surprised Claire who was very experienced in Chinese cooking.

At one point, she had sat back and smiled at him. He looked at her questioningly. "What?"

"Did you really cook this Mick, or did my mother come down during the day and prepare it?"

He put on a little pout. Juezui they called it in Chinese. "My feelings are hurt. I happen to think I'm a well rounded man and cooking is just one of the things that I do well."

Claire nodded. "You're absolutely right. The duck is perfect. You are an amazing man Mick." She reached across the table for his hand.

"I think you're amazing too Claire. That's why I wanted to share this special evening with you tonight before I leave. I know that you and I have already discussed my going offshore sailing. I know you want me to fulfill my long time dream. I know you'll wait for me to come back. I just wanted to thank you once again for giving me your support."

Claire nodded with a slightly sad look on her face. It was a difficult decision to let this man go away for so long but she had made her mind up. She couldn't, wouldn't stand in the way of his opportunity of a lifetime. She was hurting inside at the thought of him being away. But, truth be told, she needed some time on her own to deal with the demons that had taken over her nights and a lot of her waking hours. She was hurting inside but she was damned if she would show it.

Mick carried on. "I just wish that I felt better about going. I keep wondering what you're going to do while I'm gone." He leaned towards her. "I wish you would get back to flying again. I mean, there's a brand new Quicksilver in your hanger just waiting for you to fly it." Mick had arranged for delivery of the new airplane and had the factory put a rush on to get it delivered in short order.

Claire's good mood evaporated in an instant. Her face hardened and she pulled her hand away from Mick's. "Don't. Please don't go there Mick. I do not want to go back to flying and that's it. I have already told you I appreciated you buying the new airplane and I'm sure that we can find someone interested in flying it but it won't be me. End of discussion." She stabbed a piece of duck with a chopstick and pushed it into her mouth and began chewing rapidly.

Mick was too stubborn to let it go. He knew that she just needed to get back on the horse that threw her off and she would be fine again. He pressed on, oblivious to the storm signs. He simply didn't see the raw nerve that he was about to trip on. "Claire, you just need to take her out slowly, take it one step at a time. Do a little taxiing and some short little hops and then you'll be as confident as before."

Claire glared at him. She couldn't believe that he would persist in talking about her flying again. For the last month, that's all she had heard from everyone that she had run into. "When are you going to go flying again Claire?" "You're not afraid to fly again are you Claire?" "Not going to let a little accident scare you, are you Claire?" What did they know about being scared to fly? What did they know about that moment when everything that you had dreamed of, everything that you had loved and enjoyed had been turned into terror and the reality of facing your own mortality? What did any of them know and why didn't they just leave her alone?

Claire threw her napkin on the table and stood up. She put both hands on her hips and glared at Mick, her mouth a thin angry line. Mick jerked backwards, stunned by her reaction, completely and blissfully unaware of Claire's trials of the past month. So busy and caught up in his own plans and work that he had been blind to Claire's hidden pain and suffering. That she had done such a thorough job of concealing it from Mick was a gift she had learned from generations of long suffering Chinese people.

"You beast." she hissed at him. "What do you know about my fear of flying? What do you care? You're so caught up in your own ambition that you haven't noticed that all I hear these days is people telling me to go flying again. I don't care if I ever fly again. Do you hear me?" She stepped closer to him. The dam had burst and the anger and shame that she had kept bottled up ever since crashing into the trees in her airplane came flooding out. "You haven't asked how I've been doing, how I've been feeling about this whole flying business for weeks. You're like everybody else; you think it's so easy to just go flying again. But it's not. It's not." She stamped her foot and put her hands to her face and burst into tears.

Mick stood up and went to her and began to put his arms around her but she would have none of it.

"Get away from me you heartless beast. Leave me alone, go sailing and leave me alone." She turned and ran up the steps, threw open the doors and was gone. Mick stood in shock for a moment. One second they had been enjoying a great meal and warm conversation and all of a sudden, she was gone. He raced up the stairs and out into the cockpit and looked out into the rainy night. She was already half way up the ramp leading to the parking lot. He jumped over the side of the boat onto the dock and landed hard and twisted his ankle. He went down, rolling to take the load off the injured foot. Coming back up, he heard the engine on Claire's car start, saw the headlights come on and then heard the squeal of tires as she burned out of the parking lot. By the time Mick limped to the top of the dock, Claire was gone.

Later, in the cabin of Seagram, Mick sat dejectedly at the table, the plates just as they had been when he had so firmly and completely put his foot in his mouth. Half eaten duck in a congealing sauce, rice getting hard, asparagus growing limp and cold, a perfect meal ruined by a perfect fool.

Had he really been as blind as she had pointed out? She had called him a beast. That was pretty harsh. But looking back over the past couple of weeks, he had to admit that he had been so caught up in his work and preparations that he had simply assumed she was alright. "She would have told me if something was bothering her wouldn't she?" The answer was simple. No she wouldn't. She was obviously better at concealing her feelings than Mick was at paying attention to them.

Mick sighed. He had screwed up big time. He got up and grabbed the bottle of wine and took a swig from it. As he sat back down at the table he remembered a line from Eddie's letter. What had it said exactly? He went to the safe in quarter berth. Working the combination, he opened the door and peered inside.

There. On top of his new passport. He opened the envelope and pulled out the letter and read until he got to the pertinent line. Eddy was telling Mick how good Claire would be for him. There it was. He didn't really need Eddy to tell him, he already knew it. But it seemed like a voice from the grave was yelling at him now.

"If she lets you in the door, don't let her get away."

He knew what he had to do and a plan formulated in his mind. With a little luck and the right conditions, it just might work. Mick spent the rest of the night working, taking Eddie's words to heart and hoped he could pull it off.

52 SALVAGE WORK

Mick woke up, still hunched over the table. He had finished his work around three in the morning and had simply fallen asleep at the table; head down on his arms amongst a pile of sailcloth, thread and the sewing machine.

Staggering up, running his tongue around his sticky teeth, he started out by putting the coffee pot on to brew. Then, while standing in the hot shower, he planned the day. From what he could see through the deck hatch above his head, the rain had stopped and the sun had broken through. It fit into his plan perfectly.

Breakfast was eaten on the fly, an apple, some hot coffee and a couple of slices of toast as Mick buzzed around the cabin cleaning up the debris from the night's work and stowing things away. The sail that he had been working on, a huge spinnaker was taken back on deck and stowed into its sleeve, ready for deployment. Judging from the weather, there was a good chance that he would be able to pull this plan off. It just needed a little cooperation from the Gods.

Whether it was the God's day off or just more of Mick's bad luck in the romance department, his phone call to Claire's cell phone went unanswered. When he called her home, Mrs. Lu answered and with a lot of sadness and sympathy in her voice explained that Claire had gone out early in the morning with Mr. Xun in tow. She left specific instructions that she was not to be bothered and if anybody called including Mick Brese, she was not available.

Mrs. Lu said that Claire had come home in tears, slamming doors and had gone straight to her room. "She is very upset Mick. I don't know what went on with you two last night but it must have been something very big. All she's been talking about all week long was having a big going away party for you at the dock today. But from what I can gather, it's been called off. I'm sorry things went so wrong Mick but I'll come down to see you go. What time are you leaving?"

"Thanks Mrs. Lu. You don't have any idea where Claire went?"

"She didn't say a word about that to me. Just grabbed her father and left."

Mick pondered this for a moment. She might have decided to just go for a drive to talk to her father. That would be a rather one sided talk, Mick thought knowing Mr. Xun's proclivity to be on the quiet side. It was a mystery but Claire had made it clear that Mick was on the shit list. He was reluctant to leave while the situation was so bad between the two of them. But what was to be gained just sitting and waiting? He could leave and call her later. It would be a while before he was out of cell phone range and then after that, he would be on his satellite phone. "I'll be leaving in about a half hour Mrs. Lu. It would be nice to see you before I go. Claire left her coat and shoes here so you could take those back to her."

"See you soon Mick. Don't worry; I'm sure Claire will be fine. She sometimes gets this way and just needs a few days to cool off. Young people nowadays are so spoiled."

Mick went about topping up the water tanks and unhooking the shore power and singling up the mooring lines. Everything was ready by the time Mrs. Lu arrived at the dock. Mick had hopes that Claire would be with her but such was not the case. Mrs. Lu had brought a little gift for him which she insisted that he open there on the dock.

"You must wear this good luck charm." Mrs. Lu explained as she put the necklace over Mick's head and then held the pendant in her hand. "To the Chinese, a butterfly is a symbol of love. Legend has it that the butterfly symbolizes an undying bond between lovers. Maybe if you wear this, a certain young lady will have a change of heart." Mick looked at the pale green jade butterfly. He didn't know whether it would bring luck or not but it certainly didn't hurt to hope. She continued on. "I know it is possible for people to have a change of heart. Do you know what I mean?" She looked at him, waiting for his reply. He didn't know where she was going with this. "I used to think that Chinese were the only ones who were special. I felt like we had invented civilization. When I came to Canada and saw how young people seemed to care so little about their parents and grandparents, I thought we were living in a primitive culture." She blushed a little. "I'm ashamed of the fact that I told Claire that she had to marry a Chinese man. Claire's father and I arranged her first marriage. I'm not sure if she told you that or not." She didn't wait for confirmation. "But it was a disaster. And Claire is a hot headed young woman and that's why we're here in Canada. You would think I would have learned something from that experience. But it wasn't until I met you and you risked your life for my family that I realized that you, your culture is just as special as mine. You are a very special man Mick and I'm sorry that Claire seems to have forgotten that, at least for the moment." She sighed. "I don't understand why you feel that you have to go," and here she gave a derisive flick of her hand towards the ocean, "out there, but I have come to realize that there are many things I don't understand in this world. I wish you the best and I want you to know, you are always welcome in my home."

 She hugged Mick who gave her a little kiss on the top of her head. "Thank you Mrs. Lu. Thanks for coming down. I was hoping things would be very different this morning. I worked all night on a little plan to try to changer her heart but we'll just have to hope that time will help Claire to forgive me. I'll be the first to admit that I've been more focused on getting my own affairs taken care of over the last month and not paying enough attention to Claire's needs too."

 Surprisingly, Mrs. Lu rolled her eyeballs. She grabbed Mick by the arm. "Mick, Claire needs to get over herself. None of us are going to live forever. She's been going on about how frightened she is about her close call when she crashed in her airplane. Anybody who flies knows that flying is dangerous. When we were in China she worshipped Claire Chennault. General Chennault and his pilots all had accidents and crashes. Do you think for one minute that they went around moaning and feeling sorry for themselves because of that? No they didn't. They didn't have the luxury of feeling sorry for themselves. That's what's wrong with Claire. She needs something that is going to force her to fly again. When she does, she'll be just fine and she'll probably thank you for pushing her. If not, even though she is not a child anymore, I will clap her pigu." They laughed together. "I've only got so much patience for someone feeling sorry for themselves. Now get going Mick and take care. Don't worry; I'm sure that things will work out. I have a feeling about this."

 This didn't necessarily inspire confidence in Mick who had heard Claire talk about Mrs. Lu's "feelings."

Getting There

    Mrs. Lu gave Mick a strong hug and then turned and picked up Claire's poncho and shoes and walked quickly up the dock. Mick watched her and couldn't help admiring the woman for her strength. He turned and went onboard Seagram and started the engine. As it warmed up, he untied the last lines holding him to shore, stepped into the cockpit and headed out to sea.

53 GETTING BACK ON THE HORSE

Claire and her father had breakfast at the Aurora restaurant at the Poets Corner Resort and Spa in Bedwell Harbor. Because this upscale establishment was outside of their budget, they did not often frequent the place. But, from time to time situations arose and Claire and her father had an agreement that this was where they would come for daughter/father or father/daughter talks and this was one of those occasions. Mr. Xun let his daughter talk since she was the one who had dragged him out of the house.

At the next table, a man in a very nice business suit was talking loudly on a cell phone. Some kind of big business deal was more important than the breakfast growing cold on the table in front of him.

Claire noted the annoyed look on her father's face. He did not take kindly to people who thought only of themselves and the businessman had fallen into that category.

"I made a fool of myself last night father."

"It's not the first time Claire, probably won't be the last. I know you."

Claire looked at her father to see if he was making a joke but he was a hard read. He wasn't the biggest joker on the island, so he probably wasn't. It was a sobering thought.

"You don't seem surprised. Do I do it so often?"

Her father slurped his tea loud enough to attract the attention of the man at the next table. The man's look of disgust was evident but Claire turned and glared at him and he quickly went back to conducting business.

"Claire, it's not that you do it so often but you do a very good job when you do it. I taught you that. If you are going to do something, do a good job. You never really understood that you should be selective in how you apply that rule. But you are young."

"I'm worried that I may have ruined my chance with Mick. He's very special to me but I was upset that he didn't spend more time helping me with my problem."

"So, instead of having breakfast with me, why didn't you go down to the dock and tell Mick you were a foolish woman and apologize to him?"

Claire turned her glare on her father. It appeared to go right over his head. He was busy putting his egg on top of a piece of toast.

"I wasn't the only one who was a fool. Mick spent the last several weeks so busy working on his sculpture and getting his boat ready and he never really paid any attention to how I was doing. What kind of a man does that to the woman he supposedly loves?"

More slurping, more looks and finally the suit next to them moved to another table farther away. Mr. Xun looked at the man as he left and smiled.

"The idiot thinks it's ruder to slurp your tea than it is to talk loud on a cell phone in a nice restaurant like this. Go figure. Claire, did it ever occur to you that Mick was trying to "give you space", as you young people say, to get over your problem about flying? He is a smart man. Do you think for one moment that Mick doesn't understand how traumatic that crash was for you? And, I've seen the way he falls all over himself to please you when you're together. He's in love with you. He thinks you're beautiful and intelligent. I have not had the opportunity to correct his thinking."

Mr. Xun grinned a toothy grin at his daughter. Claire looked at her father and was about to make a comment but her cell phone rang. Claire knew better than to talk on the cell phone in the restaurant in front of her father. She excused herself and pulled the phone from her pocket as she left the room.

"Hello Claire, its mom. I just wanted to let you know that I had a call from Mick this morning looking for you. I told him you were in a bad mood and had gone out with your father. I went down to the dock and saw him off. I thought I should tell you, though I really don't know why. You don't seem to care very much."

"Mother that's not true and you know it. We just had a little fight. Did he really leave? He never said goodbye." Tears came to Claire's eyes and she had to choke back a sob.

"Claire, have you lost your mind? You're the one who left specific instructions to tell Mick you were not available. He might not have babied you quite enough to meet your level of expectation but what was he supposed to do? You show him that you are as tough as a man with your flying around and dropping bricks on people and you expect him to think that you're a fragile little thing because you crashed your airplane? He's doing what he thinks you expect him to do. He's trying to let you work it out yourself or ask him for help if you need it. Maybe that's one of the reasons that he loves you Claire."

At that moment, Claire made up her mind.

"Thank you mother. Goodbye." She hung up and charged back into the restaurant waving the waiter over to the table. She looked at her father who was enjoying his breakfast.

"Hurry up father. Eat, eat. Waiter, may we have our bill please?" Claire's father looked at the untouched food on Claire's plate.

"What's going on Claire? Why the rush? You haven't eaten any of your food. Do you know how expensive this place is?"

Claire made a dismissive motion with her hand. There were more important things to worry about than the price of breakfast. The waiter was back in a moment with the bill and Claire jumped up and signed the credit card slip. She pulled her father up by his arm and he had only a moment to grab a last piece of toast as they rushed out of the room.

In the car, in between bites of toast, Mr. Xun asked the obvious question. "Claire, where are we going in such a hurry? Who was the phone call from? Slow down."

Claire swerved around a bicyclist who shook his fist at them. Mr. Xun held the toast in his teeth while he finished putting his seat belt on.

"We're going flying father. Mick has already left and he must be hurting after the way I treated him last night. So, we're going to show him we can get back on the horse that threw us. That should help to make him feel better."

Mr. Xun's narrow eyes grew narrower. "What do you mean "we"?"

Claire looked over at him and grinned. Her father had sworn many times that he would never go flying in "that thing" as he called her airplane. He didn't even like flying in Captain Harris's Beaver but Claire's Quicksilver frightened him to death. "You and me Father. Everyone keeps telling me I should just get over my fear and fly again.

Getting There

You said it yourself. So, it's time for you and me to put our fear behind us and show everyone what we're made of. What do you say?'

Mr. Xun had nothing to say at the moment. The piece of toast was still sticking out of his mouth though that was not the only thing that prevented him from speaking. It was the large knot of fear that had gripped him, from his stomach all the way to his throat. He was incapable of saying anything.

Claire laughed and continued on towards the hanger where her new airplane waited. The factory had sent a technician, at an additional cost, to set the airplane up and test fly it and to show Claire all of the differences between her old machine and the new one. He had reassured her that she would have absolutely no problem flying the new airplane given her experience level. Today they would find out. As they approached the hanger, Claire watched the leaves on the trees to get a feel for what the wind was doing. "Almost dead calm. That's nice for a first flight. We'll get you seated in the airplane father and then I'll do my preflight." She looked over at him, smiling reassuringly. "We can do this."

Her father had grave doubts about going flying but he knew that this was a turning point for his daughter. He suspected that Claire was probably on an emotional roller coaster right now, caught between the decision to go flying and the doubt and fear that had plagued her for the last month. He decided that he had to put on a brave face today or risk derailing her chance to conquer her fear.

At the hanger, the airplane looked even more frightening than ever. Before, Mr. Xun had looked at it knowing that he would not have to fly in it. Today, he looked at it knowing that he was going to be high above the water in this unbelievably rickety looking collection of parts. His knees grew weak and shaky.

Claire looked at the new airplane with a critical eye and her heart swelled with pride and excitement. She was going to do it. Finally. She had laid in bed night after night dreaming, sweating, tossing and turning thinking about the crash. She thought about all the things that could go wrong and how little time a person had to react to a problem. But Captain Harris, General Chennault, they had faced these same situations and had overcome their fears. She could too. She was looking forward to feeling the new machine under her control. Today was the day.

Mr. Xun had his own coveralls in the hanger which he used when he helped Claire clean the airplane and do maintenance. As she put on her own flight suit, she helped her father put his on and then got him situated in his seat in the airplane. He was even more quiet than usual; his mouth being so dry that he would find it difficult to say anything. Claire didn't take notice, or at least pretended not to out of kindness. She knew her father was being brave for her sake. She got the four point harness on him and cinched it up snug. He cinched it up even tighter.

Claire went through her preflight checklist with a thoroughness that was really not called for. Since the airplane had been delivered, despite her fears and the belief that she would never fly again, she had been over the airplane with a fine tooth comb. She had examined every pulley, every wire, every nut and bolt from the nose to the tail. She had run the engine for several hours listening and watching the instruments for any indications of problems. It's unlikely that there was an airplane in Canada that had been more prepared for its flight than this little machine.

Claire rolled open the doors and went back around the front of the airplane and lowered the ramp into the water. The Quicksilver bobbed impatiently and Claire climbed on and gave a gentle push out the door. The airplane went straight back as Claire got her harness buckled up. With a little bit of rudder, the tail turned and they were soon in position to start the engine. "You ready father?" Claire was talking over the intercom now. Mr. Xun tried to swallow in order to speak but simply nodded his head and gave a weak smile. Claire patted his knee and smiled back. "We're going to be just fine." She clicked off the intercom and was about to start the engine but came back on the radio. "And thanks dad. I don't think I could do this without you." That brought a wry smile to his tight lips.

"What are fathers for" he asked, "if not to help their little girls?"

Claire leaned over and kissed his cheek and then went about the business of getting the Rotax engine started. Mr. Xun almost jumped out of his seat from the noise as the engine roared into life but he was holding on so hard he wouldn't have gone far. He didn't know whether to be more terrified of the noise or the prospect of the impending takeoff.

Claire taxied longer than normal, watching the engine gauges and getting a feel for the controls but she could only put off the inevitable for so long. Finally when her father could take the suspense no longer, he turned to her and gestured with one hand.

"Well? Are you ever going to fly this thing Claire?"

Claire looked at him with a slightly aggravated look and then nodded. She wriggled in her seat to get set and then pushed the throttle forward and the little airplane surged ahead and in moments they were in the air. Claire had a moment of heart stopping fear as she realized they were flying again. But that was quickly replaced by the sheer joy of freedom that comes with flight, the release from the bonds of gravity, the power and control that only those who fly experience. In that one moment, Claire was transported from the grip of demons to the embrace of angels.

Mr. Xun on the other hand had his eyes shut so tight he saw nothing and felt only the vibrations of the engine and airframe under him. His grip on his seat didn't lesson one iota as he opened his eyes upon hearing Claire's shouts of joy but his grimace of fear was slowly replaced by a small and growing smile. Claire's excitement and happiness was contagious and soon, he too was shouting right along with Claire.

"We're doing it father, we're flying! Yeeeeehawww!" Claire's grin grew by the moment and she reached over and held her father's arm.

"Thanks Dad. Thanks for coming along with me. I couldn't have done it without you."

"Claire, you concentrate more on flying and less on thanking me. To be honest with you, I didn't come willingly but now I'm glad I did. At least I think I'm glad."

Claire decided that today was a day for simple flying, just taking it easy. The first job was to figure out where Mick was. It was important to find him and show him that she had overcome her fears. He was going to be so proud of her. It had only been a couple of hours since he had left the dock, so he would only have gone about ten miles or so. He might have gone down Haro Strait or he might have decided on a more westerly course which would have taken him towards Sydney Island. She would catch up with him either way and headed first towards Haro Strait.

The weather was perfect. The temperature was mild and the ocean and the sky were as peaceful and calm as Claire's heart had become. Now she wondered why she had felt so worried about flying. It was her element, she belonged up here.

There was no sign of Mick anywhere along Haro Strait. The visibility was terrific and they could see a long way ahead. There were a couple of small sailboats in the distance but nothing the size of Starlight Two. The big boat would be easy to spot from the air. Claire decided to concentrate her search more to the west and banked gently around the tip of Sidney Island and up into Sidney Channel.

There he was. Claire pumped her fist. The light wind was behind him and he had the mainsail out to port and the large headsail out to starboard. As they closed the gap, Claire tapped her father on the arm and pointed out ahead. He looked without seeing for a moment and then nodded his head. He'd spotted Mick too.

54 THE PREPARATION PAYS OFF

As soon as Mick heard the drone of the Rotax engine and spotted the airplane in the sky ahead, he knew it was Claire. As they closed the gap, Mick was able to make out the shark's teeth, made famous by Claire Chennault's Flying Tiger airplanes, painted on the small fiberglass shroud that surrounded the cockpit on Claire's new machine. It was Claire, flying once again. Mick's heart surged with pride and joy. She'd done it.

Mick pumped his fist in the air. "It looks like my hard work last night is going to pay off after all." Putting Seagram on autopilot, Mick ran up on deck and attached the big spinnaker to the halyard. The sail was covered with a sleeve that allowed it to be hoisted to the top of the mast and then deployed quickly and neatly. He ran back to the mast and started cranking the winch, hoisting the sail up. As soon as it was in place, Mick ran back to the cockpit and got ready to pull the sleeve up. Claire was getting close, it wouldn't be long now.

As Claire and her father approached, they could see Mick run forward and start working on the foredeck. Claire just assumed he had to make a sail change and her father was simply fascinated to be seeing Mick and the big boat from this high perspective. Neither one was prepared for what happened next. They could see that Mick was back in the cockpit now and they watched as the big blue and white spinnaker seemed to inflate from the red covering sleeve and burst open in the following wind.

Claire leaned forward as she saw that there were black letters sewn onto the big sail. She was still too far away to read what it said though. "Can you make out what it says on the sail father?"

Mr. Xun had excellent eyesight and it didn't take him long to read. He was puzzled enough by the wording that he hesitated to read it aloud. It didn't matter though. Claire was soon able to read it herself. Mr. Xun heard her sharp intake of breath through the headphones. There in big black letters were the words:

      Beast to Claire
     Will U Marry Me?

55 A CARE PACKAGE

The FedEx truck pulled to a stop in front of a modest home on Yellow Point Road. The driver jumped out and went to the door just as a dog came bounding around the corner of the house. Wary from previous unpleasant encounters, the driver's hand went to the pepper spray can in the holster on his belt. As it turned out a towel would have been a better weapon against the long slobbering tongue used by the big black lab.

"Down boy, down. Come on, get out of the way, I've got work to do." The driver pushed his way past the dog and knocked on the door. Just as he was about to knock a second time, the door opened and a tired looking middle aged woman stood in front of him with a questioning look on her face.

"Can I help you?"

"FedEx delivery Ma'am. Just sign here." The driver held up an electronic pad which she signed. He handed her a flat envelope and thanked her and turned to go. The dog tagged along hoping for some more attention.

Mrs. Tom Edwards turned the envelope over in her hands wondering what bad news this was. Times had been very difficult since the death of her husband. As the sole breadwinner, Tom had brought home just barely enough for them to live on. Before his death, they had been talking about selling the property on Ruxton Island and maybe the boat too. The two children both needed a lot of dental work and there was college to save for and bills to pay. She had been stunned by his death and dismayed to learn the sorry state of their finances. There had been no life insurance and her attempts to find a job were turning out to be discouraging to say the least. It had been a hard month.

Each day when the mailman came, her stomach tied itself in knots for fear of another bill to pay and now she held a mystery envelope from FedEx. Her stomach started tightening up. The return address didn't tell her much. It was from an address on Pender Island. The good news was that she didn't owe anyone on Pender Island any money. At least, not that she knew of anyway.

Closing the door and moving into the kitchen, she sat down at the dining table. She gave a little laugh at the thought of this being considered a dining table. She had commandeered it for a work table and it was piled high with bills, paid and due along with letters from lawyers and the funeral home. There were her feeble attempts at a resume and a stack of job applications. All of it was depressing. She threw the FedEx envelope on the top of the heap and went to get dinner ready. The kids would be home from school soon.

As she prepared the evening meal, her mind kept going back to the FedEx letter. Who would be sending her something from Pender Island? Finally, her curiosity overwhelmed her anxiety of opening another possible unknown bill. She went to the table and picked up the envelope and pulled the zipper strip to open it.

Inside was a one page letter and a separate envelope with something inside. The envelope was sealed with instructions to read the letter first. It was a short letter and it read as follows:

Hello Mrs. Edwards,

My name is Mick Brese. My wife Claire and I are writing in regards to the passing of your husband, Mr. Tom Edwards. The purpose for our writing to you is twofold. First, we want to pass along our condolences on your husbands passing. We never had the opportunity to meet your husband but a friend, Stevie Taylor who lives on Ruxton Island knew your husband and yourself and has told us many good things about the two of you and your children. The man who took your husband's life was a drug dealer and was holding friends and family of ours hostage in a ransom attempt. He was unsuccessful in that attempt. We are uncertain of this person's whereabouts but we sincerely hope he is at the bottom of the ocean somewhere. Still, that might be too good for this particular devil.

Getting There

It is a great tragedy that your husband was in the wrong place at the wrong time. For no good reason, your husband lost his life and you and your children had your loved one taken from you.

The second reason for our letter is as follows. What we are about to present to you is in no way to be considered payment for the life of a good man. It is simply what we can offer to help you at what we are sure is a time of great need for you and your family. Enclosed in the sealed envelope is a bankbook. We have made a deposit in your name in an account at a bank in Nanaimo. It is hopefully enough to get you back on your feet and help you through what must be the most trying time of your life. This is yours to keep, there are no strings attached. The money can be used for anything you see fit to do with it. Sometime in the future when you are feeling so inclined, we would appreciate it if you could give us a call and let us know how you and your family are doing.

Claire and I are leaving today to sail our boat to Hawaii and will return sometime in late summer or early fall. Perhaps we will have the opportunity to meet at that time.

Sincerely,
Mick and Claire Brese

Mrs. Edwards put the letter down and opened the sealed envelope. A bankbook. Her hands trembled. It was a wonderful surprise to get a letter that wasn't another bill to pay. Instead, it appeared, good news had arrived. And as she soon discovered when she flipped open the cover of the savings account pass book, two million dollars was very good news indeed. She tipped her head back, tears streaming down her cheeks and clutched the bank book to her chest.

When the two Edwards children arrived home from school, they were very pleasantly surprised to see that their mother was dressed up and was even wearing makeup for the first time in a long time. She told them to get cleaned up. They were going out to dinner for a change and she had a lot to talk to them about.

The End

ACKNOWLEDGMENTS

I want to express my deep gratitude to all those who have given advice and encouragement...

Mom who loved this book and always told me to "go for it".

Dad and Kate who read this story and had good things to say about it and didn't hesitate to keep me on task.

Terry Matthews whose enthusiasm helped to spur me on. Thanks Bro.

John Guzzwell, an inspiration to me and a friend who took the time to read and advise me on this work.

Glenora Doherty, woman sailor and writer who read the work of someone she didn't know. Thanks for your kindness and advice.

Readers and advisors...
Lynn Capps, Teana Powell, Linda Donaldson, Sheryl Williams, Laura and Peighton Brown, Jane Boren and Michael Boren, Jenny Matthews and Ingrid Smith-McNeill, I thank you all.

If I left anybody out, forgive me and know that I appreciate every one who advised and encouraged.

ABOUT THE AUTHOR
MICHAEL MATTHEWS

    I'm a West Coast guy. I've tried living away from the coast but it just doesn't work for me. I built a sailboat and lived aboard in the area that this story takes place. The wonderful Gulf Islands of British Columbia. During my time as a sailor and boat builder, I learned all about the difficulties in trying to go offshore sailing. There are so many things that get in the way of that dream and of the many people that want to go offshore only a small percentage ever actually make that dream come true. I came very close to "getting there".

    I am married to a wonderful Chinese woman and in our travels to her home country, I have had the opportunity to learn a tiny bit about that culture. This has been difficult since I don't speak the language. But from my observations and discussions with family and friends, I have been afforded a glimpse of another world. My Chinese characters and their experiences are based loosely on that glimpse. I hope that those who know the culture better than I will cut this Laowai some slack.

Just a note on pronunciation. I pronounce Mr. Xun's name as "sun" but it is more accurately pronounced "soo-in". If you ask my wife, she will tell you that I wreck the pronunciation of almost all Chinese words but she still loves me.

There are more stories coming about Mick Brese and Claire and her parents. I have a young adult novel ready that is called "Pender Island Blues". It will be released soon.

If you have enjoyed reading this book, you could do me a big favor and write a review online. If you found things that you didn't like or if you want to just say hello, email me at:

wmm@williammichaelmatthews.com.

Thanks for reading!

Made in the USA
Charleston, SC
10 August 2012